A STOLEN KISS

Jason's face, though now in repose, glistened with a sheen of perspiration. Julia bent over further, attempting to determine the state of his fever—then exclaimed as an iron hand shot out from beneath the covers. She was jerked swiftly down, toppling her onto the bed—and the earl.

"Who are you?" Jason's voice was dangerous, with the controlled tone of a soldier.

"Oh, Lord . . ."

His eyes were slitted in mistrust. Then they widened, and a smile that discomfitted Julia as much as his prior expression crossed his face. "Thank God, it's you."

"Yes?" Julia said warily.

"I've been imagining you everywhere, Madame Sprite."

Julia nodded vigorously in relief. "Yes, yes—you know I'm only a dream, don't you?"

He sighed. "Yes, I do. But just the one I have been wanting tonight." He shifted her to the whole length of him, and Julia suddenly realized he intended to kiss her.

She swiftly inserted her hand between his mouth and hers, just in time. "Wait a minute. You—you dream too quickly. Don't you know humans are not permitted to kiss sprites?"

"Why not? I have before." Jason's chuckle shook them both. And his lips covered hers before she could object . . .

ELEGANT LOVE STILL FLOURISHES —
Wrap yourself in a Zebra Regency Romance.

A MATCHMAKER'S MATCH (3783, $3.50/$4.50)
by Nina Porter

To save herself from a loveless marriage, Lady Psyche Veringham pretends to be a bluestocking. Resigned to spinsterhood at twenty-three, Psyche sets her keen mind to snaring a husband for her young charge, Amanda. She sets her cap for long-time bachelor, Justin St. James. This man of the world has had his fill of frothy-headed debutantes and turns the tables on Psyche. Can a bluestocking and a man about town find true love?

FIRES IN THE SNOW (3809, $3.99/$4.99)
by Janis Laden

Because of an unhappy occurrence, Diana Ruskin knew that a secure marriage was not in her future. She was content to assist her physician father and follow in his footsteps . . . until now. After meeting Adam, Duke of Marchmaine, Diana's precise world is shattered. She would simply have to avoid the temptation of his gentle touch and stunning physique — and by doing so break her own heart!

FIRST SEASON (3810, $3.50/$4.50)
by Anne Baldwin

When country heiress Laetitia Biddle arrives in London for the Season, she harbors dreams of triumph and applause. Instead, she becomes the laughingstock of drawing rooms and ballrooms, alike. This headstrong miss blames the rakish Lord Wakeford for her miserable debut, and she vows to rise above her many faux pas. Vowing to become an Original, Letty proves that she's more than a match for this eligible, seasoned Lord.

AN UNCOMMON INTRIGUE (3701, $3.99/$4.99)
by Georgina Devon

Miss Mary Elizabeth Sinclair was rather startled when the British Home Office employed her as a spy. Posing as "Tasha," an exotic fortune-teller, she expected to encounter unforeseen dangers. However, nothing could have prepared her for Lord Eric Stewart, her dashing and infuriating partner. Giving her heart to this haughty rogue would be the most reckless hazard of all.

A MADDENING MINX (3702, $3.50/$4.50)
by Mary Kingsley

After a curricle accident, Miss Sarah Chadwick is literally thrust into the arms of Philip Thornton. While other women shy away from Thornton's eyepatch and aloof exterior, Sarah finds herself drawn to discover why this man is physically and emotionally scarred.

A Daring Deception
Cindy Holbrook

ZEBRA BOOKS
KENSINGTON PUBLISHING CORP.

ZEBRA BOOKS are published by

Kensington Publishing Corp.
475 Park Avenue South
New York, NY 10016

Zebra and the Z logo are trademarks of Kensington Publishing Corp.

First Printing: July, 1993

Printed in the United States of America

*To Fraser, my friend and ally.
Thank you. You know I could not
have done any of this without you.*

Chapter One
The Fox And The Hounds

The night sky was set ablaze as the flames razed the manor house in the quiet Lombardy countryside. Fog lay upon the land, cloaking the raging destruction so it appeared but a golden nimbus to the two men who sat watching silently from the hill.

"Did we succeed?"

"Yes. The Fox was in his den. He is eliminated."

"And his children?"

"They will be dead upon the morrow."

"Be sure of it. And there must be no hint it was not an accident. The Hawk commands it."

"Do not fear, little man. You may tell your English master it is already accomplished. I am the finest."

"You had best be. The Hawk does not tolerate failure. The Fox and his cubs have eluded him for too long."

The other man laughed and nodded toward the conflagration. "He need not concern himself further, your Hawk. The Fox is but ashes and his children only unmarked graves."

My Lord Castlereigh looked down at the file before him, his face impassive. "Lord Landreth is dead, then?"

"Yes sir, I fear so." The Duke of Rendon sighed. "A

chance fire takes the life of the traitor 'ere we can bring him to justice."

"Yes—very unfortunate. The man escapes us at every turn these past six months, and then perishes in an accidental fire. The whims of fate, I suppose."

"Sir, I hope you do not look upon this as a failure in our department?"

"What? That Landreth died by the hand of God rather than the will of the crown? No, no—the department has done its best and so have you. I meant no disrespect. Your brother before you proved invaluable to the king, and, since John's accident last year, you have proven the same. I know stepping into his shoes cannot have been an easy task—to take charge of his estates, his espionage work, the guardianship of his daughter was no small feat. How is Chlorinda, by the way?" Castlereigh asked, his voice gentling.

Rendon frowned, shaking his head. "She is doing better and gaining back her health, but she is still not totally recovered."

" 'Tis a shame she took her father's death so strongly. She was always a lively little minx."

"Yes," Rendon sighed. "I have tried everything I can to help her."

"Well, give her time: that is what she needs." Castlereigh returned his eyes to the paper, once again all business. "Faith, I wish Landreth had not died in a fire. I would far have preferred for us to try and execute him, but—that wish is useless."

"I do feel as if I have failed the department—"

"Nonsense. Were it not for you, we would never have discovered Landreth's perfidy. You have done excellent work; never before have we possessed such detailed proof of a traitor's guilt. These papers—they were found on the French agent, were they not?"

"Yes, my lord."

"I have always wondered why he carried them."

Rendon frowned slightly. "Perhaps he worked closely with Landreth, or perhaps they were meant to represent Landreth to another. To boast of his loyalty to the Corsican monster, as it were."

"And this from a nobleman of one of England's finest families!"

Rendon shrugged. "It could only be expected. The man married a Frenchwoman, after all, and chose to live in France rather than England. He raised his children there as well."

That may explain his treachery, but for the man to boast of it was folly. Landreth proved himself a wily and clever spy, yet he submitted his infamy to paper. Not what one would expect of such an experienced and deadly man."

"They say every great criminal will finally make a mistake."

"Yes, very true. And we cannot deny he was great. Your brother, God rest his soul, believed in Landreth. He had nothing but praise for him."

"My brother was a very trusting individual," the duke said cautiously. "Too trusting, perhaps."

"Well, we will never know why the agent had those papers upon him, since he was shot while attempting to escape."

"A true misfortunate."

"Very well," Castlereigh said, "I will see to it all. Where are his children now? That must be the next inquiry since they did not come forward upon our demand but chose to go into hiding."

"It appears to support our belief, don't you think, that even though we held no evidence against them, the boy and the girl must have aided their traitor father. But alas, news has reached me that they perished also. They evidently came out of hiding to travel to their father's funeral but were attacked by highwaymen, fatally, upon the way."

"I see. No need for an inquiry, then. Well, that rather wraps matters up neatly. Thank you for your aid in this, your grace."

"It was my pleasure." Rendon rose and left the statesman with a deferential bow.

Castlereigh stared down at the papers before him, a crease between his brows. His attendant entered. "I am finished with the last case, my lord," Ensign Trevor said. "What do you wish me to do next?"

"Something eludes me in this matter . . ."

"My lord?"

"Hmm? What?" Castlereigh looked up. "Oh, forgive me. I fear I was thinking to myself. It appears Lord Landreth died in a fire just this past week, in France."

"That fiend! Blast and damn, then he has escaped a traitor's death!"

"Hm? Yes . . . as well as a traitor's trial. Why did he never come forward? Why didn't his children? Whatever he was, the man was not a coward. He came from a proud and honored family."

"Which he dishonored in the vilest way. I only wish he *had* come forward," Trevor cried, patriotic fervor pulsing through his words. "I would have shot the cur on sight!"

"Perhaps that is the reason he never came forward," Castlereigh said wryly. "Well, the question is moot, for the man is dead now. I must inform his majesty upon this matter. Yes, and ask him whom he wishes to bestow the Landreth lands upon as well. That will certainly be a plum for some fortunate fellow."

A slight humming floated from the thicket. It was a well-modulated, lilting tone, trilling one of the latest arias. Listening, Jason, Earl of Wynhaven, halted his trusty steed Sanchos, a horse of enough hands to carry the large gentleman. The earl's dark blond hair, closely cut in a Brutus, showed him to be a military man. A

10

slight smile curved his sculptured lips, and the crows' feet and his hazel eyes crinkled accordingly. "Ah, so there is human life in this northern country after all—and female life, at that."

The earl chuckled and directed Sanchos into the very thickets from whence the voice arose. One would have been amazed at the stealth and quiet the large man and horse maintained as they wended their way through the forest. They rode until they came upon a well-hidden pool in a small ravine. Both horse and master halted, spellbound at the sight.

Amidst the cool forest greens and the shadowed blues of the water stood a tall, willowy figure, the white of skin and chemise in contrast to the woodland colors. Small wisps of curls the color of old silver coin shimmered in the glade's verdant dimness. The lithe figure cupped the sparkling water to her face and Jason caught his breath. It was a pale, piquant face, remarkable for the dark brows that flared upward over deep brown eyes.

" 'Tis no lady but a sprite," Jason murmured. He could now sympathize with the superstitions that so haunted the good folk of these parts. Sanchos, rarely verbal, whickered his agreement.

The figure in the pool stiffened. "Who is there?" she asked quickly as she spied them, her brows drawing closer in a frown.

"Merely two weary travellers, Madame Sprite." Jason prodded Sanchos forward until they came to the pool's edge.

The bather's eyes widened, for in truth, the weary travellers were of unusual size, the man well over six feet and three and the horse . . . "Faith, what a horse!"

The gentleman's rather lazy eyes lit up. "Of a certainty. This is intended, else he could not carry me."

"Of a certainty. Why have you come?"

"Beg pardon?"

"What is it you want?" The lady waded cautiously

forward, onto the land.

"Why, merely to hear you sing, sweet sprite," he said as his brows rose. Not only was her abrupt question curious, but so was her advancing towards him; most ladies he knew would rather have retreated if ever caught at their toilet by a total stranger.

"Is that all?" With a sudden swiftness, she bent over, her hand scrabbling inexplicably in the underbrush. When she arose, her actions were no longer so inexplicable. She was levelling a silver-mounted pistol directed at him with a remarkably steady hand. "Now, what do you want?"

"Certainly not what you think," the large man drawled. His posture did not alter, but his amiable eyes darkened. " 'Certes, here is an incivility. The sprite chooses to point a gun at us, Sanchos, when we really did but come to hear her rendition."

"I am no sprite and I know full well how to use this!"

"I would not care to debate the issue with you, but why point that thing at us poor, unassuming creatures? Faith, I have heard of the inhospitality of the good folk in these regions, but this is going some. I tell you the truth, we only came here to hear you sing." With placid ease he swung down from the saddle and stood before her.

"Sir, I suggest you get back up in that saddle, or I will shoot you—and in *any* place I so desire."

He studied her a moment. "Yes, I see that you would. I wonder why."

"Who sent you?"

"No one."

"I repeat—who sent you?"

"Who do you think?"

"Do not play with me." She cocked the pistol.

"Never. It is patently clear you are not of the frolicsome nature—but then, neither am I." His hand shot out with stunning speed and struck the gun from her grasp with a shattering blow. It flew into the thickets and

12

cracked as its charge shot off harmlessly. Both ignored the explosion, staring, eyes locked, at each other.

"A thousand pardons," Jason said as he retrieved the gun. "But you must understand, I have never taken kindly to guns when they are pointed in my direction. And then again, I was slightly worried as to exactly where you might desire to shoot me." The lady's eyes widened and she flushed slightly. "We men do become rather sensitive over threats of that particular nature."

"I would have shot you in the heart," the lady said coolly, her chin lifting, "since your death would have been the only thing I desired."

"Touché. But, alas, that is also an organ I cherish in some small degree." She looked away in anger, absently nursing her hand. "Oh, come now, do not look so cast down. Many have misjudged me before you."

The condescension seemed to aggravate her more, for her eyes blazed and he could hear her teeth grate. "I should not have made such a mistake!" she said harshly.

"Should you not have? What an exacting creature you are, to be sure." He stepped toward her. "Now, have I hurt your hand badly?"

"Leave me be," she said, backing away. "I am fine."

"Gad's, what a prickly sprite you are. Now do try to be polite and allow me to look at your hand."

"I told you, leave me alone or I will—"

"Will what?" He reached for her arm. "Will you strike me? You see me tremble."

"I mean it!"

His eyes lighted. "You mean it? What do you mean?"

"I mean, don't come near me or I will make you rue it."

He studied her. "You know, you are awfully threatening to a stranger just passing by. You should learn to be more civil to a man until you have determined who he is. And you certainly should not throw out such challenges, for someone like myself might just accept them." With-

13

out warning, he pulled her to him, enveloping her in a powerful hold.

"No!" She struggled against him in rage.

"Hmm, yes . . ." he said, and kissed her. A distant part of him realized that, as willowy as this sprite was, she was also rather tall, for her lips were not as far out of reach as were those of the diminutive ladies who were the fashion of the day. Her lips were at first cool, both from the water and from her rejection, but as he held the kiss, she finally leaned against him, a warm response emerging from her and enveloping him. It was not an overly passionate response, or an expert response, but the hint of the fire it banked within him caused him to draw back abruptly lest his mischief lead to something else. " 'Tis no sprite," he muttered, setting her from him, "but flesh and blood . . ."

The woman looked up at him, confusion plainly written upon her face. A flush slowly rose to her cheeks. Breathing hard, she swung back and punched him. Not a slap, which he had expected, but a true blow with her fist balled up correctly. Unfortunately, she had employed her bruised hand and she cried out in pain.

"I am sorry," he said ruefully as he nursed his cheek and she her hand.

"Sir, you are abominable."

"Madame, your swing is quite laudable," he countered, stepping back the better to view her. "You are an uncommonly aggressive wench—now why is that, I wonder? First a pistol, now a proper left. And don't tell me you learned it at finishing school."

"I'm not going to tell you anything—"

A sudden shot rang out and drowned her words. Flame seared Jason's shoulder and he doubled over, cursing. The lady matched him word for word as they dived to the ground in concert.

The lady spat out a mouthful of dirt. "Over there, to the left."

14

Jason, awash with pain, peered through the woods where she indicated. A heavy body passed through the trees. Jason raised the gun, aimed, and pulled the hammer. There was a quiet click and nothing else.

"Oh no," The woman beside him moaned. "Wait." She twisted about and snaked her way back to the thicket from whence she had unearthed the gun. The next shot followed her move but after a hair-raising moment she crawled back, holding shot in her grimy hand. She handed it to Jason without a word and he reloaded as swiftly as possible: the moments ticked by, seeming like hours.

By the time he raised the gun the shots from the dark figures were coming alarmingly closer. Jason sighted once behind the tree and fired. A satisfyingly agonized cry echoed through the woods, but the recoil of the gun sent pain darting through Jason's shoulder. His arm wavered against his will. "Damn, not again!"

"What is it?" the lady asked, inching closer. As his arm went limp she snatched the gun from his hand and reloaded quickly. "There is one more . . ." She raised the gun, her eyes narrowing in careful concentration as another bullet whined over their heads.

Jason's world began to spin; he could feel it caving in upon him. The woman beside him took aim and returned fire. "Damn, I missed him!" Then, inexplicably, she stuck the fingers of her free hand to her mouth and let loose a piercing whistle. He heard a raging animal growl and watched a massive creature lunge by them. He heard Sanchos whinny and saw a triumphant grin split the sprite's face—and then he knew no more.

Two figures stood over the unconscious body of the Earl of Wynhaven. "Are you all right, Miss Julia?" The man was of medium height, powerfully built, with an air of quiet solidness.

"Yes, John." She sighed. "They are onto us, are they not?"

"Perhaps—perhaps not. These three will not be able to tell them anything."

No, only those two are his, I believe. I do not know about this one." Her eyes darkened in perplexity as she prodded the earl with a wet, bare toe.

"It makes no difference. You had better get dressed and go back to the cottage."

"I should never have chanced this outing today," Julia said angrily. "It was foolish beyond permission. Now look what has happened."

"A person has to get out once in a while. And you were never one to stay caged in a house for very long."

"Thank you, John." She gave him a tired but grateful smile.

"Now don't worry, I will take care of these gallows-bait."

"But not this one," Julia said, frowning. She leaned down to the fallen earl. "We must see if we can help him—he still lives."

"But Miss Julia—"

"John, he is not one of them. Witness the bullet in him. He shot one of them himself and most likely saved me."

"That I cannot see. You would never have been caught unawares if he hadn't been requiring your attention."

Julia flushed. "Yes, but you cannot let a man die simply because he wished to dally with a maiden. I imagine mankind would have been long extinct if that were the case."

John did not react to the humor. "Then what do you propose to do with him?"

"I don't know—oh yes, I do. We'll take him back to Granny Esther." She looked at the recumbent man and a mischievous smile chased away her frown. "Let's see who teaches who a lesson then."

16

"Granny Esther! Now, Miss Julia, that would be twice foolish and three times dangerous!"

"Would you let the man die even before knowing if he is fair or foul?" Her eyes sparkled.

"No, I guess not." A responding gleam finally appeared. " 'Tis better than taking him to the nearest doctor; we'd both expire before accomplishing that feat."

Julia chuckled. "He is of a cumbersome size. And have you seen his horse?"

They both looked to Jason's steed and laughed. Sanchos was nose to nose with a large canine whose parentage could be easily traced to half the breeds in England. He resembled a miniature horse himself, with gray, wiry hair and a scraggly, crooked tail. A long, lolling tongue and grinning eyes, one blue, the other brown, completed the picture. "Sophocles appears to approve of Sanchos."

"Sanchos?"

Julia shrugged. "That is what the man called him. Well, my dear John, let us contrive to lift this mountain upon his steed and transport him to Granny's tender mercies. If he considers me inhospitable, he should revel in her attention."

John looked at her warily. "Now, Miss Julia, I don't like the sound of that. You know it would be better to leave him. The large gent will complicate an already dangerous game."

"Come, come, my cautious John, never say you think Grandmother Esther not up to this man's weight."

Her quiet companion smiled despite himself. "I'd never say that, Miss Julia, and you know it! Whoever he is and no matter how large, he'll not be too much for Grandmother Esther, and that I'd bet my life on."

Chapter Two

To Grandmother's House We Go

The earl knew he was delirious. Dreams of his campaign years jostled within his mind, supplanted by youthful escapades, interlaced with strange, seemingly real moments—moments that made very little sense and therefore had to be dreams as well. He opened his eyes, accepting fatalistically that what he might see was only a dream. It wasn't. It was a nightmare.

A great, blurred gray beast ravened over him, a beast that whined and jabbed a sharp, damp snout directly in his face and slathered it with a rough, wet tongue.

"Sophocles, leave him be," a voice commanded; from whence it came, Jason could not tell. The creature remained but a moment more, rendering him an oddly sympathetic gaze from its strange eyes, one of blue, one of brown. Then the monster lashed its tongue once again along the length of Jason's jaw, breathed a hot breath, and departed. Jason closed his eyes against any further phantasms.

"I can't understand it," a male voice said. "It's a clean wound."

"Then you can tend it?" a female voice asked. The voice nagged at Jason's consciousness.

"Won't be any trouble getting at the ball, but I can't figure it. The gent is out like a light, and 'tis only a ball

18

in the shoulder."

"It's the same damn place, that's why." Jason forced his eyes open. He discovered a blurred image bending over him, an image his eyes refused to bring into focus. He felt a hand undoing his shirt and attempted to brush it away. "No—"

"Oh my God, John. Look."

"Now I told you to leave the undressing to me, miss. I'll send you from the room otherwise."

"No, you'll require my help. But only look, John. How terrible."

Jason knew it was truly a nightmare now. "Sorry, madam," he mumbled, attempting to rise. "You should not have—"

"Oh, do lie still," the voice commanded, in much the same tones it had employed upon the beast. Two smooth hands pushed him back gently but firmly. "Indeed, I only meant how terrible it must have been for you."

Jason relaxed; he belived the voice, though he knew not why. The sight of his left shoulder and side would send any female shrinking in repulsion. Finally, his vision cleared and her image became defined. He groaned. "Damn, I'm dreaming again. You're the sprite in the woods—damn."

"A fine way to greet me, man," the sprite laughed. "Especially since it is you who have called me here to be your vision."

"I have?"

"Why else would I leave my woods and come here?"

"To—to finish me off, perhaps—"

"For shame, you ungrateful human."

"Sorry, it's just that—I need some reality right now."

"You'll be sampling far more of that than you wagered for, sir, in just a minute," the man said. "I'm sorry, but I must take the ball out soon. I—I see you've already seen some action, so you must know it won't be pleasant."

"Brandy?" Jason gasped.

"Yes, but only a sip," the sprite said. She left his side but returned a moment later, raised his head gently, and allowed him the slightest of tastes. "That is all. No more. You are not the patient I'd recommend to become castaway."

"You are a dream and yet give me only that? Cruel sprite."

"Have you not heard it is always a mixed pleasure to deal with the fairy folk?"

"Never believed it . . . until now."

She laughed. "You are learning fast, human. Next time, you'll not touch a sprite so freely."

He tried to answer, but he was losing his grip upon the scene, be it fantasy or nightmare. As he sank back into darkness, however, he felt the familiar, searing pain of a blade upon his skin. "Damn, now that feels real . . ."

Jason opened bleary eyes to stare at a low ceiling directly above him. He cautiously turned his head to see where he lay. It was an unfamiliar room, but cozy. The furniture was old and well-polished. An assortment of small rugs, pictures, and knickknacks gave the room a warm and pleasing atmosphere.

He turned his head further in exploration. A hunched, beshawled old lady rocked quietly in a rocker, a book in her withered hands. Her face was lined and wrinkled, obscuring her features. A pair of thick, tinted spectacles perched upon her nose and gray, coarse hair was wrapped around her head in unholy disarray.

Beside the old lady lay what appeared to be a dog. Like the ravening monster of his dreams, this dog had one blue eye and one brown eye, unmatched orbs sleepily contemplating the old lady in canine worship.

"Gads," Jason murmured. "What a beast."

The old lady looked up from the book and studied him a moment. "Which one of us do you mean?" she asked in

20

a scratchy, gruff voice.

Jason smiled. "Why, the dog—he is a dog?"

"Indeed. And a very fine one. But don't fear, he is a gentle doggie—well, most of the time he is."

"Is he? When he is not out pulling a dray cart?" the earl eyed the unique specimen with humor.

"You are referring to his size, I presume? Strange, I would not think you would be the one to cast stones."

"Being that I am such a large, hulking brute myself?"

"No, I'd never say such a thing to you, son. I know how poor Sophocles has suffered from such unkind attitudes—"

"Well, that puts me in my proper place." Jason surveyed the dog again. "Though I do think my parentage is more, er, regulated than his. At least I hope so. You call him Sophocles?"

"Yes, he's such a wise dog, you see. He has never once disagreed with me yet upon any subject that we have chosen to discuss, be it politics or the latest *on-dits*."

"I see." His head was beginning to hurt.

"Now, young man," the old lady said briskly, closing her book. "What is your name?"

"Hm? Oh . . . Jason. What happened to me? I remember the sprite at the water—"

"What? A *sprite* did you say?" The old lady's voice cracked in disbelief and she shook her head sadly. "Now, now, son, perhaps you had best lie back and rest some more. You've had a hard time of it and—"

"No, no, do not worry. I'm not daft. I called the lady my sprite, but she was human—very human," he added with indisputable lechery as he remembered her kiss.

The old lady suddenly succumbed to a fit of coughing. "Well, thank heaven for that," she said in a weakened voice. "I was afraid you were delirious again. It's not wise to be talking about sprites and the little folk, leastways not in these parts."

"So I found out," Jason said ruefully. "The hard way."

"So—you met this lady? Not uncommon for a young buck like yourself, I would wager."

Jason ignored that. "Yes, I met her down at the pond where she was bathing."

"Bathing? Dear me. Are you in the habit of meeting ladies while they bathe?"

"No, ma'am, not at all." His lips twitched at her obvious disapproval. "This was my first time at such an offence. And, I hope, my last, for that is when I was shot."

"I see. This lady took exception to your interrupting her bath?"

Jason's eyes widened at her calm acceptance of the idea, then he chuckled. "Lord, are all the females in these parts such fire-eaters? No doubt you would also have shot me?"

"Young man, ladies of my age rarely make a habit of bathing in the wilds—but yes, I would take exception to *any* man interrupting my bath."

"Then you and my sprite hold something in common."

"That we do." Jason found the crone's wicked grin oddly unsettling. "She shot you, then, and—"

"No, no, she was not the one that shot me—though she, too, wielded a gun. Two other men arrived, and it was one of them who shot me."

The old lady stared at him with a look of utter amazement. "You remember this? Son, are you positive that is what happened? You have been very ill, after all."

"Indeed, I know it sounds outlandish, but that is what happened. I do not remember much . . . but I do remember that."

"Well, son, I will not pretend that it sounds like a reasonable story, but stranger things have happened, I am sure. All I know, however, is that my man John found you at the pond, collapsed with a bullet in your shoulder. Though I should think," she said, grinning, "that if your story is half-true, you'll not be pestering females while they are about their ablutions."

Jason laughed, deciding he liked the woman's tart humor and dry wit, even if she was rather a fright to look upon. "Only too true, though I can't help but wonder why I was shot."

"You've got enemies, son?"

"That would be an interesting question, Mrs.—?"

"Grandmother Esther, or just Granny," she said impatiently. "Well, do you?"

"I cannot truthfully say, but I imagine I must. One cannot reach the age of thirty without offending someone, can one?"

"Not unless one's a pudding-heart, which I'll lay odds ain't exactly your curse."

Jason's eyes widened with feigned innocence. "But Grandmother Esther, I am quite amiable and agreeable. All my friends so say."

"A notion you try to cultivate, I make no doubt," she said with craggy shrewdness. "but one of your enemies are not likely to swallow any more than I am."

"What gives you cause to think that?" He felt rather surprised at the confidence with which she spoke.

Granny appeared nonplussed for a moment. "Well . . . anyone who had heard you in your sleep these past days would say the same. One would think you'd suffer many evil wishers after a'wooing the Señorita this, and the Dona that, and then this sprite person as well."

Jason grimaced. "Now Granny, you wouldn't throw the ravings of a delirious man in his face, would you?"

"Yes, I would!"

He laughed. This harridan gave no quarter. "For shame, Granny. You should not have listened to such scandalous things."

"Ah, yes. I should have fled the room with my hands over my hoary ears and left you to toss and buck until you ripped the wound wide open and bled to death. But of course!"

"No, no. 'Tis only that I fear that I might have said

something shocking," Jason said sincerely. He wished he could see past her spectacles to know if she understood what he meant.

"Hmph! If that is what you are worrying about, don't let it fash you." A gnarled hand waved the thought away. "I'm far past being shocked, young man. Don't you go worrying about my sensibilities and I'll refrain from worrying about yours."

"It's a bargain." Jason grinned, at ease again. "Besides, all that is in the past. You see a man about to reform."

"Indeed? If you say so," Granny murmured with blatant disbelief and returned to the subject at hand. "If those men weren't irate husbands or disgruntled fathers, who do you think they were?"

Jason frowned. "I believe they were after my sprite."

"*Your* sprite? The proprietary type, ain't you? Why do you think they were after her?"

"I told you she had a gun? Well, she returned fire."

"What? You are telling me the female shot at them?" Her rocking halted abruptly. "I think you'd best rest, son, before you have me falling into delirium. It's not good for us old folks to suffer shocks and alarms, you understand?"

"I am sorry to cause you any trouble. But—I do remember it and I am truly not a want-wit."

"No, I didn't think you were," Granny said. Jason could have sworn she said it with regret—but that was ridiculous. " 'Tis only slightly difficult to comprehend it all at once. Well, I'd best be about my chores, and you'd best be about more sleep. For such a strapping man as you appear, you're a might knocked up."

Jason's eyes became veiled, then he laughed. "Tsk, tsk. To insult a man when he's down—!"

"Hmph. It appears to me the best time to do it." The crone grinned. "You might just be too much to bullock when you're hale and hearty."

"Never, Granny. I wouldn't hurt a fly."

24

"Poppycock!" the old lady snorted. She rose painstakingly from her chair and toddled to the door, a bent and crooked figure. "But just you stay that meek, mind you. You are going to need a lot of bed rest before you're in fine fettle again, and I don't want any chariness from you, understand? You rise from there before I say you can and, old lady or not, I'll cut you down to proper size, do you hear?"

Jason laughed in amazement at her spunk. "Yes, Granny Esther. Oh, Granny?" he called, as she placed one veined, shaking hand to the door knob. "I need to know something."

"What is it, son?"

"I—I seem to remember a man taking the bullet out."

"Yes. That was my man, John."

"And now I realize that—that Sophocles was there."

"Y—yes, he most likely was."

"But I also seem to remember my sprite—the lady from the pond—being there as well."

Granny remained still a long moment, then she sighed softly. "Son, why don't you rest a while?"

"Granny, tell me." His voice sounded harsh from the tension in his body.

"Son," and her voice gentled with sympathy. "There were only John and I there when he took out the bullet, no one else. That I swear."

He lay still a moment. "I see . . . thank you for telling me. I think I had better rest now."

"I'm sorry, son—if you'll accept a word from a wise old woman, you would do better to forget all about this sprite woman—ban her from your memory completely."

Jason nodded, his face a blank. "You might be right. Perhaps I am suffering greater delusion than I ever have before . . . I will try and do as you say. I shall put her out of my memory."

* * *

25

Julia sat at the small kitchen table, gazing with a slight frown into a cup of tea. Her silver curls clashed with the age lines that were carefully drawn upon her face. Thick spectacles rested beside her saucer and a mound of shawls lay heaped upon the floor.

"So, he awoke?" John asked quietly, studying her carefully.

"Yes, and 'Granny Esther' was there to welcome him back into the world of reality—as it were."

"He did not find anything amiss with the old lady?"

"Of course not. He accepted Granny with open arms."

"That is good."

Julia's chin lifted. "Did you expect anything else?"

"No, of course not."

She smiled then, suddenly impish. "Lud, you should have seen it. He played right into my hands. Right now, the man doesn't know whether he is on his head or on his ears—he fears for his sanity, he does. As for the lady by the pond—he will believe that it was all a dream." Julia felt an odd twinge at that, but ignored it and chuckled again instead. "His face was a wonder to behold when I informed him that only Granny and you were there when the bullet came out."

John frowned. "Then he remembered that as well?"

"Yes, unfortunately—but never fear, he will not question it again. I saw to that."

"I don't know. I don't like making a May game out of this man."

"What else would you have us do? In truth, we protect the man as much as we protect ourselves in this deception." She remembered the first time she had met the earl and her mischievous smile sneaked back. "Besides, no harm will come to the man to doubt himself for once—he is far too puffed up in his own conceit as it is."

"Now Miss Julia, that's not why we are running this rig."

"No, of course not." Her eyes were deceptively inno-

26

cent. "But since we are pressed to do so, we might as well teach him a slight lesson — a philanthropic deed, as it were. Faith, I haven't had this much fun since — well, since I can't remember."

"You'll regret it if you try and bamboozle that man for too long. Besides, it's just not right."

"I'll not play him further than what is safe — I have his measure now. But that doesn't mean I can't have a bit of fun while I do so. And since when have you become his champion? Permit me to remind you that you were the one who wished him to perish in the woods."

"That was before I knew he had seen action. It couldn't have been easy, whatever he went through."

Julia shivered slightly, thinking of the scarred shoulder. "No, it couldn't have been. And that bullet he's taken won't be any help."

" 'Tis a shame."

Julia consciously shook off her mood. "Well, when a man must dally with strange women, what can he expect? I only hope that dalliance was his only objective."

"Why? Did he give you reason to think anything else?"

"He presented himself as Jason — only Jason."

"He did not use his title?" John asked. They had found his cards in his jacket.

"No, he did not. That does not denote a totally innocent man. Though it makes no sense if he is in league with the others, for they shot him."

"Wait. There may be a sensible reason why he did not give his full name. It could have been an oversight."

"In my experience, earls rarely forget their exalted station," Julia said cynically. "But I will certainly find out this next time — that is, Granny will."

"But not without me," John said quickly.

Julia looked at him in surprise. "Why not?"

"Well — it wouldn't be proper."

"Proper?" She laughed a warm, gentle laugh. "Faith, John, when will you stop thinking me a child? I'm all of

27

five and twenty and have fended for myself very well over the years. Your chick is fully fledged. Indeed, what did you expect the invalid to do to Granny, flat on his back as he is? I know you have great faith in the dauntless stamina of the English soldier, but this is going some."

"I still think I had better be there."

Julia studied him a moment, then an amused light filled her eyes. "Heavens, it isn't me you're worried about protecting, it's him! Men! You all band together. Well, never fear, I'll treat him kindly—well, as kindly as Granny can . . ."

Julia glanced up from her sewing as she watched over her sleeping patient. She discovered him awake and watching over her. "You sew very nimbly, Granny."

Her eyes narrowed, but Jason's face was innocent. "Of course. I've been doing this all my life. So—you remember who I am, do you?"

"But of course—why shouldn't I?" Then he frowned. "I am sure I appeared slightly deranged from the different stories I told you, but I'm not—really I'm not."

"I believe you, son," Julia said, after just the proper hesitancy.

"You do think I'm crazy, don't you?" he asked baldly.

"No—no, of course not."

"Good, because really—I'm not. I haven't figured out yet what actually transpired, but I'm sure I will."

"In time, son, I believe you just might." She could see she had succeeded in setting his teeth on edge.

"I intend to. I dislike mysteries and the sprite at the pond was such a one."

"I am sure . . . Speaking of mysteries, I have been passing the idle hours dreaming up a last name for you. You do have one, I hope?"

Jason looked startled. "I didn't tell you my name?"

"No."

28

"My apologies. I am Jason Stanton, Earl of Wynhaven."

"Mmm, very different from just Jason, wouldn't you say?"

"I certainly hope not. After all, what's in a name?"

"Why, in your case, a title. Something that is not easily overlooked."

Jason's eyes became wary. "Why? Does it make the rose smell any sweeter?"

Julia studied him a moment. He was serious; his concealment of his full identity had not been meant to deceive. She laughed. "Young corker, I do not care if you are a rose or a common daisy. I find I like them both equally—'tis only that I like to know which one I'm sniffing at the time."

Jason stared at her, then laughed. "I should have known you'd not consider a title of importance—after all, you've already ranked me with Sophocles there."

"Who is a prince among dogs."

"His full name would be FitzSophocles, then?"

Julia choked back her laughter. "You dastard. Do not insult my dog, for then you insult me."

"No, I would not do that," Jason said, his eyes warming. "I can only thank you for aiding me. And I do apologize if, even by mistake, I deceived you. I did not mean to do so."

"Excellent. See that you don't—ever."

"No, never. I promise."

"Remember that you swore me an oath," she said, her voice gruff in its intensity.

"It is the word of a Stanton," Jason said, looking at her in puzzlement. "And now, since we are discussing antecedents, who are you, Granny Esther? Do you too possess a last name?"

Julia was prepared for this. "Of course, though not so high as yours. It is Merton—of common stock, my lord."

Jason smiled sweetly. "Oh, no—never common stock."

"Well, perhaps not." Julia grinned her wicked granny-grin. "But it might as well be, these days. Hmm, Wynhaven . . . ah, you are a hero of the wars, then. Been mentioned in the dispatches quite a few times."

Jason looked amazed. "How did you know that?"

"I follow the news of the war, son, as any good British subject should." There was a piousness in her aged, creaky tone. "So, are you home to stay?"

"Yes. I was invalided out. Now there is nothing left for me to do other than take up the reins of my estates and become the proper gentleman again."

"I see. The Spanish señoritas will be left desolate—but it is now the fair English maidens' turn to rejoice."

Jason only laughed. "For shame, Granny. You make me sound a rake."

"Are you not?"

"Gad's no! Why, my friends would laugh to hear me described as such. Now, in truth, I am no monk, for I find the fair sex quite enjoyable. But I have been a soldier first and foremost, which leaves me very little time for ought else."

"But for Señorita Margueritte and—"

Jason held up his hand. "I cry a pax! I confess, I have had my fair share of youthful indiscretions, but I intend to settle down and set up my nursery. In fact, I am fiance'd."

"You are?" For some reason, Julia's throat tightened.

"Yes, though it is not common knowledge."

"I see . . . alas, only one fair English maiden will rejoice. But why is it not common knowledge? You aren't ashamed of her? She'd not a squint-eyed heiress that you plan to elope with, is she? Ahh, that is why you are in this area—trying to lead them off the scent, are you?"

Jason chuckled until he gasped. "Lord, Granny, don't make me laugh so—it hurts! What a shameful and lurid imagination you have for such a sweet-seeming old lady. No, my fiancée is not squint-eyed, but a delicate vision

30

of beauty; yes, she does have money, and no, there is no nefarious reason why we keep our impending marriage secret." 'Tis only that she has been in mourning this past year and will not be out of gloves until the end of this month. Her father died in an accident last year, and her uncle is now her guardian."

Julia felt a sickening premonition. "And who might her uncle be?"

"She is ward to the Duke of Rendon."

Julia's needle gouged her thumb. "Ouch!"

"What is it?"

"I—I pricked my finger, 'tis all," she said quickly, raising the injured digit to her lips. "Old eyes, I fear . . . so, your fiancée is—"

Chlorinda Everleigh."

Julia only nodded, not trusting herself to speak. Sophocles, who lay beside her, evidently sensed her tension, for he sat up and, with a whine, placed a large paw insistently atop her lap. Jason watched the dog's movements. "Is anything amiss, Granny?"

"Heavens, no. Whatever would make you think that?"

Jason frowned. "Do you know Chlorinda?"

Julia laughed shakily. "No, of course not. How—how would I know her, stranded out here in the wilds as I am?" She started attending carefully to her sewing. "Though if she is anything like her father, she must be charming."

"You knew him then?"

Julia was taken aback; she had slipped. "Ah—yes, in my salad days." Since she had stepped so far, she decided to chance it further. "Yes, I knew him then. He was best friend to the young Landreth, I remember."

"Landreth, the traitor?" Jason asked with a frown. "Yes, I recall that Rendon mentioned something of the sort once. He said that beyond that unfortunate connection, John Everleigh was the best of men." Julia remained silent. "Then you knew Landreth as well?"

31

"Yes, I did," she replied curtly.

Jason studied her curiously. "What type of man was he back then?"

"He was a good man." Her words were sharp, then she caught herself. "Well, at least, he always appeared that way to me."

Jason paused, then asked gently, "Did you perhaps have a tender for Landreth? Is that what has caused your upset?"

Julia stared at Jason's concerned expression, and then she choked. "A tender . . . for . . . Landreth?" she started to laugh. "Oh, no, no . . . never. It would be indecent for me to have one in my estimation . . . very indecent."

"I'm glad," Jason said sincerely. "He did much against England—his treachery was of the worst kind. You knew that he died recently in a fire?"

She stopped laughing. "Yes. Yes, I did."

"It was a foul business, all around."

"Very foul. Have you—heard what happened to his children?"

"His children? Oh, yes, a boy and a girl—they were under suspicion as well. It appears they fell foul of highwaymen a few days after his death as they travelled to his funeral. They perished."

"Yes, that is what I had heard. Such a pity," she said, sighing deeply.

Jason peered at her. "Are you sure you did not have a tender for Landreth? You speak warmly of the traitor and his children."

"I told you I did not, young man," Julia snapped with old-woman crustiness. "For heaven's sake, can't an old lady have an opinion upon a man without it being considered a romantic fancy?"

Jason looked at her closely. "Who are you, Granny Esther?"

"What do you mean?" Julia parried warily.

"Why, 'tis merely that you are a rare old lady. You seem to know so much about everything."

"Just because I live out here doesn't mean I'm a savage, ignorant of the outer world's doings," she said quickly. "Why, I run poor John ragged with my demands for the news and the latest *on-dits.*"

Jason laughed. "Well, that's telling me, isn't it? No, Granny, you may say what you want, but you are not ordinary, and I hope some day to hear your life story."

Julia thought that it would be cold in a certain torrid region before that occurred, but she only smiled and said, "Perhaps. If you prove to be a good patient, I might tell you—as a bedtime story. Now I'm going to leave you so that you may rest."

"Rest? But that's all I've been doing!"

"And that's all you are going to do," she warned in sugary tones as she left.

It was a distinct pleasure to close the door upon the large and rather clever man. Indeed, Julia heaved a deep and heartfelt sigh as she twisted the knob firmly shut.

John looked up from the wood he was chopping to discover Grandmother Esther advancing towards him. She wore a pensive expression. "What is it, Granny?"

"Our invalid becomes more of an enigma."

"Why?"

"Our noble guest is engaged, it seems."

"Is he? What does that signify?"

"His sweet fiancée just happens to be the ward to Converse Everleigh, Duke of Rendon."

"What?"

"Yes. None other than Chlorinda Everleigh. Is that just not our luck—to save Chlorinda's intended? Yet I've quizzed him on it all and he appears innocent. Could that be?"

"It could," John grunted, as he returned to splitting

33

wood. "The man seems to have told you everything. If he were cutting a sham, he wouldn't likely admit to an association with Rendon."

"I know. Or he could just be very clever and have decided to stay as close to the truth as possible, in case we found him out."

"It never does to make hasty decisions."

"You think it a coincidence? John, you and I both know there is rarely such a thing. Not in our line of work. Many fine men have lost their lives by thinking otherwise."

"And just as many have confused the matter by not believing in coincidence. Life does have its games to play."

"Yes—perchance you are right." Julia nodded pensively. "He did save me at the pool, after all. Nevertheless, the man bears watching—but then again, when did a man not bear watching?"

Chapter Three
In The Stew

Three days later, Julia, flinging back Granny's myriad shawls, added more salt to her stew, which did not please her taste at all. John was out doing chores; he had taken Sophocles with him, since the dog had been persistently pestering Julia in the kitchen. The creature had an underbred tendency to raid the kitchen table whenever Julia's back was turned.

Their invalid was progressing nicely, and would most likely have been up and about if his new wound had not been complicated by his prior injuries. The earl seemed reticent about those earlier experiences; he was one of those rare men who did not boast of his war exploits. Neither Julia nor John could bring themselves to ask, either — the heavily-scarred shoulder spoke eloquently enough.

He was not a common sort of man, Julia thought, pursing her lips. She decided perhaps a bit of sage could enliven her brew. The earl was all amiability to the point of being placid, yet Julia knew full well he was a man of discipline and action. He did not hold himself with the stiffness common to the military man, but there was no doubt that he was a trained fighter — his quickness at the pool demonstrated that much.

Another thing he did not boast of was conquests

within the feminine fraternity. Indeed, he claimed not to be a Don Juan, but Julia well remembered the ladies he had wooed while in his delirium. Though his reputation did not title him a rake either, she found it difficult to believe that all those women were friends or female relatives. She grimaced. No doubt his deceptively relaxed attitude also saved him from such a characterization. A lady would find it hard to cry "fiend" upon such a tall, smiling gentleman.

Julia sighed, stirring her stew meditatively. It still lacked something, but her mind returned to her confusing subject. She would not be fooled by the polite gentleman resting within the guest room. She could well remember the tones of command he had employed in his delirium when he had talked to the absent soldiers, as well as the coaxing note when he talked to the Señorita Magueritte. A proper young lady would never have listened so meticulously to the ravings of an unconscious man, nor would she hold those ravings against him. Yet she was not, she reminded herself, exactly proper; she would have been dead a long time since if she had played by the rules of propriety and decorum.

Her back suddenly tingled, and she stiffened. The unmistakable feeling of being watched crept over her. Gripping her soup ladle tightly, she spun swiftly, holding it in front of her like a weapon. The ladle smacked up against a man's bare chest.

"Gracious!" Her heart was pounding. The Earl of Wynhaven stood before her in skintight pantaloons and unbuttoned shirt, her soup spoon glued to him, surprise showing in his hazel eyes. "Oh—I'm so sorry," Julia stammered, pulling her spoon away. "Did I hurt you?" She attempted to ignore the soup as it ran down his furred chest onto a flat, muscled stomach. The bandage on his shoulder could barely be seen under the shirt, the white of it contrasting with his sun-bronzed skin. She turned away quickly, reaching for a cloth.

"No, no," Jason said. "You've only singed me a little."

Julia turned back, having secured a cloth. She became mesmerized watching Jason as he rubbed the injured area with a well-shaped hand. "Ah, here," she gulped, jabbing the towel in his direction and looking away quickly, a blush creeping up her neck. She would never have thought that the simple sight of a man's bare chest could affect her in such a manner.

"Gads, Granny," Jason laughed as he employed the towel to effect. "You are a wicked one with a ladle."

"You startled me," Julia mumbled lamely, attempting to regain control of her nerves and poise. What was she? A mere schoolgirl, to blush so? "Uh—uh—what are you doing up, young man?"

Jason evidently discerned her nervous condition. "What is it, Granny? Why, I have startled you. Here, allow me to help you." He tossed aside the towel and stepped forward, his arms outstretched to guide her.

"No, no, I'm fine," Julia said feebly, her hand instinctively warding him off. It contacted the very chest that caused her upset. Even though he was still sticky with stew, the feel of his muscles and skin beneath her hand sent an odd frisson through her. She did not pull it back immediately.

"You are *not* all right, Granny. Why—you're trembling," Jason said with concern. "Now come and sit down." He stepped closer and put his arm around her, leading her to the table. "Sit."

"Stop fussing, young man," Julia said gruffly as she slid, embarrassed, into the chair. "And sit down yourself." Suddenly, he was looking rather odd.

"I—think I will." He smiled wryly, taking a seat across from her.

"Now, why are you up, disregarding my orders? And why have you come before me in such a state of undress?"

He looked down at his open shirt and grimaced. "A

thousand apologies, but I was unable to find my own shirt." He tugged at the gaping shirt-edges uselessly and looked up. "I'm sorry to distress you. I can imagine how unsettling the sight of me can be."

Julia only stared at him, speechless. Then the true meaning of his words penetrated her mind. "You mean because of your shoulder? Stuff and nonsense. That did not bother me, nor would it ever."

Jason looked at her a moment. "Would it not? It is quite disfigured."

"They are only scars, and earned in battle. What woman wouldn't be proud of a man who had gained them fighting for his country?"

"You are very patriotic."

"One must be willing to fight for one's country," Julia said softly, "no matter the losses or the scars."

Jason studied the old woman, whose voice had turned sad and almost bittersweet. Had she lost her husband in the wars? "More women should be like you, Granny."

"Why? Would not your fiancée react the same?"

"I am—not sure. But she is a sheltered, delicately nurtured female."

"Then she does not know of your wounds?"

"No, of course not! How could she? For shame, Granny, I am not that type of man. I assure you I have courted her most properly."

"I meant only that you had talked to her about it, perhaps?"

"No, we have not—that is quite a personal matter and we have not progressed that far. I would not wish to frighten her in any way."

"What a delicate flower she sounds. You plan to marry this girl, yet you do not wish to talk to her of personal matters?"

"Why do you sound so disapproving? It is only nature, after all. Chlorinda is a good girl, and would never meet me without proper chaperonage. And my physical state is certainly something I do not plan to discuss in front of her chaperone."

"No, of course not," Julia said dryly. "Faith, it sounds as if your courtship abounds with passion!"

"Now, Granny, don't pinch at me like that. I fear I am simply not of the hot and ready nature. Faith, to see such a man as I in the throes of strong emotions might very well send the poor, gentle girl into fits."

"Well, I think her a perfect ninny," Julia said irritably before she could stop herself. Then she coughed and asked, "And you like her to be so proper?"

Jason sighed. "Granny, I have had enough excitement to last me a lifetime. Yes, I like her proper rearing — it is one of the things that I considered in my decision. I will be perfectly happy to settle down and live free from adventure. I fear I must be terribly conventional."

"Yes, you must be," Julia purred.

Jason laughed. "Ah, I disappoint you? Then your life with Mr. Merton was full of adventure and high romance?"

"Yes, it was!" Julia sputtered, nettled. "It was a grand passion with us. He did not choose me as if I were a jacket that must be a comfortable fit. Why, why, he would — kiss the hem of my dress and — strew rose petals across my bed — my boudoir."

Jason choked and laughed. "Rose petals — across your — my, you must have been one fiery minx."

"Yes, I was," Julia said stubbornly, refusing to join in his laughter. "And I hope you know, I've also been courted by princes and nobles, men who didn't want a die-away little pattern card of respectability."

Jason held up his hand against her vehemence. "Granny, please don't eat me! I did not mean any offense. I cry mercy!"

Julia glared at him angrily and then sighed. "Oh, very well, young corker. I am sure this Chlorinda will suit you to perfection. Each must lead his own life, after all."

"Thank you for such leniency," Jason said with suspicious meekness.

"Well, now, hadn't you best be getting back to your bed?" Julia said briskly. She could tell the man still laughed at her.

"No, I wish to hear about the prince who courted you."

"No, son, I am sure the sheer excitement of it would be too much for you," Julia said maliciously. "Now hie thee that large carcass of yours back to its bed."

Jason sighed and stood up. "You are a tyrant, you know."

Julia looked at him and, now that she was not so unsettled, noticed the shirt Jason wore. Not by any stretch of the imagination did it cover him; it rode up at the sleeve, pulled alarmingly over his shoulders, and hung all a-kilter. Despite her best efforts, she began to chuckle.

"What?" Jason asked, confused.

"The shirt—it's impossible! Where did you find it?"

"I obtained it from John's room. I could not find mine. Did you hide it from me on purpose?"

"Of course not!" Julia said, rising. "I was mending it. You were not supposed to be in need of it for a while."

"I know, but I thought I might go mad if I didn't get up soon."

"You are already mad," Julia said.

"I wager you never said that to your prince."

"I am not about to tell you what I said to my prince. Now do go back to bed." She noticed that he had put a hand to the back of the chair and her brows furrowed as she surveyed his every feature. His skin had taken on an ashen hue. "You're not feeling well—why did you not tell me, rather than sitting here conversing?" Her anger turned to concern as he swayed before her, and she rushed to him quickly to support him as he lurched. "See, you are as weak as a puppy."

"I—fear I am . . ."

40

"Put your arm around me. We must get you back to your bed." Jason obeyed, listing slightly. "A more foolish, caperwitted stunt I have never seen. If you weren't already so weak, I'd have your head for a washing!" Julia snapped to mask her concern.

Jason did not answer; Julia looked up at him and froze. He was staring at her and his eyes, strained as they were, scanned her intently.

"What—what is the matter?" She realized belatedly that her masquerade stood in imminent danger, so close was she to him.

"I am going mad," he muttered, shaking his head dazedly.

"Didn't I just tell you that? Let us go," she said desperately, attempting to move him.

He was granite within her arms. "Granny. What—what color eyes do you have?"

"What kind of question is that, young man? Now let us go—you are evidently under a grave strain."

"They—they aren't brown, are they?"

"N-no, they are blue," she said quickly, tugging on him.

Jason sniffed. "What scent do you use, Granny?"

Now she knew she was in trouble; at that range, the smell of greasepaint and the cornstarch she employed to roughen her skin were obvious. "My own scent; I make it myself," she said truthfully, "Don't you like it, son?"

"Er—oh, yes. 'Tis only—"

Julia did not allow him to finish. "Now, son, you are weak. Let us get you to bed—I fear you are suffering a fever again."

"No, I—"

A joyous bark interrupted him. A scrabbling of toenails upon the polished floors heralded Sophocles's approach and he galloped into the room with abandon. Spying both his idols conveniently in one spot, he barked in enthusiastic greeting and threw himself at them. This proved too much for the weakened earl and the unsuspecting Julia and they went toppling to the floor, forty pounds of dog atop them.

"Get off me, you beast!" Julia cried.

"I hope you don't mean me," Jason said. He groaned as Sophocles attempted to disconnect himself from the mass. "Damn."

"Oh, no!" Julia exclaimed. After many misplaced paws, Sophocles lumbered away dislodging Jason's bandage as he went. "Look what he did—your wound."

"Don't—don't fret. I will be all right."

"Of course," Julia snapped, angrily attempting to shuffle out of her shawls and sit up. "But I won't be. Now, how the devil am I to get you back to bed? If I have ever seen a greater pair of clunches—you," she said, pointing an accusing finger at Jason, "you had to rise before it was time! And you," she scolded, her finger swinging to Sophocles, "I've told you a thousand times not to jump up on us!"

Sophocles whined and hunkered down a safe distance away with a sheepish look. His tail thumped in a hesitant attempt at conciliation, but Julia had none of it. "If the earl dies, it will be your fault!"

"I won't," Jason protested in a weak voice. "I made it through the war—I'll be hanged if I'll let a . . . dog put me under."

"Brave talk," Julia snapped, eyeing the pale, still man beside her. "Your bandage has been mauled about and your wound is open again." She leaned over him, attempting to adjust the bandage.

There was a gasp from the doorway. "Miss—Mistress Merton, what is going on in here?" John's expression was stern as he approached the two upon the floor.

"Oh, John, thank God. Do help me get my lord to his bed."

"My Lord Wynhaven, what happened to you?"

"Sophocles," Jason grunted in reply.

"Now, my lord, permit me to help you," John said.

"Yes . . . I think that I am now ready to return to bed."

"Excellent," Julia snapped. "Now, he decides. After he has undone all our hard work to save him."

Jason grimaced as John helped him up. "Forgive me, Granny, for ever disobeying," he said through clenched teeth. John was slowly helping him towards the door.

"I do. Now go back to bed."

Jason did not even manage to reply. Sophocles, after overseeing the men's course out of the kitchen, returned to Julia's side. He lay down next to where she sat, lowered his large-boned head onto outstretched paws, and considered her with grave, sad eyes.

"Oh, don't take on so, dear," Julia said, reaching out to dig a fingernail into the wiry hair behind his ear. She scratched, and he sighed in pleasure. "He may suffer from your actions, but you certainly saved me from mine. It was very imprudent of me, and a far closer thing than I care for. We must be more cautious. I don't care if the man is dying. I won't even go near him. Ever. See if I don't!"

That evening, Julia lay in her bed, attempting to coax Morpheus to her side. She failed miserably.

John was out again tonight. She prayed that the rendezvous would be successful this time. She wasn't certain whether they could wait much longer; she was sure to be uncovered by her enemies or unmasked by the earl, and she didn't care for either fate.

She gritted her teeth in the dark. She would stay as long as possible. She had to. She didn't want to be cut loose by herself. That could only be worse.

An anguished shout sliced through her thoughts. Gasping, Julia jerked up from her bed, every nerve jangling. Silence mocked her. Then she heard voices within the house itself and fear paralyzed her. She was all alone—John had taken Sophocles as well, for the dog was an excellent ally in a fight.

She rose swiftly and flitted steathily to the bedroom door. She placed her ear to the wood, attempting to listen over her hammering heart. Finally, a slow smile eased the tension in her face; she had located the sounds. They came from the earl's room.

Opening the door quietly, she slipped down the hall. She reached his door and opened it to listen. Jason had fallen silent; she tiptoed to his side in concern. A shaft of moonlight from the window nearby streamed across his face. Julia murmured softly, for his face, though now in repose, glistened with a sheen of perspiration. She bent further over, attempting to determine the state of his fever—then exclaimed as an iron hand shot out from beneath the covers. She was jerked swiftly down, toppling her onto the bed—and the earl.

"Who are you?" Jason's voice was dangerous with the controlled tone of a soldier.

"Oh, Lord . . ."

His eyes were open, slitted in mistrust. Then they widened, and a smile that discomfited Julia as much as his prior expression crossed his face. "Thank God, it's you."

"Yes?" Julia said warily. Why did he smile like that at her?

"Well, it is about time. What took you so long?"

"Took me so long?"

"I swear I've been imagining you everywhere, even in old ladies. And then you wouldn't come here when I called. It's been hell itself tonight."

"Well—I'm sorry." She didn't know what else to say.

"First time you've ever apologized to me, Madame Sprite."

Julia nodded vigorously in relief. "Yes, yes—you know I'm only a dream, don't you?"

He sighed. "Yes, I do. But just the one I have been

44

wanting tonight. The others have been—never mind, they have only been of men's folly. I far prefer you," he said with a sweet smile. He shifted her to the whole length of his frame and Julia suddenly realized he intended to kiss her.

She swiftly inserted her hand between his mouth and hers, just in time. "Wait a minute. You—you dream too quickly. Don't you know humans are not permitted to kiss sprites?"

"Why not? I have before."

"Yes, and look what happened."

Jason's chuckle shook them both. "But she was real. You are my dream. I can kiss you," he said confidently, and did just that. His lips covered hers before she could object.

He kissed her with a thoroughness that left her trembling. His hands smoothed her body's curves to him with a devastating effect. Julia, after one languorous moment, a moment where liquid heat flowed wherever his hands had been, pulled back, gasping slightly. He said not a word, but only looked inquisitively at her, his eyes dark. Then his fingers slid up the back of her neck and wound themselves within her hair, gently drawing her lips back to his.

Julia groaned softly as their lips met again. His were soft and teasing. A warm ache filled her being, an ache that frightened her in its newness and intensity. But she remained, letting the sensuous shock course through her as his lips and tongue explored hers in a kiss beyond her imagination. His kiss stifled her gasp as his hand slid to the top of her nightgown and stroked the hollow of her throat.

Julia felt a strong desire to have that hand follow its due course. The feeling shook her so intently, it also rocked her back to reality. Faith, what was she doing? The man thought her a mere dream—if he made love to her tonight, he'd not even know her in the morning! She drew back in earnest, clasping quickly at his hand. "No—" she gasped, attempting to control her ragged breathing.

"Why not?"

"I—I told you, humans are not permitted to kiss sprites."

Jason lay still a moment, then sighed. "Even my dreams of you tonight are cruel. Why are we not permitted?"

"We sprites are not of your kind—"

"And if we were to make love?"

"You would lose your soul," Julia said softly, knowing it would not be his but hers that would be lost in such a meeting.

He did not pull his hand away. "Where would it go?" he asked softly, just as softly running his hand through her curls.

"To—to my land of the fairies. A hundred years in your world is but a moment's time in mine."

" 'Tis no matter," he sighed. "Take me anywhere. As long as it is away from tonight, and away from those other nightmares." He reached to kiss her again.

"No," Julia said, but gently this time. Her fingers rose to his face and seemed to explore it against her own will. "You need not kiss me for that, human. Only close your eyes." She ran her fingers gently over his eyelids as he obeyed. "And clear your mind. You can rest now. I will keep all other dreams at bay—but there will be no souls lost tonight."

She felt his hold relax slowly, ever so slowly. She lay there a moment more, her hand still upon his cheek. Finally, his breathing steadied, and Julia knew that he slept deeply. She slipped cautiously from his hold, feeling cold without his arms around her. She tiptoed to the door and out into the hall, closing the door quietly upon the earl. "Back to reality," she thought wryly, leaning her head against the hard wood that separated them.

46

She felt a tap on her shoulder and a muffled yelp escaped her. "What are you doing, Miss Julia?" John whispered.

"Thank goodness it's you. You nigh scared me out of ten years' growth."

"I didn't expect you to be awake. Is everything all right?"

"Yes . . . oh, yes." Julia was glad for the darkness that hid her blush. "How was tonight? Did he arrive?"

"No. No, he didn't. Why are you up?"

"The earl was delirious and I went to see how he was."

"And?"

"H—he's running a fever."

"And—"

She sighed. "And he woke up and saw me."

"Good God! Without your disguise?"

"Yes, without my disguise. But you need not worry. He thought I was the sprite from before, and only a dream."

"How could you have let it happen, Miss Julia? It's not like you!"

"I made a mistake," she snapped in response to his reproving tone. "To all appearances, the blasted man was dead to the world. Then, there he was—all of a sudden—looking at me, and—and talking to me." She paused a moment. "Can you—give him some laudanum, perhaps? He should not remember anything of it tomorrow, I am sure. And he did think me a dream."

"You are taking a big risk, Miss Julia. We've already played that game once with him. He's no block; he'll rumble to it soon."

"Yes, but by that time I plan for us to be long gone. Only do what I ask and we shall scrape by."

"I hope so," John said grimly.

Julia forced a laugh. "Come now, John, we've been in tighter spots than this. You're not going to let a single soldier worry you, are you?"

"He's not common, Miss Julia."

47

"No, he isn't," Julia admitted, shivering. "But, then, neither am I. Now please, look to him. He's truly in a fever. He's rambling like he did the first night."

"I knew something like this would happen, with him rising like that a'foretime. Excitement isn't good for him." Julia bit her lip guiltily. "Well, I'll do as you say," John continued. "A small dose of laudanum should not harm him."

"Thank you, John. Good night."

". . . Miss Julia? He only *saw* you?"

"Well—no. But nothing serious happened."

There was a pause. "What would be serious?"

"Well—let us just say that no souls were lost." The silence continued. "Oh, for goodness' sakes, John, don't be an old broody hen. Just dose him well."

"Yes, Miss Julia. I only wished to know what strength of dosage he required—I'm afraid I have my answer."

Chapter Four

Granny?

"Good morning, John," a hollow voice croaked from the bed as John set a tray of food down beside the earl.

"Good morning, my lord. How are you feeling?"

"Like the very devil."

"I would not be surprised, my lord. You did not make a good night of it, I fear."

"Lord, no. And my deepest apologies—I did not mean to drag you from your bed in order to quack me."

John looked quickly to Jason but realized he was sincere. "It was—no trouble," he said in a strangled voice.

"Whatever is the name of that dreadful concoction you gave me last night?"

"Er, it doesn't have a name, my lord. It was a recipe my master—my late master, that is—created for just such a purpose."

"Well, it certainly did the trick."

"Then—then you do not remember anything of the evening?"

"No, thank God, it is a blur. You have my deepest gratitude for that."

"No need to thank me, my Lord, no need at all," John replied, his voice gruff with embarrassment.

"I do hope I didn't wake Granny with my ravings?"

"Er—no. She is a very heavy sleeper—very heavy."

"Fortunate woman," Jason said with a frown. "John, do you know anything about the stories of sprites?"

John choked and dropped the spoon he was handing Jason. His voice was muffled as he bent to pick it up. "Sprites? You mean, like, er, fairies? The little folk?"

"Yes, fairies. Though I certainly wouldn't use 'little folk' as a description."

"Ah . . . no, sir, I do not. Why?"

"Oh, I don't know. I had the strangest dream last night."

"You did?"

"Yes, very pleasant, but very strange. Is there anything in folklore about the dangers of a human kissing a sprite?"

John wheezed slightly. *"Kissing* a sprite? Is that what you did—er, I mean, dreamed you did?"

Jason grimaced. "Something like that. But you wouldn't know anything about them? You wouldn't know what happens if humans and sprites mate?"

John turned pale. "Never—never say you did that, my lord!"

Jason laughed. "Faith, John, it was only a dream. You are white as a sheet—why, what is the legend?"

"I—I really don't know," John flushed. "But I—I'm sure it wouldn't be good. You—you didn't do it, sir, did you?"

Jason looked puzzled. "Why? What does it matter? But if it will calm your superstitious soul, no, I did not." He grinned. "I couldn't hold fast long enough to the dream to accomplish that."

"Thank God," John breathed. Then he flushed. "I—I mean, I don't know anything about such matters, but one cannot be too careful in these parts when it comes to the wee folk."

"So everyone tells me," Jason said dryly. "Even in my dreams."

* * *

Julia critically surveyed the man lazing upon the grass a few feet from her. He chewed with contentment upon a blade of grass and his hazel eyes amiably watched the clouds that wafted by overhead.

The earl looked far better than the week before, she thought with a well-earned smugness. He had not suffered any further bouts of delirium and appeared to be definitely on the mend. She certainly did not begrudge him his recovery, yet she found an ambulatory earl to be a noteworthy challenge to her ingenuity.

The fact that the earl had adopted her as his very own grandmother did not help much. She was continually pressed to keep him at a safe distance, which proved very taxing, since he had a tendency to wander quietly into a room, then tease her mercilessly at whatever task she was performing. She discovered she was often forced to take the coward's way out and retire to her room, for her supposed octogenarian naps, about which he was always understanding and solicitous.

Yet, in his own way, Julia admitted, the earl was a blessing. He kept her so bedeviled trying to uphold her masquerade that she had very little time to worry over her failure to rendezvous. Indeed, the earl and Granny had fallen into such a unique and pleasant relationship that had she had not been on tenterhooks over their prolonged stay at the cottage, she would have thoroughly enjoyed herself.

She and Jason had whiled away many afternoon hours in diverting conversations. He would tell her the most entertaining of his war stories, and since he considered her aged and wise, he attempted neither to varnish nor censure them. She, in turn, would spin amusing tales of Granny's supposed escapades in her past. She delighted in telling stories that would bring forth his deep, lazy laugh, and often as not she would blend some of her true life experience into them as well.

"What are you thinking, Granny?"

Julia started. She had not thought that he'd noticed her scrutiny. "That you are looking much haler."

"I do feel much better."

"And how is your slumber these days?"

"Capital, thank you. Perhaps the country air was exactly what I needed. I haven't once fallen into delirium this past week."

"And were you suffering from it much before?"

"Often enough. Though I think the worst is past now."

"What was the worst, my lord?"

There was a silence. "Oh, 'tis not a story you would care to hear."

"I would not have asked—son—if I did not wish to listen."

"It is no different from most soldiers' tales. A man goes to war and he fights for what he believes in, yet the agony and death that surround him make him start wondering how the things that he believes in can cause such destruction. And I, I was lucky. I did not lose an arm, or a leg, or my sight. I only took part of an explosion on my side. My batman took the full force of it, God rest his soul. And even though the doctors said I'd never live, I have. They took me for dead, or so close as not to consider operating."

"My God," Julia breathed angrily. "The fools."

"No, Granny, they were only pragmatic. And, in truth, in the shape I was in, I was waiting second by second to hear Gabriel's trump—that, or the gates of hell clanging open."

"What happened?"

Jason shrugged. "I simply would not die. I remember the doctor who operated on me saying that since I refused to give up my cot, he supposed he would be forced to look at me. He took out as much of the metal as he safely could, and now it is simply the process of waiting for more to surface and extracting that. But I feel healthier every day."

"I—I suppose you will be leaving soon, then?"

"Yes, I suppose I will be. Jackson, my valet, who I sent ahead, must surely be suffering apoplexy by now."

"I wondered about his absence."

"And never asked me? How reticent of you, Granny. No, I prefer to travel fast, while Jackson, though an excellent valet, is somewhat poor in travelling. I send him ahead in slow stages."

"And you saw no need to send him a message before this?" Julia resumed her knitting with determination.

"Gad's, no. If I did, we'd have him down on us like an old, fidgeting grandmother—no insult to you, my dear. Besides, it won't be the first time I have not arrived upon schedule. My staff knows better than to fly into a pother at my absences.

"Ah, you make a habit of disappearing often? I'm sure your bride will cherish such behavior."

Jason chuckled. "I doubt she will. But, of course, I will not continue to do so after the marriage."

"Such a relief," Julia said dryly. They sat in amiable silence then, Julia counting the stitches upon her knitting and Jason still gazing at the clouds.

"Granny, I have a question for you."

"Oh? One moment. Twenty-six . . . twenty-seven . . ."

"It's a rather excellent notion—"

"That's nice, ninety—blast, where was I? This looks incorrect for some reason."

"Why don't you and John come and live with me?"

"Twenty-four, twenty—what?"

"I said, why don't you and John remove to London with me? It is not good for you to be out here in these unfriendly territories."

"And London is friendlier, with pickpockets and thieves on every corner?"

"It's certainly less lonely. You must own, Granny, that you live a secluded existence at present. And for one who

53

cares for excitement, this life must be sadly flat."

Julia was forced to admit this was so, but she would never tell him. "My life is fine."

"You know the dowager house stands empty now that Mother has passed on."

"So you plan to move an eccentric old lady into it, one you've only just met? You require an adopted grandmother for some reason?"

"Why not?" Jason grinned. "Everyone should have one. You are far better than my real grandmother ever was. She was short of hearing and had an ear trumpet. The minute one of us would whisper something, we'd find it right in our face. It put paid to all my youthful flirtations with the young ladies, I can tell you. Thank heaven, your hearing is excellent."

"Gammon! Don't put me to the blush, young scamp. Furthermore, I doubt that you would be very fond of me for long."

"No, I won't believe that."

Julia looked at the sturdy man who spoke so confidently and something twisted deep inside her. If he ever discovered who she was, he would renounce that claim swiftly enough. "Believe me, son, I have a past."

"So I know. And a very colorful one. Though you are still holding out upon the prince that proposed to you."

Julia smiled. "Ah, that is why you invite me. You intend to cozen the story from me."

"No, Granny, it is that I have a fondness for you and will not be satisfied with you living out in these wilds with only John and a dog to protect you."

This was growing worse. "They are protection enough. And never fear, I can take care of myself. I'm not that old that I don't have tricks up my sleeve."

"That I can well believe—"

"And I'm not past the age of causing scandals and adventures."

"Perhaps my proper existence can withstand some excitement after all."

"Not my type," Julia muttered softly. "Now, son, you don't need an old lady like me to create excitement in your life. That's for your wife to do."

This truly set Jason laughing. "Lud, Granny, what else will you say?"

"Nothing more on this subject, thank you."

"Granny, I want you to come."

"And what about your young wife, saddled with a batty old shrew like myself?"

"That is not uncommon."

"But I'm not relations."

"I'll make you relations," Jason said evenly.

Julia stared at him, nonplussed. The large gentleman was determined. "No," she said as firmly as she could, though her voice shook more than she expected. "I will not batten upon you."

"Batten upon me! Granny, I owe you my life!"

Julia felt guilt-ridden. "No, you don't!"

"Yes, I do, and I want to pay you back in some manner."

"Send me a nice gift at Christmas. That will suffice."

"No, it will not. I treasure my life more than that. I am yours to command, body and soul."

Julia looked at the well-built man lying before her and swallowed hard. "Do not make such a rash offer, my lord."

"But I do. You have my oath."

Julia smiled slightly despite herself. "Word of a Stanton again?"

Jason laughed. "Word of a Stanton."

A stupid, emotional knot blocked Julia's voice a moment and then she said softly, "I thank you, my lord, for your pledge. I do not look upon it lightly, but—but I will not call you on it right now."

Jason sighed in exasperation. "Granny, would you really prefer to live here in the wilds? Come to London. I

55

promise to make you comfortable."

"No, I do not wish to become a kept woman."

"Kept woman?" Jason laughed again. Julia blushed beneath her makeup. "I promise you, no one will call you a scheming hussy. Lud, what next will you say?"

"Only the same. No, my lord."

Jason studied her for one quiet moment. "I will miss you, Granny."

Julia nodded numbly. "And I will miss you. Now let us speak no more on this." She was grateful to look up and find John and Sophocles approaching. "Hello, John."

"Hello, Granny Esther—my lord." John tipped his hat as he reached them. Sophocles plopped down in the grass and immediately resorted to eating it.

John looked to Julia gravely. "I fear, Granny, that I must be out tonight to visit a friend who's been feeling lonely."

Julia's eyes widened. What was the matter with him, mentioning it in front of Jason? "That is fine. And will you take Sophocles with you?"

"Yes, I think so. And that is why I hope Lord Wynhaven will keep an eye upon you tonight while I am gone."

Julia could see the two men communicate silently. Ire rose within her. "He need not. I will be fine as I always am."

John's eyes fell from hers. "Nevertheless, I think my lord should be aware."

"Do not worry, John," Jason said. "I will take good care of Granny. In fact, I have just been talking to her on that score."

"And both you men are ridiculous!" Julia said heatedly. "Jason, my boy, will you please leave us? I wish a word with John."

Jason grinned. "You are in for it now, old fellow," he said sympathetically, and rose. "Be gentle with him, Granny," he said with a wink. He called Sophocles to heel and sauntered towards the house.

Julia watched him go, fuming. "Now why, my dearest John, did you bring Jason into this affair by asking his aid?"

"I don't feel secure leaving you here tonight. There have been signs of men in the woods, and footprints out near the clearing's edge."

"Indeed. But why bring the earl into this? I can fend for myself — I'm not my father's daughter for nothing. Has there ever been a time when I could not take care of myself?"

"There was that time in Vienna when the Comte —"

"That wasn't my fault," Julia objected quickly. "If Armand hadn't become embroiled with that little blonde —"

"And what of the time in Brussels? That was a near thing, and your father in a proper pucker."

"Faith, must you throw that youthful folly at my head? At sixteen, one must be forgiven."

"But not at twenty-five. It's not like you to turn down protection out of pride."

"I'm not. But we cannot be sure that the earl is totally innocent, after all. And now you have warned him that I am all alone with him tonight."

"Do you really believe him guilty?"

Julia stared at John, then lowered her eyes. "No, I do not. But he was already telling me how unsafe it was out here, and then you came along with your worries. Do you know what the man wants to do? He wants to pack us up and take us back to London with him and settle us in his dowager house, no less."

"What?"

"You heard me."

"But — why would he do that?"

"Out of gratitude, I guess," Julia said bitterly. "Ironic, isn't it? It is I who got him shot, and now the man wants to take care of us for the rest of our lives."

John looked at her queerly, then lowered his eyes.

"Still, that is rather a lot to do for gratitude."

Now Julia looked away. "Oh, the big fool has taken a liking to Granny, it seems."

John watched her speculatively, a secretive smile tugging at his lips. "Has he, now?"

"Yes, and don't you dare laugh. You don't understand. This man is deadly serious, and as determined as they come."

"Is he?" John's smile became a grin. "But you turned him down."

"Of course I did. What did you think I would do?"

"If we removed to London in his train, we could go undetected and well protected. It is getting far too dangerous to remain here."

"Don't you think I had thought of that?" Julia said angrily.

"It is a golden opportunity," John said with a deceptive nonchalance. "I can stay here and wait for the rendezvous."

"No, I will not leave you here, and—and I will not go with the earl."

"Why not? It is not like you to ignore this chance."

"I am not going to do it," Julia said stubbornly. "We have taken enough advantage of that man."

"But I thought you said you'd enjoy playing him for a fool," John grinned.

Julia smiled wryly at this and nodded. Then her face stiffened. "Can you imagine what he would be like if he ever learned the truth?"

John's face sobered. "I had not thought of that."

"And if I go with him to London, and then he discovers after all his kindnesses that I-I have deceived him—"

"I don't think he is a violent man, miss."

Julia shook her head, staring off into space. "He would be, if it were for his country. But—that is not what I thought of—'tis only that . . . oh, never mind, it is of no matter. The quicker we leave him, the better it will be for us and for him."

John sighed. "Yes, Miss Julia, I guess you are right."

Julia looked up and then forced a smile. "Come, John, we are becoming unduly serious. We shall be gone from here soon and disappeared from the earl's life like wisps of smoke. He will forget all about this interlude and the waspish old Granny."

"Yes, Miss Julia—if you say that is the way it must be."

"Yes," Julia said firmly. "That is exactly how it must be. We must make sure of it."

Julia could not sleep that night. Her muscles tightened throughout her body and she lay stiff upon her bed. She hadn't changed out of Granny's costume, in case there was a disturbance. With a conscious effort, she unclenched her hands, running one gently over the pistol by her side. Perhaps it was only John's qualms that unsettled her, but she could not shake the feeling of impending disaster.

She closed her eyes and was just drifting off when the smell teased her nostrils. She sat up as if rising from a trance. Was that smoke? Oh, dear God, she prayed, not that!

Suddenly the door burst open and she screamed. Clutching her pistol, she sprang up and trained the barrel on the opening.

"Good God, Granny, don't aim that thing at me," Jason's voice said. "Faith, do all you women in these parts carry weaponry? Come on." He strode over and quickly grasped her free hand, jerking her forward. "We've got to get out of here fast."

They ran toward the front of the cottage. It was already ablaze and Jason flung up his hand to ward off the heat. "Damn, what has caused it to burn so swiftly?"

Julia choked on the smoke and didn't reply. She didn't

59

want to suggest oil as the answer.

Coughing from the fumes, they spun and stumbled towards the kitchen and the back door. Smoke made a heavy haze in the air, but the flames had not reached that far yet. Julia, her eyes streaming, wheezed as her chest constricted painfully from the lack of air. "Don't faint, don't faint," she chanted quietly to herself. Yet the sight of the flames, reminding her of another time and place, pulsed painfully throughout her body.

Jason bolted for the door. She watched him as if from a trance, but as his hand clasped the doorknob, she gasped. Warning bells shrilled within her mind. "Jason, no!" she screamed, at the instant he flung the door open.

A volley of shots riddled the air. Jason flung himself to the side and kicked the door shut. "What the hell? Definitely unfriendly, and professional. Who's out there?"

"I don't know."

"Old women shouldn't lie, Granny."

"There's more than one—that much I can tell you."

"You can count, then?"

"Here," Julia said, ignoring that. She thrust the gun at him. "I think you're a better shot than I."

"Thanks ever so much." Crouching, he went toward the door. "So you don't care if I kill them?"

"It is that or be killed," was the curt reply.

"That's just what I needed to know," Jason said grimly. He cracked the door open. The expected shots followed. "That's it, chaps, let me know where you are. They're hardly expert marksmen."

"They weren't hired for that," Julia muttered, and left him. She ran to the cupboard and pulled out another pistol and extra ammunition, which she took back to Jason.

His eyes widened. "Lord, Granny, you *are* prepared." Then he actually chuckled. "Most old ladies keep something other than guns in their cupboards." He grabbed the extra ammunition and crawled to one of the kitchen

60

windows. He shattered the glass with the butt of the pistol and opened fire.

Then came the tedious, deadly game of aiming, shooting, missing, dodging, and shooting again. It all became a blur in Julia's mind; she knew it must be seconds ticking by, but it seemed like hours. Realizing she could not help Jason, she spun, snatched up a rug from the stone floor, and determinedly went to the kitchen threshold where the flames were just starting to lick. Luckily, the large stone fireplace ranged a good portion of the wall and acted as a barrier between the kitchen and the rest of the burning house. She beat fiercely at the insidious flames as they flickered forward.

"This is no use," Jason called back after a few more futile shots. "I've only managed to wing one. We'll have to try and make a dash for it or we'll burn."

He received no answer. Looking over his shoulder, he cursed to see Granny Esther's still figure lying on the floor. Jason vaulted across the small kitchen and dragged the recumbent body away just before the flames could jump to the skirts of her dress.

Scooping her up, he flung her over his shoulder. With a prayer and a primed gun, he ran towards the door and burst through it into the midnight air. Bullets whizzed past him, but he galloped at a dead run towards the woods and cleared them safely.

He immediately took a curiously angled course through the trees, refusing to stop until the pain in his chest choked off his breathing. Wheezing, he laid his silent burden down, reflecting that Granny was not as fragile as she appeared. The old woman's face was blackened with smoke and had become oddly undefinable, as if her features were smeared.

Exhausted, he fell down beside her, attempting to catch his breath. Then he turned his attention to the still figure. "Granny?" There was no answer; he rolled over on his side and peered at her. "Granny?" He leaned over and

61

lightly slapped her cheeks in an effort to rouse her. Her skin was oily, and his hand came back with a strange residue.

He laid his head on her chest, attempting to catch the sound of her heartbeat. "Dammit, Granny, you must live!" He tore away the suffocating shawls, and reached up angrily to the tight collar about her throat, ripping it open, ignoring the spray of tiny buttons he sent flying. "Come on, Granny, breathe! Live!" He slipped his hand into her bodice, frantic to know if she still breathed.

Shock coursed through him and his own breathing stopped. He had not only discovered a heartbeat, but the swell of a smooth, rounded breast, firm with youth. His hand, frozen in place, suddenly felt the faint heartbeat increase.

"Let me go," a low voice croaked.

His eyes narrowed as he looked into brown, not blue, eyes, the thick spectacles finally lost. A dangerous look entered his eyes. "Why Granny, what remarkably youthful skin you have," he said in a voice laced with contempt. Ignoring her command, he rolled atop her, effectively pinioning her.

"No, get off me, you great lummox," Julia said, her voice raw and her head still spinning. She thought she might faint from his added weight.

"For shame. Don't you think it should be I to call the names here?"

His face was close to hers now and she looked into his eyes, only to close hers. His held the contemptuous, angry look that she had imagined and dreaded. "Please," she said quietly, unable to meet that searing gaze, "I—I can't breathe."

"I don't give a damn. Now, who are you?"

"Let me go and I'll—tell you."

"No. You've gammoned me enough. I'm not moving."

Julia blushed slightly. "Could you—could you remove your hand, at least?"

Jason looked at her and then snorted. "With pleasure. I would never have an interest of that sort in a common deceiver." He pulled his hand out of her bodice, only to reach up and jerk the gray hair from her head. Julia forced back the tears brought on by the pain.

"You are the sprite." His voice was low and oddly disappointed.

"Y-yes, I am."

"So you have duped and fooled me from the beginning, haven't you?" He was no longer an amiable, civil man.

"I had to. I—I had no other choice."

"Everyone has a choice. How you must have delighted in it, me so grateful to you while all the time it was you who had me shot. For what purpose?"

"I did not have you shot. That was an accident. Those men were after me and not you."

"I might accept that," he said, his eyes narrowed. "But then why the masquerade? Why Granny?"

"I couldn't have you know who I was."

"So you created a dear old lady who had me thinking I was going crazy all the time."

"It was for your own good."

"It is never for a man's own good to think he is crazy."

"I couldn't let you know me—but I couldn't let you die, either. So I created Granny."

He looked at her a moment, then said softly, "Perhaps the one thing I can't forgive you for."

Julia's eyes flew to his and she swallowed painfully. She understood. It was not only she who had abused his trust, but Granny as well. She only nodded, not knowing what to say.

Suddenly Jason's head rose and he listened. Emitting a low curse, he rolled away from the startled Julia, stood, and then jerked her up after him.

"What are you doing?"—she asked breathlessly, for his face was dark and stern.

"Quiet. Climb the tree behind you."

"Wh-what?"

"Climb it!" Not giving her a moment, he grasped her by the shoulders and spun her like a top, then shoved her to the tree. Rudely grabbing her beneath the arm pits, he launched her into the air. Stunned, she nevertheless snatched for the branch that loomed before her face, attempting to scramble onto it while overly familiar hands upon her posterior boosted her up. She almost overshot the branch but saved herself and secured a seat.

She leaned over to look for Jason when a furry, sooty missile rocketed up at her and smacked her in the face. Julia barely muffled her shocked yelp, shivering as the furry thing slid down her face and neck to settle into her lap. Slowly, she looked down in horror—which turned to chagrin. It was only her wig.

Once again, she leaned over to look for Jason and her eyes widened. He was nowhere to be found. How could the man have disappeared so swiftly?

The bushes to the left rustled and there was a groan as two men stumbled awkwardly through the woods, one leaning upon the other. "Damn, Josh, y'er bleedin' like a stuck pig," the one being leaned on wheezed.

"What the hell happened? The worm said it would be a simple assignment."

"Ha! Simple ain't the word. The bleeding louse lied to us."

"And I've got a bullet in me for it. Damn the bitch, she should have been ours with no trouble. Hold a minute, I need a rest." Julia watched in horror as they stopped directly underneath her tree, the injured man sliding down its trunk to sit.

"Come on, we can't be tarrying here," the other said gruffly. "We've got to find the bitch."

"In a minute."

The other man shrugged and sat down beside Josh. A silence passed while they rested. Julia prayed they would not find cause to look up.

"You think we'll find her?" Josh finally asked. "Along with that bloke carrying her out?"

"Should be simple. They can't have gotten far."

"I don't like it, I don't like it at all. I'm not for shooting people down in cold blood. Ain't professional—I'm an arsonist, fer God's sake! Never had a stomach fer blood . . . and who the hell was the blimey giant with her?"

"I don't know. Her lover, most like."

"Why couldn't she have a small gent for a lover, is what I want to know."

The two men laughed. "Well, we'd best be about it."

Josh groaned and nodded; they rose and Julia sighed in relief. But suddenly Josh put up a staying hand. "Wait!" Julia prayed once again. "Mike, what if we don't find her?"

"Could be bad for us. You know who the worm works for, don't you? He ain't the one to cross."

"I know. So—what if we don't find her?"

Mike shrugged his shoulders. "I don't know, but I'm fer not going back to tell 'em if we don't."

Josh nodded. "I'm with ye on that. Let's go."

The men performed a half-hearted search of the area about them, poking desultorily into the bushes, beating on the shrubbery, and scuffing the ground. Not once did they consider looking up.

"Well, she ain't here," Mike said, finally.

"She sure ain't. Let's go," Josh said promptly. The two men, in apparent good humor, then departed the area, muttering their future plans as they went.

Julia smiled. It was blatantly obvious that if she had called down to them, she would have severely disappointed them. Blessing their desire to protect their own hides, she prepared to lower herself from the tree when she squeaked. An ominous figure seemed to appear from the very ground itself.

"So you at least tell *some* truth," Jason said. "Someone, evidently, is after you."

Julia flushed and gritted her teeth. "Of course I do. Now help me out of this infernal tree."

For once, Julia gladly accepted Jason's hands upon her person as he pulled her down. The fears of the evening were setting in and causing her to tremble.

Jason, however, refused to let her go after that. His fingers dug forcefully into her waist and he propelled her up against the tree. "Now, mistress of deceit, who the devil are you?"

"I can't tell you. Now let me go—those men might return."

"Ha! Not likely. You know they won't return, so don't bamboozle me."

"Please, my lord," Julia said quietly, trying not to shake. "You are hurting me."

"And you'll be hurting more if you don't talk—now tell me. Who did you cheat that he sends arsonists and assassins after you?"

"I—I didn't cheat anyone," Julia gasped. "I—I am an—heiress, you see. My uncle is trustee of my money until I turn—twenty-five—and he inherits it all if I die. Accidents started happening to me—so I ran away. My uncle is—is a very powerful and determined man."

"Is he now? I can almost see why he'd like to kill you—you are a shame to your sex with your shamming, conniving ways."

Julia blinked away the foolish tears that sprang up. "I—I am sorry for that. Now will you release me?"

Jason's grin was not kind. "Leave you go? No, I'm not about to let you go until you tell me your true name, and the name of your—uncle."

"Why? So that you can turn me over to him?"

"Of course." His face was dangerously dark. "After all, I have taken a bullet meant for you; I have almost been burnt to death for you—and saved your worthless life in the process. I certainly deserve a reward for all that, don't

66

you think?"

"If it's money you want, I'll pay you. How much?"

"How much is your conniving little life worth?"

Julia suddenly felt beaten. The man not only hated her, but would take money for her life. "Not very much," she said wearily. "I could pay you, but I will probably die anyway."

Jason looked at her closely and then laughed. His hands tightened at her waist. "You won't escape that easily, woman. Not after what I've gone through for you. You'll live—at least until I've dragged the bloody truth out of you. That I'll see to."

"Why can't you just leave me alone?" Julia said, her voice shaking. "You call me a deceiver and a conniver, and maybe I am. But whatever harm I've done to you, I've tried to atone for it. The truth can't be worth your life—and you must know that if you stay around me, you could lose it, so leave."

"No."

"I didn't go through everything to save your carcass, just to have you get it killed, so just get out of here."

"And what will you do?"

"That you needn't know."

His hands were a vise. "Tell me."

"I—I intend to stay here until John returns. I will be safe. Those men won't be reporting back to—to my uncle."

"Then I will be safe as well."

Julia's eyes flew to his and she said in exasperation. "Why are you doing this? You are the most perverse man!"

"But I am only being chivalrous. How could I live with myself if I left a poor, defenseless little heiress all alone out here in the wilds, fleeing from her greedy, wicked uncle, who also means to kill her."

Julia blanched at his contemptuous tone. "I can take care of myself."

"No, woman, I am staying. I shall be a limpet by your side until I am satisfied with—your safety."

Julia knew when she was defeated. "Very well, then, but don't complain to me when you are killed."

"I do believe I will cease after that."

Julia looked at him angrily. Shoving his hands from her waist, she turned to stalk through the woods. She would never have admitted it, but the quiet tread of the gentleman behind her comforted her. Her nerves were frayed and her head buzzed; everything was beginning to take on a surreal quality.

They came into the clearing, finally, and Julia stopped dead in her tracks. She stood mutely, watching as the flames razed the cottage.

Jason studied the woman before him as she faced the fire. Horror and agony washed over her face. "Will it never stop?" she whispered. Then she seemed to shake herself from her trance and looked around in bewilderment. "We must stop it."

Before Jason could utter a word, she had turned from him. She walked to the stables across the clearing and disappeared inside. When she returned, she carried a shovel.

Jason sighed and walked up to her as she approached. "Here, let me have that."

"No. There is another in there." Her eyes trained on the fire, she began digging at the outer edge of the clearing.

He went and placed a hand gently upon her shoulder. "It won't help, you know."

She jerked her shoulder away. "I know." She stabbed the shovel into the ground nevertheless. Jason, after a moment, went to the stables and returned with the other shovel.

They dug trenches and turned dirt upon the encroaching fire as it not only devoured the cottage but sought to ignite the woods. The night was still and it seemed there were only three beings alive: Jason, Julia, and the fire. They strove against each other, bitter enemies, far into the night. The fire crackled its anger; Julia's and Jason's ragged breathing were the only other sounds.

Finally, they stood amongst the ashes of the spent fire. Together, they scanned the smoking embers with deadened eyes.

"That should do," Jason croaked through parched lips. "Come." He dropped his shovel and picked up Julia's hand. At her gasp of pain he released it quickly, then picked up her wrist and studied her palm. Blisters and raw wounds mingled with the overlying dirt. "We must tend this."

"No, leave it—"

Jason looked into her glazed eyes and nodded. Gently, he let her hand fall to her side. Taking her by the arm, he led her to the stables. She followed him dutifully, like a little child. Once in the shelter of the stables he left her.

She stood, a frozen, lost figure, while he went over and laid straw down into a bed. Then he returned to her.

Wrapping an arm about the silent woman, he assisted her over to the straw. "Lie down." She did so obediently, without a murmur, and closed her eyes.

Jason stared at the recumbent lady. Her hair was matted with dirt and sweat and her face was a blend of soot, greasepaint, and grime. Who and what was she? Schemer or victim? Either one, she was definitely a woman of courage and determination. She had not given up the fight until the fire was out. Who was she running from? Someone who had wronged her, or someone whom she had wronged? He shook his head in unfathomable regret that he did not know the answer.

Turning, he hunted through the stable until he unearthed a horse blanket. He went and gently draped it over the ragged sleeper. Julia snuggled into it, all the while wrinkling her nose in unconscious distaste at the smell.

Chuckling, Jason went and made up his own bed close to the entrance, an old habit of his. He was a light sleeper, and would know if the door was tried.

A few hours later, his eyes snapped open on their own command. He tensed, lying quietly until he could determine what had awakened him. Hearing nothing, he slowly sat up, scanning the darkness. His eyes accustomed themselves, and he discovered what had disturbed him.

The woman he had known as Granny was sitting up, her body rigid. He arose and went to her. She stared straight ahead, yet as he knelt down beside her, he discovered tears streaming silently down her face. She was evidently caught in the grip of a nightmare, yet she made not a sound. Cursing at the frozen fear on her face, he gently put an arm around her. "You are having a nightmare," he said softly, " 'Tis all. Now lie down and rest — you are safe."

She looked at him then, almost curiously. Finally, she nodded, and, sighing, allowed him to push her back down upon the straw. He lay down beside her, his arms about her. Trembles racked her body, then subsided. He felt her finally relax in his arms as natural sleep claimed her. He drew the blanket around them, and drifted off from exhaustion as well.

Chapter Five

Confusing Guardian

Julia awoke to what seemed like rumbling thunder. As her consciousness returned, she realized it was her stomach, voicing a hungry complaint. She ached and hurt everywhere.

Reluctantly, she opened her eyes, which promptly widened in shock and consternation. She lay in Jason's arms, and he was awake and watching her. His eyes studied her coolly. She blushed deeply and looked away. When she finally gained her courage and looked again, his expression was far more approachable, if not a little amused.

"Good morning," he said, his voice a little gravelly. Her stomach growled embarrassingly and he smiled outright. "I see you never need a rooster to wake you up. But you are a little behind—it appears to be noon."

"Noon!" Julia sat up quickly and groaned from the pain of it. "It is little wonder I am hungry, then," she added defensively, as her stomach growled again with unladylike fervor.

"Yes, I would imagine so," Jason said, sitting up. "Nothing like a night of excitement to raise the appetite. Though last night's was an adventure I will gladly forgo in the future; I prefer my nights of excitement to be of the more—common variety."

Julia flushed, wondering if it were her imagination that

colored his words. She placed her hands on the straw, ready to rise, only to bite back a moan of pain.

"Yes," Jason nodded, "you forgot those blisters. Now that you are rested, that is the first thing we shall attend to."

"Shall *we?*"

He grinned. "Yes, *we* shall. I haven't changed my mind, you know. You are stuck with me until I am satisfied I know the whole truth about you."

"But that could take a lifetime!"

"So be it." Jason rose, went over to where John had put his saddle, and rummaged through its bags. "Ah, here it is. I'm so glad John left my bags untouched." He pulled out a jar and bandages. "Come on, lady, we need to go and wash those hands."

Julia groaned. "Leave me alone."

"Not possible. Those hands must be attended to. Now come along like a good girl."

Julia groaned again. She was never a good riser and this morning was far worse than usual. "Are you always this cheerful and industrious in the morning?"

"Yes, always." He walked over to her. Bending down, he all but picked her up and set her on her feet. "Now let us go to the pool and wash those hands."

"Faith! I pity Miss Everleigh if this is what she has to look forward to every morning."

"Then you certainly would not have cared for the manner in which I truly prefer to awaken a woman in the morning." He turned humorously contemplative. "I wonder if Miss Everleigh will object overly much?"

Julia suppressed a growl. The man was an absolute monster in the morning. Without deigning to answer him, she stumbled out of the stables, blinking at the midday sun. She blinked even harder as her tears stung at the sight of her blackened surroundings. A large hand settled upon her aching shoulder.

"Don't stop here, woman. Keep going."

Julia bit her lip and nodded mutely as they walked past the grounds. Her aching heart began to ease as they entered the green, cooling woods. It was a bright, clear day, and the life about her seeped into her grieving soul. They were still alive and for that she must be grateful. Her spirits rose and she breathed deeply of the fresh air. Yes, dear God, she was grateful to be alive.

They came to the water's edge and she was only too happy to sit down beside the clear pool and rest. Jason wetted his handkerchief, sat down beside her, and took up her hand. He cleaned it gently. Julia fought back the urge to cry out and concentrated upon him. "Why are you doing this?"

"Why shouldn't I?"

"Because you don't like me. You said so yourself."

Jason smiled whimsically. "I know. I was very angry. But I have decided to try and withhold judgment until I know the truth about you."

"Is that the real reason?" She wished she could read his mind. Today he was the amiable man he had been before, not the cruel, tongue-lashing man of last night.

"Yes." He studied her in amusement. "It's true. Why? Are you always suspicious of people's motives?" Julia looked away uncomfortably. "Why, Granny? What kind of life have you led that you are this way?"

"A good life, my lord, but an uncommon one. I have been blessed to do and see things that other women would never dream of, and I do not regret the costs of that life."

"And there have been costs," he said quietly, returning to his work. Once again, Julia gritted her teeth against the sting. "Look at you—you are in pain, yet you will not permit yourself to show it. Why? You act more like a man in war than a woman."

"Meaning if I am a woman I must be weak and cry?"

"No, but to be human, you must."

Julia smiled wryly. "You lie, my lord. I saw you take

73

on greater pain than this without displaying your emotions. That is a manly thing to do. Yet you ask me to display my emotions, my weaknesses. To what purpose?"

Jason studied her a moment, and then he smiled. "I had not thought of it that way. Perhaps you are correct after all—I do expect women to cry. Forsooth, how can I not expect it when some fall into fits if they so much as rip a hem or miss a dance. Therefore, it only seems natural for them to do so."

"Does it? Well, it is not natural for me to cry." Jason's brow rose. "Well, leastways, it is not natural for me to show it if I want to cry. I will not pretend a weakness or display it openly, simply for the order of things. Faith, I have enough weaknesses without adding imagined ones as well."

"Like the nightmare that made you cry last night?"

Julia's eyes grew haunted and she looked away. "Did I? I don't remember."

"Very well. Pretend no pain if you wish." Jason resumed his work, salving and bandaging her hands in silence. "There, that should do for now, my stoic sprite."

"Thank you." Julia felt relieved that it was over. Then she sighed—her hands felt so clean and comfortable, while the rest of her body felt gritty and hot. The smell of smoke constantly invaded her senses. Without realizing it, she sighed deeply again, and her eyes strayed longingly to the water.

Jason's chuckle brought her eyes back to him. "I see that you are definitely female after all. If you had wanted a bath, I wish you would have informed me before I bound your hands."

"I—I had not thought of it then. I suppose it would not be possible, would it? No, it would be unwise of me."

"Why? I'll stand guard if that is what restrains you."

Julia laughed. "Will you indeed?"

"Is it that you don't trust me, then?" Jason asked, his jaw tightening.

"No," Julia said, "I do," and she realized with surprise that she truly did. "It is only the humor of the situation. We met with you accosting me in my bath and now it is you who will protect me against other intruders."

Jason grinned. "Of course. It is my philanthropic nature—I would not wish any other poor chap to suffer what I have suffered."

Julia felt foolishly hurt. She sprang up swiftly, angry at herself, and said, "I do believe, then, that I would like to bathe, if you would not mind."

"Mind? Indeed, no. Truth be told, if you had not suggested it yourself, I am sure that I would have made a push to advise you on the matter. You are something of a dishevelled sight."

"Odious, ungallant man," Julia said, even more indignant. "Now leave me be and do not dare to look!"

"Why, I wouldn't dream of it," Jason said innocently, and, with a grin that made Julia fume, rose and meandered into the woods.

" 'Why, I wouldn't dream of it'," Julia mimicked waspishly as she attempted to undo the bandages Jason had applied. "Hmmph, he must think me a mummy," she added, disgruntled at her inability to untie them. Giving up, she attempted to undo the few buttons at her front that had survived the evening's rigors. Tiny and strong, they refused to be managed by her clumsy fingers, the tips of which she discovered were sensitive and evidently singed. "Damn," she said, frustrated, as she failed for the fifth time.

She heard a laugh and looked up. Jason materialized out of the trees. "What is the matter, Granny, having difficulties?"

"No. No, I am perfectly fine."

"You don't need any help, then?"

Julia looked longingly at the water and then down at the bandages. Jason's grin was wide. "Oh, very well. Yes, confound you, I do need help."

"I thought you might."

"Then why did you leave?"

"Because you told me to, of course."

"But if you knew I would need your help, why did you—"

"A lesson to you, sprite." He walked up and gently pulled her hand into his. "A man likes to be told he is needed."

Julia's chin went up. "I don't need you. I can take care of myself."

Jason only smiled as he undid her bandages. "You are an obstinate woman, aren't you? I am not insulting your capabilities, for they are great—if a little unconventional. But accepting someone's help upon occasion and admitting the fact that you need it does not make you weak, either." He finished with the bandages and reached for the front of her blouse.

"What are you doing?" she asked sharply, pulling back.

"Did you intend to bathe in your clothes? You have burnt your fingertips and will not be able to undo your buttons without pain."

Julia cursed silently. He had noticed her injury before she had. His hand remained in mid-air, frozen, as he waited with a quizzical light in his eyes. Her anger melted. "Forgive me. I—I am rather difficult in the mornings. Please—please help me with my blouse."

"Certainly." He undid the buttons at her front with a swiftness and competency that made her eyes narrow. He then undid the buttons at the waist of her skirt as well. Julia gingerly put one hand at the top of her blouse to keep it closed and one at the side to keep her skirts from sliding to the ground. "Thank you," she said, flushing.

"Think nothing of it. Are you sure you don't require any other help?"

"No! Er—no, that will be all. Now you may leave."

"Most definitely difficult in the morning." He chuckled and disappeared.

After only the briefest of moments, Julia dropped her skirts, pulled off her blouse, and waded into the water. It felt heavenly. It not only washed away the filth and grime but the irritations and fears of the day. She took her time and enjoyed herself immensely, deciding the earl would just have to be patient.

After she allowed herself drying time in the warm noonday sun, she struggled into her blouse and skirt. Holding them together, she called out, "My lord, you may return now." She received no answer. A fear crept into her and she called more urgently, "Jason, are you there?"

"Yes, Madame Sprite, I'm coming." From out of nowhere, he appeared. "Though I fear I must insist upon a raise in my wages if I must be prompt when you summon me. And a better room, perhaps—one that will outshine those of the other servants."

"Oh no," Julia teased, ignoring her inordinate relief at finding him there. "Do not become uppity with me, my lord, or I'll turn you off without a reference and then where will your fine career as a lady's maid be?"

He laughed as he bent himself to the task of doing up her buttons; with a critical eye, he twitched out her skirts and straightened her neckline. Julia stood, embarrassed but unwilling to reprimand him. After a moment's study, he rearranged a few damp curls around her forehead. "You have the oddest color of hair," he murmured. "Is it truly silver?" Julia, finding it difficult to answer, only nodded. "No, don't move! You've missed a spot!" He pulled out his handkerchief, spat upon it, and scrubbed along her jawline. "There, that is much better," he said softly, his voice warm. "Well, my lady? Do I receive my reference?"

They stood rooted to the ground, eyes locked upon each other. Julia felt breathless with a compelling desire to lean against him. She saw his head bend toward her and she knew that he would kiss her. She gulped and

77

stepped back, breaking the spell. "Y-yes, you get your reference. Indeed, you must have 'attended' many ladies, so well practiced are you."

His eyes darkened. "That was not only unkind, but uncalled for."

Julia looked away swiftly. "Do you wish for a bath also? I will stand guard for you."

"How generous. Yes, I would like to bathe. Here is the pistol—I have no doubt you know how to use it. You do manage to shoot down people and their follies very swiftly. And don't fear I might need any help—after all, I am such an expert at undressing, am I not?"

Julia trained her eyes straight forward, scanning the area conscientiously while she did her best to ignore the splashing from the pool. She told herself that Jason had no right to be angry at her remark, but she couldn't shake off the feeling that she was in the wrong. She continued to brood until she heard a footstep behind her and swung around, lifting the pistol into place.

"For pity's sake, it's only me." Jason sat down beside her. "Faith, you are forever pointing that thing at me."

He sounded so disgruntled that Julia laughed. "I'm sorry. 'Tis only that you creep up on one so."

"It couldn't be that you are an overly skittish person?"

"No, of course not," Julia said, her face not betraying a hint of humor.

He smiled then. "Oh, do put that away and let me try and bandage your hands again." Julia put down the gun in surprise and pleasure. She thought after her rudeness he'd not care for her hands, even if they fell off.

"You know," he said, his eyes upon his work, "you have a rather mistaken image of me. I am no lecher. I realize that I might have said certain things to you while I thought you were Granny that I should never have said to a young female. That is something I cannot change, and I do not think it fair for you to hold it against me, under the circumstances."

"No, I didn't mean to do that," Julia said quickly. "And I apologize for—for what I said. I valued your confidences to Granny and your honesty. I am sure I learned much more about you than I ever would have if we had met at the proper social functions."

"Much more!" The corners of his mouth twitched.

Julia bit her lip. "Does it always have to be that way?"

"Be what way?"

"That you would do me the honor of being honest if you thought me an old lady, but would not if you thought me a young female?"

He studied her a moment. "You do have a unique way of looking at matters. But I understand what you ask, and I don't know. Our society does not encourage honesty between the sexes. But I am not sure that if I had not taken an instant liking to Granny I would have been so candid about my life."

Julia felt unaccountably pleased. "Thank you."

"In truth, I shall miss her."

"I think I will also." She would not meet his eyes. "I enjoyed the ability to be as free as Granny was in what she said and did."

"Something you are not accustomed to?"

"Something I am not accustomed to," Julia admitted. "I know you believe me a deceiver and perhaps I am. In my life it is necessary, even enviable. But Granny wasn't all deception; there was a true part of me in her."

In a gentle movement, Jason lifted his hand to her chin, turning her face so that she was forced to look at him. "I would like to think so. Perhaps that is why I've stayed—and why I have not strangled you before this."

Julia grinned wryly. "Then I must be grateful."

He smiled. "You did do an expert characterization." Then he sighed gustily, his hand falling away. "But now, alas—"

"What? What is it?"

"I always wanted to hear about Granny's proposal from

a prince, and now I never will. It was all a hum."

"Oh, I wouldn't say that."

"Why, sprite, don't jest with me. Do you have such a story?" Julia only smiled. "I see you do. Now tell it to me."

"No, I will not. A young lady does not tell of those things."

"Then be Granny for a moment and tell me."

"Neither does an old lady," Julia retorted, blushing. "You noticed that Granny never told you."

"I'll get it out of you somehow," Jason growled.

"Along with all the other stories?" Julia teased.

"Yes," Jason nodded, growing intent. "Along with all the other stories."

"And how do you propose to do that, my lord?"

He grinned. "Why, I'll torture it out of you. We are alone out here."

"Beast!"

"Ah, first you call me lecher, then beast. Is there no end to your calumny?"

"I never said you were a lecher!"

"You implied it."

"You cannot deny that you are an engaged man, can you?"

"No, no I can't," he said evenly. Suddenly, he rose. He bent and took the pistol from her lap. "I believe, madam, that it is time to eat."

"What are you going to do?"

"Hunt, of course. Why don't you go back to the clearing and make a fire."

Julia shuddered. "Must I? I don't ever wish to see a fire again."

"I'd reconsider, unless you enjoy your game exceptionally rare."

"On second thought, I think I will start that fire."

"I thought you would see it my way. Any preference as to rabbit or squirrel?"

Julia's stomach growled at the mention of food. "No, no preference. It could be a horse for all I care. But I warn you, I am no expert at cooking over an open fire."

"That is of no significance, for I am." Jason held up the silver-mounted pistol. "Though I do feel odd, using such a weapon upon a mere rabbit. Oh well, I'm off to challenge the surrounding wildlife . . ."

Jason succeeded in hunting down a squirrel and a rabbit, though it was late into the afternoon before they finally ate. Julia supposed it was the hunger, but she couldn't remember food ever tasting better, even in the houses of the French nobility.

They sat quietly while dusk fell. Julia was somewhat anxious about what might be delaying John, but despite the turbulent past and the uncertain future, she felt at peace. Jason had unearthed a pack of cards from his saddlebag and they sat beside the fire, playing every imaginable game.

Though the shadows were darkening, they continued to play. Neither seemed to wish to end the strangely comfortable time they had shared. The pistol lay close to the discard pile, and Julia often lost a card or so as they slipped through her bandaged hands, but still, the time seemed idyllic. Julia attempted to conceal a yawn as she picked up the next set.

"Perhaps we should end this game," Jason said lazily as he observed her. "This hand was not my finest, anyhow."

"No, no, I am all right—and my cards are excellent."

"Liar."

"Why do you say that?"

"You wouldn't be yawning if they were so wondrous. You have a definite enthusiasm when you think you have a chance to trounce me."

"Are you saying I give myself away?" Julia asked, amazed.

"Oh no, you have a perfect cardsharp's demeanor. 'Tis only that I can feel your excitement over a good hand." Julia only stared at him, stunned. "Well, now, it's been a long day, and we needs must get our rest."

Julia laid down her hand, pulling herself out of her surprise. Rarely could anyone read her when she did not wish it. "Perhaps you are correct." She picked up the pistol instead and asked casually, "Who is to take the first watch?"

"First watch?"

"Yes. I realize that I was no help last night, but I am certainly able for tonight."

"Your offer is quite laudable, but I think I will have to take the watch for the night."

"And just why should you do that?" Julia asked.

"You need not fear for your safety," the earl replied, shuffling the cards. "I am a very light sleeper and awaken swiftly. There will be no need for you to help—and you look burnt to the socket."

Julia flushed but her eyes narrowed. "I refuse to allow your insults on my looks to concern me. In any case, you are not looking any more the polished dandy than I am the ravishing debutante."

Jason's brow rose appreciatively. "*Debutante*, sprite? You? Never. Giggles and bows would never suit you."

"Is that to be another insult?"

"No—in truth, it isn't. Were you ever a debutante?" he asked almost whimsically.

Julia stared into the fire for a moment. "No—not unless I choose to be, that is. But I am not exactly an ancient ready for a bath chair, either."

Jason laughed. "No, that you are not. Now do stop taking snuff at everything I say and go to bed. You could use the rest."

"And so could you."

"There's no sense trying to bullock me, you know," Jason said firmly. "It might have worked when you were

Granny, but I know you better than that now."

"Ah, we come to the crux of the matter. You don't trust me."

"Yes—we come to the crux. I don't. Is there any reason that I should?"

"No, of course not," Julia said curtly, springing from her seat abruptly. "I purposefully saved your life and nursed you back to health just so I could savor the pleasure of personally putting a bullet through your thick hide in the dead of night. Ah, but perhaps I might do it the silent way. I'll just slit your throat with a nice, sharp knife! Of course, how clever of you to discover my plan!"

Jason stood and caught Julia's arm as she swung away from him. "So hot at hand, sprite? I did not think that. I am grateful you saved my life, but I would not be surprised to wake up and find you vanished, disappearing just like the creature I call you."

Julia's eyes widened, and then she looked down. "And would that be so monstrous? You know you are not safe while around me."

"True. But my curiosity will not allow me to let you go. Come now, sprite. If you truly are a fleeing heiress, I would think you would be glad for my protection during these trying times."

Julia gazed at his amused face, seething, and pulled her arm from his grasp. "You deal with something you know nothing about, my lord." She stalked angrily away toward the stables.

"But I am willing to find out," Jason called.

Julia froze in her tracks, stiffening, then turned slowly around. "Willing to find out, yes. But willing to understand? No, I don't think so."

"Try me."

She shook her head sadly. "You will not trust me with a night's watch yet you ask me to lay my life in your hands? Unjust, my lord." She left him standing there.

Julia entered the stable, grimly determined to remain

calm, and found the blanket from the night before. She laid it down upon her bed of straw, feeling it a horrible ending to a lovely day. Getting into bed, she closed her eyes resolutely.

A half-hour went by before Julia heard Jason enter the stables and close the door. He must have taken the precaution of quenching the fire and clearing all the remains away; he was efficient, she had to concede that. She kept her back stiffly toward him in feigned slumber while he moved about the stable.

Then she felt him come and stand behind her. "Granny, are you awake?"

"No."

"Your anger is unjust, you realize. It is merely that I am a seasoned campaigner and have always preferred keeping watch myself."

"Liar," she muttered under her breath.

"What did you say?"

"I said I'm sleepy. Good night. Enjoy yourself guarding against them—and me."

"And should I not?" Julia gritted her teeth and refused to answer. "Well?"

"You are disturbing my beauty sleep, of which I am in dire need, as you so kindly pointed out. Good night, my lord."

A tense silence ensued. Jason broke it. "Damn." Julia relaxed slightly, sensing he had walked away from her.

She lay there then, tense and irritated, for the next half hour. The man was too infuriatingly fixed upon the truth, a truth that might cause him to betray her to the crown. He was a loyal soldier. And he was becoming too much of a threat for her to stay and await John's return. She sighed at the thought of what she knew must be done; it would not be easy, but she would escape.

Julia closed her eyes to catch what little sleep she could. She awoke an hour later but lay still, attempting to determine where Jason might be. Feigning sleep, she turned over and peeked through her lashes. A night lantern gave only a dim light, but she saw Jason still awake, sitting upon a bale of hay. She should have known he would not be one to fall asleep on duty. He was wide awake and, to her surprise, smoking a cigar. He must carry everything in his saddlebags, she thought, truly an old campaigner. Still, it surprised her that he would risk smoking at a time like this.

Realizing there was nothing she could do at the moment, she settled down for another hour's nap. The next time she awoke, it was well past her intended hour. That was uncommon for her, for, unless she knew that John or Armand stood watch, she was very much like Jason in wishing to stay alert and awake. She frowned slightly at the thought. Somehow she always felt safe around this man, a very dangerous emotion, considering his power to send her to her death if he discovered who she really was.

Once again she located the earl, and very swiftly at that. He paced the small stables like a caged panther, his large stride encompassing the small space in a few steps. Slowly, a smug smile twitched at Julia's mouth. Her watchdog was displaying signs, not only of weariness, but of turmoil. His self-imposed guardianship was, evidently, breaking down the granite of his composure.

Julia quickly snapped her eyes shut as Jason stopped his pacing of a sudden and peered at her. She could sense it when he came and stood over her. What was he going to do? He seemed to be standing, just staring at her. A seemingly interminable time passed. Julia, unable to accept what she imagined was his scrutiny, turned over again in feigned sleep so that her face, at least, was not exposed to him.

Still he did not move. "Damn the woman," she heard him mutter. Then she heard a rustle, felt a presence, and he was alongside her, wrapping two encompassing arms about her and pulling her to his side. Shock coursed through her and stifled any speech.

She heard him sigh in exasperation and understanding struck her. The Rock of Gibraltar was indeed tired. He no doubt planned to acquire some sleep and didn't want her too far away while he did so. It showed that he did not fear intruders as much as he did her escape.

Julia knew she should have been angry, but couldn't seem to stir up her ire. The man had his own cunning and she was never one to begrudge her enemy a small victory. In fact, an amused smile spread across her lips. "Excellent decision, my lord," she whispered impishly. "Else I would have been gone come morning."

The arms about her stiffened sharply, but then relaxed. A deep chuckle tickled her ear as he pulled her closer. "Vixen. Now go to sleep or it will be I who slits your throat and no one else."

Julia chuckled, too, and, yawning, drifted back into slumber, thinking that she had seen many strange things, and experienced many situations, but this one had its own unique twist.

Chapter Six

Comings And Goings

Julia awoke the next morning as she had the morning before, snuggled in a man's arms and completely disoriented. She wondered what the hour was and attempted to move. The arms tightened.

"Where are you going?" Jason asked without opening his eyes. His voice was low, sleepy, and suspicious.

"Oh, I was just crawling away to uncover the axe I hid in a bale of hay so that I may use it upon you." The mistrust in his voice set her back up.

"Very amusing." One hazel eye opened, then closed. "Now go back to sleep."

"I don't want to sleep anymore."

"But I do."

"Well, then—you sleep. I'll go . . . and make the fire."

"No, you'll stay here with me. I'll rest far better with you right here."

"How flattering." Jason didn't even bother to open his eyes. "My lord, it is morning, and it is time to wake up."

"No."

"No, what?" she replied with sweet malice. "It isn't morning or it isn't time to wake up?"

"No to both. Now be quiet and go back to sleep."

"This is impossible," Julia said, sitting up. "Are we to be joined at the hip merely because of your fears?"

"Woman." Jason growled, and finally opened his eyes, threatening and bloodshot. "I have barely had any sleep for two nights now and what little sleep I have had has been on a hard stable floor. I warn you, I am in no mood to argue."

"And I am in no mood to sleep with you." Julia attempted to rise; Jason's hand grasped her shoulder and shoved her down. She hit the straw hard, sending the dust flying.

"Odious man," she said, sneezing. "I do not wish to simply lie here, doing nothing, while you get your sleep—sleep, mind you, that if you had not been so pigheaded last night, you would have gotten."

"Then make it worth my while," Jason snapped, opening his eyes again.

"Wh-what?"

"Make it worth my while to stay awake." He trained his eyes on her.

Julia flushed. "Cur."

"That's it!" Jason's face expressed his fury. "I've had about enough!" With lightning speed he suddenly rolled Julia atop him.

"Wh—what are you doing?"

"You called me *cur*. Hasn't anyone ever told you it is best to let sleeping dogs lie?" Jason grinned and wrapped his hand behind the back of her head, entangling his fingers in her hair.

"No!" Julia gasped. Her breathing had suddenly become erratic.

"For two nights I have been a perfect gentleman, never once importuning you, yet all I receive is abuse. Why? Are you angry? We can change the situation if you want. I thought it an unbeneficial arrangement myself." He pulled her mouth down to his.

Fear washed over Julia as her lips touched his. Here was a man who could make her lose herself. Here was a man who held power over her deepest emotions. Here was a man dangerous to her very being, and yet she kissed him.

"You are just like my dreams," Jason whispered, his lips

brushing the side of her mouth.

The words drifted through Julia's passion-filled mind and then her lulled fears turned to panic. She had been his dream and heaven help her if he found out.

She acted instinctively. Her hand slid up to his shoulder and with grim determination she pressed cruelly upon his wound. Jason groaned sharply and in his moment of pain, Julia rolled away from him, coming to her knees. She watched him, her breath coming in ragged gasps.

"Gad's, woman," he panted finally, rolling over slowly to look at her. "That was unnecessary."

"Was it?" She was panting herself.

"It was. I would not have ravished you, for goodness sake."

"But you would have seduced me?"

His gaze did not flinch. "Perhaps. Would that have been so terrible?"

"I—did not wish it."

"You have a very efficient but cruel way of saying it. A simple no would have sufficed."

"I said no twice."

"Then the third would have sufficed."

Julia stared at him, at a loss for words. She would never have found the strength for a third denial. Then she noticed that he was truly in pain. "I've hurt you! Here, let me help!"

"No, you've done enough," was the cool reply. Jason gritted his teeth and rose very slowly. "If you will excuse me, I think I will go shoot something—for breakfast, that is."

He left her kneeling there without another word. Julia stared determinedly ahead, refusing to watch him leave. She didn't know whether to laugh or cry, but decided on neither. She merely eased down to the floor and sat there pondering upon the perplexities of the man. Had he harbored fell intentions before or had she unwittingly triggered his ill behavior? Would she ever find out now?

An anguished shout from outside shattered her reverie. Springing up, she caught herself before she ran out of the stables into dead center of whatever danger was out there. She forced herself instead to go to the stable door and crack it open slightly. Receiving no obvious retaliation from this action, she opened the door wider and slid out.

Then she saw him. The young man's back was to her and he stood before the charred husk of the cottage, a tragic figure.

Julia choked back the emotion that swelled inside her. "Armand!"

The man turned; the agony masking his face tore through her. "Armand, dear, I'm here, I'm safe." She ran to him and threw herself into his arms.

He hugged her tight, lifting her and swinging her. "Lord, Ju, I thought —"

"Hush, I know," Julia said with a quaver. "I know. But I wasn't."

He grinned weakly and set her down. "Should have known you'd escape. We Landreths don't seem to take well to burning."

"No, we don't," she laughed through tears of emotion. "Thank God you are finally here. We have been waiting ages for you, you beast. Where have you been?"

"Leading our beloved enemy a merry dance. Well, if not him, at least a few of his minions, a few of whom we must mourn, dear sister."

Julia laughed at his cheerful tone. "Then I pardon you for your overlong absence. Now, if it had been merely some delightful damsel in a cozy little harbor town —"

"For shame, Ju. I'm past those irresponsible days," Armand said with mock sternness.

Julia looked up at the tall, lithe youth before her, his dark hair ruffled in the wind, his brown eyes sparkling, and she laughed. "Yes, the gray hairs of age are apparent."

"Minx. And you are a fine one to talk, young lady. What is this I hear from John about you harboring an earl upon the premises?"

Julia's smile slid away and she looked around quickly. "Oh, my goodness. What are we going to do? He will be back soon."

"What? You mean the man is still here?"

"Yes, yes. He is the most obstinate, odious man in existence.

90

He refused to leave after the fire and —"

"And you would not leave until I arrived?" Armand said gently. Then his face took on a sterner cast. "Faith. Do you mean to say that you have both been alone here?"

"No, of course not. I invited the surrounding neighborhood to a soirée."

"Now, sister, don't eat me. I have a right to worry over your honor. It is a brotherly thing to do." He looked at her piercingly. "Did he importune you in any fashion?"

"No. He's been a perfect gentleman," Julia said quickly — too quickly. Armand looked askance at her. "Well, he was."

"He *was*?" Armand asked suspiciously. "Usually you have to beat them away. Is the man made of ice then?"

"No. He's — he's fianced, you know. And, besides, he does not like me," Julia added. "He did not like me making a May game out of him."

Armand nodded. "Only makes sense. No man likes to be made a fool of. Then why is he still here?"

"Because the blasted beast is determined to find out what I am doing."

Armand whistled. "That is not good. How much does he know?"

"Nothing. I told him I was a fleeing heiress running away from my wicked uncle."

"What, you tried that old hum on him? Whatever possessed you?"

"I couldn't help it," Julia retorted defensively. "At the time, I was hard-pressed for an explanation."

"You? Hard-pressed? Zounds, I've got to meet this man," Armand said, glancing about.

"No!" Julia almost screeched. "Things are bad enough without you doing that. Now, what on earth are we going to do?"

"What do you want me to do?" Armand said, amused. "Shall I go and shoot down the man? Then he will not dare bother us again."

"No," Julia said — again too fast, before she realized her brother was jesting. "Oh, do not pinch at me so. Besides, we can't shoot him. He saved me from the fire."

"He did? Then I do have to meet this man."

"Armand, you can't," Julia said, clutching his arm as he turned to search. "We would never be rid of him then, and I have no doubt he would not hesitate to turn us in if he ever knew who we were. Let us just leave before he returns."

"Is that what you wish? You seem uncertain."

"I'm not. There is nothing else to do, after all. He will think me an adventuress, no doubt, but that is better than his thinking me a traitor. Oh, why do we even tarry here? It is not as if I will ever see the man again."

"Oh, I don't know. One never knows when one might meet up with another again."

Julia looked at him suspiciously. "Why do you say that?"

"The earl resides in London, does he not?"

"Yes. But we aren't going to London," Julia said confidently. Armand didn't answer. She shook her head in growing fear. "No, Armand, don't say we are going to London. Please don't say so."

" 'Fraid so, my dear."

"Well, then," Julia said, shrugging. "I still will not meet him. London is a large town, and I know I won't be travelling in his exalted circles." Armand was once again silent. Julia looked at him and gulped. "Armand. Don't say it, we can't travel in his circles."

"All right, I won't say it. But we are going to do it."

"Oh, no, Armand. It can't be true. Sir can't wish it of us. Why, we'd be right under the Hawk's nose—or beak."

"I know," Armand laughed. "Isn't it a grand scheme? The Hawk would never think of it."

"Neither would any other right-thinking person," Julia said numbly. "It's ridiculous."

"I don't know. They say that a bird's eye sees from side to side, but doesn't focus upon center—so directly in front of the old bird should be exactly where we should be, don't you think?"

"No, I don't think," Julia snapped. Then she sighed. "Oh, very well, let us make haste, then."

Armand gave her a bear hug. "I knew you'd not balk at it.

Just you wait, sis. We'll turn the tables on the old vulture soon, see if we don't."

Julia laughed. "I only hope so. It is certainly time. Are we to meet Sir in London, then?"

"No. He and John remain in France. He still believes there is a clue that we have overlooked there."

"Then what are we to do in London?"

"Nothing much. Merely make our curtsy to the upper class, befriend the Everleighs, and look for any possible information that we may use . . ."

"Is that all?" Julia said dryly. "My, I do hope I am not bored."

Armand grinned. "Come on, Ju. We shall have a grand time."

His grin was infectious and Julia laughed. "Oh, very well, so we shall. Though I fear this game may well get out of hand."

"My dear, it is already out of hand. The scheme merely matches the stakes this time. Now, let us be gone before your cumbersome earl returns."

"He is not my earl, and he is the one man I hope do not meet in London."

"Don't fash yourself, my dear. I haven't known a man yet who can see past one of your disguises," Armand said confidently.

"Let us only hope it remains that way," Julia muttered, not so confidently, before she and Armand turned to leave.

Jason, highly irritated at himself, returned to the stable, another squirrel in his pouch for dinner. What was the matter with him, to have taken off and left the woman just like that?

He frowned, for he knew the answer. She was driving him insane. From the moment he met her, she had been doing that. She was playing some deep game and every time he thought he might have a thread to unravel her mystery, she proved to be one step ahead of him. Just when he was coming to grips with the image of her down at the pond, he discovered she was the old lady he was so fond of. Always, she was masquerading.

Now she claimed to be a fleeing heiress, a story he could not believe.

All of which made her an adventuress, most likely. Yet she did not act like an adventuress. She had saved his life when she could have left him for dead. She had nursed him patiently, even though she had done it while masquerading as Granny Esther. And she had never once used her feminine wiles on him to get her way, as an adventuress would.

He grimaced; perhaps that rankled the most. She made him think her an innocent when, in all probability, she was not. Yet why else did she rebuff him so? He swore. What was the matter with him—that he should become so lusty over a lady of such questionable motives? He was fianced, after all. Perhaps that was it. Since his engagement, he had abstained from any liaisons, feeling it was only proper in a man soon to be married. That was his problem. Perhaps he should not be so noble if he was to make it to the wedding without becoming a raving ravisher.

As he walked into the quiet clearing, he looked around. Julia was nowhere in sight and no fire was started. "Granny?" He walked toward the stables. The door was ajar and he swung it wide. The stable was empty, except for Sanchos. "Damn." He dropped the squirrel and ran outside. "Granny?" he called more loudly, scanning the area. He loped toward the woods, calling as he went near the pond. He reached the clear pool, but she was not there.

He sighed and sat down to think. He told himself that she had taken advantage of his temper and escaped in his absence. Indeed, the whole scene that morning might have been for that purpose only. He should be glad that she was gone, with no possible way for him to follow.

Yet a niggling worry filled his soul. What if she had been taken against her will? What if she did have a wicked uncle who had captured her? He peered into the water and swore deeply. Was he now always to wonder what had happened to his mysterious sprite, the woman who had endangered his life only to save it? Was he never to know the truth about the woman who, despite his best efforts, enthralled him in every one of her guises?

He rose slowly. After one more look into the water, he slowly walked back to the empty stables.

The sound of a carriage could be heard as it drove by the elegant townhouse on Half Moon Street. The afternoon sun was waning but a stray breeze still held enough strength to billow the curtains as it whispered into Lady Manchester's charming drawing room. It failed, however, to ruffle even a hair of the three occupants who sat comfortably upon blue and gold brocade chairs while taking tea from a delicately wrought silver tea set.

"Thank you for aiding us, Lady Manchester," Julia said as she tasted the aromatic brew. She had great respect for the resplendent hostess sitting before her. Though the woman was in her fifties, she had a beauty not only unfaded, but all the greater for her maturity and confidence. Her chestnut hair was perfectly dressed, her green gown the latest fashion, and her blue eyes highly intelligent.

"Don't thank me, dear," Lady Daniella said with a wave of her white hand. "I am quiet pleased to be of service—I had a great fondness for your father." She noticed the significant look that passed between Julia and Armand and gurgled in delight. "No, no, you absurd children, it is not in the way you obviously imagine. Good gracious, so Robert still attracts the ladies' attentions."

Armand smiled sheepishly. "Yes, my lady. Do forgive us."

"No need to apologize. The ladies always did lose their hearts to your father, though a lot of good it did them. He never had eyes for anyone but your dear mother, Nanette. A preference I could never fault him upon, for I loved her dearly myself." She sighed. "I still miss her. You two would be surprised at the escapades your mother and I embroiled ourselves in. It was well that we both married men with a penchant for—for adventure, let us say."

"We must warn you that this love of 'adventure' could place you in grave jeopardy," Armand said.

95

"Never mind that, dear boy. I have a passion for intrigue— indeed, I believe my whole generation does. It is only you younger people who seem to spurn excitement and cling to the staid and mundane as the epitome of life. A shame. It shows a decided lack of spirit, in my opinion."

"Yes, it does, doesn't it?" Julia agreed, quite in agreement with her hostess. "But we must warn you, it could be a matter of life and death if you're found harboring traitors. A death that is not pleasant, either."

Lady Manchester returned her steady gaze. "Don't distress yourself, my dear. I've lived with the knowledge for far longer than you, child. Your father saved my husband from such a death once, you know. Now, unfortunately, the circle has come full swing, and it will be my privilege to help him as he did my dear Quentin."

Armand rose and, with a courtly gesture, raised the lady's hand to his lips. "Agreed, dear lady. You have our deepest gratitude."

"There, now," Lady Manchester said after a moment's silence, "what is your papa's plan? I only received a message telling me to expect your arrival and to aid you if I could. What has come to pass? All I've heard was that Robert was a heinous traitor and that you must fall under suspicion as well. All of which I know to be poppycock. Yet the crown has labelled Robert such a traitor that his deeds must not even be discussed."

Julia nodded, her eyes pained. "In truth, you now know as much as we. A French spy was taken and then shot supposedly while trying to escape. On him he held papers, supposedly in Sir's handwriting, boasting of his deeds. Needless to say they are forgeries."

"Excellent ones at that, we assume," Armand said, grimacing. "Of course, the forger would have had plenty of Father's documents to study."

"How is that?" Lady Daniella asked, her eyes sharpening. Robert Landreth was a man who had lived his secret life as a phantom, a phantom who did not commit much to paper.

"They were his letters written to John Everleigh," Julia said softly.

"John!" Lady Daniella exclaimed. A sadness filled her eyes. "Someone found them after his death and used them against you."

"The same someone who killed him," Armand said.

"Killed him?" Lady Daniella gasped. "My God, it wasn't an accident?" She froze, and her mouth quivered. "Who?"

"His grace, the new Duke of Rendon," Julia said.

"Converse," Lady Daniella said softly. A stillness settled upon her and her face seemed dead. Suddenly her eyes were alive, alight with a fierce energy. "How?"

"We had finally acquired bona fide proof that Converse was selling secrets to the French," Armand said. "We had known he must be involved for quite some time. Perhaps we should not have let it go on so long, but in the beginning his dealings with the French were more illegal than treacherous. Then he began selling our secrets as well. One would almost believe him a true French patriot if one didn't know that with Converse only money counts."

"And power," Lady Daniella added. "His desire is almost demonic." She seemed to shake herself, then her eyes cleared and she looked at Armand. "So you found the proof against him. What went awry?"

Armand looked away; he would not meet Lady Daniella's eyes. "We sent all the information to John. You know he was our contact here in England. Things were such that we could not leave France. Indeed, it was John who would need to present the information to Castlereigh." He stopped, unable to continue.

Julia went on. "Father also sent it to John so that he would know beforehand – so he would be prepared."

Lady Daniella shook her head. "John always did love Converse, always believed in him, even when everyone else knew that Converse cared nought for John and only used him. It was strange – John was always such an intelligent man – no one could fool him easily. Yet it seemed he was blind to Converse. He could never see the envy and hate in Converse's eyes."

"You understand," Julia said. "Then you can understand that John confronted Converse."

"My God!"

"I don't know why." Julia's voice shook. "Maybe he thought Converse would have an explanation. Maybe he thought Converse would do the honorable thing and confess."

"Oh, no." Lady Daniella's eyes teared. "Poor John."

"You do not know the half," Armand said, his voice thick. "Converse told John that he—he was framed and that he would prove his innocence."

"He could not, of course."

"He didn't need to," Armand said in clipped tones. "Chlorinda Everleigh, John's sweet daughter, his pride and joy, removed herself from John's house without explanation and went to Converse's."

"Oh, no. She didn't."

"She did. Converse told John that Chlorinda believed in him and not her own father—that she called her father the traitor. He also said that she wouldn't come home until John had handed over the evidence to him and promised not to destroy the family as he was intending to."

"No," Lady Daniella said, shaking her head vehemently. "She should have known John would never do that—that would be betraying his country. That he informed Converse of the charges against him beforehand, I can see—he had his own strange view of honor and brotherly love. But no—he would never do the rest."

"He didn't," Julia said. "It became a stalemate. John could not get near Chlorinda—nor would he turn the evidence in. Converse did have Chlorinda, after all—even if she was a willing hostage. By this time John fully knew of Converse's perfidy, but it was too late. And Converse—Converse just waited."

"Like the spider he is," Armand said. "Until he had sweet little Chlorinda write to John that she wanted to meet him alone by the back gate to Converse's estates—that she had decided she believed in him no matter what and that she wanted to see him. God," he said, his voice shaking with rage. "You

wouldn't believe the joyous letter John wrote to Father over it."
His little girl believed in him and wanted him to come to her,"
he said, his voice turning ugly.

"And he went to her," Lady Daniella said as if mesmerized.
"And died in that terrible carriage accident."

"Yes," Julia said numbly. "Yes."

"The rest was simple after that," Armand said, clearing his
throat. "With John dead, Converse only needed to rid himself
of us. However, he was not foolish enough to think he could
just kill us; he knew we had family and friends and he couldn't
be sure who we had told."

"So he destroyed us by turning us into traitors," Julia said.
"The crown is hunting for us rather than Converse and the
only evidence they will care to see would be proof of our innocence—not of Converse's treachery. Which evidence, since we
are not in possession of the facts, is extremely difficult to come
by."

"Even if we had the time," Armand snorted. "The last six
months have been dedicated merely to staying alive. Converse
is a very busy man and he is sparing nothing in his endeavor to
exterminate us. Only Father is free of Converse's 'attentions'
now." His smile was not pretty. "But then, he believes Father
burned and dead in that fire he set."

"Let me help," Lady Daniella said, coming out of the trance
she seemed to be caught in. Her eyes snapped. "Tell me how I
can help."

"You must consider very carefully before you commit yourself to the undertaking," Julia said, her eyes serious.

"Well, what is it then?" Her ladyship's fine brows rose in
sudden amusement. "Do I get to murder Converse for you?"

"I fear it is nothing so easy and enjoyable, my lady. We must
clear our name before that fortunate event," Armand drawled.
"Therefore our sainted Papa desires that you introduce Ju and
me to the *ton*."

Lady Manchester's composure fled. "You jest, do you not?"

"Indeed no," Julia said, smiling wryly. "He deems it time we
bring the battle to English soil."

"English soil, yes, but the English drawing room? My dear,

what cheek." Lady Manchester sat a moment in consternation but slowly, ever so slowly, as the two siblings watched, amusement seeped back into her blue eyes. "Faith, I don't know why I am surprised. Robert was always a daring one. Lud, he surpasses it all. If only Quentin were alive to see this. But then, if he were, perhaps things would never have become so desperate. Your father would have called upon him for aid far sooner than he did me."

She sighed and her eyes became distant. Then she brightened. "So it is to be a masquerade, then? Or do I presume? Please do not say I am to present you as the Landreth heirs."

"Oh, no. That, at least, is one cross you need not bear," Julia said with a grin.

Armand chuckled. "Though you *will* have the pleasure of introducing Sir Horace Farouche."

"Sir Horace Farouche?"

A peal of laughter came from Julia as she studied her brother. "Excellent, excellent. I do so love Sir Horace." She turned in delight to Lady Manchester. "I promise you, my lady, you are in for a rare treat. T'will be an exquisite bird of rare and colorful plumage that you patronize."

"But then — you wish to draw attention?"

"What better way to confuse matters?" Armand laughed. "And you, sis, who shall you be?"

"I think Miranda shall do nicely," Julia said, eyes sparkling. "She will be a perfect foil for Sir Farouche."

"Oh Lord, have pity on me," Armand said, laughing. "You know how Miranda sends me into whoops."

"And who might Miranda be?" Lady Manchester asked warily. "Or dare I inquire?"

"Miranda?" Julia grinned. "Only the most complete skitterwit imaginable. With a total lack of fashion sense as well. She is so absent-minded that you will find her wandering off into the strangest situations."

"And asking total strangers the most ridiculous questions," Armand added.

"Good gracious," Lady Daniella said, frowning. "But, then, how am I to present you to society? I will lose my standing with the *ton* forever and you will never succeed in circulating with the elite."

"Shall we not? Not even with all Miranda's wealth?" Julia asked innocently.

"Wealth? You are to be an heiress, then? Well, in that case, we should not have too much difficulty after all. But faith, the magnitude of the masquerade—it takes the breath away."

"Yes, does it not?" Armand asked. "But I assure you, my lady, it is not something we enter into lightly. We know the dangers, but we also know it is time. Past time. Every avenue in France has been closed to us. Converse, has seen to that! No, it is past time that we settle matters with his grace, "The Hawk"—and this should give us the perfect vantage point."

"But of course. You will be so close, he can trip over you," Lady Manchester observed.

"I have no grievance with being Rendon's stumbling block," Armand said with a smile. "Do you, Julia?"

"Indeed no. In truth, I look forward to it."

Lady Manchester laughed. "Very well. Count me in. If it will help foil Converse I will present you—faith, I would present a hunchback himself to the *ton* if it would help."

"Well, you need not do that," Armand said, a smile hovering upon his lips, "though we might create just as much stir."

"We will not fail you, my lady," Julia added. "Whatever may come to pass, there will always be a way for you to deny all knowledge of our identities if it becomes necessary. Indeed, it is something you must promise to do if our masquerade is uncovered.

"I promise, child," Lady Manchester said dutifully, if not with great sincerity. "However, I do not fear that. Something tells me that all I need do is sit back and watch a fine play unfold."

Chapter Seven

In Society

"Od's blood, never!" a high, finicky voice exclaimed. "Never consider such a color, my dear Madame."

Lady Manchester turned from the bolt of cloth that Madame Celeste's little helper held out before her. Her eyebrows rose haughtily, for the veriest fop stood before her, resplendent in puce, teetering upon red heels, his nose definitely in the air due to his excessive shirt points. This while he surveyed her with a quizzing glass raised to his eye. The man was actually wearing paint! His splendor was topped off, so to speak, with a straw hat bedecked with flowers. In a day when Beau Brummell had at least added a touch of sanity to men's dress, not to mention a pleasing understatement, this dandy was a positive jolt to the eye.

"I beg pardon?" she said, at her most frigid.

"Why, certainly you may," the tulip said benignly. "For I know, in the deepest depths of my heart, that if given but a moment to meditate upon it, you could never, never, bring yourself to don such—such a cloth. Why, the color—so weak, so insipid, so unequal to the strength of your beauty."

"And who said it was to be for myself?" Lady Manchester found herself asking.

The exquisite allowed his glass to fall and clasped his hands together in delight. "Oh, there, you see! I knew it, I positively knew it! My dear madame, you have restored my faith, yes, you have. I knew such an exceptionally well-dressed woman as yourself would never sink to such a color. Gadzooks, but never!"

Lady Daniella was fast losing her starch. "But, my dear sir, how dangerous for you to have made such a decision when you do not know me."

The man tittered and put his hand to his mouth, then. "Forsooth, now, what an ill-mannered boor you must be thinking me. I assure you, madame, you may rest easy on that score, for I am not."

"You are not what?"

"Why, an ill-mannered boor. I am a man of superb refinement, after all. Can you not tell?"

"T-to be sure," Lady Daniella said, swiftly attempting to cover the little shop girl's loud gasp of disbelief.

"I made sure you would understand and forgive my little faux pas. Alas, I was so overcome by dread that you would perhaps purchase such a color for yourself. Why, my dear madame, it would not have done. I knew then that I must make a push to save you from such a fate, no matter if it went against my nature."

"Indeed?"

"Why, yes, if you were to present this –" He jabbed the offending cloth so furiously with his glass as to make the little attendant start and squeal. "If you were to present this cloth to your bosom beau you would have lost his affections forever. Indeed you would! But never fear, I am here to prevent such a disaster. You, girl," he said, sniffing at the now-trembling attendant. "Remove that most unfortunate bolt of cloth from our sight upon the instant."

"But – but 'tis a very f-fashionable color, sir," the attendant whispered bravely.

"Fashionable! Oh, my stars! Can I believe my ears? You poor, poor ignorant child, you must not be seduced by what some misguided people call fashion. Why, look at what half of mankind has sunk to, wearing shabby, genteel clothes. And then they parade around, truly believing they are well-dressed. Oh, the poor, benighted souls." He sighed profoundly. "But let us not dwell on such depressing matters."

The man looked so sad that Lady Manchester took pity on him. "Oh, do take the cloth away," she ordered the attendant. "I will find something else."

"One moment, please," a vague voice interrupted. "Did I hear you say that color is fashionable?" All three turned to the lady speaking. She was a tall maypole of a woman, wearing an unpleasant dress of burnt orange, which did little for her pale, sallow skin and mousy brown hair.

"Sink me," the tulip breathed in evident pain. "Madame, you would never hear it from my lips, I assure you. I was just informing this fine lady of its inadequacies."

"Oh dear," the newcomer sighed. "And I thought it such a pretty color. Now whatever shall I do?"

"Why, that is simple," the fop replied. "You will put such dreadful thoughts from your mind. After we have found a proper cloth for this dear lady's friend," he went on, waving to Lady Daniella, "we shall expend all our efforts into finding something to replace that—that—I fear I must say it—that abominable dress you wear, which I strongly advise you to burn the moment you arrive home. My dear lady, you should never consider umber a proper color—"

"Umber? What is that? Oh, is that what I am wearing to-day?" The lady stared down at her ensemble in surprise. "Odd, I had thought to be wearing the blue outfit—but I see you are correct. I'm not." She sighed as if deeply disappointed, then turned appealing, myopic eyes toward Lady Manchester. "Do you like your lady's maid?"

"Why—why, yes."

"I do not like mine. She never dresses me in what I wish."

"But, then, why do you wear it? You should tell her that it is not correct, and that you wish the outfit you asked for."

"I—I fear I never notice that she has dressed me in what I didn't ask for until it is too late. I am always quite out of the door and on my way by then."

"Faith, never say you are so—so cavalier toward your attire as not to notice what you wear?" The tulip's voice rose to a squeak.

"I—I fear I am a jot absentminded."

"Zeus!" the fop exclaimed. He spun with great determination upon the silent, wide-eyed clerk. "Quick, begone with that dreadful cloth before this poor woman forgets and — and buys the stuff. *Out* I say! Out!" The little clerk, clutching the condemned pink cloth to her bosom, fled.

"Now that, I am sure, was unnecessary," Lady Daniella said, but her lips twitched.

"Madame," the man said sternly, "can you truly look at this woman and say that?"

Lady Daniella studied the woman before her; she had the distinction of wearing one of the ugliest dresses her ladyship had ever seen. "Well . . ."

"See? I knew you would agree! Now, let us attend to your friend's gift. And then we shall look to you."

"How kind of you," Lady Manchester said, biting back her smile. "But do not fear, pink is not a color I would ever wear."

"Ah, the gods be praised." He lowered his voice, all the while swinging his glass. "I own that in certain circles, it is considered an acceptable color for the lady of brunette hair, but that is sheer fustian. Only the blonde, and then the *jeune fille* should ever wear such a color. Now a fuschia, perhaps, would be permissible for you." He raised his glass in grave contemplation. "Yes, yes, fuschia would be magnificent." He frowned at the bolt of pink cloth again. "You do not intend this cloth for any female but a blonde, I hope? Now do not disappoint me. Do say it is for a sweet young blonde."

"I — I regret that it is not," Lady Daniella said.

The dandy's face twisted in anguish. "Oh no, no. A cut to my heart, a very cut. But — but — " His face cleared and he tittered. "Oh, silly me, I perceive what you are about. You clever lady, you. You intend it for a lady you hold in abhorrence, true?"

Lady Manchester gurgled in delight. "No, of course not, you absurd boy. It was meant for a dear friend of mine."

"But no, no, my dear madame. You rend my poor withers, indeed you do. Then it was destiny that I would save you from your own destruction," he concluded, with a minatory look to the other lady, who only smiled upon him in unfocused gratitude.

"But sir," Lady Daniella protested, "I am sure I am honored by your offer, but I do not know you—"

"Oh, good gracious, where have my wits gone wandering? Why, pray, permit me to introduce myself." The dandy performed an extravagant bow. "I am Sir Horace Farouche, at your service."

"And I—I am Miranda Waverly, if you please," the other lady said in a kind tone.

The little clerk in the back room heard a shriek and ran to the curtain. She peered out in fear, only to discover the three customers all clasping hands and laughing. She shook her head, trembling; her ma was right, the quality were a queer and strange lot. Indeed they were!

A grand coach rolled along the evening street at a spanking pace. The Manchester coat-of-arms could be seen upon its glossy side.

The occupants presented a stunning, if unusual, collection. The elder lady was dressed with a flair that told even the dimmest observers she was of the first stare. Beside her sat an awe-inspiring dandy in pea-green satin evening clothes. He gently wafted a matching lace handkerchief under his nose as they passed through one of the town's lesser streets. Upon the squab across from the two sat the antithesis of the dandy. The woman wore a sallow gold gown that spoke clearly of money, but of nothing else. Except for her execrable taste in dress, she appeared nothing out of the ordinary, unless it was for the disconcerting vacancy that filled her brown eyes.

"Well, my dears, we've done it! Imagine! The doors of Almacks are open to us this very evening."

"We could never have done it without you," the gentleman said in a rich voice that did not fit with his finicky movements.

" 'Twas easy with Miranda's and your considerable wealth to brute about," Lady Manchester laughed. "I'd not have thought you two would become so readily welcomed, but see, the world comes calling."

The vacant eyes of the girl leapt to life and filled with intelligence. "While all my eccentricities go overlooked . . . is it not amusing?"

"Lord, child, and such wicked things you do. To wander off and leave that poor young viscount holding your parasol and reticule for a full two hours at the Tarrington picnic! Why, he looked a proper quiz—it was shameless."

"And not very fruitful." Julia frowned. "Tarrington keeps a very clean desk. One would never know he was in the war department; either he is very conscientious about hiding his papers or he is so lazy he never sees the need to bring work home. I fear it is the latter. And you are right, it was unkind of me to leave Edmond in that fashion. Poor man, it truly is bellows to mend with him. He complains constantly that he cannot sleep due to the duns at his door, even during the evening. I really think I must uncover a true heiress for him to court."

"Tut, tut, Miranda," Armand drawled. "It won't do for you to be warning off your beaus. You have precious few as it is."

"Yes," yawned Julia, "only the most hardened fortune-hunters now, and you, of course, Sir Horace."

"Yes," Lady Daniella said, patting her hair. "You two as a couple are becoming a proper *on-dit*."

"Which suits me just fine," Julia said. "Most of the men that court Miranda bore me to death. I'd rather have Armand's company in truth."

"Ain't I just one with the ladies," Armand remarked, smiling wickedly.

"I own I feel rather sorry for leading poor Edmond on so," Julia added. "He really is not a bad sort, though shockingly blunt about his financial difficulties."

"Do not fret, Ju," Armand said. "I believe I have the perfect heiress for him."

"You mean that cit's daughter, Miss Carson?" Lady Daniella inquired, amused. "He doesn't have a chance. Why, he dresses far too plainly for her taste, I make no doubt. Now you, Sir Horace, are far more in her style. She told me so herself. You dress just like a king, don't you know, and your top-lofty manner is precisely what a nob's should be, in her opinion."

"Sink me," Armand replied in die-away tones. "I knew she was a woman of unusual—ah—delicacy. I do believe she would suit our impecunious friend Edmond wondrously. Yes, yes—we must introduce them. For I have set my sights on Miranda Waverly." He waved his handkerchief at Julia flirtatiously.

Julia laughed. She looked out the window and straightened. "We are almost there. Rendon is still out of town?"

"I had it from his butler the other day," Armand grinned. "And word had it in the club that he should have arrived yesterday. But Melcher informed me his visit is extended, though he did not know until when."

"Must be that he did not accomplish whatever had drawn him to France." Julia laughed. "But Chlorinda Everleigh will be present tonight?"

"Yes, Lady Jersey told me so," Lady Daniella replied with a nod. "This will be her first engagement since she has thrown off her blacks."

"Excellent." Julia hesitated. "And we still have no word from her fiancé?"

Armand laughed. "The mammoth remains absent from his beloved's side."

"Thank heaven."

"Come now, surely you do not fear the gent, do you?"

"Of course not," Julia said quickly. "But I far prefer his absence while I corner his little fiancée."

"Would you prefer it if I drew the little Miss Everleigh out?" Armand asked, his tone hardening.

"With the attitude you harbor toward the child? No, indeed not. Sir's orders are to befriend Chlorinda so that we may watch her and gain her confidences. I fear that your opinion shows too clearly."

Armand's brow rose haughtily. "You believe that I cannot hide that?"

"Normally I would say yes," Julia said gently, her eyes open and warm toward him, "but with Chlorinda I am not sure."

"She betrayed and killed her father . . ."

"Don't start, dear," Julia said, her hand reaching for his. "You do not know for sure. You know how wily Rendon is, how he can lie. He may have fooled her—indeed, she might just be Rendon's pawn."

"She went with him, Julia," he said angrily.

"She might honestly have believed it was family duty—she might not have known the seriousness of it all."

"How can you overlook the fact that she invited her father to his own death, for God's sake? The letter was hers!"

"I know the letter was written in her hand. But that could have been forged. We know about his talent in that direction."

"Children, children," Lady Daniella interrupted, raising her hands. "Cease this brangling on the instant. We have arrived and it is time to prepare. You must both give your best performances this evening. Keep your minds focused upon the matter at hand—do not let your emotions override your objective. And pray, do not fail me, or my credit with the *ton* will be ruined."

Chlorinda, the Duke of Rendon's ward, daughter to the deceased Lord John, was—much to Julia's displeasure—exactly as she'd pictured her. She was petite, blonde, and possessed of the bluest eyes. At least those eyes, Julia mused, claimed her as Lord John's offspring, so very much like his were they. She appeared, however, to be of a retiring nature, for though she smiled and chatted quite properly with her partners, she showed no signs of flirting as many other women of her beauty and station would have done. Indeed, her lack of vitality was pronounced.

Yes, Julia thought acidly, she would be a perfect wife for the Earl of Wynhaven, comfortable and staid. Why, he could set her upon the mantel shelf and need only take her down for an occasional social dusting once they were married. She shook her head to clear it of the uncharitable thought. She had warned Armand not to let his emotions interfere, and here she was thinking similarly dangerous thoughts.

Marshalling her straying wits, Julia positioned herself at the edge of the dance floor. As Chlorinda stepped by, Julia purposefully trod upon the girl's flounced hem. It tore quite easily.

"Oh, good gracious me," Julia breathed. "Look what I have done! Do, pray, forgive me. I fear I was not watching where I was going."

"Do not tease yourself over it," Chlorinda said in a soft voice with a polite smile. "It is of no significance." She made as if to move on.

"Of no significance — you are only saying that to be kind," Julia said swiftly, clasping the other girl's arm. "After all, I have torn it quite dreadfully." Which was only the truth, for the flounce trailed upon the floor as if Chlorinda possessed a tail. "Do permit me to help you. Do you think we might pin it? I have some pins in my reticule."

"Do you?" Chlorinda asked, looking relieved.

"Yes, indeed, I never go anywhere without them. I fear I am such a clumsy that I find recourse to them often enough."

"Oh, I know who you are," the girl suddenly exclaimed. "You are Miranda Waverly, are you not?"

"Why yes, yes, I am. However did you guess?"

Chlorinda looked down at her hem and looked away. "Oh — it was nothing in particular."

Julia understood her embarrassment. "I see you have already heard of me, perhaps. Then you must know that I am sadly lacking in wit — quite buffleheaded, in fact."

"Oh, no, I am sure —"

"Now there is no need to deny it," Julia said kindly, warming to the girl despite herself. She could see why the Earl of Wynhaven had offered for her hand. "For it is the simple truth. I have tried not to show it, but I fear it becomes apparent every once in a while. Like stepping on your gown just now. It is not bad enough that I tread upon my own hems,

110

but I also now needs must tread upon yours as well." Julia sighed. "Oh well, there is nothing for it, I suppose."

Chlorinda giggled, the first spark of enjoyment she had shown. "Do not tax yourself upon it. I did not care for this dress, anyway. Is it true that you—oh, pray, do forgive me."

"Is it true what? Do go ahead and ask me. I have very few sensibilities so you need not fear offending me."

"Well, I had heard that you left the Baron Von Haven right in the middle of the dance floor. Was that true?"

"The baron? . . . Oh yes, I remember now. Yes, yes, I did."

"Why? Were you angry at him?"

"Oh no, it was only that I had suddenly remembered something I had left undone—and I fear that I rather forgot the baron. I can't figure how I became so skitterwitted as to do so."

"I can," Chlorinda said, an enchanting smile peeking through. "The old baron does pinch one so."

Julia was surprised into a laugh; Chlorinda flushed and looked swiftly around, as if fearful of attention. "Do forgive me, I should not have said such a thing."

"Why ever not? I thought it funny. And I assure you, I am so birdwitted that I will never even remember you said such a thing ten minutes from now. I do hope you will not mind?"

"Not at all," Chlorinda smiled shyly. "In fact, that is what I would prefer."

"Now what were we about to do?" Julia asked with a show of perplexity. "Were we going to do something?"

"Yes, we were going to pin on my flounce. Do come to the retiring room with me. I am beginning to feel that we shall deal famously together and I—I would so much like a friend." She added, more quietly, "My name is Chlorinda Everleigh, by the by."

The two ladies slipped from the dance floor, hunting until they discovered an empty chamber. Julia pulled out the pins from her reticule and bent to Chlorinda's dilapidated flounce. "I do hope I have not destroyed your dress completely, Chlorinda." Julia said. Then she feigned surprise. "Chlorinda . . . why, you are the Duke of Rendon's ward, are you not?"

Chlorinda stiffened, and she did not reply immediately. "Yes—yes, I am. I am—was—the daughter of John Everleigh."

"Why, then I have heard of you also! My father knew your father."

"D-did he?" Chlorinda's eyes grew oddly lost. "Did he know him well?"

"No, I don't think so. I only remember Papa mentioning him in passing." Julia did not have to feign her sudden hesitancy. "Your father—he passed away last year, did he not?"

Chlorinda gasped sharply; looking up, Julia saw she was trembling, but the expressions that rapidly crossed the girl's face were unreadable. "Yes," Chlorinda said, her voice dull. "He was—was in an accident."

"I am so very sorry," Julia said truthfully. "How stupid of me to mention it."

"No, no. It is all right. But—let us not talk of it."

Julia studied Chlorinda's face. There was grief there, deep grief, but something more. What was it? She was masking her emotions, Julia realized, but what were those emotions? "Of course. I understand. You must miss him."

"Yes. But Uncle says that I must put off mourning. He says that my father would not have wished it."

"Then that is why we have not met before—you were not in town? I feared that I had merely missed meeting you. I, myself, have just arrived this past month, and have not stopped running since."

Chlorinda laughed. "I used to be the same. But—but I have not been well of late."

"I see," Julia said politely, returning to her work. Chlorinda was becoming more reticent by the minute. "I hear that you are engaged?"

"How—how did you? It was to be a secret until after my mourning."

Julia cursed herself for the error. What was she thinking? She knew what she was thinking and it was not helping. She swiftly displayed a perplexed face. "I really don't remember

112

where I heard it. Then you are not engaged to – to Viscount Salford?"

Chlorinda relaxed and giggled. "Lud, no! That is Tiffany Meadows."

"How tottyheaded of me. But you just said – "

"Yes, yes I did. And you must promise to tell no one. I mean until it becomes official."

"Of course not. But who are you to marry? Or should I not ask?"

"I am fianced to the Earl of Wynhaven."

"You are? How romantic – though I do not know the gentleman, or at least, I do not think I do. Do you love him deeply?"

Chlorinda flushed. "Uncle says that I will come to love him, afterwards."

"Oh, I see."

"I mean, that is the way it is to be, isn't it? I mean, that is what everyone says, after all, and surely those who are older and wiser would know. And it is only natural for us to – to be shy of – of the men, is it not?"

"But would it not be difficult to marry a man you are not sure you could care for?"

"I – I believe that I can grow to love him – once I know him better – don't you think? And it would be far better than – " Chlorinda suddenly flushed and stopped whatever she was about to say. "Oh, never mind. Do you intend to marry for love, then?"

"If I ever marry, yes," Julia said, wondering what Chlorinda had almost said.

"*If* you marry? What do you mean? Don't you wish to marry?"

"Why – why, I guess I do. I am not sure, though. I mean, who would be comfortable with such an addlepated female as I am?"

"Nonsense," Chlorinda said staunchily. "I find you delightful. Any man would be fortunate to wed you."

"Would he?" Julia asked, amused. "That is debatable. But thank heavens I have never found a man I wish to wed – that

113

way, it has never been put to the test."

"Then you have never been in love before?"

"No." Julia said, sighing. She then thought it prudent to add, "Though I have a beau I find I like very much. I—I might be falling in love with him." She attempted to look casual. "And you?"

"No—no, I don't think so," Chlorinda said, her eyes clouding. "I—I suppose that sort of thing only happens in books, don't you think?"

"I imagine so," Julia said softly. Both ladies sighed just a little and, the flounce finally pinned, they returned to the ballroom in a rather subdued mood. As they entered, Julia heard her name called.

"Oh, yoo-hoo, Miranda. Gadzooks, I could not find you anywhere, my dear, and it is my dance." Armand trotted up, waving his looking glass as if it were a baton.

Chlorinda gasped beside her. Julia looked at the girl, expecting the expression of disbelief Armand's appearance usually occasioned. Instead, there was more an intense curiosity upon her face.

"Who is he?" Chlorinda whispered.

"He is the man I was talking about," Julia replied, as her brother executed a deep, flourishing bow before them. "He's my very dear friend, Sir Horace."

"Ladies, I am at your service," Armand tittered, yet his eyes were at variance to his tone, running over Chlorinda with a coolness and particularness that could only be offensive.

"Sir Horace, permit me to introduce a new friend of mine," Julia said swiftly, stunned at his lack of discretion. "This is Miss Everleigh."

"Indeed? She is a new friend of yours?" Armand drawled. "Well, then, I am sure I can find her nothing but charming, for any friend of Miranda's is a friend of mine to be sure."

"You are too kind, I fear," Chlorinda said quietly, though a sudden sternness threaded her voice. "And far too magnanimous to bestow your favors so swiftly. You must beware, lest you bestow them unwisely as well."

"I could not have stated it better," Armand nodded. "The little English rose speaks the truth."

Chlorinda flushed. "English rose?"

"Why, yes, a rose. They do hold their thorns despite their deceptive beauty, do they not?"

Julia gasped. "Sir Horace!"

"No, 'tis of no moment, Miranda," Chlorinda said quietly, flushing. "It is apparent Sir Horace took exception to—to something I said, perhaps. Though I meant no insult, I only meant . . ." and her eyes were fully on Armand now, "that there was no need for you to pretend a friendship towards me—if you do not feel one, sir."

Armand tensed perceptibly, his eyes locked with Chlorinda's. He then tittered and raised his looking glass. "Tut, tut, we have both misunderstood each other. As I said, any friend of my dear Miranda's is a friend of mine."

"Indeed," Chlorinda said and nodded.

"Chlorinda," Julia said promptly, for the air seemed thick about the two. "Would you like to go to the museum tomorrow?" she giggled. "Actually, Lady Daniella planned it. I am not a hand at art."

Chlorinda smiled at Julia. "I thank you but I have a fitting tomorrow."

"Oh," Julia said, allowing her face to fall.

"But you are welcome to come with me if you would like. I would enjoy the company," Chlorinda said almost shyly.

"Oh, my darling Miranda dearly loves clothes," Armand said drolly, "though she does much better with my advice and my expertise. She does have a tendency towards the unfashionable."

"Oh, would you plan to attend?" Chlorinda asked. She gazed directly at him. "I assumed you would be otherwise engaged."

Armand was speechless. Chlorinda's meaning was quite clear, and the cut masterful. Armand looked to his cuff and straightened it. He then looked up at the girl and smiled wide. "Indeed, I go to the tailor tomorrow."

Chlorinda paused just a moment and then said, "As I

would have thought." She then turned her attention to Julia and her eyes warmed again. "Do allow me to go and inform Mrs. Bendley, my chaperone, of our plans."

Chlorinda smiled at Julia and, without another glance towards Sir Horace, left their side.

"She certainly handled you, my dear," Julia murmured. "Far better than you did her, I would say."

Armand's eyes followed the small blonde, his face expressionless. " 'Tis only the first round, I believe."

Julia felt concern. "And I do hope it is the last. We are to befriend her, not alienate her."

Finally, he looked at her and smiled wryly. "I fear you were right—I must leave the 'befriending' to you. I find it quite an impossibility."

Julia frowned. "You know, I do not find it difficult at all—which, I own is surprising. But—she is not all she seems. I find I have a liking for her."

"You will allow the chit to take you in, then?"

"No," Julia said slowly. "But I will wait before condemning her out of hand. We cannot afford to allow a bias to enter into it. Emotions will cause us to make errors and you and I have both made slips this evening in that direction."

"Do not allow her to betray you as she did her father," Armand said softly.

"No, I will not. But enough of this; only time will tell us the answers, and you did promise me this dance—and it's a waltz."

"Women! God protect me from them. The world may go hang if there is a waltz playing," Armand said in exasperation as he gave her his arm. Julia only laughed lightly and permitted him to lead her to the floor.

Jason rode down the streets of London, his eye upon the hustle and bustle. It felt good to be back in civilization. It was what he needed to forget the past month, to forget sprites, to forget fires—and to forget adventuresses who disappeared.

116

He had racked up at an inn outside London the night before, not wishing to arrive on his doorstep late or to send the staff into a flurry. He had seen them earlier that morning to inform them he would remain in town for the rest of the season.

Now he was on his way to see Chlorinda Everleigh, the woman he was to marry. A sweet, comfortable, biddable woman who would never play games upon him, never lie to him, and certainly never get him almost killed.

He dismounted in front of the Duke of Rendon's elegant townhouse and rapped the knocker. The Duke's butler opened the door promptly.

"Good morning, Filton." Jason nodded to the thin-faced butler. "Is Miss Everleigh receiving?"

"I regret that Miss Everleigh is not at home," Filton said solemnly. "She and another young lady are shopping at Madame Celeste's this morning."

"I see. Permit me to leave my card." He reached for his card, then hesitated. Somehow, it seemed important to see Chlorinda as soon as possible; it was time to focus on the future and erase the unfortunate past. "On second thought, do you have the directions to Madame Celeste's?"

Filton delivered the directions in a proper monotone. Jason thanked him and, more determined than ever, rode back through the streets until he arrived in front of a row of elegant shops.

He entered the quiet, elite atmosphere of the one boasting of being Madame Celeste's. The shop was spacious and had the subdued, peaceful atmosphere that is the hallmark of money. Female fashions, laces, and frills abounded, and Jason felt overly clumsy and overly male in this obviously female domain. He cast a dour eye over the dainty, gilded chairs that were the only furniture. He guessed he'd remain standing in this establishment.

Then his eyes fell upon his fiancée and her everfaithful chaperone. Chlorinda's blond hair shone, and she appeared a sweet angel dressed in the palest of pink. Ah, here was what he needed—an angel, not an adventuress.

He trod softly up to her. "Good morning, Miss Everleigh, Mrs. Bendley."

Chlorinda started and turned. Her blue eyes widened, then she blushed attractively and her lashes fluttered low. "Good morning, my lord. I—I did not know that you were in town."

"I just arrived." He smiled warmly. "I'm glad you still speak to me. I have been absent so long. But I assure you, only the most unavoidable circumstances could have kept me from your side."

"Think nothing of it," she said, appearing nonplussed. She hesitated as if she did not know what to say. "Ah—permit me to introduce a new friend of mine—Miss Miranda Waverly." She directed his attention to the store's sole other occupant; the woman had her back to Jason, yet a quiver ran through him. Something in the woman's posture reminded him of his sprite.

"Miranda," Chlorinda said, "I would like you to meet the Earl of Wynhaven." Jason could have sworn the woman stiffened—could it be—?

And then she turned, just as she was donning the most obnoxious hat imaginable. It sat perched upon her bird's nest of dull brown hair; from under its surplus of fuschia bows and pink flowers, brown, vapid eyes gazed at him.

The difference between the image in his mind's eye and the vision before him was so stunning he almost gasped aloud. No, this creature was most definitely, most positively, not his sprite. Disappointment settled in him.

The woman focused myopic eyes upon him. "I beg your pardon, Chlorinda?"

"Certainly," Chlorinda replied, nodding. "I said I would like you to meet Jason Stanton, the Earl of Wynhaven."

"My lord." The woman's slight curtsy set the hat wobbling and swaying upon her head; she reached up and clutched a pair of satin ribbons to steady it.

"Madame," Jason said, his disappointment nudged aside by amusement.

At that moment, the proprietress, Madame Celeste, emerged from the back. "Miss Everleigh, we now have that dress ready for you, if you would please come this way."

"Do not mind me," Jason said, seeing Chlorinda's hesitation. "I shall wait."

"Thank you. I'll be back shortly," Chlorinda said, softly smiling. Mrs. Bendley watched Chlorinda go, looked at Miss Waverly and Jason in consideration, then promptly turned on her heel to follow Chlorinda. Evidently, Jason mused, she did not fear Miss Waverly was in imminent danger of seduction.

He surveyed Miss Waverly anew. An apparent attempt to tie a bow had left her hands hopelessly entangled in the hat's ribbons. "Do you need any help?" Jason asked before he could stop himself.

"N-no," she mumbled. Her hands fell away, and a drunken, topsy-turvy bow appeared. "There. How does it look?"

Unconsciously, he stepped forward. "It needs—a slight adjustment," he said, deftly righting the bow. The woman stood mute and obedient under his ministrations—and he froze. A sudden and strange desire engulfed him, as if stepping close to her had swept him up in a secret current. Lord, what was the matter with him? He stepped back quickly. "There you go," he said with a swift nod.

The girl—Miranda—trod quickly to the mirror. "Oh yes, that is much better. How expert you are at it."

Jason stiffened; his face became still as he eyed the woman warily. Yet she didn't turn around, nor was she castigating him as his sprite had; she simply gazed happily at the bow. He shook himself, forcing a smile that could not help but be wry. "So I have been told before—though not in a complimentary manner."

"Whyever not?" Miranda frowned, wide curiosity in her eyes. "To have such expertise in women's dress must be marvelous."

"Some do not see it so."

"Why not?" she asked innocently.

"Er—it is nothing you need understand," Jason said. He certainly did not care to go into the ramifications of his experience; perhaps it was better to have a woman knowledgeable enough to be angry at him than to face such innocence.

She looked as if she were about to question him again, but then she bit her lip and turned to the mirror, twisting this way and that. "Do you like the hat? Shall I purchase it?"

With a jaundiced eye, Jason considered the large fake strawberries decorating the brim. "Perhaps not—isn't it frightfully expensive?" he added quickly at the sight of her crestfallen face.

"Oh, money is of no consideration." She smiled brightly. "I am an heiress, you see."

His smile vanished. "Oh, God!"

"You do not like heiresses? Most people do."

"Most people do not meet the ones I do," he said grimly. Then he realized the girl had an odd, tight expression upon her face. "Forgive me, I did not intend to insult you—you, I am sure I will like."

The girl's smile seemed to lighten her sallow face, and once again Jason felt drawn to her. "Then that's all right."

Forgive me," he said, as if mesmerized. It was the woman's smile that entranced him. "You—do not have an uncle, do you?" he asked rather stupidly.

The girl frowned, her eyes crossing deeply as she concentrated on the question. "No—but I do have some aunts," she said eagerly. "Does that count?"

He laughed then, amazed he had even asked. "Forgive my foolishness. Indeed, it is fine."

"I am glad you do not mind heiresses." She turned back to the mirror for another glance at the hat. "I fear I am not a hand at anything other than that." She looked down, fidgeting. "I mean, I am not clever or anything."

"Clever women can be the very devil," Jason said as seriously as he could.

She smiled. "Thank you. Though I wish I could have more sense about fashions. Sir Horace says I am impossible."

"Who is Sir Horace?"

"He is a particular friend of mine." Her voice was stupidly fatuous. "He is like you and knows—oh, so much about

120

dressing women." Jason almost choked, but she rattled on. "But he is not often pleased with my clothes."

Jason was not sure he cared for this Sir Horace; evidently this woman was infatuated with him, and all he could do was insult her taste. Granted her taste was — well, poor — but could the man not see past that? "Well then, let us surprise your Sir Horace. Choose a different hat."

Miranda obediently untied the hat and set it aside; she gazed about intently and unerringly strode to the second-worst creation in the store. Its crown of virulently blue-and-green peacock feathers waved and danced as she picked it up. Smiling delightedly, she plopped it swiftly upon her head, disarranging her mousy brown hair all the more.

Placing her face but a few inches from the mirror, she screwed up her eyes and peered into it. "Oh, dear." She choked slightly. "It's not the thing, is it? I look like a bird of paradise."

Jason's eyes widened in shock and then he laughed. She swung around swiftly with such an embarrassed expression upon her face that his laughter only increased; her precipitous turn had set the feathers dancing like the tentacles of an enraged octopus. That image set Jason laughing all the harder, and he sat down swiftly upon one of the store's gilded chairs.

"No, I meant I must look like a peacock," the girl said quickly, only to have a long feather catch the wave of her breath and swoop into her mouth. She spat it out indignantly, blowing and puffing at the offending feathers. "Pshue!"

Jason leaned back, shaking with laughter. A crack split the air and Jason's dainty repository toppled over, spilling him onto the floor.

"Oh, let me help you!" Miranda exclaimed, rushing to assist him. She thrust her hand out and bent over — and the hat slid over her eyes. "Gracious!"

Jason choked again but grabbed her hand nonetheless. Once he was standing, he said, "And let me help *you*." He righted the mass of green feathers in order to see her eyes —

and then froze. Without warning, he felt it again—a strong physical desire. An urge to kiss her.

A look of consternation eclipsed the laughter in the woman's eyes, and she suddenly turned them upon his cravat. She swallowed; her tongue crept from her mouth and ran nervously across her lips. His own lips wanted to follow that path . . . he knew he should move, but he did not.

Voices suddenly drifted into his fogged mind. Jason, as if fighting a powerful force, turned from Miranda to see Chlorinda and the other women returning from the back of the store.

"I hope we did not keep you long, my lord," Chlorinda said as they approached.

"Er—no," Jason said. "Miss Waverly and I were discussing hats. We—" He turned to include Miranda in the discussion and halted. The girl was nowhere to be seen. Neither was the broken chair—only the telltale broken leg still lay upon the floor.

Miranda then appeared from behind a mannequin supporting Madame Celeste's prize ball gown, its wide folds encrusted with jewels and pearls—and, Jason realized, suspiciously wider and fuller—and lumpier—than they'd been when he entered.

Miranda smiled somewhat sheepishly at him; she walked swiftly toward him, then stopped with her skirts effectively covering the chair leg upon the carpet. "We were discussing hats. But I fear I—I do not care for this one."

All the women merely stared, mouths agape. She still wore the monstrous hat crookedly. Madame Celeste frowned. Clearly, she did not blame her creation, but rather found fault with the creature who wore it.

"Are you ready to go, Chlorinda?" Miranda said, her voice odd.

"Yes, if you are finished here," Jason said promptly. "Do permit me to buy you ladies some ices."

"I—I cannot," Miranda said. "I must meet Sir Horace in two hours."

"Then we must not tarry," Chlorinda said, her voice tarter

122

than Jason had ever heard it. "I would not care to have him think I detained you." Aha, Jason thought, another one who does not care for this Sir Horace.

The goodbyes and arrangements were swift. As the small group exited the shop, Jason suppressed a laugh. He wondered when Madame Celeste would discover she was missing one gilt chair. Or when she would discover her prize creation was now pregnant with that chair!

Later that afternoon, Julia sat in the salon, a forgotten book before her. It was the first moment she'd had time to think since her visit to Madame Celeste's.

Her emotions were all jumbled. She should be upset that Jason was back in town so soon; after all, it would complicate her masquerade immensely. Indeed, the obvious disgust he harbored for her true self should have infuriated her.

Yet, after the first fear of his recognizing her, she found herself—well, happy to be back in his presence. Just to hear his voice and see him had been a pleasure. And when he had laughed at Miranda's hat—the emotion she felt was indescribable. She sighed. If only he could laugh as warmly with Julia Landreth as with Miranda Waverly.

"Miss Miranda?" a voice called from the salon entrance. She looked up. Lady Daniella's butler, Hinton, stood respectfully at the door with what appeared to be a hatbox in his hands. "This was just delivered to you." He approached her and set it in her lap.

It was indeed a hat box. "Thank you, Hinton," she said. He bowed and left her, wearing a grin that made Julia blush despite herself.

After staring at the box in wary suspicion, she undid the fancy ribbons and lifted the lid. Nestled in its tissue paper lay the most exquisite little black hat. With no bows, and only enough fine netting to lighten its severe tailoring, it was dashing.

Beside it lay a card. She lifted it to read:

123

Miss Waverly,

In appreciation of your kind assistance of today. You saved me from no end of embarrassment. I believe this should meet with your Sir Horace's approval.

The Earl of Wynhaven

Sir Horace's approval be hanged—it met with *her* approval! A feminine, feline, purely-satisfied smile spread over Julia's lips. Placing the card aside, she reverently lifted the hat from its nest, ran to the mirror over the fireplace mantle, and gently placed it upon her curls. With an efficient movement, she tipped the hat to a rakish angle.

"My, how modish," her brother's voice suddenly observed from behind her.

Julia spun quickly. "Armand! I didn't hear you enter."

"Of course not." He grinned. "You were too busy admiring yourself and that daring hat. A little too dashing for Miranda, don't you think?"

"I didn't buy it!"

"You didn't?" Armand's brows rose. "Who did, then?"

"The Earl of Wynhaven."

"The Earl of Wynhaven?" Armand stared at her. Then he choked and began laughing. "He's obviously back in town."

"Yes," Julia said curtly.

"And already sending you hats. He doesn't let any grass grow under his feet, does he now?"

"He does not know it's me—he's sending it to Miranda. I—I met him with Chlorinda today."

Armand frowned. "Indeed. His fiancée—yet he sends you hats." His mood lightened. "Well, this should certainly liven things up a bit." Julia threw him a dark look that made him smile all the more. "At least he has excellent taste."

Julia turned back to stare at herself in the mirror. "Yes, he does at that," she said grimly. "The man knows far too much about women's apparel. Far too much!"

Eight

Aristocrats, Shepherds, And Ensigns

Jason tooled the carriage slowly through the crowded park, nodding at the fashionable passersby. Chlorinda sat quietly beside him, her groom properly behind them. They had exhausted all the usual polite topics in record speed. Indeed, the weather had been discussed down to its last possible drop of rain.

It seemed the only one interested in the conversation was the groom, who coughed and nodded throughout the discourse. Chlorinda sat quietly looking out across the park, and he focused upon his cattle.

Faith, how Granny would cackle at the situation, Jason muttered to himself. She'd say it was too dull by half. What was he thinking? There was no such person as Granny, only an adventuress who had lied and used him.

He looked at the lovely, contained creature beside him. Had she always been so quiet? Or was it that the adventuress had planted a seed of doubt in his mind about what he wanted in life? No, how could he judge Chlorinda so — it was the other woman he should condemn!

"There's Miranda," Chlorinda said, her face brightening considerably. Then her smile tightened. "And Sir Horace, of course."

Jason trained his gaze toward Miss Waverly, precariously seated upon a docile mare and dressed in an extremely dull maroon habit. Yet, perched upon her head was the hat he had

125

sent her. Indeed, it was the only thing that seemed correct and exciting about the woman.

His brows rose, however, when he observed her companion. The man was actually dressed in a canary-colored coat, with inexpressibles of the same color. His face was painted, and he wore a wig. "That is Sir Horace?" he asked, trying to keep his voice neutral.

Chlorinda must have read his thoughts anyway, for she giggled. "Yes, that is Miranda's beau." She frowned. "She—she says she is very attracted to him."

"Indeed."

"I—I do not think they suit," Chlorinda said hesitantly. When Jason did not respond negatively, she continued, "Miranda seems such a bufflehead, and she'll say the strangest things—but she truly does have an intelligence. It is simply that she is absentminded and becomes distracted. Why, last night she lost herself at Lord Brewster's ball and I discovered her in the study . . ."

"Never say she was reading?"

"No, she was just sitting at his lordship's desk with the most distracted air. I asked her if she was looking for something and she promptly replied, yes—her dinner, for she was terribly starved."

Jason threw his head back and laughed.

"You see, she does not have much of a care for convention—yet she is accompanied by Sir Horace."

"It does not appear that he has much care for convention either," Jason said gently.

"No, indeed not. All *he* cares about is his dress. He is the veriest fop," Chlorinda said, then she gasped as if she had said too much.

Jason looked at her. This was the first time he had ever heard an unkind opinion from his future wife. "You do not like him, then?"

Chlorinda sat very still, her face unreadable. "I do not think he and I agree," she finally answered.

Jason's eyes roved back to the man, whose eyeglass bounced as he used his hands to emphasize something to Miss Waverly.

The earl felt in complete charity with his future fiancée.

The dandy must have felt their gaze, for he suddenly froze and lifted his glass to his eyes, looking about haughtily until he spotted him. He returned their regard pompously, then leaned into his companion and said something. She peered across at them. Her smile, Jason realized, was Miss Waverly's saving grace. She waved at them.

After repeatedly kicking her stolid mare, Miss Waverly and her colorful suitor made their way over to them.

"Chlorinda," Miss Waverly said warmly, "it is a pleasure to see you again. And my lord," she said, nodding to Jason, "permit me to introduce you to my friend, Sir Horace Farouche. Sir Horace, this is the Earl of Wynhaven."

"How do," Sir Horace drawled, and waved his fingers in Jason's direction. Jason felt Chlorinda stiffen beside him. He failed to hide his amusement. "A pleasure to meet you as well." He turned his gaze to Miss Waverly. "And you are looking particularly dashing today, Miss Waverly." The smallest of blushes rose to her cheeks.

"Yes," Sir Horace said, leaning a little back upon his mount to eye her critically, "she is looking in fine fettle. Though that hat — 'tis not in her style, I fear." He shook his head. "Why, I was totally astounded when I saw her wearing it."

"I — I thought you would be pleased," she said. Her eyes wavered to Jason's, as if for support.

"Come now, Sir Horace," Jason said. "Do you tell me that you think the hat is not fashionable?"

Sir Horace seemed to consider a moment, his eyes appraising Jason meticulously. Perhaps he was a dandy, but few men would openly study or challenge Jason so — his size usually forestalled it. A rare smile crossed the fop's face. "Indeed I do, my lord. Why the hat is simply delicious, but it was meant to be worn by a rogue no less, a temptress. And if you knew my Miranda as I know her, you would realize that is not in her line."

Jason's smile was bland. "Perhaps it is — now."

"Yes," Chlorinda said stoutly. "Miranda has the right to change styles whenever she wishes."

"But of course." Sir Horace's tone sounded unaccountably tart as he gazed at Chlorinda. "A woman's prerogative, is it not, Miss Everleigh? And we poor mortal males must but suffer until the weathervane of their affections swings in our direction." Then he laughed. "Aren't women just too, too intriguing, my Lord Stanton? They appear the sweetest, most understandable of creatures, and then—surprise! You suddenly discover unplumbed passions, as it were. Even secrets, perhaps? Hmm?" He turned his sharp gaze from Chlorinda to Miranda. "But that is not so with my Miranda."

"Oh dear," she gulped. She was looking as guilty as a dog with a chicken in its mouth; Jason did not have to guess what she was thinking, and he drew in a deep breath as she went on. "Then I must tell you, Sir Horace—"

"—That every woman has a right to her own mysteries," Jason supplied, for he could tell she was about to confess he had sent the hat.

Sir Horace's painted brows rose in amazement. Then he laughed. "Egads, I believe I could become fond of you, my lord. Pon rep, but I do!"

Jason's eyes glinted. "Of which I'll be forever grateful, I am sure."

"Touché." Sir Horace feigned lifting a sword. "And if you say we must let the women have their little mysteries—so be it. Only remember, my lord," he said, his eyes bright, "you were the man who said it. May the words not come back to tease you.

"Now, my marvelous Miranda and I have detained you long enough. Come my dear." It was the same tone, Jason reflected, he would have used to address his favorite pet.

"Yes," Miss Waverly said obediently. "We shall see each other again, I make no doubt."

She prodded her horse ineptly. The beast snorted its displeasure but followed in Sir Horace's wake; for all his effeminate manners, he sat a horse well.

"He is the most—" Chlorinda's words choked to a halt.

"The most what?" Jason prompted, hoping to hear his fiancée once again say something that was not polite form.

Chlorinda blushed. "Nothing."

Jason sighed. "Very well. Let us be going as well." He prodded his horse forward. He and Chlorinda left the park as they had entered it, quietly.

Jason's thoughts, however, were not so tranquil. His attraction toward the eccentric Miss Waverly was impossible; his dissatisfaction with Sir Horace was surprising. He rather liked the unconventional fop—but not in connection with Miss Waverly. Was that why he had stopped her from confessing he had sent her the hat? He did not fear Chlorinda's misunderstanding the situation—but he did not want Miranda suffering if Sir Horace took offense.

He shook his head. It was all a mystery to him—even his own behavior. Sir Horace did not need to doubt that Jason recognized the mysteries of women—that seemed to be all he encountered these days.

"You fool!" the soft, aristocratic voice lashed out. "You incompetent fool! How could you have let this happen?"

"I do not know how it h-happened," the man whined, cringing before his master. "But—but we were looking for the widow as well, and—"

"And you have not found her, either. But that is another matter. This—this is a far more heinous mistake. Do you realize that I have informed Lord Castlereigh that they are dead? And why did I do such a thing?"

"Because—because I sent you a message."

"Exactly."

"But I believed it. I took the man's word in good faith."

"You took a common assassin's word in good faith?"

"But he is the best! He has never failed us before. He has always, always been loyal. He is a professional, after all—I still do not see why—why he lied."

"Do you not? You forget that they are some of Britain's finest agents and they have their own ways. Forsooth, The Fox and I have circled for years because of his wiliness."

"But you found him. You killed him. That I do know. I was

there."

"Would that you had been there at the childrens' execution," the voice said mercilessly. "God, I cannot believe your folly. I killed The Fox just before he killed me—do you not comprehend that, worm? He had uncovered me, the bastard! And if it had not been for my foolish, sentimental brother, I would never have known. He was Landreth's only folly. And my ace." He laughed. "That, and the fact that The Fox had taken such pains to cover his tracks over the years. It was child's play to bury them completely. But now, now you tell me that the children of the man I have killed still live. Damn your soul!"

"They—they are merely children," the shaking man stammered.

"Merely children? My poor, deluded little slug, do you still not understand? They were his partners. He trained them, you fool." The angry aristocrat grasped the perspiring man by his collar, pulling him forward until they stared eye to eye. "Does your gnat's brain have difficulty understanding the magnitude of the enemy and the vastness of your stupidity? Here was a man who, with the help of his brats, had spied successfully for the British government for years. Successfully enough to pass himself off as a French agent! One must admit the enemy's intelligence, and accept that he always, no matter what his role, worked for our mad king. One could have respected the man—if he had allowed himself to be bought.

"But alas, he was like my foolish brother, an 'honorable' man—and therefore, of necessity, a man to be slain. Do you know," he said musingly, while his underling still dangled in his grasp, "that The Fox had managed to keep his activities so secret, even those fat British officials did not know of his work. Not even the fattest of them all, old Prinny. They drooled for his information, never knowing from whence it came. Only one man knew that—my dear brother. That was The Fox's downfall."

"Yes—yes," the henchman managed to gurgle through choked vocal chords.

"But now—now you tell me his children live! A fact, my foolish cockroach, that you failed to tell me for some time."

"I—I had not realized the bastard's betrayal, and then—then I thought we would have overtaken them without delay."

"Without delay? Two months is without delay?"

"Th-they were not—not easy to follow. But we did, and—"

"And have five men dead for the effort."

The man gurgled again. "I—I am sorry. I did not understand."

"It was not your place to understand, insect. It was expected that you follow orders, nothing more. Orders that you have failed miserably to carry out."

"Please, have I not served you faithfully these many years? Have I not done everything you have bidden?"

"Yes, you have served me faithfully—until now." The aristocrat released him and strode back to his desk. "And that is why I forgive you your sin." He reached his hand into a drawer. "And why I say goodbye to you, beetle, personally."

He raised a small pistol. The trembling man cried out and sank to his knees.

"No need to thank me," his master said indulgently. "I knew how grateful you would be if I attended to your execution personally. Never would I have sent a stranger in my place—not after all these years."

With that, the Duke of Rendon cocked the hammer and pulled the trigger. Only the slightest death rattle arose from the kneeling man, his hands still clasped together in a plea as he fell forward with frozen, astonished eyes.

Two French peasants sat before a small campfire, a bare pinprick of light in the vast night. They talked in low tones as their flock of sheep settled down for sleep, rustling and bleating. A large, rawboned dog that lay beside the men had apparently already reached that state, though occasionally one blue eye and then one brown would wink open to ensure the party's safety.

"Well, my John, it looks to be a clear and quiet night," the fairer and taller of the peasants said. His hair was dark as bootblack against a light complexion, while piercing blue eyes glimmered in the meager firelight.

"Yes, if the lice would but be still."

"Come, John, let us hear no complaints. Everything is well in hand."

"That it is, my lor—André. I've no doubt those two scamps are enjoying their frolic in London town."

"A sure bet. My only regret is that I cannot be there for their entry into society. Strange, I have introduced them to many elite circles, and now they must enter England without me."

"You do not fear for them?" John asked incredulously.

"No, they will find the *ton* an easy playground. Polite society is very much the same in every country—they know the rules. It is not that. 'Tis only that I had always planned to—well, never mind. It cannot be helped." He sighed. "Things move too slowly, I think."

"Are you not the one who says patience is your specialty?"

"True, but not in this instance. Never in this instance. There should be no respite for the man who killed my dearest friend."

They sat quietly then, contemplating the stars. "André" said softly, "It has all come to an end, John. They have been good years, though, have they not?"

John sighed. "That they have—the best."

"And we've accomplished much. But now it must all come to an end."

"I only hope that *we* do not come to an end."

"Never fear that. The Hawk is no match for us. We shall expose his villainy."

"Do you think the man might resume his traitorous activities? We could get him that way."

"I doubt it. Why should he? His goal in all his treachery has always been money, and he does not need to steal secrets or smuggle anymore to have that. He has the dukedom, stolen from the brother he killed, the brother I sent to his death."

"How can you think that, André? You had nothing to do with Rendon's treachery."

"Yes, I did. I should have known if I sent the information against Rendon to John, he would feel honor-bound to approach him with it before turning him over to justice. How could I have asked John to betray his own brother?"

There was a derisive snort. "Rendon had no such difficulties, that's for sure."

"And he shall pay for that, my friend. I swear it to you upon my honor—and Lord John's grave—that he shall pay dearly. And he shall know he is paying for it at the time of his death, for it shall be I who presents the bill and only I."

"It will be no easy task. He has swept his tracks clean."

"Which is nothing we have not done for many more years than he. We shall have him yet, make no mistake. But first we must discover the charges he has laid at our door. They must be clever to have turned England against us so."

"They must be forgeries."

"There is no question of that." André shook his head, the blue of his eyes shadowed. "But for one brother's trust and another brother's betrayal . . . No matter, it is far past the time to settle down as it is."

"Settle down?"

"Why, yes. Settle down and live as all other Englishmen do. It is our birthright, after all."

"But how will—"

"You do not think I have played this cat-and-mouse game for nought? The honor of our family name shall be regained first. 'Tis the only reason our enemy still lives in his folly. No, it is time to see the children settled."

"S-s-settled? How—how do you mean?"

"Why, how else? It is time my Julia married. Since she has not found a man she desires in France—or any other country, for that matter—we must find her an English husband."

"But my lo—André. Miss Julia has never shown herself interested in that subject. Has she ever truly looked for a husband or—or love?"

"My dear John, one does not look for love. It is love that finds one."

John nodded his head dubiously and refrained from comment. He did not wish to point out to the proud father beside him that it could be no easy matter for love to find a lady who moved about in constantly varying disguises and who had rarely ever shown an inclination toward that tender emotion.

André, however, cocked a knowing brow at John and chuckled. "John, where is your faith? You must have trust in me. Julia is a woman with the ability to love deeply. She is very much like her mother, underneath." He sighed. "Nanette would say it was time for Julia to come out from amongst the shadows and marry."

"And Armand?"

André smiled wryly. "He is like me. He needs a special woman who will understand his hot-at-hand nature. A woman who will keep him happily by her side as my Nanette did me."

"She was a fine lady," John said reverently of his late mistress.

André's eyes grew softened at the memory. "That she was . . . perhaps all that has happened has its reason. This may prove the best way — for how else would I have gotten Julia and Armand out of the game?"

"Of their own free will? Never."

"My precise thoughts. This way, they have no other choice."

"I only hope they are not taken out of the game in the wrong way."

"Ah, John, that is the rub. That is the rub, indeed."

"I cannot believe it, Miranda. If the world could only know that Castlereigh is your idol," Chlorinda said with a laugh as they walked down the long hall to stand outside Castlereigh's office.

"Oh please, please do not mention it to anyone. I would sink if they knew," Julia said. "The world, as you say, thinks me a perfect quiz as it is. But alas, he is such a fine figure of a man, do you not think so? It — it is his nose, I feel, that makes him so."

"His nose? Oh, Miranda, he is the finest statesman of our time, and you can only sigh over his nose!"

"You do not understand —"

"No, and I do not wish to understand." Chlorinda giggled,

rapping upon the door with her dainty gloved hand. "I will go as far as to introduce you to him, but to listen to any more of your transports over his—his nose—I will not."

"I—I am so grateful that you are doing this," Julia said with a sincerity that had nothing to do with romance.

"Then promise me that you will not ask any questions out of the ordinary? None of your unusual ones that always seem to send people into a pucker."

Julia looked penitent. "No, indeed. I know what a sad trial I must be to you."

Chlorinda smiled warmly. "Of course not, you goose. I am very glad to have you as my friend. You always make me laugh somehow—and I never thought I would, ever again, after—" Her eyes became haunted and distant.

"After what?"

"What? Oh—I don't know why I said that. Now it is I who am being a goose."

Julia studied her a moment, then said, "It is amazing that you may wander these halls unescorted as you do. Why, any other visitor would be marched about by those stiff-looking guards that one sees at every turn."

"Poor dears," Chlorinda giggled, "they are only doing their duty. I know most of them, you see. I practically grew up here; my father's whole world revolved 'round this building."

"Did that not make you jealous of all this?" Julia asked casually.

Chlorinda's eyes widened. "Heavens, no. I was always so proud of him—you'd not believe how even the greatest men deferred to him." Julia said not a word, for she *did* know how well respected her father had been.

Chlorinda, blushing at her boasting, rapped upon the door again. It opened to her as her hand raised for the third knock. Alas, it was not the great statesman who stood before them, but a very grave-looking ensign. His eyes widened at the sight of Chlorinda, and he breathed a reverential "Miss Everleigh."

"Good afternoon, Ensign Trevor. Is Lord Castlereigh here, perchance?"

"I'm sorry, Miss Everleigh, but he is in council with the Regent at present."

"I see," Chlorinda said with pretty disappointment. "I had wished to introduce a particular friend of mine to him."

Ensign Trevor, in spite of his infatuation, stiffened in disapproval. "I know what you must be thinking," Julia gushed immediately. "That we womenfolk should not have come here to waste his lordship's precious time. And—and indeed, you must forgive us our presumption, for it is I who begged and begged poor Miss Everleigh for an introduction until she could no longer gainsay me. You see," she said with worshipful eyes, "I have thought Lord Castlereigh one of the greatest men of our times."

The ensign unbent enough to nod his head in agreement. "That he is, miss. No man should know better than I, for I am his aide and secretary."

"Goodness, never say so?" Julia exclaimed breathlessly, her hand coming to her chest. She knew that Chlorinda watched her in amazement, but she ignored her, and fixed her astonished gaze upon the ensign. "Then you are the man who supports and helps Lord Castlereigh in all his great affairs."

Trevor definitely softened and his chest swelled. "True, true, and it is a great responsibility."

His eyes strayed to Chlorinda, who only stared in fascination. Julia, under cover of her skirts, pinched the silent girl. Chlorinda squeaked slightly and jumped. "Uh—er—yes, we have no doubt, Ensign Trevor." She glared at Julia.

"Please, call me Edward."

Chlorinda slapped at Julia's hand before she could pinch her again. "All right—Edward."

Trevor's smile was beatific. "Lord Castlereigh is not present, but—perhaps I—I could arrange a meeting with him after all."

"Oh, no," Julia said. "I realize now how utterly inconsiderate and foolish I was to beg Chlorinda for a moment of Lord Castlereigh's very important time. Just being here—just seeing the actual place where all the important affairs of England are performed, is—is inspiring."

"Perhaps—perhaps I could show you around," Trevor said deferentially. His eyes went to Chlorinda in spaniel-like adoration.

Julia did not give her a chance. "Oh, please!" she squealed in excitement. "You are so very wonderful, is he not, Chlorinda?"

Chlorinda shot her a threatening look. "Yes. Indeed he is."

"Ladies . . ." The now-smiling ensign waved them into the office.

His smile did not last long, however. The minute Julia passed the office threshold, she exclaimed in utter delight at the surroundings, then raised her hand to her brow. "Oh, my! I fear that—that the excitement is too overwhleming." Her voice changed radically. "I—oh, dear, I fear I feel faint." With one more sigh, she gracefully crumpled to the ground.

"Oh, I say," Trevor said, his face a mask of horror.

"Miranda!" Chlorinda exclaimed, flying to the recumbent figure. "Miranda!" She gained no response. Lifting the stricken lady's head to her lap, she looked at Trevor, who stood in frozen confusion. "Quick! Do you have any smelling salts? I—I no longer carry mine."

"Smelling—salts?" Trevor mouthed, staring stupidly about the office as if Lord Castlereigh might be hiding some.

"No, of course not," Chlorinda muttered, helplessly patting Julia's face.

"W-w-water," Julia murmured, her eyes still closed.

"Water," Trevor said happily. "I can get her water—should I get her water?"

"Yes," Chlorinda said, frowning. "Please do so."

"I'll be right back—just wait."

"Of course—where do you expect me to go?" Chlorinda said, ruffled. "Please do hurry."

Trevor tore out of the room. Chlorinda frowned down at the recumbent girl. "Miranda? Miranda, what are you doing?"

Julia, catching the suspicion in the girl's voice, peeked her eyes open cautiously. "Chlorinda?"

"Don't Chlorinda me!" she whispered. "What in heaven's name are you doing? I know you aren't really faint."

Julia did not move. "I—I am not really faint—but I have a problem."

"What?"

"It—it is rather personal and I did not know what to do."

"What is it?"

"My—my garters were coming untied. I—I must not have tied them properly this morning."

Chlorinda's face cleared and she giggled. "Miranda, only you could be such a noddy. I'm surprised you remembered them at all."

"I—I didn't until this moment," Julia admitted truthfully. "But I didn't know what else to do with Ensign Trevor in the room."

"Oh dear, and he'll be back soon."

"I need some time. Couldn't you—" Julia did not have a chance to finish, for the ensign burst into the room, a dripping glass of water in his hand.

"Here it is, Miss Everleigh." He presented it to his goddess, then stepped back to a safe distance, as if Julia had not just fainted, but died of some deadly disease.

"Oh, yes—thank you," Chlorinda said. "Ah—Miranda, dear, do you wish to drink this?"

Julia had closed her eyes on Trevor's entrance, but opened them feebly now. "Ohh—yes," she said hesitantly, rising to her elbow. She took the glass from Chlorinda, and after taking a deep breath, brought it to her lips and drank it down, all eight ounces. There was an amazed exclamation from the ensign and a suspicious half-chuckle, half-cough from Chlorinda. Sweetly giving the glass back to Chlorinda, Julia then dramatically collapsed backward again. "More," she whispered weakly.

"More?" Ensign Trevor's voice squeaked. "B'gad's!"

"Yes, you heard her," Chlorinda said, her voice shaking. "More. It—it is the best thing for a fainting lady. Here, allow me to accompany you." Chlorinda shoved Julia from her lap, rose, and drew her hand through the startled ensign's arm. "Let us hurry."

"My God, yes," Trevor gulped. "If—if my Lord Castlereigh were to come back now—"

"Heavens, don't even *think* that," Julia heard Chlorinda say soothingly as the door closed firmly behind them.

Julia did not waste a moment. She sprung up and flew to the filing cabinet with a surety that she had gained from a close study of the office floorplan beforehand. Employing her best lockpick, she quickly entered the cabinet marked "K-L," rifling through the files, she found the one she desired. A large CASE CLOSED in red was scrawled across it.

"And about to be opened," Julia murmured as she pulled the inner papers out and returned the gutted file back to its place. She slid the drawer shut and relocked it.

Folding the papers, she bent down and lifted her skirts. It was not, however, her perfectly-tied garters that she attended to, but the secret pocket within her petticoats. She had just barely secured the papers when the door to the office opened. Julia, her skirts still lifted, looked up in consternation.

"Oh, no," Chlorinda squealed, her face comical in its dismay at catching Julia thus. She stepped backward quickly and the door slammed shut.

"Madame, watch out!" Ensign Trevor could be heard to say on the other side.

"Oh, dear," Chlorinda said sweetly. "Look what I have done—do forgive me. Quick, we must get her another glass of water."

"Another one? Bedamn!"

Julia's shoulders shook in laughter. Chlorinda evidently was the quick-thinking John's daughter, after all. She dropped her skirts, scanned the cabinet to ensure all was as before, and made a quick dive to the floor, resuming the position in which Chlorinda and Trevor had left her. In fact, Chlorinda must have been harrying the poor ensign slightly, for Julia had a few extra minutes before the door opened once again.

"I do thank you for your assistance," Chlorinda was saying. "Oh, my poor Miranda," she exclaimed in endearing tones.

"Yes." The ensign's tone was not so endearing.

"Here, allow me to give it to her," Chlorinda said. Julia waited for Chlorinda to settle beside her and lifted her head before she opened her eyes slowly, with a feeble moan. "Here—drink this, dear."

"Yes, please do," Ensign Trevor said. "We must hurry before my Lord Castlereigh returns."

Julia, thinking the very same thing, sat up quickly. She sipped a quick mouthful and said, "Ah, yes, that made me feel better. Yes, indeed, I am much revived." She quickly handed the glass back to Chlorinda and without further ado, sprung up, dusting herself off.

"Er—is that all you need?" Ensign Trevor asked, looking at the still-full glass in Chlorinda's hand as if it had insulted him personally.

"Yes, thank you," Julia said sweetly, turning to the man, only to gulp as her eyes widened appreciatively. Trevor stood before her, his face a study, with a wide, wet spot across his chest.

"Yes, thank you—Edward," Chlorinda said prettily, rising. She walked over and handed him the glass. "And I do apologize for my clumsiness in spilling that water on you."

"Th-think nothing of it," Ensign Trevor said with far less fatuousness than he had before.

"And I do apologize for my delicate sensibilities," Julia said. " 'Twas only that the excitement was—was too much."

"Miranda, dear, do you still wish to meet Lord Castlereigh—perhaps we could still make an appointment," Chlorinda managed to say with innocent tones.

"No!" Trevor all but shouted. "I—I mean, Miss—Miss Waverly must—must of course be tired after—after this."

"Yes, I do believe I am slightly pulled about," Julia said dutifully. "We must go now. I—I am not sure I would be able to control my—my excitement if I met my idol now."

"My God." Ensign Trevor's eyes bulged. "No—no, we couldn't have you fainting with—with my Lord Castlereigh here. You must leave. Now!"

"Yes, I fear I must," Julia said meekly. "Thank you so much for showing us about his offices, Mr. Trevor."

"Do not mention it," the ensign said, paling. "Please, do not mention it to anyone!"

"If you wish," Julia said with only the slightest smugness. Then, after the proper goodbyes, the two girls left the office and the water-bearing ensign.

Two heads bowed over the papers spread out upon the table. A fire crackled in the grate and a gold-leafed clock marked the passing minutes. There were no other sounds.

A sigh was finally heard through the room. "Well, he is very neat about it all," Julia said quietly.

"That he is," Armand nodded. "Now we know why all of England is turned against Sir. Gad's, it would turn *my* stomach if I'd been such a knave and traitor."

"How can we ever combat it?" Julia asked, a trace of defeat in her words. "He has hung every crime of his upon us."

"Yes. As you say, the man is very neat. He has not only created a traitor in father, but has totally obliterated his own past in so doing. Since they are actual crimes, actual deeds, they can be documented. They will be believed."

"Which means we cannot just negate them," Julia said wearily. "We will have to prove that it was he who committed these crimes and not us."

"And how can we do that, sister mine? All the true evidence has been destroyed. Only this—this bilge is left," he said in disgust, picking up one sheet amongst the many and crinkling it in an angry fist.

"I don't know," Julia signed, idly lifting another sheet. Her brows lowered as she caught a line upon the paper. "Armand?"

"Hm?"

"Do you know which French spy was serving as courier for these papers?"

"Who?"

"Lecroix."

"What?"

"And do you know who shot him while he tried to escape?"

"Who?"

"Rendon himself."

"Are you sure?"

"It is recorded right here, in these papers."

"But how would Lecroix have become involved with such a

scheme? He was far too loyal and honest a French agent to lend himself easily to Rendon's plans. Indeed, I had total respect for Lecroix—even if he *was* French."

"I know. Yet consider this: Lecroix's involvement is what made this all so plausible. Rendon was no fool. If he had presented it directly, we would have had the right to an inquiry—not a trial. But to have one of the finest French agents have the evidence about him—when he was 'accidentally shot'. . ."

"It blackens us immediately." Armand's face twisted in bitterness. "And Rendon is the hero for shooting Lecroix. Damn his soul to perdition."

"Yes, but how he managed to involve Lecroix is still amazing. Perhaps Sir can make something out of it. It might be a lead, but I do not see how."

"No. In fact, it is damn depressing. These papers almost have me thinking Sir a scoundrel. Well, I'd best get this information passed along."

"Where is it tonight?"

"The Arms and Shield."

Julia smiled. "Then I need not expect to see you until just before dawn."

Armand grinned back. "Sorry, Ju. I can't help but enjoy myself—at least there I hear the news of the war secondhand."

"I know, dear. I miss it all, too. Well—lift a glass for me as well."

"My pleasure, sister. I'll even lift two if you want me to . . ."

Chapter Nine
The Bakery And The Ballroom

Jeanne Lecroix glanced out the window of the small bakery shop where she worked. Her eyes automatically searched for, and found, her son, who was playing with a large gray dog in the street. Tiny worry lines suddenly marked her brow.

The shaggy dog had mysteriously materialized four days ago. Her son, as small boys will, had become fast friends with it the minute he'd seen it, and now the dog appeared every day to play with Michael. Jeanne wondered for the twentieth time if she should permit her son to play with the unknown dog, yet Michael took such pleasure in playing with him that she found it hard to deny him. He had had very little chance to be a child, and the dog seemed to make him able to be one.

Dusting the flour from her hands, she went to the door to call Michael in for the lunch they were allowed to eat in the back room every day. Michael, after waving at her and giving the dog a departing stranglehold meant to be a hug, came running into the shop.

He was a sturdy boy, though small for his age of eight, with the black hair and eyes that always conjured up his father's image for Jeanne. She determinedly pushed back the emotions that swelled within her at that thought and smiled as her son clattered into the shop, dirty and breathless.

"Maman, may I feed Sophocles something after we eat? We've been playing all day, and he must be hungry."

"Perhaps. Now go and wash that dirt from your face – and do not forget behind your ears."

"Yes, Maman." Michael grinned, already placing a grimy finger to the offending spot. Rubbing at it, he disappeared into the back of the shop.

Jeanne returned to the back of the counter and straightened the freshly-made loaves that were set out to cool. She breathed in the fragrant aroma with satisfaction. Today, they had risen and baked perfectly, with the crust just the right golden-brown.

The sound of the bell above the door interrupted her self-congratulations. She looked up with her usual "customer smile" – which tilted slightly in confusion. The man who had entered was tall, and since Jeanne stood no higher than five feet and two, his height was imposing. He dressed as a peasant and his shock of black hair was unkempt, but the way he held his body contained no hint of the downtrodden. Jeanne was a quick judge of character and the slight contradiction bothered her.

"May I help you?" she asked pleasantly, attempting to ignore the odd nervousness that was overtaking her.

"I do hope so," the man said with a charming smile. His French was that of a common peasant; there was nothing amiss there. But then he looked directly into her eyes and a frisson ran through her. His eyes were blue – blue! English blue, if she did not mistake the matter.

"I am finished, Maman," Michael chirped as he entered. "And I even checked my nails, which you forgot to remind me of before," he added meticulously, before stopping and looking at the stranger. A welcoming joy leapt into his eyes. "Ah, Monsieur André, it is you? You have come to meet Maman like I told you to! Is she not as beautiful as I said?'

Jeanne flushed; only a child could approach matchmaking with such forthright ruthlessness.

"Indeed she is," André said, his eyes sparkling at her embarrassment. "But have you not forgotten something, Michael?"

Michael frowned in concentration. "Oh – yes! Yes, I did!

144

Maman, permit me to introduce Monsieur André," he said with quaint courtliness. "Monsieur André—Maman."

"Good day, Maman," the peasant said, obviously amused.

"I am Madame Pendon," Jeanne said quickly.

"Madame—Pendon, then," he amended, fully smiling.

"He owns Sophocles," Michael said happily.

"Does he?" Jeanne replied. "You have never mentioned Monsieur André before, *mon ami.*"

Michael giggled and cast a conspiratorial look at the man. "I know. We wanted to surprise you."

Jeanne's fears crystallized at that. "Michael," she said slowly, attempting to control her voice. "Why not go and—and invite Father Jaton to break bread with us?"

"But Maman, if I do that, the food will get cold."

"Do as I say," she said sharply, refusing to look at the tall man.

"But Maman—"

"Do as your mother says, Michael," André said gently. "I am sure Father Jaton will be pleased to join you at table, no matter how cold the food might be."

"Yes, Monsieur," Michael said with a grin and an obedience that Jeanne resented. She watched as her son left, then turned her full attention to the man. He was watching her very carefully.

"He is a good boy," he said gently.

"Yes, yes, he is," she replied mechanically. Her hand slid along the counter until she touched the wooden handle of the bread knife. It was only that, but she grasped it, nevertheless. "Now, how may I be of service?"

"I have but a few simple questions."

"Do you? Then I am sure I can answer them for you. Our bakery is the finest and we are able to create anything you wish. Perhaps you wish a bridal cake?"

His laugh was deep and appreciative. "No, indeed not, Madame Lecroix—"

"My name is Pendon," Jeanne said firmly, her hand clutching at the knife handle.

"I must beg to differ with you—Jeanne."

"Who—who are you?" She thought she knew.

"Landreth," he said ever so softly.

Her eyes widened. It was not the answer she had been expecting—and dreading. "Landreth? I know no Landreth," she said in true confusion.

"I should think not," the man said kindly. "But intimates and—no-so-intimates—have often called me The Fox."

"The—The Fox," she gasped, turning pale. "Non, non, you cannot be he."

"No?"

"Non," she said more forcefully. "What an imbecile you must be to tell me that. I am no fool—The Fox is dead."

"Yes, but I've come back from the grave."

"Sweet Mother of God," Jeanne breathed, for the truth was there in the man's eyes. Without hesitation, she lifted the knife and threw it at him. He sidestepped it with humiliating ease.

"Now, just a few questions," he murmured, advancing.

"Non," Jeanne spat. She grabbed up her so-perfect loaves and threw those as well. He ducked and dodged them, looking very much like a bobbing block.

"Please, Madame Lecroix, strive for some decorum," he said as her final doughy missile flew past him to bounce off the wall behind him, a crumbling mass.

"Decorum! You English bastard!" She grasped a full jar of flour. "You should be dead!"

"No, not that," he ordered sharply as she hefted the jar up. Lunging over the counter, he grabbed at the jar before she could muster the strength to fling it.

"Y—you still live," she accused, struggling to pull the jar from his constraining grasp. It suddenly tipped and flour poured out—on her, not him. "English pig!" She coughed and sputtered as her eyes were clouded by the white dust.

"Temper, Madame. I control mine and it was your husband who attempted my downfall."

Jeanne froze and the flour fell from her fingers and crashed to the floor. *"Nom du nom,* you are here for revenge."

She jerked back from him and made a mad dash. Clearing the counter, she darted past the man, toward the door. His long arms reached out and clasped her around the waist, dragging her away before her fingers could touch the doorknob. "Let me go, you filth, you beast," she sobbed, turning to his arms to scratch and claw at him.

"Not until I have my answers, little madwoman," he said, grabbing at her flailing hands before her nails could score his face. He forced them down and pinned them to the small of her back, all but cracking her ribs as he restrained her to him. "I—"

The bell over the door jangled and it opened. Jeanne, still caught in the Englishman's arms, craned her neck to see. Madame Seaton, one of the pillars of the small community, stood upon the threshold, shock painting her face. "Madame Pendon, what is the meaning of all this?"

"Madame—Madame Seaton," Jeanne gasped. "Help me, help me, this man—"

"Madame Seaton?" Landreth asked, the sternness of his face replaced by an enchanting smile, while his grip on Jeanne forced the air from her lungs as well as the words from her mouth. "Please, do forgive my little dove and me. We have had a quarrel, you see? My darling, it seems, has not taken kindly to my—my overlong absence."

"Is this true, Madame?" Madame Seaton asked, her eyes trained on Landreth. Her voice was already mellowing. "We have been wondering upon your husband's absence—even if it were true that you had one."

"Oh, she has one—" he said, grinning.

"But he is not my husband!" Jeanne cried.

"Not your husband?" Madame Seaton exclaimed.

"Tsk, tsk, sweetings. Now the cat is out of the bag." The charm exuding from Landreth was a nauseating sight for Jeanne to behold. "I do hope, Madame Seaton, that you will take pity on us and not inform Monsieur Pendon of our—our liaison. As you say, he is rarely home and my poor darling becomes lonely. And I—I cannot resist her." He said it with such warmth that Jeanne's cheeks flamed.

To her horror, Madame Seaton looked at her, and then at the man gazing at her with passionate eyes and — and chuckled. Yes, the respectable Madame Seaton chuckled, and then sighed. "Ah, I understand, Monsieur. After all, her husband neglects her shamefully — and she is still so young and beautiful. And you — you, I am sure, are far more attractive than her husband, yes?"

"I would like to think so," Landreth said with a wink.

"Well," Madame Seaton said with ruffled pleasure, "never let it be said that I am a woman who does not understand amour. Indeed, there was a time when my Émile did not attend me — and a woman must have love, must she not? Well, I see that I intrude. I will come back another time." She smiled, her tone conspiratorial. The good lady winked and turned to leave, but stuck her head back in. "By the by, Madame Pendon, you have flour upon your nose."

Jeanne, stupefied, watched as the lady waved again and hastened out of sight.

"That is what I have always admired about your countrymen," her enemy said. "They have such sympathy for the affairs of the heart."

Jeanne looked up into those *blue,* blue English eyes and crumbled. It had all been too much for her — even the powder upon her nose. She burst into tears with a wail. "I hate you! Why, oh why, did you not die?"

"There, now," he soothed, his viselike grip becoming soft and comforting. "I understand. It was very inconsiderate of me not to die, and very unobliging. Just cry it out."

And Jeanne did just that. She buried her streaming face into the rough-clothed chest of her enemy, and cried as she had not at her husband's death. She cried for the past and the uncertain future. She cried for the utter uselessness of it all. Finally, the racking sobs subsided, and, refusing to look up, she muttered wearily, "As long as you were dead, there was a reason for my Paul's death. Now there is none."

"But there still can be."

This did make her look up, sniffling. "What — what do you mean?"

148

"I mean," Landreth said, gently pushing her away from him, "that his death can be the undoing of the man who betrayed him." He led her gently over to the counter and lifted her atop it as easily as if she were air. "You can destroy The Hawk and avenge Paul's death."

A shiver ran through Jeanne and she shook her head. "Non."

"Why not?" He pulled out a rough handkerchief and dried her eyes. "The Hawk betrayed your husband, did he not?"

"I — I don't know." Her eyes flitted away from his.

"But The Hawk is the reason you quit Paris so hastily and moved to this little place and took up the name Pendon, is it not?"

"How did you know that?"

"People who have been involved with The Hawk in some fashion or another have the tendency to do so — at least, those who still enjoy breathing. And why would you do that unless your husband was involved with him? I do hope you were not involved with him as well."

"I would never have had anything to do with that *canille!*"

Landreth's lips twitched. "I am glad to hear it."

"I told Paul he could not trust that man — he had the look of the devil, that one. So cold-eyed." Jeanne shivered.

Landreth's smile disappeared and his eyes grew piercing. "You saw The Hawk?"

"Why — why, yes. Though I did not know his name — my husband told me he was The Hawk later!" Jeanne said quickly, for Landreth's look was dangerous.

"My God, 'tis better than I expected. You actually saw him! How did you see him?"

Jeanne looked down in embarrassment. "I — I knew that my Paul and this Hawk person were to meet to discuss something that was to — to aid all of France."

"My death?"

"Yes, or at least your downfall. I knew when they were to meet, and — "

"And you spied upon them?"

"Well — yes."

"Did The Hawk know that you saw him?"

Jeanne drew herself up in indignation. "Of course not. I am not such an incompetent."

"But then why did you go underground?"

"Because — the night Paul carried the papers about you, he felt very troubled and nervous, though he could not think why."

"His instincts finally came to the forefront. It still amazes me that your husband would deal with The Hawk."

"Me, I thought the same. The Hawk is the so-obvious Englishman from what I saw. He claimed loyalty to France, but you cannot trust an Englishm . . ." Her voice trailed off.

"Yes, we are pig people." The man nodded, obviously undeterred by her disgust. "Continue."

"I —" Jeanne looked down, slightly embarrassed. "I sent a good friend of mine to follow Paul, to help if there was trouble, you understand?"

Landreth only stared at her. "Gad's, woman, it sounds as if you did as much spying as your husband did."

She stiffened. "To be the wife of a successful spy, one must. Where would my Michael and I be if I had not spied, eh?"

"I am not sure — continue with your story."

"My friend — who is very discreet, you must understand, followed Paul. He saw the English dog capture Paul, which was part of the plan. But then — The Hawk did not take Paul into his personal custody as he had promised, but — shot him instead, crying out that Paul was attempting to escape. And this I have never understood, why he wanted my Paul dead."

"Paul had seen who The Hawk was. Just knowing him as The Hawk signed his death warrant. I could have told you Paul was marked for death the minute he allowed Paul to see him in person."

Jeanne turned white. "Oh, my God. It was Paul who demanded to meet with The Hawk personally. He said that the scheme was too dangerous to walk into it blind, that he'd not be set up to be captured by the English if he did not know the man who was to rescue him."

"If only he had known the man," The Fox said tightly. He looked curious. "Did Paul know exactly what was in the papers he carried?"

"But of course. That was the whole purpose. To carry papers that would turn the English against you and hopefully cause your death. Your Monsieur Hawk said he would have the best forgeries possible."

"I can understand Paul's wish to cause my death, but why such a complicated scheme? I understand The Hawk's purpose, but why did Paul agree to it? Why did Paul not just hunt me down and kill me if he knew I was an enemy of France?"

"He would have, but he did not know who you were or how to find you. The Hawk said that he did not know either, but this surely would settle matters."

"I see."

"It is not as if we did not know of the information you sent, but we could not be sure of your identity." She laughed. "Indeed, there have been many theories about that. Some thought you were just a myth."

"But The Hawk knew who I was—and my name."

"But he did not tell Paul this," Jeanne said angrily. "The whole scheme was created so that the English, who did know who you were, would turn against you and hopefully execute you, since we could not."

"That was Paul's scheme. It was not The Hawk's. His was the conclave suit. He was using your husband to get at me. He already knew who I was."

"Treacherous dog," Jeanne said, her eyes darkening.

The man considered her closely. "The Hawk did not know you saw him, but you went into hiding anyway?"

Jeanne held back her sudden tears. "Yes. The friend who had been investigating for me disappeared suddenly."

"He did? Damn. Then The Hawk must know of you—or have his suspicions—according to how strong your friend was."

Jeanne's eyes moistened. "He was very strong, Monsieur."

"Excellent." His blue eyes warmed. "And you were very

151

wise. I compliment you on your abilities—it was not easy to find you."

"But how did you? The Hawk has not."

Landreth laughed. "I have played this game far longer than he has, and far longer than you have."

Her eyes snapped. "I am thirty-nine. How old are you?"

"Older than that," Landreth parried dryly. "Now, will you help me?"

"Help you?"

"Yes. Don't you understand? You can recognize The Hawk—a very rare thing. And you, my dear, can also testify that it was he who framed me—you are my only chance of proving my innocence."

"Are you mad?" Jeanne said, amazed. "I am to help you? You, who are an enemy to France? You, whom Paul died to destroy? I am to throw in with you against the man who already seeks me? *Nom du nom,* you are mad!"

"I am France's enemy, but not yours. It is The Hawk who betrayed not only France, but your husband as well—and who will find and kill you if you do not act against him."

"But even if I were so foolish—how could I help you? Who would believe my story? Certainly not your English butchers—I am the wife of a French spy!"

"Allow me to handle that."

"No."

"Then you will not help me?"

"No. Definitely not."

Landreth looked at her with a confident smile. "You'll change your mind—and when you do, I will be here." He handed her the handkerchief and was gone.

He departed so swiftly and without argument that Jeanne wondered if, perhaps, he was a figment of her overly nervous imagination. Her eyes fell upon the crumpled loaves that lay upon the floor and the bread knife, its tip snapped off from striking the wall, and she sighed. No, he wasn't a ghost—but he could be the devil . . .

152

It was the very devil, Jason thought, entering the Cambinton's glittering ballroom deep in meditation and depression. Day by day he had become more and more unsure of his impending engagement to Miss Chlorinda Everleigh. Even now, as he stood at the entrance to the ball, his eyes roved the room for the sight of Miss Miranda Waverly—not for his fiancée.

Therein lay the rub! Women rarely confused him, rarely unsettled him. He truly enjoyed their company, but his other interests—the war, his estates—had always held the prime position in his life.

He was not one to suffer an excess of emotion. He had not lied when he told Granny Morton that his was not a passionate nature.

Then how had he landed in a position where his hand was offered to a perfectly marvelous and beautiful heiress, while his attention and desires ran towards an abstracted, ill-dressed twit? He sighed. Miranda Waverly could only be called a twit—no one could claim she was a heavyweight in terms of gray matter.

He shook his head. If only he had never answered his sprite's singing in the woods. Ever since then, his life had turned topsy-turvy. He grimaced; at least he was no longer attracted to an old woman. Ah, but that old woman had been as sharp as a tack; now his blood ran hot for a witless young woman. And he still could not seem to touch hearts with his fiancée, the one who should command his devotion.

Jason squared his shoulders, and a determined step was added to his already-firm stride. That was one condition he could change; it was time to communicate with his future bride. He spied her across the room and directed his path to appear before her with a polite bow. "Miss Everleigh, you are looking beautiful tonight, as always."

Chlorinda smiled up at him shyly—or was it apprehensively? Now, why had that notion entered his mind? He asked for her hand in the dance; both Chlorinda and Mrs. Bendley granted it. Jason moved his partner through half of the line, then he pulled her away and down the nearest hall.

"My lord! Whatever are you doing?" Chlorinda exclaimed

in surprise.

"Looking for an empty room." He grinned, opening a door and peering within. "Empty. Excellent."

He dragged her in despite her objections. Then he released Chlorinda's hand and smiled down at the petite blonde. "I wish to talk to you. I promise that is all. I know better than to go beyond the line."

"Wh—what do you wish to talk about?"

Jason was slightly nonplussed. How to start a private conversation with this child? "Perhaps our impending engagement. Are you still of the same mind as before? Do you wish the engagement?"

"Of course," she said nervously and swiftly. She sidled away and sank into a chair. "That is—if you do?"

Faith, what a passionate response! Once again he could hear Granny's jeer. "Of—course," he said mechanically, moving to sit in the chair across from her—they were both, he noticed, avoiding the cozy settee. " 'Tis only that—I know I have been away, and we have not been able to talk since my return." When had they ever talked, he thought wryly. "It is still not official, you know."

"Yes . . . but we must wait for my uncle's return," Chlorinda said anxiously. "Mustn't we?"

"Indeed we must," Jason replied gravely. An uncomfortable silence formed between them.

Time to push forward. "Chlorinda." She jumped at the sound of her name on his lips; he'd never used it before. "There is a matter of some import that we must discuss before we continue our engagement. It is something I feel you must know before you consent to marry me."

"Y-yes?" Chlorinda looked at him as if expecting him to announce that he devoured little children for nuncheon.

He drew in his breath; he was insane to try and talk about this. It hadn't been so difficult with Granny—but this was different. However, the need to know her response was all-consuming. "As you know, I was in the war and was almost killed."

Chlorinda's face took on a frozen expression. "Yes. The

154

war is a terrible thing. Let us not discuss it any further."

"No, I fear we must," Jason said gently. "You see, I was greatly scarred."

"S-scarred?"

"Yes, upon my shoulder and my back. It is not exactly a pretty sight. I – I wanted you to know that so you wouldn't be shocked upon – upon our wedding night."

"Stop!" she said sharply. She sprang from her seat, a frantic, odd expression upon her face. There was an unfocused stare in her eyes as she looked wildly about, as if she were retreating into another world. "I – I will not think of this. I must go back to Mrs. Bendley." She shook her head as if in severe pain. "Excuse me, I – I have a headache."

With that she stumbled from the room, leaving Jason sitting in his chair, frozen and numb. How long he sat there he did not know.

Slowly the feeling that he was not alone pervaded his consciousness. He looked wearily about the room, then his eyes trained themselves upon two slippers peeking out from behind the drapes – an eavesdropper! Marvelous! "You may come out!" he said roughly. "I know you're there."

The curtain slowly drew back. Miranda Waverly stepped out from behind it.

"Oh God, no," Jason groaned. Of all the people in the world, it had to be her!

"I – I got lost," she said in a small voice, her brown eyes wide and agonized. "You entered so swiftly and I did not know who it was – so I hid. And then you began . . ."

"Spilling out my most private secrets," he said bitterly. He eyed her speculatively. "Well, do you not wish to run screaming from the room as well – I truly am a terror, you know."

She opened her mouth, then clamped it shut tightly and approached him slowly and deliberately. "You must give her more time, my lord." She placed a gentle hand upon his shoulder. "She was merely surprised."

"Indeed? Is that what it was? Strange, it looked more like stark horror to me. Especially at the mention of the wedding night – now that *would* be frightening."

155

The hand upon his shoulder tightened; the unfocused brown eyes were somehow too knowing and understanding. "Never mind me, Miss Waverly," he said gently, reaching up and clasping her hand. "I did not mean to berate you—it does not matter." He kept looking down at her hand, lest she see in his eyes that it did matter.

Gazing at that hand he noticed it bore light scars. How had that happened, he wondered absent-mindedly. "I mean . . ." He turned it over to view the palm. ". . . You are probably right." Unblemished, but for a rough, scarred patch on the tender skin at the base of the thumb.

A scar from a blister, he thought with sudden, certain knowledge. A blister from a shovel she had used to deaden a raging fire in a wood. "You are correct . . . Chlorinda only needs time," he said slowly.

"Of course," the woman who was now Miranda Waverly replied, her voice odd.

"Thank you for your concern." He raised the telltale hand and kissed its palm softly. Just a kiss of recognition.

"My lord?" Her voice rose nervously as she jerked her hand away. "I—believe you need a moment by yourself," she said tightly.

She escaped as swiftly as Chlorinda had. "Well, old man," Jason muttered, "that's two women you have sent scuttling from this room in the course of an hour."

But it was upon the second one that his thoughts focused. He shouldn't feel so positive that it was she. The thought was mind boggling. Many women might bear such scars—yet deep down, he felt no doubts. He knew that hand. He knew that woman—*women,* he corrected himself.

He stood up and stretched. The pain that had been in his eyes was gone, replaced by a brighter, expectant light. Indeed, when he left for the ballroom, he was humming slightly—a song he had heard once when riding through a wood . . .

Julia sped out of the room and back to the dance floor as

fast as her slippered feet permitted. Her heart thumped and pounded like a savage's drum.

And why? Because some man had kissed the palm of her hand! Lud, she was becoming as silly a nodcock as Miranda!

Yet that kiss had been so intimate, offered so gently, it had reached the very core of her. She shivered. Staying to console him had been a mistake; she should have known her best course was to flee far away from him.

"Miranda, my sweets." She heard her brother's voice behind her and turned, attempting to erase the emotions upon her face as he approached.

His piercing gaze told her she had failed. "What has happened?"

Julia sighed. "I was caught in the room while Jason and Chlorinda were having a tête a tête."

"Jason and Chlorinda?"

"None other."

"I see. Then you are privy to why the English rose is in full blush and acting as if she might faint?"

"Yes." Julia's lips tightened in aggravation.

"What, then? Did the mountain rush his fences with her?"

"What?" Julia said blankly.

"Did he imposition her or not?" Armand's voice was sharp.

"Heavens no," Julia said. "He isn't that type." Then she blushed. It was *her* hand that still tingled from his kiss, after all.

"Then why is the rose acting the way she is?"

"He—he told her about the scars he bears from the war. And—she just fled the room."

"Faith, you mean she turned from him because of that?"

" 'Twas odd. I mean, she could have been responding from abhorrence at the thought . . ."

"Most likely," Armand said contemptuously.

"But I don't believe it was that alone. It seemed as if something else was . . . oh Lord, he's coming toward us!"

"He?"

"Jason."

"Ah, *that* he." He raised his quizzing glass. "And positively making a dead set at you, you lucky girl." He chuckled at Julia's quiet but deep groan.

"Miss Waverly," Jason said without preamble, "Would you care to dance? I was to dance with Miss Everleigh, but I fear she desires to rest a moment."

"Well . . ." Julia looked pleadingly at Armand for assistance; Jason's eyes had an odd gleam to them that jangled all her natural instincts.

Armand, the beast, merely shrugged and said, "Do dance with him, my dear." He then smiled at Jason. "Only beware, my lord, my pet does have a kick to her stride." Armand tittered and left Julia and Jason with a slight wave of his hand.

She peeked up at Jason, who was considering her with a very confident smile. She forced a smile to her lips. "Sir Horace is correct, my lord, I am not a graceful dancer."

"I am sure you are excellent," he said placidly as he drew her onto the dance floor and deftly swung her into the dance.

The man was too overbearing, Julia thought rebelliously. She smiled her special Miranda smile—abstracted and silly—and trod sharply upon his toe. "Oh, I am so sorry," she murmured, looking down in supposed regret.

"Think nothing of it." Jason stifled a groan and smiled tightly. "Perhaps you are merely nervous." He pulled her closer without warning.

"Wh-why should I be nervous?" Julia asked with an inane laugh, though being drawn up so snugly to the length of him did shorten her breath.

"Because of my confession in the room," he said. "I must have shocked you. I assure you, I did not mean to."

"No, of course not," Julia stammered, attempting to pull back. Nary an inch did she gain. The man appeared totally oblivious to the fact that he held her absolutely glued to him. "You didn't know I was there, after all."

"No." Then he actually grinned. "You could have knocked me over with a feather when I realized it was you."

"I do feel embarrassed at being caught there—'tis only that I—I get lost so easily." Julia said. "But as for the rest—do not think you shocked me. I—I do not shock easily."

"Strange . . ." Jason's voice was silk. "I remember a little old woman telling me the same thing." Without warning, he clutched Julia up and twirled her about the room in breath-snatching circles.

"My Lord—you're—" Julia stammered as he finally slowed, allowing her slippers to touch the dance floor.

"Yes indeed," he continued as if in fond memory, "she was a rare old tartar." He propelled Julia into another spiral; she drew a quick breath when he slowed again. She knew she would need it. "Indeed, it was she who suggested I confess my, er—drawbacks—to Chlorinda."

Julia, despite her best resolve, clung to him. Her head was spinning madly. "Scars are not a drawback," she snapped without thinking.

His arms tightened about her; she could feel him ready to toss her into a spin again. Did he think her a top, for goodness sakes? "No, my lord," she gasped, and pushed him back. "You are holding me far too closely. We are drawing attention. You do not wish that, I trust?"

"You trust, Miss Waverly?" he quizzed. "Beware, trust is a tricky thing." She groaned as he hefted her up and sent her into another death-defying whirl. Julia barely stifled an un-Miranda-like curse when he finally settled her upon the ground. "Indeed, people are not always what they seem." He smiled kindly as she panted. "Some, you see, are charlatans, masqueraders—fakes, if you would."

"Indeed?" Julia gritted through clenched teeth. She planted her slipper sharply into his instep. Jason yelped. "Soooo sorry," she cooed, crossing her eyes.

"Of course," he grunted and promptly picked her up before she completed another kick. He sent her into orbit.

"My lord," Julia snapped, her head reeling, "set me down. I do not feel well."

"Forgive me," Jason said. However, regret was not among the tones in his voice. He brought her to a proper landing. Even better, he set her at the proper distance. "My incompetent dancing, I fear."

"Oh no," Julia gasped, merely grateful to be on her own two feet. "I would never call it that."

"What would you call it?"

"I don't know," Julia said, biting her lip and looking myopically up at him. "I fear you are roasting me. You know I do not possess that much wit."

"Never say so," Jason said with a grin. "I do not feel that way about you. Indeed, you remind me of that little old lady I told you about. And she was sharp as a tack. Of course, she had me thinking I had lost my sanity for a while."

"Did she?" Julia asked, her eyes widening to saucer size.

"Yes." His smile was slow and wolfish. "But I have found that sanity—again."

"How—how fortunate," Julia said weakly. "Well, here is the end of the dance. I thank you," she said swiftly, pulling away from his arms and walking toward the retiring room as steadily as she could. Her head was spinning and so were her thoughts.

Fortunately no one was in the retiring room at that moment. She sat down shakily and gazed at herself in the mirror. Her hair was as scattered as her thoughts.

Damn the man! Look what he had done to her. Worse, think what he could do . . . if he knew. If he didn't—he had the largest suspicions possible. As hulking as he was, she thought bitterly as she rested her aching head on her hand.

Still, he had not denounced her as he could have. He had toyed with her, but he had not denounced her. She breathed in deeply. That meant she was still in the game. A calm settled over her. If she was still in the game, she still had a chance. He wanted to play—well, he'd find out that she played better. That was all.

After all, this was her field of expertise and she'd been at this a far sight longer. She smiled. She'd roll that gentleman up yet, see if she didn't.

Armand, upon deserting Julia, directed his steps toward Chlorinda.

He knew he shouldn't attempt being near her. His antipathy was too strong. And curse the woman, she knew it. It seemed every time he tried to fake it, she knew. Her clear skin would flush and her delicate little body would stiffen imperceptibly. Not imperceptibly enough, however. He knew.

So why did he want to go to her now? That was one thing he didn't know. She was obviously upset. The look of pain and bewilderment upon her face did something to him inside. It should have made him happy, but that was not what he was feeling.

He told himself it was a perfect time to approach her. She was vulnerable. Perhaps she would let something slip.

He flourished a deep leg before her. "Madame, would you care to dance? I find myself bereft of a partner, you see. Your mountain has commandeered my dear heart."

Chlorinda blushed. "If you speak of the Earl of Wynhaven, then you are mistaken. He is not *my* 'mountain'. "

"Is he not? Then my love was confused—not an uncommon occurrence I own. You see, my sweetings was under this absurd impression that you and my lord were . . ."

"That was to be a secret," Chlorinda said, cutting him off sharply.

"Miranda and I do not have secrets from each other," he said pointedly. "Though you need not fear. 'Pon my honor, no one else will ever hear your little secret from me," he mimed, locking his lips and throwing away the key. "I, after all, can be the very soul of discretion. Now, shall we?"

"Shall we?"

"Why, shall we dance?" Armand drawled. He tittered. "I certainly was not asking anything else than that."

"I am well aware of that," Chlorinda said stiffly.

"Indeed, I would do nothing untoward. Only think if it overset the earl. Great Zeus, the thought of the mammoth enraged sends positive chills down my spine, indeed it does. Turns my knees to jelly, s'truth." She was refusing to look at him. "Shall we dance?" he said more sharply. "Or do you wish to remain and moon over your beau?"

Her blue eyes flew to his. "I am not mooning," she said coolly as she rose and followed him to the dance floor.

"No?" Armand quizzed as he took her into his arms. "Then what has sent you into such a pucker?"

Chlorinda looked stunned at his bluntness. "Sir, that is none of your affair."

"Tut-tut, your thorns are showing, English rose," Armand chided, though a smile did slip through the dandy's paint. "From the demure, sweet demeanor you always present to Lord Stanton, I would have thought it safe to participate in a dance with you. And here you rip up at me. Hm? I wonder if his lordship knows of your thorns. Perhaps the poor fellow should be warned."

Chlorinda's eyes widened and then looked lost. "He knows now."

"Aha! Do allow me to guess. You've had a lover's tiff. Indeed, that would explain that distracted brow of yours."

"No, we did not," she responded too swiftly. Then she sighed. "I—I acted like a ninny. My lord had broached a-a particularly delicate subject, and while he was talking, I started thinking about . . ." He could feel her body shake. "About something different . . ."

"What?" Armand asked, holding her closer.

"I hate the war," she said softly. "I hate the maiming, the killing, the death . . ." She halted and looked at him then. Her previous dark expression seemed to submerge within the blue of her eyes, and she shook her head. "Never mind, let us not talk on this."

"Gads no," Armand said. He knew he should push her for answers, but all he wanted to do was drive the tormented look from her face. "It's such a nasty thing. And the uniforms—so restricting. So unimaginative. I would simply go mad if I was forced to wear the same dreary dress every day."

She looked at him as if he was crazy. Then a bubble of laughter rose to her lips. "Only you would look at it in that fashion."

"Oh indeed," he drawled. "Killing someone is not worth it if one must mess one's clothes."

She flushed. "Must you always be so sarcastic?"

"Ah, such a fall from grace," he countered. "Is that the eleventh commandment? Thou shalt not be sarcastic?" His eyes suddenly widened as he looked across the dance floor. "Ods Blood! Do not look now, but *your* beloved is positively mauling *my* beloved."

Chlorinda looked just in time to see Jason swinging Julia off the ground and into a twirl. "Why, how very odd."

"Indeed. And he had appeared such an accomplished dancer."

"He is," Chlorinda snapped. "I find him an excellent dancer."

"Zounds," Armand said faintly. "I do hope you do not cherish expectations of my performing such feats. I simply cannot swing you about in that energetic fashion. Why, it would be far too enervating—and could possibly render grave damage to my jacket."

"I do not wish it! And my lord has never done that with me, I assure you."

"Done what?" Armand quizzed, his painted brow raising. "Never spun you about or never mauled you—for that is surely what he is doing to my dear."

"Neither!" A flush creeped up Chlorinda's cheeks.

"He's always behaved with perfect circumspection then?"

"Yes. Of course."

"Has he?" Armand asked, unconsciously holding her closer. "Has he never stolen a kiss from those delectable, soft little lips or run his hands through those silken, golden curls or sworn that the blue of your eyes is the only true blue in the universe?"

Chlorinda only stared at him. "N-no, he has not," she gulped out. "And—and I would not wish him to do so." She looked up at him. "Why, is that what you do with Miranda?"

"No. I always swear that her eyes are brown."

Chlorinda gasped. "Then—then you *do* do that?"

"Is that not the way a gentleman courts a lady?"

"I-I have never seen it so."

"Ah, the mountain is made of the sternest stuff then. Such

163

control . . . masterful." Armand sighed. "Now with me, I fear, when love's powers sway . . ."

Chlorinda bit her lip. "Then you do love Miranda?"

"Yes, all my life," Armand said with complete truthfulness. "Why must you ask?"

"I care for Miranda, 'tis all. After all, she is very wealthy."

"And you think I might seek her wealth? No, English rose, mine is a sincere attachment. It has nothing to do with selfish gain."

Chlorinda's chin lifted. "Neither has mine."

"Has it not? Then you love the mammoth?"

"I — I, oh why must you ask?"

"Why, I am only showing my concern. I am a man who desires truth."

"Truth?" Chlorinda asked quietly, her face paling. "There is no such thing as truth."

"Yes, there is, and in this case, I intend to find it," Armand said, his voice suddenly implacable.

Chlorinda seemed to flinch. "Find it?"

"Yes." Armand forced a smile, for the blue eyes were hauntingly lost. "I'd like to know all about you."

"About me?" Her face became stern, her voice dulled. "No, there is nothing about me you need to know."

"I would not believe that."

"And why would you wish to know about me anyway?"

Armand grinned. "My Miranda believes in you."

"And you do not?"

"I never said that," Armand said swiftly. " 'Tis only that I care . . ."

"Care?" Chlorinda said in suddenly angry tones. "All you care about is the set of your coat, the tying of your cravat, and the shine of your boots. What would you know about the love you speak of? Or truth? You wouldn't know . . ." Chlorinda bit her lip.

"Wouldn't know what?"

"Nothing. Nothing at all. Only someday I would relish seeing that smugness wiped from your face and just once — just once — seeing your fine cravat askew and your — your fine clothes—oh, never mind."

"Thank heaven," Armand breathed. "I was afraid, yes, deeply afraid, that you would say something drastic—that my clothes might be creased. I could not have borne the thought. Indeed no, I could not have borne the thought at all."

Chapter Ten
Flee The Hawk

Jeanne glanced up from the accounts she was tallying and bit back an exclamation as the door opened. Landreth, whom she had thought gone for good, entered without preamble. "You again!"

"Come, you must leave." Landreth held out his hand. No hello, no greeting, just a curt order.

"I beg your pardon?"

"Is there a back way out?"

"Only a window, but you must be crazy if you think I am going anywhere with you!"

"We have no time for your temper. The Hawk is coming this very minute. Do you really wish to sell him your bakery? *You* are the sweetmeat he wants, after all."

Jeanne's arm shot convulsively over the counter and she grabbed at his outstretched hand. "Non, non, it cannot be true."

"It is. Now hurry." He pulled her toward the back.

"Michael!" Jean halted immediately.

"He is safe with John." Landreth jerked her into motion again.

"Is he? Why, you were just waiting for this, were you

not?" She planted her feet again, arms akimbo. He had already pulled her into the back room, where a pile of crates covered the only window. Landreth tossed them aside with ease.

"No time to rip up at me," he said with a grin. With panther quickness, he secured her wrist, yanked her to him, and shoved her toward the opening. "Now, out you go." He not only assisted her, he literally thrust her through.

"Ugh! Evil man!" Jeanne pushed herself out of the muddy gutter she had landed in, recoiling from the mound of rotted cabbage just inches from her nose. She was looking at her grimy hands, fuming at the high-handedness of certain Englishmen, when Landreth's tall, lean body thumped down beside her.

"Come on, you can check your nails later." He chuckled and grabbed her smarting hand, dragging her away from the mud.

"Just one moment," she said, firmly digging her heels into the muck. "How do I know you speak the truth, that this is not just a ruse?"

"My God, woman, can't you find a better time to question me? I have no desire to take on The Hawk and his men right now."

"Why not?" Jeanne grinned. "They cannot hurt you. You are a ghost."

"But you are not. Faith, woman, show some sense. If I had wanted to, I could have abducted you the first time we met."

"But you wanted my cooperation," she said, shaking her finger at him.

"And he wants your death," Landreth retorted in exasperation. "Oh, very well, you stubborn woman, learn for yourself." Looking up to heaven in weariness he flattened himself against the bakery back wall and motioned her to do the same. "Be quiet," he mouthed, as voices came to them through the open window.

"She's not here," a deep, heavy voice said.

"And why, pray tell, is she not?" asked a cool, emotionless one.

"I don't know. We've been watching her this past week, like you told us. She was here just a few minutes ago, else we would not have come and got you."

"Incompetent fool! You should have had one watch while the other fetched me. Enough. I have wasted far too much time upon this matter; I still must find the bastard's children, which is a matter of more import."

"Have you found where they have gone?"

"Of course not, buffoon, else they would be dead by now. No, the beetle had lost their trail by the time I was notified of their continued existence. Pity, for I did not wish the beetle's demise. I find I miss the sycophantic gnat."

"I will not fail," the coarser voice snorted.

"You had best not. And pray, do not ever, ever call me out on a wild goose chase again." The voice had dropped to a deadly pitch.

"No, I w-won't."

"You have three days in which to locate the widow and bring her to me, is that understood? I have been extremely lenient with you and far more patient than I need to be. She is a loose thread that I do not wish to let dangle further, *n'est-ce pas?* She must be eliminated before my return to England."

"England?"

"Yes. I was far too kind to The Fox's brats before. And then—my poor beetle's folly. Alas, I had not anticipated such stupidity from my underlings.

"Nevertheless, it is something I shall mend promptly. Indeed, it is time to get the hounds upon them, and I do believe that can best be done in England. Now let us go—and bring me the woman soon."

"Yes. Must she be alive?"

There was a pause. "Yes, I do believe she must be. I have a few questions for her."

"But then I may kill her?" the other voice asked hungrily.

"But of course. And in any manner you find most entertaining," the aristocratic voice said indulgently.

"I will not fail you, I will not fail you." The voices grew distant.

"Heard enough, Madame Lecroix?" Landreth asked dryly.

"Yes," Jeanne said, smiling grimly. "That pig person with the nasty, thick voice — he will die within three days time."

"Will he?"

"But of course, for he will not find me, no?"

"No indeed."

Jeanne laughed. "And The Hawk, he will be so disappointed, so downcast, that all he can do is slit the man's liver and feed it to the birds, oui? That, I think, will please me."

Landreth's laugh was deep and rich. "You do not take kindly to threats, then? I believe, Madame, that we shall make excellent allies."

Jeanne frowned, still hanging back. "You understand, Monsieur, that I go with you, but whether I will help you — this, I do not know."

Landreth smiled, amused. "Understood. Even if you do not, just keeping a tasty little shrew like you from The Hawk's dinner table is a reward in itself. Now may we go?"

"Indeed, yes," Jeanne nodded. "For I do not like the odor in this alley. No, not at all."

The Earl of Wynhaven smiled wryly as he opened the door to the small establishment known as the Shield and Arms. It was not a very fashionable place, this haunt of his. In fact, it could be safely considered a boozing den of the lower orders. Yet it was comfortable for him, for here he could meet men from his regiment and hear the latest developments of the war. Not the news published for public consumption, but the real news of what happened to old Sergeant Humphries, and who survived the latest battle.

He nodded to various acquaintances and smiled at the barmaid as she came over to him. She smiled back with all the flirtatiousness she could muster and sighed when he politely ordered a tankard of ale and nothing else. But then, that was all he ever ordered from her.

His eyes roved the dim, smoke-laden room, looking for the other acquaintances. They froze and narrowed. In the far corner, in the most shadowed place of all, an old lady sat huddled in conversation with a man. The man was small and wizened, apparently a resident of the London slums. The old lady, Jason knew.

"Damn." Then his frown changed to a calculating smile. The debutante Miranda Waverly had skillfully outmaneuvered him at every function in the past week, always slipping out before he could accost her. He was not exactly sure why he played the cat-and-mouse game with her: partly because her endless ingenuity amused and intrigued him, partly because he'd already experienced his mouse's ability to vanish if followed too closely.

He watched as the little man leaned over the table to the old lady and unobtrusively slipped her a package. If Jason had blinked, he would have missed seeing it disappear into her voluminous shawls. But he hadn't blinked. Smiling grimly, he picked up his tankard and quietly wended his way through the roistering, chattering throng to the small table in the darkened corner.

"Why, Granny," he drawled as he neared the whispering couple. "What a surprise to discover you here."

Julia froze at the sound of his voice and looked up in amazement and disgust. She had avoided Jason safely for a week, and now he had discovered her here, as Granny! Blast Armand anyway, she thought bitterly. It was he who should have made the pick-up, but he claimed he had other business to attend. "My lord," she finally managed. "I can truthfully say the same. What brings you here? Slumming it, are we?"

The wizened little man cackled at this, but subsided quickly as the large nobleman stared at him intently.

"Why, I wouldn't say that exactly," Jason said coolly. "How have you been, my dear old Granny? Are you sure you are feeling the thing? You are looking a great deal older than when I last saw you. A good forty-or-so-odd years, I'd say."

"You must forgive the flash cull his witticisms, Jem," Julia said. "He has a balmy sense of humor."

Jem had lived by his wits since the age of five, when his mother had run off to the Indies with a sailor. He knew when a situation was beyond his understanding; this one was, and he did not care for the looks that passed between the old lady and the large toff. It made him think of naked steel, so he rose and made a hasty departure, glad his business had been finished before the newcomer's arrival.

Jason immediately sat down in Jem's place.

"Did I say you could join me?"

"No, but I just knew you would welcome my company," Jason said, eyes glinting. "After all, what is a drink good for, if not sharing with friends?" Rather than taking a draft from his tankard, however, he lifted Julia's glass and sniffed. "Forsooth, blue ruin? You do go for the strong stuff."

"Jem ordered it for me. I do not like it above half, and never have."

"A relief! The tippling of that can lead you down the path to destruction. But then again, that path appears to be quite familiar to you already—perhaps even well-traversed?"

"Oh, do put a damper on it," Julia said in an un-grandmotherly tone.

"Tsk, tsk, and you appeared to be such a sweet old lady when in the country."

"As it does to many women, London town has

changed me considerably."

"What brings you to town—or rather, to this part of town."

"That is none of your business," came the curt reply. "It was so nice to see you again, my lord, but I fear I must be running." She stood swiftly, only to have one of her myriad shawls catch itself on her rickety chair. "The devil!"

"Permit me." Jason grinned, rising to her aid. Yet, as he solicitously leaned over to pull the shawl from the half-rung it was snagged on, he reached under the cloth and snatched the package she was holding.

Julia gasped and grabbed for it. Jason held it out of her reach, then swiftly deposited it in his vest. He smiled down at her from his Olympian height. "Well, Granny? Are you about to importune a man young enough to be your son right here in front of this good company?"

"Give that back to me," Julia ground out, voice low, eyes shooting the daggers she did not possess. "Or I'll cry *thief* right in front of this good company."

"A shame—it's sure to clear out half the clientele, since they'll fear you mean them. Well, as you said, I really must be running." With a smile, Jason turned his broad back on her and strolled from the pub.

Muttering angrily, Julia hobbled after him, hampered by the necessity of maintaining her guise as an old lady, though she dearly wanted to pick up her skirts and leg it after him at all due speed. By the time she exited the Shield and Arms, she could not see him anywhere. Sighing, she turned to toddle down the craggy, narrow street.

Suddenly, a long arm shot out of an alley and dragged her into it. Julia immediately kicked out, flailing furiously. She opened her mouth to scream when it was muffled by a large, well-manicured hand.

"Now Granny, don't be missish. I am sure the alleys and the back streets are just your venue."

Julia relaxed in great relief. She pulled her mouth

away from his hand. "What do you mean by scaring me like that? And why that remark?"

"Why not? I've read your message."

"Have you? How nice. Mind telling me what it said, since it was meant for me?"

"Not at all," Jason replied, his eyes cynical. "It says that your favorite old bird is due back in town and that you are to treat him most tenderly."

Julia tensed. She pulled away from Jason, lest he feel her tremble, and went and leaned against the alley wall. Rendon was returning to England! "I see."

"I imagined you would. There is roughly two hundred pounds here, as well."

"Thank you so much for counting it for me," Julia said sweetly, some of her strength returning.

"Think nothing of it. I found it interesting to discover what your sort gets paid."

"My sort?" Julia asked warily.

"Your sort. Who's the 'old bird' due back? Your protector?"

"Protector?" Julia asked, bewildered. Then she understood and she laughed bitterly. "No, he's most definitely no protector of mine. Far from it. And I'm not what you think—I'm no prostitute."

"No, I suppose not. They are generally quite honest about their occupation while you—you are a different kettle of fish altogether."

"And just what kind of kettle am I?"

"I don't know." His hazel eyes perused her. "You are certainly an adventuress, and unmistakably an exceptional one."

"*Merci beaucoup.* I am elevated from a prostitute to an adventuress—an exceptional one, at that—and all in one brief moment. My head spins."

"I don't consider it an advancement," Jason said curtly. "As I said, a prostitute is at least honest. Now, what is your game?"

Julia bit her lip. "I cannot tell you."

173

"All right. Who are you really?"

"I am . . . I am . . ."

"What, stumped? Running out of characters? Now, let's see. You are not a kindly old lady—a true shame. She was the best of them all, except for her slumming habits and her partiality to blue ruin."

"I told you, I don't like blue ruin," Julia protested.

"And you are not an heiress. Or if you are, you receive your funds in the most peculiar way."

"No, I—I am no heiress."

"Which means Miranda is on the catch for a rich husband, rather than the other way around."

Julia's eyes narrowed. "So you did know. How?"

"At the ball. I saw the scars from your blisters on your hand. Remember, I helped bandage those hands. Then when I held you in the dance—I knew your figure, and it only took lifting you to know it was your weight. Though I think you have lost a few pounds—"

"You beast! So that is why you kept picking me up in that dreadful dance!"

"Oh, I don't know." Jason chuckled suddenly. "I particularly enjoyed the dance. And I think I behaved very well—since my first instinct was to strangle you, which still might be the best answer," he said meditatively, putting his hands upon her shoulders.

Julia gasped and stiffened until she caught a glimmer of amusement in Jason's eyes. She smiled, shakily. "I—I am not what you think I am."

"No? Then you have not befriended Chlorinda in order to use her?"

"Indeed no," Julia said swiftly, a tinge of fear running through her at that. She must be careful here. "I just ran into her, literally—I'd accidentally stepped on her gown. Faith, it would not have made sense to meet her on purpose, would it? I mean, since you would be around? Only—well, she and I have become good friends . . ."

He studied her carefully. "Good," he said with a nod.

"Otherwise I would have been forced to tell her the truth about you."

Julia's heart stopped. "But you won't, will you? It would hurt her so. And—and I am sure you would not care to—to explain your past experiences with me."

"No, I would not only look the fool, but she might be upset at how long I remained unchaperoned with you." Surprisingly, he grinned. "Though actually, Granny was our chaperone." His eyes became speculative. "So, is it that you are on the catch for a rich husband?"

"No." She looked away. "That is not why I am Miranda. It has nothing to do with money."

"It best not," he said, his face becoming stern. "Else I will warn Sir Horace of your entrapment."

Julia's eyes flew to his in amazement, and then she gurgled in delight. "Entrap Sir Horace? Me? Oh heavens, no!"

"Does he know of your deception?"

"No—not yet," Julia said breathlessly. "But I plan to tell him. I would never hurt him, ever!" She said it with an honesty that could not be mistaken, and the hands on her shoulders tightened.

"Then you do love the fop?" Jason's voice was inexplicably tense.

"I always have."

"And this 'old bird' due to arrive? What of him? How tenderly do you intend to treat *him?*"

Julia's eyes blazed. "You are despicable." She reached up and tried to pry his hands from her shoulders. "Now let me go."

His hands remained implacable. "Don't try my patience. What is this all about if it doesn't involve Sir Horace?"

Julia's expression became opaque. "I can't tell you, my lord."

There was a long pause while their eyes locked. "Perhaps I should take you to the Bow Street Runners," Jason said slowly. "They might be able to shed some light

175

on the matter."

Julia flinched as if he had hit her and her eyes fell from his. "Do that and you will sign my death warrant."

"My God," Jason muttered, "so it comes down to this. You are nothing but a common criminal."

"No." Her eyes returned to his. "I am no criminal, that I swear to you."

Jason stared down into her brown eyes, eyes that were pained, but honest. "Dammit, woman, what am I supposed to do with you? Who are you, you little witch?"

"No one you would want to know," Julia said sadly. "But I promise you, I am no criminal. And all I ask of you is that you give me some time. Nothing more. Please do not betray me."

"It is I who betray you now?"

"Please." Her eyes pleaded where her voice could not.

"How long?" His voice was curt.

"I don't know. But it cannot be long now, not if this note is correct."

"How long?"

"I don't know, honestly—but soon." Her smile was bitter. "Either I will be able to come to you with the truth, or you will be able to come to me—in a graveyard."

"You ask a lot of me. How do I know you won't just run away again?"

"Because I've run as far as I can," she said simply. "There is no other place now."

"Dammit, everything I know about you tells me you are dangerous."

Julia smiled wryly. "I used to think I was. But not anymore. Now, I'm only *in* danger."

Jason looked down into the face of an old woman—and the haggard, weary lines were not due to make-up alone. Somehow, they compelled him. "You will be in worse danger," he said—not unkindly—and his hand rose to her tired face. "You will be in worse danger if I give you this month and then find out you lied to me, that you are wanted by the Runners ... and if the crown jewels are heisted, I'll be suspicious."

Julia's eyes lit up. "Then you will tell no one? Not even your fiancée or her family?"

"No, of course not."

"Thank you, my lord." A sweet smile transformed Julia's face.

"Mind you, you had better come to me in a month's time with the truth," Jason warned her sternly—but Julia's happiness was contagious and he smiled. "And if it is that you are a mere lightskirt after all, I'll—"

"You'll what?" Julia asked, teasing him out of sheer relief. "Will you turn me in at Bow Street? I'm sure our men of law would be overly taxed if they were to book every common straw damsel."

Jason grinned. "But we have already determined that you couldn't be a common one." Surprising Julia, he bent down and kissed her firmly. She was too offset to protest, and allowed him to tug on her shoulders and draw her against him. The warmth of his body was far more pleasant than the brick wall at her back had been, though it was equally as hard; the gentleness of his questing, teasing kiss was far better than his taunting, hurtful words had been. She leaned into him for one spellbound moment, as if his kiss could heal.

Then she shakily pulled back, securing a hand's breadth between them, for she knew she'd need something more than just his kisses if he were to heal the deep wounds she bore. "Well," she said with a tremor, "until you prove my guilt—as a lightskirt, that is—please refrain from such behavior."

Jason grinned. "A month, sprite, that is all."

"I—I almost believe you'd like to discover I'm a lightskirt."

"Perhaps. For then I would know what kind of punishment to mete out. And I'd not require the thief-takers for it." Julia ducked quickly as he swooped down for another kiss. His lips shied off her cheek.

"Hey, Gov!" someone called from the street. Julia and the laughing Jason looked and saw a dirty urchin standing a few yards away, his grimy arms akimbo. "What ye want to be kissin' that old hag fer—I've got me a sister that's much prettier—younger, too," he added, with an insulting eye on Julia. "And I can take ye to her fer a shillin'."

Jason laughed again while Julia gaped in outrage. "Be off with you, young varmint. This is—my grandmother."

"Cor," the urchin breathed, his eyes bulging. "Ye flash coves are a bad lot, that ye are—slap and tickle with yer own granma? Disgustin', s'what I say." He shook his head in disapproval and ran from the alley.

Jason was still laughing. "Well, we all see the world differently. He'll sell his sister for a shilling, but he takes exception to me kissing my own grandmother."

"And so do I," Julia said breathlessly. "I must be going. It was not wise for me to be here as Granny, but it was necessary."

"I will see you at the Grasons' ball two days hence, will I not . . . Miss Miranda?"

"Yes, of course," Julia murmured, untangling herself from his arms.

"Then save me the waltz."

Julia looked at him suspiciously. "Why?"

He smiled. "Don't think I do not intend to keep my eye upon you this month, for I do."

"But will that not raise talk?"

"Not any more than if I denounce you as an impostor."

Julia sighed and nodded. "Very well. I will save you the second dance." She turned, head bent, to depart.

"Come now, I am not that difficult to be around."

She turned back to him. "And I am not so wicked. Only believe that. Whatever happens, whatever comes to pass, please remember that. And whatever you hear, come to me first; don't betray me, I beg of you."

Jason stood quietly a moment. "No, I will not betray

178

you, but I beg of you the same boon."

Julia gave an odd, quaint little shake of her head. "I would not betray you if I could. Just remember that, my lord, for it is the truth." She turned, and with the most careful gait, tottered from the alley, leaving Jason staring after her.

Armand raised his glass to study the hats in the shop window before him, but his thoughts wandered elsewhere. This trailing of The Hawk's ward had proved a futile exercise, bordering upon the dull. Either Chlorinda Everleigh led the most nondescript existence imaginable or she was the most cunning of schemers. For five days now, a lad had been assigned to follow her; the urchin had reported nothing but the usual activities of a young debutante. Fearing the child had overlooked something, Armand was following her personally today.

From the corner of his eye he saw Chlorinda leave the lending library and head down the street. Her constant companion, Mrs. Bendley, was nowhere in sight. Chlorinda seemed totally unaware of the people around her. There was no doubt of that, for even dressed in Sir Horace's clothing as he was, Armand had not once drawn her attention.

He pretended to study the ladies' articles before him, but all the while his eyes followed the retreating figure, dressed in a fluttering jonquil ensemble that made Armand think of the sun. His eyes sharpened as he observed a stocky man appear from the crowd and fall into step beside the girl. Aha, here it was! She was meeting someone! Finally!

The man took hold of her arm quite possessively. Chlorinda seemed to stiffen at this familiarity and pull away. Then the man leaned close to that golden head and whispered something in her ear. Chlorinda stopped resisting.

Armand turned slightly to discover a hackney slowly trundling down the street from the opposite direction to halt beside Chlorinda and the man. It was a common, unmarked cab. The ruffian furtively looked around and then, swiftly tugging open the door, assisted Chlorinda into the vehicle. The minute the door swung shut upon them, the hackney's driver whipped up his horses. As they drove by, Armand caught a fleeting glimpse of Chlorinda's face within the window. It was a pale and drawn face — a face of fear.

Armand cursed, then paused in consideration; what game did the little wretch play now? Not a second slipped by before he let out a whistle. The urchin he had hired appeared from the back alley. "My horse, and be quick about it."

The urchin nodded in surprise and ran back from whence he had come, returning shortly with the animal. Armand flipped him a coin and mounted.

He caused quite a stir upon the streets as onlookers observed the polished tulip, that pink of the *ton,* Sir Horace, gallop by them, neck for leather upon the busy thoroughfare. One man idly commented as he passed that he hadn't known the dandy could even ride, let alone so bruisingly. His companion but grunted and remarked that the poppinjay was most likely late for an appointment with his tailor, for what else could it be? The other nodded and agreed.

Armand, however, did not stop at any of the dress shops along the way, and he soon caught up with the hackney as it left the city behind. He followed it for a short distance, but turned off into a byroad after a mile.

It was a half-hour later that the driver of the hackney squinted against the sun and cursed. He slowed his horses to a trot, for a dandy, resplendent in a puce jacket, sat quietly upon his mount, squarely in the middle of the road. His hands rested lightly upon his saddle horn as he all but lounged atop his steed. The driver emitted a more fulsome and sulphurous oath as he reined his horses to an abrupt halt, not inches away from the man—who had not twitched a muscle. "Hey, you! What in blazes are ye doin' in the middle of the bloody road? This ain't Hyde Park, fer God's sake!"

The man lifted a gauntleted hand to his mouth and yawned. "Why, I do believe I am holding up your hackney," he said in effeminate tones. "Yes, that is exactly what I am doing. Let me see—there is something I ought to cry out in uncouth tones, isn't there? Now, what is it? Ah, yes—stand and deliver, old man. Stand and deliver. Do I have the right of it?"

The driver laughed in amazement. "Cor, Gov, ye must be castaway. Now let me pass, my pretty little man, before I'm forced to wrinkle your pretty clothes."

"Ah, dear me, this man is a slow-wit," the fop sighed, dismounting before the chuckling driver. "I fear, sir, you are one of those poor beings who lack the intelligence of a common flea and must have everything repeated. I said—stand and deliver." The dandy's hand went to his chest; he pulled out a pistol and shot the driver very neatly in the arm.

"You goddamn fool!" the man cried out, clutching at the wound. "Ye shot me, ye bleedin' shot me!"

"Come, come, my man," the dandy sniffed. "Don't carry on so. I only nicked you. Now do be a good boy and get down from your perch." The driver stared at him and opened his mouth to speak. The tulip drew a second pistol and aimed at the bemused man's head, cocking the hammer. "You really must not demand that everything be repeated, you know. It is extremely fatiguing to me. Now get down, and quietly."

The driver, nodding nervously, climbed down one-handedly from his perch, never taking his eyes from the pistol that followed his every move.

"Rob, what the hell ye doin'?" an irritated voice called from the bowels of the carriage. "What's stoppin' us?"

The fop raised his hand to his painted lips and said, with a sly wink to the flabbergasted fellow trembling before him, "Shh, you wouldn't wish to ruin the delightful surprise in store for your friend, now would you?"

Rob shook his head vigorously.

"Ah, you are a brighter fellow than I thought. Your mama must rejoice exceedingly. Now, if you do not wish to have me send you to your dubious rewards post haste, I suggest—now it's only a suggestion, mind you—that you walk away from here and don't look back. And don't you be a naughty boy and peek or you'll force me to put a hole in your jacket." The dandy frowned. "Though I really think I ought to now, for it is a hideous affair. No *savoir faire* whatsoever."

"N-no, I'm going, don't sh-shoot! I'm going." Rob turned quickly and loped off down the road without another word and nary a peek back.

"Rob, you no-good lout, answer me—what the hell is going on out there? Do I have to come out myself?" the man inside called out again.

Sir Horace smiled grimly and pocketed his pistol. He pulled out a dainty handkerchief and, after collecting his beribboned cane from his horse, minced up to the hackney window from which the man had stuck his bullish, red-faced head. With the window so blocked, Chlorinda could not be seen. The man's belligerence turned to suspicion and then to contempt as he took in Armand's full, foppish glory.

"No need to grow upset, old man," Armand tittered, waving his handkerchief and leaning upon the cane. "Our good friend Rob appears to have departed on some—er—pressing business."

"What?" the man asked, peering around to no avail. "This ain't no time fer him to be taking relief. And I thought I heard a shot."

"Ah yes, you must excuse me, I fear that was my gun—it accidentally went off, you see. Boom! I thought I'd die from fright, and now I have powder burns on my gloves!"

"Gun?" the man snorted. "Blimey, a cove like you

182

oughtn't to be allowed a barking iron. It could be damn dangerous."

"Strange, that is what all my friends say whenever I dare to pick up one of those nasty things—er, don't you think you ought to come out of there? Your horses are quite unattended, you know. Now I'd be glad to help, but—"

"No," the man exclaimed. "You stay right where you are. Don't touch my cattle. Can't think what's gotten into Rob," he muttered. He threw a cautious glance over his shoulder and then opened the door and descended, shutting it very quickly. Scratching his head and swearing, he walked past Armand to the horses.

Armand took the unguarded moment to peer into the hackney. A forlorn figure huddled in the corner, bedraggled and quite the worse for wear. The blue eyes above the gag widened at the sight of him and there was an unmistakable, muffled squeal. He raised his fingers to his lips; the tousled golden head nodded slightly and Armand left her, trotting up to where her captor held the horses. The man was looking off in both directions, an ominous frown upon his rough visage.

"Can't figure it. Which way did Rob take off?"

"That way," Sir Horace said, pointing his cane down the road. "A direction I would heartily advise you to take as well."

"Oh yeah? Now why would he do a thing like that, I'd like to know?"

"Why, because I told him to," Sir Horace said simply.

The man doubled over in laughter. "Rob left because you told him to—cor, that's a whoop! You're a blooming jokester."

"Faith, that there should be two such imbeciles," Sir Horace sighed, looking up at heaven with a suffering eye. "Yes, my good man, I told him to leave and he was wise enough to see the strength of my argument."

"And why would he listen to the likes of you, you bleeding fag?"

"It was quite shocking and very upsetting, as I told you, but when my gun accidentally discharged, the confounded contraption hit his arm, as it were."

"You little bastard." The man pulled out his own iron. "You shot Rob."

Sir Horace's pretty cane swung up and struck the man's gun arm a cracking blow, sending the weapon flying into the dirt. "Sorry, old man, but I do dislike those nasty things."

The enraged thug charged, but Sir Horace neatly danced out of the large man's way. "Egads, such brutish energy. It does make my knees weak."

"Damn you to hell!" The man lunged and grappled the air. He looked stunned.

"Yoo-hoo, handsome, over here." Sir Horace stood a few feet away, waving his handkerchief. His foe growled in frustration and lumbered forward, his mammoth fists clenching as the dandy pranced away, always out of reach. "Whee, look at me, I'm the Pied Piper—leading the rat!"

"I'll get you, you little Mary Jane!" The man lunged forward, but misjudged again. He flew past Sir Horace, who stuck out a well-heeled foot. The man tripped over it and plummeted to the ground.

"Eeks, now look what happened. A smudge, a veritable smudge on my shoe!"

"I'll smudge you," the man snarled, rising.

"Tut-tut, such fervor. You really ought to save it for the ladies, don't you think?"

"You bleeding little fag! Stop running and fight like a man."

"Fight like a man? Ah, like you are doing? But no, no, you fight more like a bull, don't you?"

And just like a bull the man charged again, and missed again. "My, my, whatever am I going to do with you?" Sir Horace sighed. "Oh, very well—if you insist that we stoop to the lower, more primitive levels, so be it. I fear that elsewise you will suffer an apoplexy." Sir

Horace threw down his cane, shook out the ruffles at his wrist, and raised his fists. "Have at it, bull."

The ruffian grinned in feral satisfaction. "Now I'm going to kill you." He rushed in, large, hamlike fists windmilling. Sir Horace, with simple ease, met him with a swift, clean left to the jaw and a cruel, curt jab to the breadbasket. The man doubled over in surprised agony. Sir Horace stepped back, allowing the wheezing man to recover his breath. He finished coughing and finally straightened up, his eyes red with anger.

Lifting his fists, he attacked again. Sir Horace welcomed him with a punishing series of blows, the last of which sent the ruffian spiralling to the ground.

"Forsooth, the man has no science," Armand complained, studying his fallen adversary. Then he shivered. "And his excruciating taste in clothes. 'Tis inhumanity to wear such apparel. And as for his personal toilet," he sniffed, "it definitely lacks something. Soap and water, I do believe. Yes, soap and water is what it lacks. But alas, I doubt he even understands the concept." He shook his head and turned to the carriage.

As he had rightly guessed, Chlorinda was watching him. She fairly hung out of the window — at least, her upper portion did, while her face was as gray as the color of the gag between her teeth.

"Ah, Miss Everleigh, what a pleasant surprise to see you again," Armand said politely, his gait every bit as foppish as usual as he teetered up to her on his heels. "Though I must object, I must strenuously object, to your choice of travelling companions. What? What's that you say? Oh, I see, silly me. You would like me to take that rather unclean cloth from your mouth." He tittered inanely and untied the gag.

"They are not my companions," Chlorinda said angrily after working her sore mouth a moment. "They were abducting me!"

"Were they? Dear me, such incivility one finds these days. Then I'm quite glad I had my little disagreement with the chaps." He raised a hand and studied it with a frown. "Though I've dirtied my nails and I fear my poor valet, Cedric, will pack his bags and leave when he beholds my jacket. That naughty Lord Petersham has been trying to steal him away for ages now. And only Cedric knows how to do a cravat the way it should be done. Well, never mind, it must be accepted."

Chlorinda smiled wanly. "I think you look fine."

"Now that is a fib if I have ever heard one. Shame on you, Miss Everleigh. Now, if you would pull your—er—torso back in from the window I will strive to undo the rest of your bonds. At least, I assume you are bound?"

"Of course I am!" Chlorinda flushed. With her hands tied behind her back as they were, she realized the only view she was rendering to Sir Horace was of her face and bosom—and from his point of view, she realized, her neckline was gaping. She pulled herself in from the window with alacrity.

Sir Horace opened the door and climbed in beside her. His nose wrinkled. "Faith, what an unpleasant odor this carriage contains—no doubt from your objectionable companions."

Chlorinda nodded, though she could not find her voice. Sir Horace was once again the consummate dandy, yet she could not forget the force with which he had subdued her captor. He had made it look like child's play. A sudden shyness overtook her.

"Hi-ho," Sir Horace said crisply. "Do let me see your wrists then, Miss Everleigh."

"Oh, yes," Chlorinda murmured, turning hesitantly so that her bound hands were to him. In a second, the rough, scratching ropes were gone.

"Gadzooks," Sir Horace said, pulling her wrist to him as she turned back around. "He has bruised your fine skin. The villain deserves to be run through," he said curtly. Chlorinda gasped; his hand flew to the door handle and he appeared about to step outside and do just that.

"Oh, please, no," she begged, her hand touching his. "Please leave him be—I'm fine now, honestly."

Her touch must have stayed him. He raised her wrists before him and looked at her intently. "Who did this, Madame?"

Chlorinda gasped at the question and looked away. "Why—what do you mean? They did."

"I know that. But whose creatures were they?"

"I—I don't know."

"Methinks you lie, Miss Everleigh." The voice was no longer lazy and effeminate—it was implacable.

"I don't know, I tell you!"

"I see—then your guardian must be told of this, in order that he may take stronger measures to protect you."

"No, oh no!" Chlorinda gasped. "Please don't. It's only just now that I have gained any—he must not know."

"I beg your pardon?"

"I mean—why tell him? He—he would worry so." She was unable to meet Sir Horace's suddenly intent gaze. "I do not wish him to know."

"I see. Then you are protecting someone. Very well. So be it."

Chlorinda's eyes met his at this, and she paled. She read contempt within their depths. Even though he was a fop, and had shown a dislike of her from their first meeting, tears welled up and she was helpless to stop them. "I—I'm sorry." Her furtive attempts to brush them away were like those of a little girl.

Sir Horace expelled his breath in apparent exasperation. Chlorinda sniffed back her tears to no good purpose, and he cursed. Suddenly, she was pulled into his arms in a strong, comforting embrace, and it undid her. She fell to weeping as she had not done for a very long time. "I—I'm so sorry. I—I'm just so tired. And such a coward!"

Sir Horace did not say a word, but rocked her gently.

187

Slowly, the waves of sorrow, loss, and fear subsided, leaving only a few forlorn sniffs and hiccups. With the cloudburst waning, Chlorinda began to notice that Sir Horace smelled good. He did not smell of the heavy perfume most dandies favored. He smelled of soap and water and—he smelled masculine. Furthermore, the arms about her were comfortingly strong, while the chest beneath the ruffles she was crying upon was—hard. She sniffled in embarrassment at her straying thoughts and glanced up at him in bewilderment.

He looked down into her eyes and after a breath-snatching moment, when Chlorinda thought she saw a different, compelling man, he tittered in his high-pitched voice and shattered the image. "Well, now, I am sure you are feeling much more the thing, aren't you?" He asked firmly setting her from him.

"Yes," she said quietly, though in truth she had felt better with his arms still around her. Now she felt shatteringly bereft. "Pray, I hope you will forgive my foolish outburst. I am not usually such a watering pot."

"Yes," he drawled, drawing out his dainty handkerchief and handing it to her. "But then again, even English roses must be allowed some leeway when abducted, wouldn't you think?" Chlorinda gave a watery laugh. "Now, are you positive you would not care to tell me who these naughty men were?"

"No." Her eyes fell. She unconsciously knotted and unknotted Sir Horace's delicate handkerchief. "I—I do not know. And I do not wish anybody to know of this—this debacle. I would not care to be grist for the gossip mill. And my guardian would only worry so."

"And we wouldn't want *that*, now, would we?" her companion said in a lazy drawl. "Well, then, let us return you as soon as possible. Wherever is your chaperone, by the way?"

"Good gracious, I left her in the library. I had just intended to visit the shop next door. What will she think?"

"Only the good Lord and Mrs. Bendley know. Now do lean back and quiet down. I will drive you back to town."

Chlorinda's eyes widened. "In this?"

"But of course, what else?"

"But—but can you drive a hackney?"

Sir Horace shrugged. "La, child, if the common hoi polloi can manage the art, I make no doubt that I can. Yes, indeed, I should make a splendid coachman, don't you think?"

Chapter Eleven
The Hawk's Arrival

Faith, what a mad little performance this evening was turning out to be, Julia thought wryly, looking at the ladies in the Earl of Wynhaven's elegantly decorated drawing room. Lady Daniella sat before the fire—musing on what, Julia did not know. Chlorinda sat at the piano, absently picking out a tune. The boring Mrs. Bendley sat next to her, bending her ear about something or other.

And the puppet master in charge of the evening's farce? The Earl of Wynhaven. He was most definitely keeping his promise that he would be watching her; this dinner party must have been his opening salvo.

Thus, they all sat there after Jason's marvelously prepared dinner—and while they sat there, Julia thought irritably, the puppet master tarried over a glass of port with her brother.

She frowned, wondering what was passing between the two men. She did not fear Armand would be unable to handle Jason; what she feared was that Jason might not be able to handle Armand. She had not told Armand that Jason knew Miranda the fluff was also Granny Merton of the woods, and she was afraid that Jason, in some form or another, would tip Armand off.

A deep pain suffused her. She never kept secrets from Armand, especially secrets so vital to their operation. Yet that was why she kept her silence. Their task was vital, and if Armand thought it necessary to decamp because of Jason's discovery, Julia did not think she could bear it.

The road to the truth lay here in London. She felt it deeply. At first, she had thought her sire reckless in this escapade, but now she agreed—here was where the battle must be joined. Here was where they must make a stand, if they were to clear their name and survive.

And clearing their name was becoming all-important. She had always enjoyed the masquerades and games before, but now, now she wanted desperately to be just Julia Landreth and no one else. She wanted to be Julia Landreth, and stand before the earl as herself—not a traitor, not an adventuress, but Julia Landreth, faithful servant of the crown.

"Her nervous indisposition is back." Mrs. Bendley's whispered voice drifted through Julia's thoughts.

Something in the woman's tone brought Julia back to reality. "Whose indisposition?" Julia asked.

"Why, Miss Chlorinda's." Mrs. Bendley shook her head in obvious displeasure at Julia-cum-Miranda's slow-wittedness. "You see, my dear, she was dreadfully ill after her father's death. We all feared for her sanity then."

"You did?" Julia asked. The woman's attitude always grated upon her nerves. She did not know why she could never warm towards Mrs. Bendley, for she seemed to feel deep concern for Chlorinda—even if she did smother the girl in the process.

"Yes indeed," Mrs. Bendley said. "That's when the dear duke sent for me to help." Her reverence for Rendon could hardly have been greater had he been a saint. "Poor, poor child. She seemed to improve after she came to town. But these past few days," she said softly, "it's happening again. Her mental disposition is erratic and—"

"I am sure it is nothing," Julia said curtly. The woman was all but calling Chlorinda insane!

Mrs. Bendley offered Julia a pitying glance. "I'm sure

you would not see it as such."

Julia responded with her most inane smile. Fortunately, before she could say anything she would regret, the door to the drawing room opened and Jason and Armand entered, laughing gaily.

Julia's eyes narrowed. What had those two been talking about? Nevertheless, she plastered her lips with a silly smile to greet them as they approached.

"My love," Armand drawled, "Jason has just too-too many comical stories."

"Does he?" Julia asked.

"Only war stories, Miss Waverly." Jason's eyes glinted at her. "Nothing you ladies would care to hear."

Julia noticed Armand look to Chlorinda, whose playing had stopped upon the mention of war. He shrugged at Julia, then said, "Miss Everleigh, do you know of the latest aria—"

"I am sure I do not." Chlorinda replied, cutting him off.

"Oh, you really should know it." Armand pranced over to the piano. "Do allow me to teach you." Julia peeked at Jason; rather than watching Armand with Chlorinda as she had expected, he was studying her.

"Do excuse me," said Mrs. Bendley, who was watching Armand and Chlorinda. She rose abruptly, hurrying to join them at the piano. It appeared her little chick could be left with no man save her betrothed.

Jason promptly took the vacated seat beside Julia. "Jealous?" he asked as he saw her eyes upon Armand and Chlorinda.

"Indeed no," she said coolly.

"Your Sir Horace is quite an original," he said. "In truth, the man can be quite witty, once off the infernal subject of fashion."

"Is that what you talked about?" Julia asked as innocently as she could.

He chuckled. "Never fear, I gave no clue away to your

192

suitor. Your secret is safe with me—for now."

"You are far too kind." Julia cooed.

"Yes, I believe I am." He smiled back.

Julia decided to turn the tables. "And how have you been faring with Chlorinda? Have you been able to talk to her?"

"Oh, I've talked to her," he drawled. Julia's eyes flew to his expectantly. "I've talked to her about the weather, the latest play, the soirée—"

"Do stop it. You know what I meant."

He studied her. "For a woman who indulges in masquerades you do believe in stripping others of their secrets."

She paled. "I am sorry. I had no right to bring the matter up."

"The matter up?" he quizzed. "You mean the matter of my disfigurement?"

"Would you stop that," Julia retorted. " 'Tis only scars."

"Miss Everleigh evidently doesn't think so."

"I do not believe she—she was responding to that," Julia said slowly. "I truly believe something else was affecting her. Some other memory."

"And you would know?"

Julia looked him straight in the eye. "Yes, my lord, I would."

He looked away, gazing at the couple at the piano. "Then you truly believe it was not the thought of my horrendous scars?"

"They are not horrendous," Julia said softly. "You forget, I have seen them."

"Yes," he said stiffly. His eyes returned to her and the slowest of smiles crossed his face, catching Julia's breath. "And you smacked me with a ladle for it, if I remember correctly."

Julia blushed. "Well, you surprised me." His chuckle only made her cheeks flame all the more. She was grateful that Jason's butler, Canton, entered at that moment.

Canton cleared his throat and intoned, "His Grace, The

Duke of Rendon, and the Right Honorable Edward Carstairs."

A crash of discordant chords resounded through the room. Julia jumped, despite herself; she quickly noted that Chlorinda sat frozen at the piano, her face pale. Armand rose beside her, seemingly poised — but Julia could feel his intensity. Lady Daniella was no longer lazing by the fire, but sitting straight, her eyes trained upon the doorway.

Lud, Julia thought, there could not have been a finer entrance for a villain, not even upon the boards of the most dramatic play. "You invited him, my lord?"

"I left a standing invitation in case he had arrived in town," Jason said, rising.

"Eager to draw up the settlement papers?" Julia taunted softly as Rendon entered with another man she had never seen. Jason looked sternly at her, but she only returned Miranda's vapid look.

She turned that same gaze upon the man who had created such pain in so many lives. Her smile widened and became fluffleheaded, even as she thought, *"En garde,* your grace, *en garde."*

"Your grace." Jason crossed the room to meet the two men at the entrance. "It's a pleasure to welcome you back to town. I hope you had a pleasant journey."

"An uneventful one," the duke replied. Julia thought he sounded disgruntled — excellent! "I can stay but a moment. I did wish, however, to accept your invitation and to see how my dear niece fares."

"I am fine," Chlorinda said, though her voice was weak. Her eyes were wide upon the man beside the duke; the man seemed unable to return her gaze. "I — I am fine."

"I fear the dear child does not wish to alarm you, your grace," Mrs. Bendley gushed. "She has not been herself these last few days."

"Indeed?" Rendon asked in his polished tones. "Are you ill perhaps, Chlorinda?"

"No, no, of course not." She flushed.

"For shame, child," Mrs. Bendley tutted. "You know your nerves have been all overset."

A silence filled the room. Julia could not allow it. The old harpy, Mrs. Bendley, would be talking of insanity next! "Oh, it could not be her nerves," Julia breathed. "I've always envied Chlorinda her calmness—she never flies into the boughs over anything. She's such a knowing one."

All eyes turned to her; Julia widened her own and presented them with her twittiest expression. She noted with pleasure how the duke stared at her as if she were a troll crawled out from beneath a bridge. Perhaps he didn't care for the olive green dress—with orange flounces and bows—that she wore this evening. It matched her complexion very neatly.

"Your grace, may I introduce Miss Miranda Waverly," Jason said promptly, his voice lightly threaded with amusement.

"How do you do, your grace?" Julia squinted her eyes as if she couldn't really see him. "Chlorinda speaks so often of you—it is a pleasure to meet you."

"And you," the duke said in a monotone. Clearly her inane manner had already displeased him.

Jason smiled. "And her chaperone, Lady Daniella."

Rendon's eyes went to Lady Daniella and remained there. "No need to introduce us—Lady Daniella and I go back some years. How are you, Daniella?"

"I am fine, Converse. Or—forgive me, it is 'your grace' now, is it not, since John's unfortunate demise?"

"Indeed."

"And last but not least," Jason continued, still the polite host, "may I introduce Sir Horace Farouche?"

Armand flourished an exaggerated leg. He wore peach satin this evening, with black lace at his sleeves. "Your grace, such a pleasure," he said in his finicky tones. "Truly."

The Duke stiffened, as men were wont to do around Sir Horace. "Ah yes." He turned swiftly back to Jason. "And may I introduce Edward Carstairs, an old friend of the family. Particularly—" he added, his eyes turning to Chlorinda, "—of my niece's."

Chlorinda flinched, scattering the music sheets, some falling off the bench.

"Tut, tut," Armand murmured; he bent down to assist Chlorinda as she picked them up.

"I can do that." Carstairs crossed the room in a trice, all but grabbing the sheets out of Armand's hands.

"Gadzooks," muttered Armand, rising. "Do have them old boy, do." The man stood almost too close for courtesy, frowning at Armand fiercely. "A music afficionado, I take it?" Armand inquired sweetly.

The man stiffened and turned toward Chlorinda. "Here you are, Chlorinda." His use of her first name was pointed.

Dead-white, Chlorinda folded her shaking hands in her lap, as if refusing to accept the music from Carstairs. What was the matter, Julia wondered; she'd never seen Chlorinda act so. Mrs. Bendley watched the girl with pity-filled eyes; the duke, however, frowned.

"Oh faith, you have that tune," Armand exclaimed abruptly, peering at the extended sheets, then snatching the music from Carstairs's hands. "Jason, 'tis famous!" He waved the sheets aloft. "I play this piece to perfection—indeed, you will hear the angels sing. Shall I?"

"Er, I fear we cannot stay," Rendon said swiftly.

"Ah, you think I do not play," Armand chided, shaking his finger playfully at Rendon. "You do not know me, your grace—I play masterfully! I am not puffed up in my own consequence—indeed, I am not. I do not need to be. Tell them, Miranda."

Julia nodded. "Indeed, everyone says he is most talented; I fear I have no ear for music, but Sir Horace does."

"Some other time, perhaps," the duke said, even more

196

coolly. "Edward and I," he continued, casting the younger man a minatory look, "have unfinished business at the department tonight."

"Ah, 'tis a shame," Armand sighed. "I would dearly love to play for you, your grace; I am sure you are a man of exquisite tastes. Cannot your work wait until tomorrow?"

"Indeed, Converse," Lady Daniella added in gracious tones. "What could be so important that you must do it tonight?"

"It is grave business, pertaining to the welfare of our country." Rendon's blue eyes flared with an unkind light. "You will hear of it tomorrow, Daniella, I am sure. All of England, I fear, must hear of it tomorrow. But tonight—I cannot speak. I am sure you, of all people, will understand." He faced Chlorinda. "And I will see you tomorrow, my dear. I fear you have been overtaxing yourself. Perhaps a lighter schedule would be helpful."

Chlorinda's eyes rose to his face. "But I feel fine . . ."

"We will discuss this later," the duke said in clipped tones.

"Allow me to see you out, your grace. I do thank you for dropping by." Jason said it as politely as if the room did not quiver with electricity, then diplomatically shepherded the two men out, leaving silence behind.

"Excuse me . . ." Chlorinda rose from the piano and ran from the room.

"Oh dear, oh dear," Mrs. Bendley clucked. "I must follow her." The door closed behind her a second later.

Julia looked swiftly to Armand, rose, and went to his side. "What was that all about with Chlorinda and Edward Carstairs?"

Armand shrugged. "I am not quite sure. Not sure at all."

"You have not met him before, have you?"

"No—'tis strange."

Lady Daniella drew close to them. "He seems to have taken you in extreme dislike."

197

"I know." Armand frowned. "I believe it has something to do with Miss Everleigh—but what, I do not know."

"Mrs. Bendley insinuated earlier that Chlorinda is not fully in her right mind," Julia said quietly.

"What?" Lady Daniella exclaimed. "What fustian!"

"What do you think, Armand?" Julia studied his odd expression.

His eyes were guarded as he looked at her. "I don't know, Ju. But I believe I will find out."

"Perhaps I should try to find out instead," Julia replied. "I know you do not care for Chlorinda—"

"No," Armand said. "Allow me to do so. It is important to me."

"Very well," Julia sighed softly, not sure if she had made the right decision, yet certain Armand meant his request seriously. "If you can do so, do it. And do it fast. Rendon has something up his sleeve."

"Yes, but we will find that out on the morrow," Lady Daniella said dryly. "Of that we can be certain."

Armand, who had been frowning, looked at the two women and smiled. "Then I will find the information out tonight, of course."

Chlorinda sat upon the stone bench and gazed up at the night's stars. Blankly, her eyes scanned the silent garden about her, the leaves painted in silver moonlight. This was her secret—her quiet place. If Mrs. Bendley had ever discovered that she slipped down to the townhouse's private garden in the middle of the night, that good woman would have swooned dead away. Yet she had never been caught out, and she often thought that if she didn't have the garden to come to, she would lose her sanity.

A slight sob caught in her throat. Perhaps even the garden could not keep her from going mad. Perhaps Mrs. Bendley was correct in her estimations. She lowered her

198

head as another sob escaped and the hot tears stung her cheek. The pounding and pain in her head was beginning again, along with that strange, disembodied feeling she always felt with it — as if she were removed from playing any part in the proceedings around her. How crazy was she?

"Why the tears, fair fatality?" A man's voice suddenly sounded from the darkness, and Chlorinda's head snapped up. What was she imagining now? "Forsooth, I hate to see a lady cry," the voice sighed. It was not imagination. Chlorinda gasped, and she spun upon her seat towards the voice.

There, perched atop the garden's high, thick wall, sat a man. He was in black, all in black. A black cape swung from his shoulders and a black mask covered his eyes.

Chlorinda blinked, and blinked once more. The romantic character, straight from a Radcliff novel, for certain, was still there. "What — what do you want?" Chlorinda asked when she had retrieved her voice. "Th — this is a private garden."

"I should think so," the man said, scanning the garden with an amused eye. " 'Tis not large enough for a public affair."

Chlorinda's hand flew to her chest, clutching at the green silk she still wore from Lord Wynhaven's dinner party. "You — you should not be here. How did you get up there?"

"I climbed, of course." Swinging his legs completely over the wall, the man pushed himself from the bricks to land with fluid ease upon the ground.

Chlorinda, her tears quite dried now, sprang from the bench. "Stay away from me," she warned, nervously. "Or I'll scream — I will!"

"No, you won't." He shook his head surely. "For if you do, you'll bring your chaperone down upon you — I'm sure she doesn't know of your nocturnal visit here. Now for me, I don't see anything wrong with a midnight stroll, but I'm sure she won't see it in the same manner."

Chlorinda's eyes widened, but she did not scream. The stranger was appallingly correct. She would far rather face a man in a mask than Mrs. Bendley and her vapors. "Who—who are you?"

"Only a masked stranger." The man found himself a tree to lean his slim length upon. "Come to discover why such a lovely lady cries here, all alone."

"I—I'm not a lovely lady," Chlorinda denied, her chin lifting. She shook her aching head to clear it. "And I'm sure it's none of your business why I cry."

"Isn't it?" the masked man asked in an odd tone. "Well, then, let me see. Why would a lady cry? Mmm . . . I know, one of your suitors has the mumps; one has fled the country from a duel over you; another has gone to the Indies to raise a fortune for you, and the other fifteen or so? Why, they are simply out of town. Leaving you, of course, all alone, here."

"Don't be ridiculous."

"Then what tragedy could it be? Come, it is a perfect evening for midnight confessions." Chlorinda started, then turned from him. "You must leave, now. Or I swear I shall scream."

"Sometimes 'tis better to talk to a stranger than to no one," said the man, kindness in his voice.

Chlorinda froze. After a moment, she turned back to the man, who remained relaxed against his tree. She was losing all sense of reality anyway. What matter if she talked to this stranger? She had no one else to turn to—no one who wouldn't most likely throw her in an insane asylum. She knew her uncle often worried that that was where she belonged.

And oh, the softness of that voice. It was so soothing; it eased that ache in her head. "Very well," she said gently, and drifted back to the bench.

"Wait!" the stranger commanded as Chlorinda was about to sit. He leaned away from the tree. "This should help," he said, undoing his cape and walking over to the bench. He draped it over the cold stone. "Now, sit. The night is damp—you really should have worn a cloak, you know." He took a seat beside her. She stiffened slightly but he seemed not to notice. "Now, tell me what distresses you."

Chlorinda clasped her hands together. "I—I think I am going mad," she blurted.

There was a slight pause. "Why?" the stranger finally asked.

"Oh—for many reasons."

"Like what?"

"I don't know why," she said desperately. "I have these fears. So many of them. And—I no longer know which ones are real. Which ones are not."

"Ah, you are mad because you have a surfeit of fears?" The stranger's voice lightened. "My dear, everyone has fears. It's only when you stop having them that you know you have truly gone mad."

"But I can't control them anymore!"

"Madame, you are fortunate I came along," the stranger said gravely, and Chlorinda looked to him. "For I, fair damsel," he drawled, "am a great slayer of fears. Why, I'm sure I've killed at least fifty or sixty of the beasts in my lifetime! I'm just the one to help you: present me your fears, and I'll behead the fellows."

"You're being absurd," she said thinly.

"Ah, you want them boiled in oil, is that it? Fine choice. We'll do that instead."

Chlorinda stared at him, though amazingly, laughter did rise within her. "Sir, I believe you are madder than I."

A strange smile tipped the man's lips. "Perhaps. But permit this practicing lunatic to advise you upon the matter. I do not wish to insult you, but you appear a novice madwoman to me. Quick!" he said. "List a fear! Don't think! Just say it!"

"I was kidnapped," Chlorinda said in a rush. "And I-I . . ."

"And you fear you might be kidnapped again, do you not?" the man supplied easily. "Why, 'tis a reasonable fear. Nay, I would consider you mad, or quite unwise at least, if you did not consider it."

Chlorinda could not meet those eyes. She shook her head. "You do not understand. There would be no reason for me to think it should happen again. But the fear of it still remains with me."

"I see." The stranger rose abruptly and walked away. After a moment, he turned and his eyes measured her from behind their mask. "And who is your kidnapper?"

"Wh—what do you mean?" Her heart stopped.

"What do you think of your kidnapper?"

Chlorinda seemed to jerk, but then she lifted her chin. "How could I think anything? I don't know who my kidnapper was, so how could I think anything of him?"

"Yes, you do! You are lying to me."

Chlorinda gulped. "How did you know?"

The man took a quick step towards her, then halted. He shrugged and smiled. "I can tell it in your beautiful eyes. I can tell it in the way you hold your body and in the tone of your voice."

"But—you couldn't," Chlorinda insisted wildly.

"I can. Don't ask me how—perhaps I have magical qualities where you are concerned. Only tell me, fair one. I am but a stranger—you can confide in me."

Chlorinda looked down. "Very well—you are correct. My kidnapper was someone I once knew. I—I was once affianced to him, but—but decided I could not marry him."

"His name?" It was almost a command.

"I beg your pardon?"

"I want the man's name."

"No."

"He is one of your fears, isn't he?" the man asked sternly.

"You think he may attempt kidnapping you again, don't you?"

"I don't know," she said softly, attempting to regain control. "I truly don't know."

"What is his name?"

"I can't tell you," she said, turning from him. She felt trapped by this man. Then why did she not run? Why? Because she could talk to him. She could not talk to anyone else. "I — I shouldn't have told you in the first place."

"Why not?"

"Why — because I don't know you. And I do know him — he's not an evil man. It's just that I — I decided not to marry him. I shouldn't have spoken of this to you, you who are a stranger."

"Would it help if you could see my face?"

"Perhaps." Chlorinda said. A sudden, sharp thrill ran through her at the thought.

Chlorinda gasped as he stepped before her and knelt. "Then, madame, please — untie this mask." Chlorinda sat, staring. Suddenly she was immobilized. "What is the matter, are you afraid?"

"No — no, I'm not." Yet still she could not move.

"Very well then, don't." The man started to rise.

"No!" Chlorinda's hand shot out to stay him. She slowly reached for the mask's strings. Untying them, she allowed the mask to fall and stared into the man's face, mesmerized. She did not know the man, but the face was compelling. His brown eyes were even more so, for they were warm eyes, eyes that already looked at her as if he knew her, knew her deeply.

"Who are you?" she asked, slightly breathless.

"No one but your fool," he replied quietly, an almost bitter twist to his fine lips.

"Why do you say that?"

"Because I am. But I am no longer a stranger to you. Tell me who your kidnapper was."

"His name is Edward Carstairs," she said softly, dumbly staring into those compelling eyes.

"Ah, I see. It explains much."

"What does it explain? Do you know him?"

The man rose and walked away. "Perhaps." He turned. "Why do you not tell your uncle? Surely he will protect you."

"You know me?" Chlorinda gasped.

The man turned towards her. "No, I see I don't." He came to sit beside her, confusing Chlorinda all the more. "Why will you not tell your uncle?"

Chlorinda flushed. "because it might be at Edward's expense. I—I would not want that. After all, I had promised to marry him at one time. I know I disappointed him and—led him to believe something that—that would not happen. But I was sick at the time and—both my uncle and he desired it. It wasn't until I became better that I thought differently. I displeased both of them greatly, and I must have hurt Edward deeply for him to have tried to kidnap me, even after my uncle told him I was engaged to another, and that he would sanction that match instead."

"How kind of your uncle." The stranger's tone was dry.

"Yes, yes, he is kind," Chlorinda said, but her hands clenched.

"Do you love your uncle?" the stranger asked quietly.

"I did," Chlorinda said sadly. Then she gasped, her eyes flying to the man in alarm. "I mean, I do. Of course I do."

"I don't think you do. What happened to change you?"

"I don't know." Chlorinda shook her head, sighing. She was so tired of her pain and confusion. "He has always been nothing but kind, and I should be very grateful to him—but sometimes I feel trapped, almost a prisoner. And I know it is only his concern, and I know because—of the past—he has reason to be cautious—but sometimes I think I will go mad with all the restraints."

"What happened in the past?"

Chlorinda looked at him with suddenly-tormented eyes. "My—my father died in a carriage accident last year. He was coming to visit me at my uncle's, and as he passed over the bridge at the back part of the property—it went down. All of it. He—he and the carriage and the horses went, too."

"My God, you were there?"

Chlorinda nodded. "It's not—not something I've been able to talk about. Uncle has never told anybody, for he knows how it upset me."

"Talk to me," the stranger said hoarsely. "Tell me what really happened to your father, please."

"I—I had gone to meet my father at the back way to my uncle's home. I had asked him to come to see me there." Chlorinda began to tremble. She saw the vision before her; she was no longer really talking to the stranger beside her. "If—if it wasn't for me, it would never have happened. He would never have come to my uncle's estate, never have come by the back way. Uncle told me later that the bridge was weak, but I—I didn't know that at the time. I never suspected. It was all my fault—my father's death."

"No, don't believe that," the stranger said firmly, his arms coming up to hold her close, rocking her gently as the tears came. She could not stop them, she had no control. "Your—your father would have died anyway."

"No, you don't understand!" Chlorinda shook her head wildly. "He would never have set foot on Uncle's property. They—they had a fight, an awful fight. Father only came because I was there."

"Hush, it's over . . ."

"But it's not." She clutched the man's shirt. She needed desperately to explain the formless terror that haunted her. "I can't forget! I play it over and over in my mind. Do you know horses can scream?" There was a horror in her voice. "They can scream—I'll always remember hearing them. But I can't remember hearing anything else. I never heard my

205

father."

"You wouldn't have," the man's voice whispered softly, close to her ear.

She froze and then lifted her head to gaze into the stranger's eyes, eyes strangely as anguished as hers. She drew in a ragged breath. "No, I wouldn't have heard him, would I? He wouldn't have screamed, would he?"

"No." He raised a hand to her face and brushed away the stray hair that had fallen on her forehead. "He was a strong man and a brave man. And you are his daughter, after all. Do not torment yourself so; it wasn't your fault. You couldn't have stopped it. You must let it go."

"I can't." She withdrew from him, standing and drifting away like a forlorn waif in the moonlight. "I try, but I always feel I'm forgetting something. I feel I could have done something—wanted to do something—but I can't remember what!" She spun around and ran back to the man, sinking to the ground and clasping his hands. "It haunts me, and when I try and think on it, I become filled with fear. Do you think I am going mad?" she looked pleadingly at him, desperation running deep within her.

"No—no, I don't," the man said, his voice a soothing balm. "But tell me what you can remember."

"I think I remember everything—and then, sometimes, I think I don't." Wearily, she laid her head upon his lap, as if he were her lost father, as if she were in a dream where she could do as she desired. Nothing mattered but resting her aching head. "I remember the carriage and seeing it come over the bridge. Father had the team well in hand, and then—then there was creaking, and—and it all caved in.

"After that—I can't remember. I must have fainted. The doctor said that when I fell, I must have hit my head upon a rock; I remained unconscious for quite some time afterwards. They say I was so distraught, even after I awoke, that I had to be carefully watched and dosed with medication."

"They say?"

"Yes. I can't remember any of that time. Just like I can't remember anything before I went to see my father at the bridge. I can only remember the—the actual scene; anything before or after is a void. The doctor said it is perfectly normal for a person who's been traumatized and suffered a concussion not—not to remember things."

"Yes, it's true. Some forget their whole lives."

"I wish I could forget mine," Chlorinda said desperately. "Or else remember what haunts me. It is this living in-between and—and always feeling that it was my fault. My uncle tells me to stop trying to remember. And I know it's for the best—but I can't help it."

"Is that why he watches you so closely?"

"Yes—when I was sick, they feared for my life. Uncle brought in his own doctor to attend me. He brought in Mrs. Bendley, who is a relative of his—he made all the arrangements for me when I was unable to attend to matters. And he did his best to save my—" Chlorinda stopped shortly.

"Save your what?"

"Nothing, nothing at all," Chlorinda said, suddenly pulling back. She stood swiftly, shaking out her skirts.

The stranger was suddenly beside her, clasping her arms and looking at her intently. "Save your *what?*

Chlorinda gulped. "My—my finances."

"What do you mean?"

She looked down, embarrassed. "I know that everyone considers me an heiress. I—I was to have in trust not only an inheritance from my father's family, but one from my mother's as well, that first my father held in trust and then my uncle."

"I see."

"But—but it is not as large as many think it is. You see, Uncle explained it all to me—something about stocks, and the exchange, and faulty investments that my father and his man of business made. Though he says it was my father's man of business more than Father himself, since my father merely over-trusted the man. Uncle has fired the man now for his gross incompetence and is working to help me, as my trustee, to gain better investments. Of which I can only be grateful."

"Grateful?" The stranger's voice was oddly angry. "You are grateful to him?"

"But of course I am. He is trying to do the best for me."

"And you feel you must please him?"

"As much as I can. He has never failed in his efforts on my behalf. I mean, he arranged the marriage with Edward Carstairs with my interest in mind—it is not as if I come as high-dowried as one would expect. And I—I know I disappointed him when I refused Edward, but at least I can please him in regards to Lord Stanton's suit. I believe I can like him, and Uncle seems quite satisfied with the match. Lord Stanton does not care if my dowry is small, either."

The stranger dropped her arms abruptly and moved away. "So now you are grateful to Lord Stanton as well?"

Chlorinda, shaken by his tone, immediately went to sit upon the stone bench. "Lord Stanton was not only kind about my lack of dowry, but generous upon the settlement as well."

"And are you pleased to allow yourself to be a commodity? Is love not a factor in your life?"

Chlorinda stiffened. "Uncle says that love is not required before marriage, and that a woman will grow to love her husband."

"And do you know how a woman will grow to love her husband?" the stranger asked softly, walking slowly towards her. Chlorinda blinked, for the stranger's kind eyes that had so drawn her were no longer the same. They glittered dangerously.

"No," Chlorinda whispered as he stopped but a breath away.

"She will, of course, grow to love his touch." He reached out and ran his hand against her cheek, his palm a rough velvet to her skin. She pulled back, a shiver coursing through her. "And she learns to love his kiss." He was suddenly beside her on the bench, drawing her to him in an embrace. His kiss was not gentle, and his hands slid up the column of her neck to turn her head and lips fully to his. Still, the shock that ran through her was a thrilling one, as commanding as his kiss.

She remained a moment, enthralled. Then she broke away, gasping. "Sir, unhand me!"

He rose abruptly and strode away. After a moment, he turned and said softly. "Is that the way you will learn to love Lord Stanton?"

His words struck her as if he had lifted his hand to her. With a small sound she turned from him, hiding her face as sudden, confused tears sprang to her eyes.

"Forgive me, madame," the man said after a tense moment. "I have overstepped the bounds of decency and taken advantage of the situation—which I did not intend. I will leave you now. You need not fear that I will invade your private garden again." Chlorinda refused to look at him. "Though I have abused your hospitality, it was no lie when I said I am your fool. Much more of a fool than you would ever guess. In recompense, I will make it my duty to insure your safety. Do not fear Edward Carstairs.

"And do not fear for your sanity. Only trust your fool in that." She heard but a whisper of movement from behind, and the veriest sound of "Farewell, fair fatality."

Relenting, she turned quickly to say goodbye, but her stranger was nowhere in sight. She searched the garden almost longingly, then stood and lifted the cloak he had left. Without thinking, she held it close, rubbing the fabric against her cheek. It could have been a dream for all she knew—but for that cloak. Tears slipped down her cheek once more. She did not think it was he who was the fool.

Chapter Twelve
Donnybrook On The Docks

Nothing felt right, Julia thought nervously. Her eyes scarcely took in Lady Pembroke's magnificent foyer as the butler held her cloak and Armand's coat, informing them that the musical would be held in the yellow salon. Armand delivered his greatcoat to the butler with a sniff. The butler appeared somewhat surprised at the brilliant blue satin that Armand wore, but Armand stared him down with a ruthless ease.

Julia attempted to hide her smile at the interplay. Though Armand appeared the finicky dandy with not a care in the world, she could feel an odd energy emanating from him on this evening. She had asked him if he had discovered anything about Chlorinda. He had said that he had discovered nothing that would matter. His manner had been strange and closed. She sighed. There seemed to be a distancing between them. She knew it must arise from her own secrets regarding Jason, but it bothered her, nonetheless.

She nodded in distraction to a passerby as they walked toward the salon. As she entered the room, Julia's tension evolved into a feeling of impending disaster. She was experienced at gauging a social atmosphere and tonight the room buzzed with an uncommonly high energy. Matrons' turbans collided with each other in conference, and feathers wagged furiously. Men's snuff boxes were held out but went unnoticed as their owners discussed a subject that evidently held more interest.

"Armand, I have a bad feeling," Julia murmured to her brother as they stood on the threshold.

"One of your premonitions?"

"Yes, exactly. Look at the room."

"Tongues are wagging, aren't they?" Armand smiled. "Most likely it's over some deb who ran off with her dancing instructor."

Julia looked at him hopefully. "Do you think so?"

"No. Not with Rendon being so pleased with himself last night, and what he needed to tell all of England."

"I thought the same thing."

"Well, let us sally forth—whatever has the room so wrought should be of interest."

Julia replied with an indelicate snort. "Very well. Chlorinda is over there. I'll go and see what she has to say."

"You do that." Her brother's tone was frigid. Julia looked quickly to him, and found herself shocked by the look in his eye as he watched Chlorinda. "My dear," she said, "what is the matter?"

Armand looked back at her, the intense emotion leaving his eyes. "Nothing. You go visit Mistress Everleigh and I will check the men's conversation."

Julia stared after him in concern, but then set her mind to the task. She wended her way between the clumps of muttering guests, and various words and phrases flitted by her—words such as *outrage, scoundrel,* and *heinous.* The word *traitor* fell from behind and it was all Julia could do to keep walking. A pain gripped her chest; what had the duke done?

Unconsciously, her eyes began searching for the figure of a large man. She found the man she was looking for—the Earl of Wynhaven.

Jason stood nonchalantly, his head bent to hear a shorter man who gesticulated rapidly to match his speech. Jason's eyes, however, were on Julia, and his brow rose with mild curiosity as she met his gaze.

Julia forced a smile to her numb face along with a cross-eyed look; Jason smiled wryly and returned his attention to the excited little man beside him. The steel band about Julia's chest eased. Whatever was transpiring in the room, Jason had not directed condemnation towards her. The amused smile upon his lips said as much. It righted her rocking world.

She straightened her resolve and went to sit by Chlorinda and Mrs. Bendley. "My dear Chlorinda," she said in unfeigned concern, "what is the matter? You appear ill." Chlorinda's skin was pale and dark circles rimmed her eyes.

"Yes, yes, that is what I have been telling the child," Mrs. Bendley said, her head bobbing up and down rapidly. "She's been overdoing it—all this racketing about is very unhealthy for the sweet dear. Yet she will insist she is fine and desired to come tonight."

"I am fine," Chlorinda said with unaccustomed sharpness. "I—I merely have a slight migraine."

"It is most likely the weather," Julia said sympathetically. "It is quite oppressive, really. I fear it will storm before the night is out. Lady Daniella could not attend this evening, due to a migraine."

"Yes, that is it exactly," Chlorinda said quickly.

Julia then cast her eye about the room in seeming innocence. "My gracious, the Signora Santini who is to sing tonight must be wondrous. Only look, the room is abuzz with excitement for her performance."

Mrs. Bendley shook her head and leaned over to pat Julia's hand condescendingly. "You are quite mistaken, dear. It is obvious that you have not heard the latest dreadful news."

"What? Has the Signora fallen ill or something?"

"La, child, it has nothing to do with the Signora—she is of no moment. It is our national welfare that is at stake."

"Signora Santini is involved in our national welfare?"

Julia asked with a determined show of bewilderment.

"No, no, do forget that woman for a moment," Mrs. Bendley said in exasperation. "We have just received news that the blackguard Landreth's children aren't dead, but live, and are now at large somewhere in England."

"Oh, they live now?" Julia asked, looking confused, though her heart skipped out of rhythm. "And has their father returned from the dead as well?"

Chlorinda chuckled a little at this, and Mrs. Bendley cast her eyes to the heavens, as if to pray for Julia's small intelligence. "Of course not. He is truly dead. And the children didn't return from the grave. They never left it, you goose!"

"But you said the children had been dead but are now alive," Julia repeated solemnly.

"No, no, that was a mistake. They were never dead. It was all a sham. The dear duke discovered their plot — and do you know what else he discovered?"

"I can't imagine."

"The children were not innocent, but traitors with their father!"

Even though she had expected the words, Julia turned pale. The pain was great. Mrs. Bendley, misunderstanding, exclaimed and patted her hand. "Now, my dear, don't be upset. I know it is a frightening prospect, but the dear duke has vowed to rid England of these traitors, so you may rest easily."

"To be sure," Julia said mechanically.

"I hope he discovers them soon," Chlorinda said with unwarranted wrath. " 'Tis a pity they didn't die with their father."

"But they haven't been tried yet," Julia said, amazed at her gentle friend's force. "The evidence could be misleading."

"No, they are traitors," Chlorinda said sharply. "If it wasn't for the Landreths, my father wouldn't have —" She stopped.

"Wouldn't have what?" Julia asked sharply

"Nothing," Chlorinda said, shaking her head. "But my father trusted Landreth—and Landreth betrayed him."

"Are you so sure?" Julia asked softly. Her eyes pinned Chlorinda's, and it was Chlorinda's that were the first to fall.

"There, there," Mrs. Bendley said soothingly. "Don't you girls be worrying over all this. Your uncle will see that those devil-spawn meet their just end. Why, even the prince regent has put his faith in your uncle." She leaned over in excitement. "The prince says that if his grace uncovers the two traitors, he will give him the repossessed Landreth lands as a reward."

"My God," Julia breathed, stunned. Her world was crashing about her.

"Yes, isn't it marvelous?" Mrs. Bendley nodded. "Of course, it is only fitting—it's his grace that has undermined that monstrous family. He certainly deserves to be rewarded."

Bile rose in Julia's throat and she forced herself not to retort. Her eyes desperately searched the room until she caught Armand's gaze. He'd heard the news, she knew it—his eyes mirrored the stricken pain that she felt. "Excuse me," Julia murmured. Rising quickly, and without another word to Chlorinda or Mrs. Bendley, she left the room, her head held high as if she was already facing the accusations.

She entered the first empty room she could find, closing the door. Walking to a high-backed chair, she gripped it for support, her nails digging deep into its patterned brocade. She stood there, lost, until she heard the door open and close behind her.

Armand stood waiting when she turned. With a few steps, she flung herself into her brother's outstretched arms.

"You heard," she said raggedly. "I don't think I can bear it, Armand. I cannot bear it."

"Hush, my dear, hush . . ."

Julia drew in a great, gulping breath. "Why can't he

214

just leave it alone? Will it never be over?"

"It will—with his death," Armand said calmly. "And he will surely die before he ever sets foot on Landreth lands."

"You heard that, too?"

"Of course. All the world praises the Duke of Rendon tonight. But all the world will not protect him when we bring him down."

Julia breathed easier. "We shall, of course. I just grow so weary of it all. Even though we could have expected it, I didn't think he'd dare admit we still lived—or accuse us of treason as well."

"The man will dare everything if it gains him what he wants. But he'll not get it with us. Now, we'd best warn Sir. I have complete faith in him, but I'd prefer that he didn't stumble into the guards when he arrives this evening."

"What guards?"

"You didn't hear? Everleigh is having all the ports watched this evening for anyone entering or departing the country."

"Good gracious. The man is definitely serious, isn't he?"

"Yes, and imagine his apoplexy if he knew that he is calling out the best of the British Army when we are right here under his nose." Armand grinned engagingly.

Julia laughed shakily. "Lord, but I'd like to see his face at that." Then she sobered. "We'd best be going, though, for Sir should arrive in a few short hours. We'd best warn them at the port and the Shields and Arms in case he has changed any of his plans. Which do you wish to take, the port or the tavern?"

"I think I'll take both."

Julia frowned. "Why? We waste time that way and could miss sending the message."

Armand sighed. "I know—but neither place stirs brotherly confidence in my breast for you."

Julia's eyes narrowed. "This English climate is not

215

healthy for you, mon frére; it is seeping into you and making you a prim and proper dunce! Soon you'll be telling me to stay at home and tend to my tatting and mending."

"Never! I value my life too much."

"Well, then. Let us flip a coin as we always do."

Armand grimaced, but he pulled a coin from his pocket nevertheless. He grimaced even more when the toss went to Julia. With a triumphant glitter in her eye, she said she would take the docks.

"Very well," Armand said, sighing again, "but I do wish you would reconsider."

Julia chuckled. "Don't worry, dear brother. I have been in far more dangerous places than that and you know it."

"Yes, but not with an entire country ravening for your lovely head. It's generally only half the populace that wishes you hung."

Julia laughed. "Never fear—they'll be too hot on Julia Landreth's tail to consider an old decrepit woman of any consequence."

"All right, we'd best be—"

He stopped in midsentence as the door handle rattled. The siblings sprang swiftly into action as the door swung open, Armand pulling Julia to him in a mock embrace while she slid her arms to his shoulders. They positioned themselves in such a manner that it appeared they had just disengaged from a kiss; they had performed this little scene many a time and their pose was meticulously correct. To be discovered in a lovers' tryst was far more acceptable than to be discovered in an assignation of espionage.

A woman's shocked cry echoed in the room. Julia and Armand, displaying all the proper confusion for such a delicate situation, disengaged and turned towards the door.

Julia's heart plummeted to her toes. Chlorinda stood within the portal, hand clenched and raised to her quivery lips, eyes wide and aghast. A grim, cold-eyed Jason towered behind her. Julia blushed fiercely.

"Ex—excuse us," Chlorinda stammered. "I—we—were worried about you, Miranda."

"W-were you?" Julia asked.

"Yes, you had appeared somewhat er—upset," Jason said coolly. Julia's eyes flew to his. The man could read her emotions far too easily.

"Well, she is not," Armand drawled. He reached over suddenly and pulled Julia back into his arms. "She is only slightly bowled over. I have asked my pet to become my wife." Julia looked swiftly to Armand, attempting to cover her shock. His eyes were locked challengingly upon Chlorinda's. She just about groaned. This was no time for Armand to kick over the traces, merely because he disliked Chlorinda.

"And has 'your pet' accepted?" Jason's tone was calm, Julia observed as she glanced at him and swallowed hard. But his look was not. In fact, it was rather threatening.

"Well, I said . . ." She prevaricated.

"She said yes, of course," Armand offered swiftly. "We are deeply in love and one marries when one loves, does one not?"

"One should," Jason murmured. Cynicism ran rampant upon his face. Julia's eyes sparked. Who was he to look at her as if she were a toad just hopped out from under a log? His match with Chlorinda was not exactly the grand passion of the century.

"Yes," she sighed, fluttering her lashes. "We intend to throw convention aside. We want a love match, don't we, Sir Horace?" She gazed lovingly into her brother's eyes. His twinkled back as he pinched her gently. She giggled, though her heart raced. She was playing with fire. Jason's eyes told her so.

"And so do we," Chlorinda suddenly said, her voice breathless. Her little chin lifted. "That is why—why Lord Stanton and I intend to announce our engagement as well. We can no longer deny ourselves, either."

The subsequent gasp was not from one individual, but

rather a collective response. The atmosphere is the room crackled and popped as glares and stares flashed back and forth.

"I must congratulate you," Julia said. Her lips hurt as she cracked them into a smile. Jason's gaze turned impassive.

"Thank you," Chlorinda said nervously, refusing to meet the others' eyes. "And I—we—wish you both happiness as well."

"Yes," Jason said, his tone controlled. "I am sure a celebration is in order."

"Indeed," Julia said. "But—but first, Sir Horace and I must go and inform Lady Daniella of the—the good news, since she was unable to attend tonight."

"So must we inform Uncle Converse," Chlorinda said, a strained smile upon her face. "He will be so pleased to hear this."

"I wager he will," Armand said dryly.

"Well, then," Jason said, "we shall see you later this evening, perhaps. We really must get together and celebrate our engagements." His look was anything but congratulatory. "This is indeed a momentous night."

Julia smiled sweetly. "Perhaps another night . . ."

"Yes. Sorry, Stanton," Armand said swiftly. "I am sure Lady Daniella won't take kindly to our just popping in and delivering our announcement, only to pop out again."

"We quite understand," Chlorinda nodded. "Well, we must be leaving." She turned swiftly, only to run into Jason's chest. "Oh!"

"Faith, already your fiancée embraces you, my lord," Armand said sardonically.

"Let us be going, dear," Julia said quickly. She refused to look at Jason as the two couples finally left the room. She realized she could no longer withstand the look in his eyes—the look that showed he thought her an adventuress who had just entrapped the rich Sir Horace. She grimaced; the man could go to Hades for all she cared. She had much more important things to worry about, after all.

Julia slipped out the back door of Lady Daniella's townhouse. Granny's wig covered her silvery hair and she wore the shabbiest of Granny's dresses. She directed her small, doddering steps toward the London docks.

Fog rolled onto the streets, blown by a wet wind, and Julia greeted the fog as a friend rather than a foe. She needed its protection. She needed to be but a shadow in the mist.

Julia's mind raced, but she forced the measure of her steps to remain slow and even. She attempted to train her mind to the task at hand, even though it kept retreating as she thought of prior events. What had Armand done and why? What was Jason thinking? How did Chlorinda feel? She knew better than to try to determine how she felt.

All of a sudden, her steps faltered. The back of her neck tingled as if someone was following her.

Julia disappeared into the nearest covered doorway. No one appeared. Still she waited. Still no one came.

She shrugged to herself. Her nerves were playing games with her, evidently. She resumed her journey to the seedier side of London.

Once she reached the docks, Julia proceeded to hobble back and forth. She did not approach any particular vessel, nor did she call out to anyone. On her third revolution, she stopped to adjust her shawls. One slithered to the ground; exclaiming, she bent to retrieve it.

"Hey, old lady," a tall, thin sailor called from one of the moored crafts. It was Carl, a man whom she had often worked with in the past. They called him "Cautious Carl." Tonight she was glad he was on watch. "I'll help you!"

Julia straightened up slowly. "Thank ye, sonny, me old bones ain't what they used ter be." The man dropped

219

from the deck and ran to help her. "It's a frightful night out, ain't it?"

"Ain't that the truth," the sailor said as he bent and picked up her fallen shawl. "Storm out there's keeping our cargo from coming in. Reckon it'll be in come midnight."

"Ye poor man, having to unload it then, and looking like there be more holdups, what with them planning to set the guards to checking your cargo."

"What ye mean?"

"Ah, they says they're looking for a pesky traitor so's they're checking all yer vessels coming in and out. Thought ye'd 'ave heard it by now."

"Ah, hell, I ain't going to see my bed all night, then. The captain ain't going to like this."

Julia shrugged. "All we can do is warn the man of the tangle and see what 'appens."

"That I will," the sailor grinned. "Well, ye have a good night, old woman."

"Ye too, son, ye too," Julia said with a wave of one withered hand as she arranged her shawls with the other. The sailor sauntered back from whence he came and she resumed her constitutional along the docks. Her father would be duly warned.

She peered out at the black waters; lightning flashed far off on the horizon. Her father must be having a rough journey. She shrugged, and a smile crossed her lips. Her father was an excellent sailor and rough weather would make no difference to him. Indeed, he'd probably exult in it.

Her smile was quickly extinguished and she exclaimed as a rough arm circled her neck, choking the breath from her and drawing her up sharply against foul-smelling, scratchy material. "All right, old woman, heave over yer dibs," a just-as-scratchy voice demanded.

"I—I don't have any!"

"Listen, ye old bat, I ain't the man ye can fool. No sir, ye can't fool Old Jake, so hand it over."

Julia attempted to twist from her captor; alas, Old Jake truly wasn't the man to fool and his grip only tightened. "I—can't breathe!" Julia wheezed as her world grew blurred.

"Then stop yer fightin'." Old Jake's grip eased marginally.

"A—all right," Julia said, her thoughts racing. "Let me loose and I'll give ye what I got—which ain't much. I ain't flush in the pocket, ye know."

"Sure, sure, all you old biddies say that. But I knows better—yer always saving fer a rainy day. Guess I'm yer rainy day, eh? Now where's ye hiding it, grandma, under your petticoats?"

Julia looked wildly about. Enshrouded with Old Jake in the fog, she could not see another living soul: yet, even if there were another person out there in the mist, she couldn't expect much. Aiding old ladies in distress was not a common pastime on the docks.

Her heart sank, though her mind still worked feverishly. She truly did not have much money, and Old Jake was just the man to check her petticoats if she handed over such a paltry sum. Her harried thoughts, however, were interrupted by a loud, off-toned and slurred singing that drifted to her through the fog.

"Oh, Sweet Mary sells such lovely fruit," the voice crooned, coming closer. "Her peaches are so-o-o round and soft."

"Oh, Lud," Julia moaned. She was praying for help and it seemed the only other person in the vicinity beside her seafaring captor was a tone-deaf drunk.

"Damn." Jake's arm tightened around her. "Be quiet or ye'll be sorry."

Julia thought she was already sorry. She made not a sound as the two stood in waiting silence.

"And p-ret-t-y P-o-ll-y," the voice caroled with deafening, off-key force. "Owns the b-brightest ch-cherri-es, red ripe laddies." A dog yowled in the distance. "Never tasted b-bet-ter-r-r . . ."

Julia cringed and her captor began to chuckle. "Be-Jesus, the bloke's tap-hacket." He laughed as the voice came closer. A large, swaying shadow emerged from the mist.

"But of them al-l-l, the v-very b-best is M-i-r-and-a." A drunken nobleman, voice booming, weaved towards them. "S-p-rite-li-est of — them all!"

Even if Old Jake hadn't been squeezing Julia's vocal cords to pulp, Julia couldn't have squeaked out a word.

"How-do," the drunken Lord Stanton slurred as he began to pass them.

"How do,"Old Jake chuckled.

The earl suddenly stumbled, ramming into them at full velocity. As the trio rocked over, Julia quick-wittedly rolled loose from Old Jake's slackened hold. Completely surprised by this, Old Jake howled in surprise as the supposed drunk drove an iron fist into his stomach. "Help!" he howled, scrabbling away from Jason and springing to his feet.

Jason was up with surprising agility for a drunk, and attacking Old Jake in a flash. But the man had been a long-time denizen of the docks and he stood up to Jason's hammering blows gamely.

"Damn," Julia muttered as the tattoo of running footsteps echoed out of the mist. "Damn, damn," she repeated as three more dark shapes broke through the fog.

"On him, men," Old Jake wheezed — before he spiralled to the ground. The three shapes converged upon Jason. Julia stood rooted to the spot, amazed as Jason greeted the new ruffians with startling vigor. The group became a brawling mass, first one figure flying from the roiling core, then another, only to pelt back into the melee immediately.

"That's the way!" Julia shouted to Jason. She quickly sidestepped one of the dock rats as he rocketed past her and crashed to the ground. He bounded up, shook himself with a terrier growl, and charged back to the brawl. Julia clasped hold of his coattails as he passed and jerked him back rapidly. Curses split the air and he spun, his arms windmilling about. Julia released his coat and dodged a flailing fist. She backed up hastily as the man advanced towards her, anger in his eyes.

She looked quickly about, sizing up her options. Suddenly, she turned back to the snarling little man with a knowing, diabolical grin on her face. With malicious intent, she stuck her tongue out at him.

His eyes bulged in outrage and he swore, then sprang at her, arms reaching, hands ready to strangle. Julia hopped from his charging path and thwacked him on the back as he sailed past her. The man cursed again in the split second before he discovered what Julia had found out only moments before—they had been fighting perilously close to the edge of the wharf. He tumbled beyond the edge into the murky water below.

Julia, without hesitation, turned back to check on Jason's progress. He battled only two attackers now, but they, too, had brawled their way to the edge of the wharf. Fearing the outcome, Julia bent down and snatched a dainty pistol from a strap at her ankle. As she brought the gun up, however, the two attackers realized their sudden advantage and slammed Jason over the edge. A sickening splash followed.

"We've got him now, mate!" one man chortled.

"Take one step and I'll shoot you," Julia commanded. Both men spun about to discover a little old woman training a pistol upon them with a rather nasty eye. "Now, you may both choose to leave here upon the instant, or I will shoot one of you and the other—well, he may take his chances with the large gentleman in the water." The men cast each other frightened glances and Julia wasn't quite sure which threat of hers had carried more weight. "Well?"

"We're going," said one of the men, who had a split lip. His companion, whose eyes were beginning to swell shut, nodded vigorously. They vanished into the fog as if they had been apparitions.

The moment she could no longer hear their running footsteps, Julia ran to the edge of the wharf. Kneeling, she peered into the dark void. "Jason?" Frantic, she leaned further over, yelling his name. "Oh, dear lord, please don't let him be dead. He just can't be dead!"

"I don't know why not," a wry voice said from behind her.

Julia, gasping in relief, twisted about on her knees. "Oh, no . . ." she breathed. Jason's satin dress jacket was ripped to tatters, his cravat dripped seaweed, and his face sported a wealth of cuts and bruises. Julia drew back in dismay—and screeched as she felt herself falling backwards.

Jason, moving swiftly, grabbed her and, after a moment's suspension in limbo, dragged her from the edge and pressed her securely to him. "Th-th-thank you," Julia stammered, pushing herself away from his wet male body.

"Think nothing of it," Jason said kindly. "It's been a lovely evening's entertainment."

"What are you doing here?"

"I could ask the same of you."

"You were following me, weren't you?" Julia turned stiffly and began to walk away.

Jason fell into step with her. "Yes, but I lost you a few times."

"I wish you hadn't followed me."

"Indeed? You wanted Old Jake all to yourself?"

"No, I was glad of your assistance, but I do not wish you to follow me anymore. It's not as if it's beneficial for your health."

"Or my tailoring."

Julia noticed how he sloshed beside her with a dignified grace, and chuckled. "Lud, you present a sight."

"So do you. Your wig is askew."

Julia's hand flew to her coiffure. "Why didn't you tell me?"

"And a glow of youthful skin is beginning to wear through the wrinkles." He ran his large thumb over her cheekbone. "Yes—definitely youthful skin."

"Then we must hurry," Julia stammered, increasing her pace. "I don't want to be seen this way."

"Ah, yes, Granny Merton rushes home before the stroke of midnight, lest her hair turns to shimmering silver and her wrinkled skin becomes smooth and young at the witching hour. You confuse the tale, I believe, but then, you confuse many things—me included."

"Only because you persist in following me," Julia snapped. "You must stop following. You—you're an engaged man now and shouldn't be endangering yourself."

"I could say the same. Do you intend to change your—er—habits, whatever they may be, now that you are engaged to Sir Horace?"

"Not yet," Julia said, looking away. "But that is my choice. I'm not the one who said he wanted to lead a quiet and comfortable life."

"Did I say that?"

"Yes, you did," she replied firmly. "Repeatedly. And I'm afraid peace is the last thing you have had since you met me."

"True, but perhaps I was wrong. Perhaps some excitement in my life is not all that bad. I find shootings and bashings and dunkings are becoming quite an enlivening pastime."

Julia halted a moment, her eyes suspicious. "You are in a fey mood tonight."

His grin was wry. "I've been too long around a sprite, I fear." Julia frowned. He smiled, snatching up her hand and holding it. "Come, sprite. 'Tis the last night before we are both officially engaged. Cannot you smile for me?"

"My congratulations," she said tightly. "Chlorinda is a sweet girl."

"She is," he said. Slowly he drew her hand to his heart and held it there. She thought she could feel the very beat of it through his wet shirt. "Are you happy?"

Her hand trembled. "You are happy with her, that is

225

all that matters."

"And are you happy with Sir Horace?" he said, his voice low.

Julia's hand trembled and she tried to pull away. He only held her hand more firmly. "I must be going."

"I cannot let you do it," he said roughly. He swiftly captured her other hand and held them both to his chest.

"What?" Julia said, her eyes meeting his. She was intent on what he might say.

He opened his mouth to say something and then he closed it. His eyes became guarded. "I cannot let you hurt Sir Horace and lie to him."

Julia felt as if she had been doused in ice cold water. "Let me go." she said angrily. "How dare you? Let me go."

He dropped her hands and clasped her shoulder. "Tell me, dammit," he said. "Tell me who you are. What you are. You want to marry this fop—you must tell me that."

Julia found her eyes tearing, and she shook her head. "I can't." The sound of approaching hooves sounded along the street. "Someone comes. Please, you must let me go."

"Tell me."

"Tomorrow I will. I must go now," Julia said shakily.

"Damn." His hands loosened slightly and Julia swiftly slipped out from under them. She ran as quickly as she could, but she heard his low voice through the fog very clearly: "Tomorrow, sprite, tomorrow." She shivered and continued through the mist that swirled about her.

Out in the ocean, in the storm that had not made landfall yet, a vessel tossed and tipped. In the vast, rolling water, it looked like a toy, small and insignificant.

Jeanne, resting in one of the toy cabins, felt the same. She bit back a weak moan as the four walls about her swayed and rolled. She clutched the side of her berth as her head spun accordingly. "Peste', I will kill him," she promised herself. "I shall think long and hard. He must die a cruel death, that one." She groaned and clutched the coolness of the basin, which had not left her side since the English monster had brought her upon the craft. "Think, Jeanne, think!"

A low, mournful howl penetrated her feverish vision of Landreth tied to a rack while she turned the wheel and he pleaded. It was such a pitiful sound as to cause Jeanne to slowly turn her head in the direction of the groan.

Sophocles lay supine across the cabin from her. His head rested upon two outstretched paws and he turned miserable eyes towards her as he emitted another sick whimper. His large, furry frame shuddered.

"Ah, pauvre Sophocles," Jeanne commiserated. The dog's body began to heave. "Oh no, no, wait!" With superhuman will, she rolled from the berth and toppled to the cabin floor. "I'm coming, wait!" She crawled towards the nauseous dog with her basin. He howled and Jeanne lunged, sliding the basin under his snout just before he cast up his accounts.

Dog and woman then laid their heads down on the floor with deep sighs of contentment. "Pauvre Sophocles, your master is a beast," Jeanne breathed. "You must attack him, really you must. I know you are loyal, but only consider . . ." Sophocles whined as if he did.

She heard the cabin door open and a cool draft brushed her face. "Jeanne, what are you doing on the floor?" a voice asked in concern. Jeanne recognized the brute's voice. "Up! After him, Sophocles, attack!"

"You ask too much of him, madame," Landreth said with a chuckle. She felt, rather than saw, him lift her into a sitting position. "Are you all right?"

Jeanne opened her eyes in irritation. "But of course! I like to sleep with the dog on the floor. We keep each other company."

"Allow me to assist you—"

"No!" Jeanne cuffed him feebly. "Leave me be. I wish to die here. Only tell me why? Me, I understand if you wish me to die, but the poor doggie? He is your own!"

"I do not wish you to die," Landreth said soothingly. He picked her up in blatant disregard of her wishes.

"Leave me be!" She tried to fight, but the nausea weakened her swing. Landreth quickly settled her upon the bed, and she felt a warm hand on her cheek. Like a sulky child, she turned her head from him, despite the ache it caused.

"I know how difficult this must be for you," he said. *Mal de mer* is never comfortable, but it will soon be over."

"Yes, for I will be dead! Then how will you feel, M'sieur Fox?"

"Desolate," Landreth said calmingly. "Here."

Jeanne opened her eyes. Landreth was offering her a new, clean basin. She stared—the man was a fiend! In one sentence, he said he'd be desolate if she died and in the next, prosaically offered her a basin.

"Monster!" She struck the basin angrily. It flew from Landreth's hands and crashed to the floor a bare six inches from Sophocles. "What need do I have for that?" Jeanne cried wretchedly. "There is nothing left of me."

"Except your temper," Landreth said, amused.

Jeanne's eyes filled with tears. "I'm sorry—I feel miserable. I hope I did not hit Sophocles."

"No, he is dead to the world."

"What?" Aghast, Jeanne sat up swiftly.

"He's only sleeping." Landreth placed two solid hands upon her shaking shoulders and firmly pushed her back. "As you should be."

"But how can I sleep? My stomach, it hugs my backbone. My head, it pounds like a cannon. No, I cannot sleep—c'est impossible!"

"If you will drink this, I promise you, you will be able to sleep."

Jeanne looked warily at the draft Landreth produced from a tray outside the cabin door. "What is it? Do you intend to poison me? Is it not enough that you torture me on this pig boat?"

" 'Tis naught but a sleeping potion, I promise. Now be a good girl and drink it." He held the glass to her lips and, after a moment's hesitation, Jeanne sipped the bitter liquid. The boat suddenly lurched again and the rest of it trickled down her front.

"Ah, me," she said miserably. "I cannot even drink my poison right. You must think me a great stupid."

Landreth was silent a minute. "No." He reached to brush the liquid from her lips and chin. "That is not what I think."

"You think me weak."

"No, I do not think you weak. Now rest, my little French spy."

Jeanne closed her eyes at his gentle command, but then they snapped open. "Michael?"

"He's in fine fettle. Much better than his mother, in fact. He intends to become a sailor when he grows up."

Jeanne groaned. "Men!"

"Yes, we are a rather scurvy lot, aren't we?"

"Yes, you are," Jeanne said with a yawn as the draft took effect. "I think, Fox, you must need me to live very much, non?"

"Yes. I need you to live—I want you to live." She heard him say it just as she entered the comforting mists of sleep.

Jeanne did not know anything, and mercifully, did not feel anything, until a persistent shaking of her shoulder dragged her from her dreams. She attempted to ignore it. It continued, however, until it forced her to open her eyes.

A stranger loomed over her. He was a distinguished-looking gentleman with light brown hair and moustache, and Jeanne blinked in alarm. "Who—who are you? Does Lord André know you are here? Unhand me, sir!"

"Yes, he knows—for he is me." The man's voice sounded like Landreth's.

Jeanne studied him muzzily, then gasped. *"Voyens,* it is

you. I cannot believe it. But why do you dress like that?"

"We are soon to arrive in port."

"Impossible!"

"Not impossible. You have been sleeping for quite some time."

"Oh, but how wonderful!" Jeanne sat up. "I cannot wait to be on land."

"You might change your mind about that," Landreth said, an odd note in his voice.

"And why should I do that?" Jeanne asked suspiciously.

"It appears we shall have a welcoming committee."

"Who?"

"All passengers and cargos are being searched upon docking, and they must all show their papers."

"Merde, then we cannot land. I have no papers, I am French! It will be the death of me." She gulped. "But if I must stay on this boat—*that* will be the death of me."

Landreth laughed. "Do not concern yourself—we will land. Only—" He stopped and eyed her carefully.

"Only what? Tell me, I will help. I will do anything to get off this pig boat, anything!"

"Anything?" He continued to study her. "Hmm, no, I don't think you should be my mistress."

"Certainly not! I am not that sort of woman, m'sieur!"

"No, that's obvious. Besides, you could talk then. I must arrange it so that you cannot talk."

Jeanne began to tremble. "Wh—what are you going to do to me, English monster?"

Her horrified tones drew Landreth from his reverie. "What? Oh, no, I won't be doing anything to you. I only want you to dress up and play-act."

She looked at him suspiciously. "Only that?"

"Only that."

"That's all?" She thought a moment, then glared at him, affronted. "And then why, m'sieur, do you not think I would make you a good mistress, hmm? Do you think I am not pretty enough?"

Landreth laughed. "No, you're pretty enough."

"Merci," Jeanne replied, slightly mollified.

"With a pretty enough accent, as well."

"You do not like my speech? Ha! I have been told that I speak English most perfectly."

"A Frenchman told you this, non?"

"You—you do not think I speak your English well?"

"No, I think you speak it delightfully."

"M'sieur, now you confuse me."

He smiled. "Don't let it concern you—however, we must think of something for you. You certainly must not be allowed to talk." He sat staring at her until she felt like a rare specimen being studied by some collector—some mad collector, she thought as he smiled at her.

"I know just the thing," Landreth said, snapping his fingers. "Yes—yes, it will do nicely. Perfect!"

Perfect, the man had said! Impossible, Jeanne fumed as she clutched desperately at the silky, iridescent folds of the layered robe that was far too long for her—a sari, Landreth had called it. It was formed with so many intricate folds that Jeanne had not been able to master it; she flushed as she remembered Landreth laughing at her futile attempts, then pulling her hands away and arranging the folds himself, just as if she were nothing more than a mannequin!

Then he had instructed her to keep the veil well over her face, her eyes cast down, and to walk three paces behind him at all times. Perfect, he had said—for whom was it perfect?

Finally securing a stranglehold on the folds of the sari, Jeanne looked up as she walked down the gangplank behind Robert Landreth—three irritating steps behind him. At the end of the plank, two soldiers awaited them, and Jeanne felt the chill of fear. She didn't notice the last step from the plank to the dock and stumbled, falling head first, unable to keep her balance in the strange and voluminous wrap. Worse, she fell directly at Landreth's feet as if she were worshipping him.

"Watch out, there!" the younger of the guards cried.

Stunned and embarrassed, Jeanne waited for Landreth to come to her rescue; alas, the man merely stared down at her with an uncaring, critical look. "My dear," he drawled in a bored tone, "I have told you that it is not the custom here in England to bow before my feet, and I have asked you to refrain from doing so. You may resume when we reach my house, of course."

Jeanne, astonished at his rudeness, pulled in her breath to tell him exactly what she thought, when she gagged on a mouthful of veil. She spat it out and was about to speak when Landreth spoke. It was in an incomprehensible language but the command in his voice was unmistakable.

She bit back her ire as she peeked up to see both guards watching her with curious eyes. She scrambled to her feet and, clenching her fists, stared down at the ground determinedly.

Landreth turned back to the guards. "I am sorry, gentlemen. She's not been trained very well yet, has she? How are you tonight? Is there anything I may do for you?"

"Er, yes there is, sir." It was the older guard speaking — though in truth, both were fresh-faced. "We must see your papers."

"Indeed?" Landreth's brows rose. "If you must see them, you are certainly welcome to them." He reached inside his vest pocket and withdrew a packet, handing it to the guard. "I have not been in my native land for many a year — been in the Indies, in fact — but is this surveillance by the army now customary?"

"No, sir, but we are at war with France, as you know, and have been alerted that there are two very dangerous traitors loose who may attempt to land here."

"Indeed? Well, I hope you catch the scoundrels."

"We will, Mr. —" The young soldier looked down at the

papers. "Mr. Hanover. These are in order." He delivered them back to Landreth. "And now may I see the lady's?"

"Lady?" Landreth looked about in confusion. "What lady?"

The officer coughed in embarrassment. "Why—*that* lady's," he said quietly, jerking his head towards Jeanne.

Landreth turned and looked at Jeanne in surprise and then turned back to the now-reddening officer. "Ah, I see. You are mistaken, sir, this is no lady."

"No lady?"

"No, of course not. She is a gift."

"A—a gift?"

"Yes, from the maharajah, for a trifling service I had rendered him. He gave her to me just before I left: in fact—that is the explanation for her lack of tutoring."

"The maharajah gave her to you!" the younger guard squeaked, his eyes bulging.

"Yes. Now, you wouldn't have expected me to have turned his gift down, would you? One does not deny the maharajah anything, you understand—not if one values his life and freedom. Besides, she is an excellent slave— she would have brought quite a fee in India, I hope you know."

"A slave! Bloody hell!" the younger soldier exclaimed. The other officer glared at him fiercely.

"Why, yes—a slave," Landreth said slowly, as if to a lack-wit. "You have heard of them?"

"Yes, sir, we have—but I would still like to see her papers. Madame," he said, raising his voice as strangers do with foreigners, "I must see your papers."

"You need not raise your voice, corporal," Landreth said kindly. "She can hear—she simply cannot speak."

"A mute?" The soldier examined the silent Jeanne suspiciously. "The maharajah gave you a mute slave as a gift?"

"Certainly. It does increase her value, does it not?"

"Why would it?" the younger one asked, wide-eyed.

"Son, think on it. Would you not prefer a woman who

233

will do your bidding and cannot speak back? Now we in India recognize the value of such a gift."

The two young officers stared at him in astonishment. Then both broke into silly grins—in Jeanne's estimation—and even sillier guffaws. "I see your point, Mr. Hanover—but she does not have any papers."

"The maharajah's slaves never have papers. Why should they? They only travel when in their master's train. You would not ask me to show you my horse's papers, now would you? Why should my slave have papers?"

"Of course," the older boy said hesitantly, "but it just doesn't seem right."

"The customs in India are far different from here, 'tis all. Though if you would care to go to your superior, merely to ask over the status of my slave—"

"Er, no." The officer felt slightly overwhelmed by Landreth's blasé, sophisticated attitude. "I—I'm sure you are right. You may proceed."

"Gentlemen," Landreth said, bowing politely. He proceeded to walk away from them, leaving Jeanne to grab up the folds of her dragging sari and chase after him.

Landreth hailed them a hackney and with not so much as a look back at her, climbed into it directly. He left her to negotiate the ascent into the vehicle by herself.

She managed to climb into the carriage, then tripped over the trailing sari. She toppled ignobly onto Landreth, whose arms promptly circled and steadied her. "Are you all right?"

She backed from his embrace like a spitting kitten. "No, I am not all right. I have never been so embarrassed or humiliated! To be called your slave! Ha! You did not tell me—"

"Well, no, but it did work out, did it not? Thought it helped to have two such young and foolish men—"

"Mon Dieu!" Jeanne's eyes narrowed. "Understand this, M'sieur Fox, I will not play that part again. Me, I am no one's slave, n'est-ce pas? Perhaps you are used to

234

women like that, but I am not that sort! Do your English women follow behind you unspeaking, eh?"

Landreth laughed. "No, the English women are not like that, either. Perhaps they are not so volatile as you Frenchwomen—"

"And this is what you like?"

"I did not say that." Landreth's eyes became distant. "Else I would not have married a Frenchwoman, would I?"

"You—you married a Frenchwoman? This I did not know."

"You didn't know? How is it you did not ferret out that snippet of information? You seem well informed about me otherwise."

Jeanne's chin lifted. "That was not information spies require."

"My dear, a good spy should know everything about his opponent. Down to the last detail."

"Ha! And do you think you know everything about me, monsieur?" Jeanne's voice dripped with sarcasm.

Landreth considered her. "No—but I will."

Jeanne stared at him, her heart racing from the look he gave her. Then she sniffed in disdain and turned to look out the hackney window. "Well, the one thing you may know about me right now is that I do not like this England of yours. It is so damp and cold and its people are great stupids."

Landreth chuckled. "You have not seen England at her best. It can be—quite beautiful at times."

Jeanne snorted, ignoring the loving tones as he spoke of his country. "Say what you will, I will never like this damp country. No, never!"

In another area of town, Armand Landreth leaned back, lifted a tankard to his lips, and set it down. His eyes were trained upon the man sitting across from him. "Our awaited visitor is still scheduled to arrive tonight?"

"Yes," the little man replied. Like Armand, he wore shabby clothes, spotted and ripped to mere tatters. His beard, though, was long and full, whereas Armand sported only a stubble.

"We can but hope he is warned, then. There is nought else to do tonight."

"No—but I am sure he will survive."

Armand snorted. "He will. I wonder if I will, however. This inactivity is wearying."

The little man grinned. "Perhaps another tankard of ale will ease your pain. And while we drink, I can tell you a story you might like to hear."

"Indeed?" Armand's eyes brightened, and he immediately signalled a passing barmaid for another round. "Then this meeting will not be wasted."

"Perhaps not," the other said. "It seems there is a clerk in the department who has been voicing small but vicious remarks about his exalted employer—a man we all know very well. The clerk is hinting at duplicity and fraud."

"Excellent. What does he say, exactly?"

"He hasn't said much of anything, as yet. He's keeping it vague, saying nothing that couldn't be taken for a disgruntled underling's carping about a demanding overseer."

"But you think there might be more?"

"Possibly."

The barmaid set down two large tankards, and Armand spoke crisply as soon as she walked away. "Follow up on it. If you can persuade this man to do more than just hint, I would care to meet him."

"I will see what can be arranged." The small man lifted his drink in a salute. The two men enjoyed their ale, exhibiting every outward sign of being friends sharing boasts and jokes while becoming bosky.

The little man was the first to slap his tankard upon the table and leave, remarking loudly about his nagging wife, then weaving away. Calling good night, Armand got up and wobbled away in a different direction.

Chapter Thirteen
Ace Of Swords

Edward Carstairs was having an unfortunate night. Lady Luck had mistreated him at cards, and now at faro. Conversation about him lulled, and he heard a high, effeminate laugh behind him.

"No, Petersham, I believe I shall try my hand at faro first," the voice drawled. "I find the game such a simple pleasure — and so simple to win."

Irritated, Carstairs turned. Sir Horace and a companion of his, Petersham, stood directly behind him. His eyes inadvertently met the dandy's, who raised his painted brow at him.

"Well, bless my stars," Sir Horace said. A white hand came to his ruffled chest. "If it ain't Mr. Edward Carstairs. Good eve to you." He flourished a magnificent leg, displaying a calf that Carstairs was sure he padded with sawdust. "Do you play, my dear fellow? And dare I join? The one time I met you, I feared you did not care for me. Can't say why I thought it, perhaps the way you hurried off so swiftly. But, there you have it — one does get such strange and unusual notions."

Carstairs stiffened and anger shot through him. Indeed, he did not like the dandy. The tulip had interfered in his life where he shouldn't have. "I do not play anymore," he muttered softly, for they were drawing attention.

"Ah, me, a wise decision," Sir Horace said, nodding solemnly, "since I feel lucky tonight and would not care to fleece you."

"I doubt you would find it an easy task," Edward said tightly. The dandy's whole demeanor was insulting.

"Tsk, tsk, no reason to raise your hackles at me, dear fellow. Just have to tell you, I'm one of the luckiest men in the world. Yes, indeed. You can't believe how I can stumble upon situations — situations that always turn to my advantage. Especially with the ladies. 'Fear you don't have the same kind of luck, now do you, old man?"

Carstairs's shoulders jerked back. Such an insult, and from a fop like Sir Horace, could not be tolerated. "I do not think you would be swift to speak so if we talked over swords."

"He's right, you know, Horace," Petersham said quietly. "He's devilish fine at the foils. Come, let us go."

Sir Horace shrugged Petersham's restraining hand from his shoulder. "For shame, my dear friend, it appears you listen to rumors about Mr. Carstairs's powers. Now I, on the other hand, rarely consider what the gossips say as the truth."

"I can believe that," Carstairs retorted, rage overcoming common sense as the room fell completely silent, "else you'd know that your dress and manner are the subject of common jest. Lord, you wear more paint than any doxy and only look at your jacket — pink satin, with more ruffles than any woman's."

"And yours, sir, is a pain to any discriminating eye. I have tried to look the other way, not wishing to consider your deplorable taste, but, alas, for the comfort of society, I must tell you that you are in dire need of a new tailor. Now I have just the man that could be of service. He could give you more distinction; he's also very good at hiding a man's defects."

"B'gads," Carstairs snorted, "your dandified airs would give any real man a disgust of you."

"And do you consider yourself a real man?" Sir Horace asked in dulcet tones. "Real men don't require the aid of

238

bullies, do they?"

Carstairs paled suddenly. The man knew all, evidently. But how? "I don't know what you are talking about. Now, I am a patient man—"

"Are you? Ah, me, what a commendable trait. Now I, I fear, am not a patient man." He turned to Petersham and reached for the glass of brandy Petersham absently held. "Mon ami, do pray excuse me." He took the glass and, swinging around, dashed the contents into Carstairs's surprised face with a delicate flick of his wrist. "Such a waste of good spirits. Petersham, do let me buy you another."

Carstairs stood amazed, even as brandy trickled down his face. "You shall pay for this!"

"Of course. Did you not hear me just promise Petersham I would?"

"No, poppinjay," Carstairs snarled as a snicker ran through the crowd. "I mean you shall pay *me*."

"You? Whatever for? It was not your drink, my dear fellow."

"I am challenging you to a duel! Can you understand that?"

"Oh, is that what you are doing?" A beatific smile suddenly lit Sir Horace's painted face. "Well done—you do catch on after a while, don't you? Here I thought I'd be forced to toss another drink in your face, which I would have done, mind you, though I would have hated to waste more good brandy."

"Name your weapon!" Carstairs's hands clenched and unclenched in anger.

"Very well." Sir Horace frowned at his arm and paused to flick a minute piece of lint from it. His eyes rose to meet Carstairs's. "Let us make it foils."

A concerted gasp ran through the room. "Foils it is." Carstairs snapped. "You've just signed your own death warrant, fop."

"Have I? Ah, me, and here my old professors swore I'd no hand for the letters. Do be a good fellow and choose your seconds. I fear I am growing fatigued and would like to finish this business as promptly as possible." He raised a white hand to his lips to cover a yawn.

"You mean you wish to do it now?"

"But of course. Why wait until morning? Beastly things, mornings. Besides, I'd not wish you to forget our little meeting — it can be so devilishly hard to remember such affairs after a night of fun and frolic, can it not?"

"Danford? Carlton?" Carstairs rapped. "Will you act as my seconds?"

"My good Petersham," Sir Horace said gently, "would you be so good as to second me?"

"My pleasure."

"Excellent, and let me see . . ." His gaze roved the expectant room, and he raised a finger to point at a young tulip in the crowd. "And you, sir, I have held nothing but admiration for your cravat all this evening. Would you be so gracious as to second me?"

The young man, blushing and unable to speak, but pleased to be brought to attention, nodded mutely. "Marvelous. Faith, and here I was afraid this evening would be dull. Shall we meet in the park within — let us say, twenty minutes? The faster we settle this, the faster we all may return to the gaming, which I am sure none of us desires to forgo?"

"But how will we find a doctor at such short notice?" Danford objected.

"Why bother to knock one up? According to Mr. Carstairs here, there is no doctor alive who will be able to aid me after he is finished. Toodle, all." Turning, he took Petersham by the arm. "Come, my dear, do let me buy that drink for you first. And you, sir." He addressed the young tulip. "You who are so kind as to second me, allow me to buy you one also. I simply must toast your skill with the cravat."

Carstairs stared after Sir Horace as he and his seconds departed. Adrenaline pumped through him. He could not wait to draw the insufferable dandy's blood. Furthermore, he would not need to hold back; any man in this room would forgive him for running the tulip through. He smiled; Lady Luck had returned to his side.

Blood pounded in his head, thrummed in his temples, burgeoned in his heart. He parried the menacing foil once again, but it disengaged and licked thirstily at his arm. The damned dandy was merely toying with him now, playing with him like a cat with a mouse between its paws. How could this nightmare have happened?

Carstairs blinked the sweat from his eyes and met Sir Horace's flashing blade. He couldn't answer his own question. They'd begun the duel in full accordance with the rules, half the club present to watch. At first, it had been a mild surprise to discover the dandy possessed even a modicum of talent for the foil. As the play continued, surprise had been erased by dawning fear. He fenced with a master, a master who had held back, letting him expend all his power and skill in the opening feints and parries.

Carstairs raised his eyes for just a second from the flashing foils to meet his opponent's gaze. A shudder that had nothing to do with exhaustion streamed through him. He faced death—he saw it in the dandy's implacable gaze.

Pushed to the very edge of desperation, Carstairs attempted an elaborate feint in third, followed by a swift disengage, and for one thrilling second, as his foil thrust for the fop's heart, he thought he had succeeded. Suddenly, excruciating pain wrenched at his wrist and his foil, his only protection from death, flew from his grasp. It arched through the air to land far away.

Carstairs, his breathing ragged, froze as the dandy's sword point came to rest lightly at his throat, pressing against his adam's apple. "Be done with it for God's sake!" he rasped after a moment, terror clawing at his chest.

The tip of the blade dug in harder, then the pressure eased. The dandy sniffed. "Forsooth, is it not enough that you make me become overheated, but now you ask me to view the sight of blood as well? Really, that's doing it too brown. Now what I want of you, sir, is for you to back up—I wish to have a private word with you."

Carstairs, cold steel gently pricking at his throat, nodded, stepping back carefully. "Excuse us, gentlemen," Sir Horace called as they drew away from the surrounding crowd.

"Here now," Danford called. "This is irregular—"

"Let him be," an older man said. "Farouche won fairly. He has the right." The other men solemnly agreed and a deep silence fell on them as they peered into the darkness at the now-distant figures.

"This is far enough," Sir Horace said at last. "You may stop."

"What are you going to do?" Carstairs rasped. "If you're going to kill me, be quick about it."

"It would be my pleasure to oblige you, but then, alas, I would be forced to flee the country. Something I would not care to do. Travelling is so exhausting. And heaven only knows how I would find a decent tailor in those foreign parts. Therefore, it must be you who leaves the country."

"What?"

"I said, it is you who will leave the country. After all, it is apparent that you won't miss your tailor very much. I would prefer it if you leave tonight. I believe an extended trip—for at least a fortnight—would be sufficient."

"Why—why are you doing this?" Carstairs gasped, his mind numb.

"Why? My dear man, 'tis simple. You committed a crime that requires punishment. Though you chose to commit your crime in private, I prefer to administer the retribution in public, n'est-ce pas? You attempted to take by force that which was not yours, nor freely offered. Do you understand?"

"Yes," Carstairs said finally. "Yes, I understand."

"You caused a lady a great deal of pain and fear." His voice was strong in its condemnation.

"I did not mean to! I love her—I have always loved her."

"I know, else I would have killed you. Now, you will leave

242

town for an extended stay, never to contact or harass the lady in question again."

"But—" He made to object, his heart hurting in a new fashion. The foil's tip pressed in hard. "Yes, very well!"

"And you will never speak of this to anyone—ever. That includes her uncle. Do I have your word on this?"

Carstairs nodded solemnly. "You have my word."

"Very well," Sir Horace said, lowering his foil. "Let us go."

Edward watched, amazed, as the dandy turned and minced from him. In a flash of insight, he called out after the tulip. "You love her, don't you?"

Sir Horace halted, turning to look at him. It seemed as if he would not answer, but then he said, softly, "Only a fool loves his enemy."

He turned and was gone.

The Duke of Rendon leaned back in his leather chair and tapped his fingers gently upon his desk. "An amazing story you tell me. I find it difficult to credit."

"So does everyone," Danford said, "but I saw it with my own eyes. The dandy bested Edward—I'd never seen the likes of his swordplay before."

The duke's fingers ceased their tapping. "What do you mean? What style was it?"

"It is difficult to say—"

"Was it English? French?"

Danford frowned. "Both—as well as Italian. The combinations he used were incredible—he used a parry-riposte-disengage I could not even fathom."

"Indeed? Strange . . . I have known of one man whose style was such—but he is dead." His eyes narrowed. "You say the fop would not kill Edward?"

Danford grinned. "He balked at the last minute. Said he couldn't stand the sight of blood."

"What?"

"It's true. I think the man mad myself; faith, he threw a

drink in Edward's face only because Edward commented on his coat—it was pink satin, mind you."

Everleigh frowned. "Where is Edward now?"

"He set sail. Said he wouldn't remain to be the laughing-stock of town."

"Understandable—to be bested by such a one. Tell me, Danford, do you think any man could be so frivolous as Farouche and yet possess such a skill at the duel?"

"The man's a damned eccentric, that's what he is," Danford snorted in contempt.

"A very unusual eccentric. He may bear watching."

"That man-milliner? The only thing you'll discover about him is that he practices the foils because it allows him to play with the men."

"Perhaps . . . now, if you'll excuse me, I fear I have much to do."

"Certainly. I'm off to the club. I only wanted to warn you that Edward's bolted."

"I thank you. And Danford, could you please ask Filton to send my ward to me?"

"Of course."

It was but a few minutes before Chlorinda, dressed in a morning gown of the palest blue, softly entered the room at her uncle's command. "Filton said you wished to speak with me, uncle?"

"Yes, my dear—please, come in and have a seat. I thought it best if I were the first to inform you of what has transpired, before the gossips tell you."

"Tell me what?" she asked worriedly.

"It is about Edward Carstairs. He fought a duel and fled the country last night."

"Oh, no—" Chlorinda's thoughts immediately raced to a figure in a garden who had told her he would take care of Edward. "Did Edward kill him—I mean, his opponent?"

"No. His opponent bested him."

"He did?" she asked excitedly, and the duke looked at her in surprise. She quickly attempted to hide her relief. "Who—who did he fight?" She knew it was foolish to ask, for if it had been her stranger she would not know it. She did not know his name.

"Sir Horace Farouche."

Chlorinda couldn't help but stare. "Sir Horace Farouche? But that is impossible."

"Why do you say that?"

"Why—why—because—" Her uncle trained piercing eyes on her. "He's—he's such a fop. And everyone knows that Edward is one of the finest swordsmen in all of England."

"Yes—well, it seems this fop possesses even greater skill. Tell me, my dear, has this Sir Horace ever given you reason to believe he is anything other than what he appears to be?"

"What do you mean?"

"In your meetings with him, has he ever displayed other surprising talents or manly skills? Perhaps his fiancée has mentioned something of the sort."

"Manly skills?" Chlorinda asked hesitantly, her face becoming unaccountably flushed.

"Yes. His skill with the sword, for example. Where does it come from? Does he indulge in any of the other manly sports? Perhaps he has shown you a strength of character not obvious to the public eye."

"No, never," Chlorinda said swiftly. "He is exactly what he appears: a vain, malicious, mincing fop! Why, he's never—" She froze. What was she saying? She had seen another side of the man. One that had compelled her, and yet frightened her in some manner. She looked up to find her uncle's gaze upon her; she could not tell him that story. "He has never shown me any other side than what everyone else has seen."

"Are you sure? It appeared you had thought of something."

"No, indeed not," Chlorinda said quickly. "Why, the man cares for nought but his attire."

"And fencing, it would seem. It is a small wonder he was not afraid to challenge Edward."

Chlorinda gasped. "Edward didn't challenge Sir

Horace?"

"Yes, but it was Farouche who started it."

"But that doesn't make sense," Chlorinda said. "I could see why Edward would challenge him—but for Sir Horace to challenge Edward?"

"Why would Edward wish to challenge Farouche?" Everleigh asked sharply.

Chlorinda looked up and gulped. What was she doing? "I—I only meant that—well, I just never thought Sir Horace was the type of man to—to start a fight with anyone."

"Well, he did. He threw a drink in Edward's face."

"He did?"

"It seems Edward insulted his jacket."

Chlorinda stared. Then her lips twitched. "He threw a drink in Edward's face because Edward insulted his jacket?"

"That is what I said."

Chlorinda could not stifle it. She giggled. "Oh, my." Her hand flew to her mouth to muffle her outright laughter.

"You find that amusing?"

"Er . . . no." She attempted a serious face. "Perhaps Edward should not have insulted Sir Farouche's coat; he—he takes his dress—er, rather seriously."

"So it seems," Everleigh said sternly as a giggle escaped Chlorinda again. "Very well, that is all. You may leave. I have wasted too much time over this farce as it is."

"Yes, uncle," Chlorinda replied, quick to leave her guardian's presence before she disgraced herself once more. She simply could not contain her desire to laugh. This particular story tickled her senses. Oh, what a pleasure it would be to call a man out for nothing more than insulting one's dress. Faith, if the ladies were to behave so, they would be dashing drinks in each other's faces every hour upon the hour! She giggled all the more.

Sir Horace was not aware of it, but he had unwittingly rendered her a great service; Edward Carstairs was no longer in the country and she need not fear him. She laughed once more. She could imagine Sir Horace's dismay if he ever discovered that he had aided her to such a great extent. Yes, indeed, he would be aghast . . .

At the same moment that morning, in another fine London residence, another interview ensued — only the lady involved in this meeting was not sitting quietly. She was pacing the breakfast room's carpet while her brother sipped tea and partook of a hearty breakfast.

"I cannot credit it," Julia said, spinning on her heels. "How could you have been so rash? Were you moon-mad last night? First you announce to the world that we are engaged, then you fight a duel and send your man fleeing the country. You have certainly dipped us in the scandal broth now! I don't think this is what Sir would like!"

Armand shrugged. "I only did what I thought necessary. We were caught in a compromising position; we wouldn't want Miranda's reputation sullied, would we? Besides, the mammoth seemed suspicious that we were plotting something — I thought a marriage t'would be the better choice."

"Perhaps. And is that why you fought a duel with Carstairs?"

"No." Armand shrugged coolly. "The man irritated me, 'tis all. Would you care for some eggs? Cook has surpassed herself this morning."

"So have you. Faith, what caused you to do it? As if having all of England after us is not enough, you needs must go and fight a duel with The Hawk's closest friend!"

"Do not fear," Armand said as he applied preserves to a scone with a critical eye. "Carstairs has left the country and will not contact Everleigh."

Julia stopped her pacing and sat down beside Armand. "Dearest, what are you doing? Can you not tell me the truth?"

Armand studied his scone. "We have orange marmalade this morning. Are you sure you wouldn't care for any?"

Julia clasped Armand's hand as he replaced the knife.

"Please, Armand. We have never kept any secrets from each other before."

Armand finally looked up, his eyes hooded. "This has nothing to do with our operation. It is nothing to concern yourself over."

"But you are unhappy—that is my concern. Are you sure I cannot help?"

Her brother smiled wryly. "I am afraid not. It is only this interminable waiting that has me blue-devilled." Julia studied him and then sighed.

There was a scratch at the door and Lady Daniella's butler, Hinton, entered. In service since Lord Quentin's time, Hinton was a trusted employee. "Miss Miranda, this letter has arrived for you. The messenger awaits a reply."

"Strange . . ." She took the missive and broke the seal.

"Is it from Sir?" Armand asked.

"No," she replied as she read the contents of the note:

We must continue our discussion from last night. Where shall we meet today, and when? Do not ignore my request.

Lord S.

Request? More like demand, Julia thought angrily. She bit her lip; she dared not avoid him. Armand had created enough of a stir last evening that she daren't have Jason causing more. "Please bring me paper and ink, Hinton."

"What is it?" Armand asked as Hinton left.

"It is from the Earl of Wynhaven. He wishes to call upon me."

"Why would he want to do that?"

"I don't know . . . perhaps he wishes to congratulate me on our engagement. Faith, but things become more complicated."

"It's not so complicated. Refuse the man. He is engaged to Chlorinda now, so it will be best not to deal with him any further."

"Look who is cautioning me to be circumspect," Julia

said tartly. She was saved from further questioning by Hinton's return; looking guiltily at Armand, she took the writing materials from the butler. Luckily, Armand appeared immersed in the newspaper. She quickly scrawled. "Be prepared for your distant and widowed relative to arrive at noon." She did not sign it, but folded it and returned it to Hinton, who left to deliver it to the awaiting messenger.

Armand lowered his paper. "You are frowning. Is the earl a possible threat?"

"Nothing I cannot handle," Julia said with false bravado.

"There is something you aren't telling me."

Julia could not meet his eye. "It is nothing of significance—I do believe I would care for that marmalade after all. You say the eggs are fine this morning?"

Armand looked at her, his eyes narrowing. Then he smiled. "Very well, I deserved that. Would you care for bacon, too?"

"Yes, I believe I would," Julia said gratefully.

Brother and sister then busied themselves with their breakfasts. It was as Julia was lifting a forkful of eggs to her mouth that she stopped, slowly lowering them to the plate again. "You will tell me the truth if I can be of service, won't you, dear?"

Armand grinned. "Only if you tell me as well."

Julia nodded, then she frowned. "But who is going to tell Sir?"

Armand suddenly choked on his food. He reached desperately for his water glass and took a long draught. Then he looked at her. "I don't know about you, but I'm not intending to tell him anything I don't have to."

Julia laughed, finally picking up her fork again. "I agree with you there. Let's hope it never comes to that."

"My, lord, Mrs. Hargrave has arrived," Jason's butler said quietly upon entering the earl's personal library.

Jason glanced up from the book he was reading beside

the fire. "Mrs. Hargrave?" He paused and then smiled. "Ah, yes, Mrs. Hargrave, the bereaved relative I told you about."

"Certainly." The butler nodded gravely. "She is on your mother's side."

"On my mother's side?"

"Yes, the Hargraves are from your mother's branch." Canton delivered it as a statement, rather than a question; he was well aware of every family delineation of the Stanton dynasty.

"Why—yes, so they are," Jason said after a second. "Would you prepare for the luncheon in here, as I ordered, then please leave us in quiet. I would not wish for a disturbance of any kind."

Canton had earlier frowned upon Jason's irregular request, but now he nodded in approval. "A wise decision, my lord. The dear lady seems quite distraught, but I am sure you will be able to assist her, will you not?"

Jason's hand froze in mid-air as he reached to set his book down. A definite note of fatherly concern laced Canton's voice, a note rarely bestowed upon visitors to the earl's abode. "Of course I will, Canton. You may depend on that." With that assurance, the butler bowed and departed.

The next time the door to the library opened, it was to admit a lady in deepest mourning. Her costly dress was black, as was the full veil that flowed from her black hat and hid her face. She held a dainty black handkerchief, which she gently twisted as she entered with subdued grace.

"Thank you for your kindness, Canton," a soft and wistful voice murmured from behind the veil.

"Think nothing of it, madam," the butler said indulgently. "You may trust my lord to take care of you." He left, closing the door gently.

Jason could understand Canton's unusual behavior; the willowy woman in black seemed to evoke a man's tenderest chivalry. He rose and walked over to the silent figure. "Welcome to my humble home, madam."

"Said the spider to the fly?" The voice was still gentle, but suddenly questioning.

Jason smiled. "For shame. Did you not hear Canton say that you can trust me to take care of you?"

"Yes, but in what manner? That is my question."

"I only wish to assist a poor, bereaved widow—on my mother's side, of course. You don't miss a trick, do you?"

She shrugged. "It was easy enough to look up, and details matter."

"I quite agree," Jason said as he lifted the heavy black veil from the "widow's" face. His breathing ceased for a moment.

Deep brown eyes gazed up at him from under flaring brows. Her skin was clear and luminous, devoid of any artifice. It was the true face of the woman, a face Jason still dreamed of in the dark hours. "I am truly honored," he said huskily.

Julia flushed and looked away. She could not say what had driven her to meet Jason as herself. Except for the dark veil and the brown wig, she had not been able to bring herself to masquerade any further. "I was—pressed—to invent another character at such short notice."

"I am glad of it. Your true face is more beautiful by far than any character you could create."

"You've only seen Granny and Miranda, who are certainly not the most comely of my characters. I can do much better."

"You could never create a more beautiful face than your own," Jason said quietly. Julia's eyes widened and he swiftly spun away from her. He walked over to the windows of the library and began drawing the thick velvet curtains.

"What are you doing?"

"Wait." A knock sounded at the door and Julia hastily drew her veil over her face as Jason bade them to enter.

Canton arrived with two maids, carrying platters. Next, three heavily-laden footmen staggered in. Julia watched in amazement as they proceeded to set down a table and bedeck it with crystal and china. She smothered a laugh as

251

another little maid toddled in with a fine bottle of wine and placed it lovingly upon the crowded table.

"I thought perhaps you would care for a light nuncheon, Mrs. Hargrave," Jason said solemnly. "One must keep up one's strength, after all, even in one's time of bereavement."

"Yes, I—I see I must keep up my strength," Julia said forcefully as she watched Canton place two long candles upon the table and light them. "This is far more than I expected, my lord. Far too thoughtful of you—."

"It was my pleasure, madam," Jason smiled. "My only wish is to make you as comfortable as possible."

"Indeed?"

"Will there be anything else, my lord?" Canton asked, after surveying the table with pride.

"No, that will be all."

"I should hope so," Julia murmured under her breath.

Canton bowed. "I hope you will enjoy the nuncheon, Mrs. Hargrave."

Silence filled the room after the butler left. Julia lifted her veil and trod softly over to survey the impressive array. Delicate pheasant steamed in its platter, silver glittering in the candlelight. "I marvel that Canton would dare leave a grieving widow in your care with such a display as this."

"Why ever not? You're a relative—on my mother's side, no less." Then he laughed. "In fact, you have evidently won Canton's heart. The candles were his idea."

"And the wine? Was that the maids' idea?"

"No, it was mine. Though now I wish I had ordered champagne." He walked over to the door and locked it.

"Why did you do that?" Julia asked suspiciously.

"Calm yourself. I am merely locking out all intruders."

"And not locking me in?"

"Of course not. I know how skittish you are, sprite."

"And I'll be more skittish, for this hints of seduction."

"Don't be afraid. I have no plans to attack your virtue," Jason said whimsically, walking back to her. He reached out and gently lifted the veil from Julia's face. "Only to attack your honesty a little." She stepped back at this.

"No—don't move," he said. His fingers slid up to pull the hairpins from her wig. He had it off in a second, while Julia watched him with wide, wary eyes. "Come now, sprite, you are looking at me as if I am something dangerous, when you know I am not. You have always been one turn ahead of me, haven't you?" Julia swallowed as he reached over and fluffed out her silver hair. "It is such a pity you cover such fascinating hair." He fingered a curl. "When will your masquerade stop that we may always see these curls?"

The question finally penetrated Julia's befuddled mind, and she pulled back from him swiftly. "Nice try, my lord, but you will not seduce any answers from me."

Jason gazed at her intently, then laughed. "Lord, sprite, don't be so cruel. I'm a new hand at this game after all."

"Indeed?" Julia looked pointedly at the table. "You seem very experienced to me."

"Anyone can set a table—but come, let us eat."

Julia stared at him suspiciously, but then she relented. "Very well." She sat in the chair Jason so solicitously held out for her. "I would not want Canton upset that his efforts went to waste."

"And not one care for me—correct, sprite?" Jason said with good humor and smoky eyes as he joined her at the table.

"You are quiet capable of taking care of yourself. Besides, it is not I who needs must care for you—that is your fiancée's duty."

"As it is *your* fiancé's duty. Does he know what an onerous task he is setting himself?"

"I do not think he considers it as such," Julia said tightly.

"But of course not. He does not know that you are not the buffle-headed Miranda, does he?"

Julia was caught. If she admitted Sir Horace knew of her masquerade, it would incriminate Armand in Jason's eyes. "I do not care to talk on that matter. Only suffice it to say that I will tell Sir Horace when necessary. I am not an adventuress; I will not hurt him."

"So you say."

"I will make Sir Horace an excellent wife!"

"And will he make you an excellent husband? Somehow I cannot envision him strewing rose petals across your boudoir or kissing the hem of your dress. Now, I can readily see him kissing the hem of his own jacket—but not of your dress."

Julia flushed. "Do not be ridiculous."

"Is that not what you wanted in a marriage? I distinctly remember you saying that."

"I believe, my lord, those were Granny's words, not mine."

"Ah, then that is not what you want in a marriage?"

"I only said that—or Granny only said that—to prove a point. Marriage should have passion and not be just a convenience."

"And you possess this sort of passion for Sir Horace?"

Julia looked at his amused expression and swallowed hard. "That is personal. Let us not talk on this anymore."

"Has he ever seen the real you, sprite? Does he know your hair is silver and that you are a fine shot with a pistol?"

"I do not care to discuss this."

"You promised to tell me last night."

Julia's chin shot up and she stared at him defiantly. "Then I lied."

Jason, his eyes mild but curiously determined, rose from the table and came silently over to her. She was forced to lean back to look up at him.

"What are you doing? I haven't finished this lovely meal you prepared for me."

"Yes, you have," he said firmly. "I see that food does not loosen your tongue: therefore we shall move on." He reached down and grasped her hand.

"Move on? To what?" Julia's voice faltered as he pulled her to a standing position.

"I have failed at attacking your honesty; let us try another tack. Your virtue."

254

"But you said you wouldn't!"

"Then *I* lied," he retorted, mimicking the very tones she had used before.

"Don't be silly," Julia said, attempting to pull away. "What do you hope to gain by this?"

Jason's eyes glinted and he shook his head. "That is far too naive a question for you to be asking."

"I mean—"

"I know what you mean." He smiled and drew her into his arms. "I told you I want the truth. And there is always a certain amount of truth," he murmured, lowering his lips almost to hers, "in a kiss." His mouth covered hers and an instant flame flared within Julia. After a searing moment, she jerked back. "Stop it!"

"See, there was a little truth there. You do not kiss like a woman who has given her heart to another. But . . ." he said, reaching to draw her back into his arms, "I'm not so certain . . ."

"All right." Julia breathed quickly, backing away while keeping a hand firm against his chest lest he pull her to him. "I—I don't love Sir Horace—in a passionate way. He's my brother—I mean, I think of him as a brother." She gulped as Jason inexorably shortened the space between them, his arms securing her firmly.

"Are you going to marry him?" his lips came down, not on her lips as she had expected, but rather they grazed her cheek and then continued to her ear.

"No," Julia murmured without thinking, too enthralled with that pleasurable liberty. "But—but I would never have denied his proposal in public. I'll stay affianced to him until we—I mean—until it won't be so embarrassing for him."

Jason's head came up so he could look Julia in the eye. She sighed in relief and slight regret that he had stopped nuzzling her ear. "You are being honest?" the earl asked.

"Yes."

He smiled. "Yet another truth appears. We progress."

"Certainly far enough," Julia said tightly. "Now, I think

it is time for me to go."

"Not yet. I need to know one more thing."

"What?" Julia asked nervously, for his eyes had darkened.

"A question that has haunted me since we first met."

"Y-yes?"

"What kind of woman are you, sprite? Who are you?"

Julia shook her head slowly, trying to pull away. "How can I answer that? There are certain things I can't tell you."

"Then don't tell me. Let me find out—you'll not have to speak a word." Julia wasn't allowed a word, for with stunning speed, he scooped her up into his arms and carried her to the sofa.

"What are you doing?" she gasped as he dropped her unceremoniously upon the upholstery.

"Hush, darling, you don't have to say a word." Julia tried to rise but he pushed her back down until he was atop her—or halfway atop her, for a man of his height was far too large for the sofa. However, neither participant noticed whether they were on the sofa or not, for Jason immediately set about kissing Julia with a passion that defied such irrelevancies.

For a time, Julia could not deny the pleasure of Jason's touch, which brought her body to a quivery life of its own. Yet, regardless of the passion, the passion that was not hers alone, her mind recognized Jason's motives and her heart cried out. She slid her hand into his hair and, with a viciousness born of hurt, she jerked hard, not only snapping his head away from hers, but eliciting a small groan from him.

"Cad," she spat, whirling into a slapping fury. With emotion-ridden force, she shoved him back and he fell to the floor with a crash. "You despicable—"

"Cad," Jason supplied. Unbelievably, a lazy grin crossed his face as he sat, sprawled on the floor. "I certainly know what kind of woman you are now."

"And I know what kind of man you are," Julia retorted, springing from the sofa. It cut her deeply that the man she had come to trust had treated her this way and was still smiling about it. She swiftly sidestepped him and rushed to the door. it was not until she grabbed the knob and turned it that she remembered and her back stiffened. "Unlock this door."

"Not yet," Jason said, rising.

"Yes, now!" She turned to him with seething anger.

"You forgot something." He walked over and picked up her wig.

"Damn!" Julia muttered, and darted over to grab it from him. Her hands shook as she attempted to place the wig properly.

"Allow me," Jason said quietly, gently setting it straight. Julia stood before him, mute with anger. "You are not going to trust me after this, are you?"

"No. I was a fool to have trusted you."

"Perhaps now you can understand my confusion regarding you." He leaned over and picked up her veil. "Yet now I trust you all the more." He placed the veil's hat upon her head.

"You had better not from now on!"

Jason merely chuckled. "Until we meet again, sprite." He lowered her veil and handed her her reticule. She felt thankful for the veil, which covered her face as Jason walked her to the door. She waited in silence as he unlocked it.

"Goodbye, Mrs. Hargrave," Jason said solemnly as he opened the door. "Only remember that I will be only too glad to assist you in this difficult time."

"Thank you, my lord," Julia said coolly as they entered the hall and discovered Canton standing at his post. The butler went swiftly to open the foyer door. "I am sure the 'assistance' you have already offered me will be more than I will ever desire."

"Think nothing of it," Jason said with an innocent face. "It was truly my pleasure." A hiss came from Julia before she exited the house and descended the steps.

Canton closed the door promptly and turned to Jason. "I shall have the repast removed on the instant, my lord. I hope the lady enjoyed it."

"What?"

"I hope the lady enjoyed the nuncheon. Was it prepared to her liking?"

A slight smile hovered over Jason's lips. "I cannot say—she did not eat much."

"Quite understandable in her saddened state. Such a shame. She seems to be a fine lady."

"Yes, I think she is," Jason said. "I do believe she is."

Chapter Fourteen

Discoveries

There were times — not many, but they were there — when Julia wished she had not been reared as a spy, wished she had learned sewing and the pianoforte and married a fat, balding squire, and led quiet life where a crisis would have been nothing more than an undercooked meal or a child's toothache. Tonight was such a night, for she sat at the Vauxville Gardens dining at the Duke of Rendon's party, a party to celebrate the Earl of Wynhaven's betrothal to Chlorinda, as well as hers to Armand.

She could barely taste the famous paper-thin slices of ham as she watched not only Rendon, but the Earl of Wynhaven as well. She found it difficult to determine which man engendered more anxiety within her. She noted Armand, too, was toying with his food, while the discussion revolved about the impending nuptials of the two couples. Lady Daniella and Mrs. Bendley seemed to be the only ones talking.

Looking at her, Armand smiled slightly and raised a hand to his lips as if to suppress a yawn. Julia, knowing full well that Rendon watched Armand tonight with particular interest, kicked Armand under the table and frowned.

"Are we perhaps boring you, Sir Horace?" the duke

259

asked.

Armand smiled benignly. "Forsooth, no, not at all, your grace. A thousand apologies for my teensy faux pas—indeed, I find the talk of bridals, above all things, intriguing. Unfortunately, I suffered a slightly more fatiguing evening than common last night—but it is of no significance, I assure you."

There was a pause at this, for though everyone there knew of Armand's evening, as did every gossip in town, no one had considered it a topic for polite discussion.

"Fatiguing?" the duke queried, his brow rising. He frowned forbiddingly at Chlorinda, who had choked at Armand's words and appeared to fall into a coughing fit. "Is that what you call it?"

"Yes," Armand replied without batting a lash. "But please, please, do not let my meager enervation deter us from the far more important discussion of what our ladies shall wear upon their wedding. S'truth, I fear, I am most anxt over the matter. It rends my poor withers, yes, it does. My sweet Miranda here believes she would care for a wedding dress of white with lace. Now I truly think, yes, most positively think, that nothing would serve her but perhaps a cream, not a true, harsh white—and perhaps seed pearls? Discreetly employed, mind you, nothing in excess, lest you say it would overpower my dear love. But the color of the dress itself? Hmm? A taxing riddle—white or cream? What do you think, your grace?" Armand leaned forward in serious anticipation of Rendon's next pronouncement.

Rendon only stared. "I am sure I couldn't say."

"Ah, me, I quite agree." Armand sighed, leaning back in dejection. "It is a soul-searching question that one would hesitate to answer without the deepest consideration. But never fear, I am sure with much more thought we shall hit upon the most superior of choices. Of more import, a subject about which I am all curiosity, is the question of when you mean to hold Miss Chlorinda's and Stanton's engagement ball? Unless, that is, it is too bold of me to ask?"

"No, it isn't," Rendon said stiffly. "I intend to hold their engagement ball the same night that the Prince bestows the Landreth lands upon me."

"Forsooth." Armand clapped his hands together while the rest of the table appeared stunned and speechless. "You, sir, are an absolute marvel, a master of cunning indeed."

"I beg your pardon?" Rendon's eyes narrowed.

"Come now, you naughty man, confess. You intend to steal everyone's thunder, don't you? Yours will throw every other event into the shade. None will be able to rival it! B'Gad's!" Armand turned a bright and challenging gaze toward Chlorinda, who sat as if frozen. "Aren't you the most fortunate of fortunates, Madame, to possess such a man as your uncle? Your betrothal will be the social exploit of the year—nay, of the century. Of course, it means you must wait until those nasty traitors are apprehended before joining hands with your 'beloved,' but surely the wait will be all worth while."

"Yes, of course," Chlorinda murmured softly. She glanced hesitantly toward Jason. "If it is acceptable with you, my lord."

"I assure you, Lord Stanton," Rendon said, smiling, "it will not be a long wait."

"Of course," Jason nodded, his expression unreadable.

Julia was so deeply involved in the conversation that she screamed in utter shock when a large body suddenly crashed against her chair, rocking her and the table. She heard a loud "Excushe me," as she futilely snatched at her tottering wine glass. It capsized and the red liquid rivered onto her dress. She gazed up through everyone's attentions to discover a flashily dressed sailor well into his altitudes, swaying precariously next to her. "Excushe me, Lady," the drunk repeated. Though his eyes were very watery, they were also very blue—and familiar. They were the eyes of her beloved sire.

"Here, here, misshy, let me help," he slurred. He

grabbed up her napkin and ineffectually swiped at her stained dress.

"Gadshounds, you clod," Armand yelped. "Watch what you are about. You'll but rub the stain in all the more."

"Freddee!" a petite lady shrilled out in a French accent, advancing on the group with her impatient eye trained upon the drunk. She was dressed in a virulent cherry-striped gown that shrieked as much as she did. "Come. I wish to see the fireworks." She seized his arm and yanked determinedly.

"Moment, love. Gotta help thish lady," Julia's father shouted and flung the little woman off. She cursed with Gallic fervor as she reeled and lost her balance. Jason arose adroitly and caught her about the waist, spinning her around and saving her from an ignoble fall.

"Tiens," the little woman said breathlessly, looking up in awe as he held her, "but you are grandiose."

Julia's father, as Freddy, desisted in his ruthless scrubbing of Julia's gown and barked irately, "Sheree, stop that, you trollop!"

Sheree gave Jason a flirtatious wink and then shrugged sadly. "Alas, he is a very jealous man." She disengaged from Jason and with surprising grace curtsied low to him, exposing much of her small but fine bosom to the company. "I thank you, kind, kind sir." She attempted to rise from her curtsy when, apparently, her heel snagged in her dress, for she teetered once again. Jason failed to save her this time and she fell backward—directly into Rendon's lap.

There were no flirtatious winks or gracious gestures this time. Sheree looked into Rendon's cold and disdainful eyes and screamed in horror.

"Freddee" responded with astonishing speed for such an inebriated fellow. He was beside the trembling and shrieking Sheree within an instant and had her jerked from Rendon's lap and safely enveloped within his arms even more swiftly. "Keep yer bloody hands off her, Gov," he growled as his little lady wound her arms tightly about him and hid her head upon his shoulder.

"I had no intention of molesting the—this female," Rendon said, slowly rising. "Now, sir, you will leave immediately. This is a private party."

The drunk, still hugging the petite woman, looked blearily around at the mesmerized group. "You call this private? 'Tain't what I calls private, is it, Sheree?" He rendored a healthy pat upon her posterior.

Sheree, evidently calmed from her shock, suddenly giggled. "Oooh, no, Freddee."

He chuckled. "Come on, we ain't seeing no fireworks, we're going to the long walk."

Sheree squealed in delight and the couple meandered off, billing and cooing, not giving the amazed table watching them a backward glance.

"Zounds," Armand exclaimed. "The gall of the man. He utterly destroys my sweet Miranda's dress, then walks off to dally with his *chére* as if nought is wrong. Unbelievable. Such gaucheness from the lower classes. I cannot for the life of me understand why their mothers simply don't murder them at birth and have done with it. Faith!"

"Would some water take it out?" Julia asked, crossing her eyes as she studied the red stain on her front.

"Water? By the saints, that will be useless," Armand exclaimed. "But now, vinegar—yes! Ah, brilliant me, vinegar will do the trick. Do not fear, there is hope after all!" He rose and extended an imperious hand to Julia. "Come, my beloved, we daren't waste a minute more—nay, not even a second. We must find vinegar!"

"Very well, Sir Horace," Julia said with a sigh, rising. "If you think it might help." They, too, wandered from the table, Armand tut-tutting as they went.

"My," Lady Daniella said, her voice husky with amusement, "you do supply the best of entertainments, Converse."

"I find no humor in this situation. The management shall hear of this," Rendon said, his voice icy.

263

"I believe the fireworks are about to begin," Chlorinda said softly, a hesitant eye on the grim duke.

"Indeed, shall we go?" Jason asked, rising swiftly.

"I suppose we should," Lady Daniella said. "Though I make no doubt we have already witnessed the best display of the evening. It is always so crowded at the fireworks."

"Then allow Mrs. Bendley to go with the children," Rendon said, leaning back. "We may finish our meal, preferably with no more interruptions."

"Enjoy yourselves," Lady Daniella called as Jason and Chlorinda left quickly, Mrs. Bendley trailing behind them. "Perhaps they will be able to join up with Sir Horace and Miranda—after Sir Horace has acquired some vinegar, that is."

"You amaze me, Daniella," Rendon said, his voice low. "How could you dare to foist that girl upon the public?"

Lady Daniella's hand froze as she reached for her glass of wine. "What do you mean?"

"Your *protégé,* of course, this Miranda. How could you have introduced her to the *ton?* She is a half-wit! Why, her sense is no greater than that of those two drunken idiots who interrupted our party."

"You might be right." Lady Daniella sipped her wine. "But she's of good birth, Converse, that I assure you. She may be an unusual debutante—quite unconventional, at that—but she is vastly amusing, do you not agree?"

"No, I do not."

"You do not seem to find anything amusing tonight, do you? You lack a sense of humor, I fear."

"Mine is a more serious nature, it would seem," he said stiffly, then his eyes became intense. "Even now, I worry over our nation's welfare."

"Ah, yes—the hunt for Landreth's children. You can't receive the lands until they are found, can you?"

He studied her, his hand toying with the stem of his wine glass. "You would not know where they are, would you, Daniella?"

Lady Daniella laughed, setting her glass down. "Lud,

Converse, if I did, I certainly would not tell you." She looked him directly in the eye. "But no, I haven't heard from them. Why should I? Now I might have heard from their father, for old times' sake, but he is dead, isn't he? No," she said, looking away from him, "I am no longer in the world of intrigue. I haven't been since Quentin's death."

"You should have married me, Daniella," Rendon said softly.

Daniella controlled the shiver that passed through her at his words. "but I didn't," she said succinctly. "And I was happy with Quentin, very happy, despite the many uncertainties that came with his way of life."

"He asked for danger," Rendon said coolly.

"Sometimes," Lady Daniella said, her eyes darkening. "And sometimes it was foisted upon him. Now," she said, rising, "I believe I have changed my mind and would care to see the fireworks after all."

"Certainly." Rendon rose and bowed. "I would be pleased to accompany you."

In the darkest corner of the long walk, a man put a protective arm about a woman.

"Are you all right?" Landreth asked quietly.

"Yes," Jeanne nodded. "Forgive me, I am an imbecile to have behaved that way. Only that man—when he touched me . . ." She shuddered.

Landreth chuckled. "No, never a pleasant prospect. Imagine Rendon's chagrin if he ever discovers you had landed right in his lap after all his searching."

"That man would never feel chagrin. He is a monster."

"Does that mean you will help? You have seen him; you are the only one who can identify him as The Hawk, and as the man who has framed us."

Jeanne pulled back from him, turning away. "No, I will not help you. I—I told you that before. There is no doubt that it is he. I have come here and done what you wished, seen him once again. But I will do no more."

Landreth sighed. "Very well. I thank you for that much."

"May we leave now?" Jeanne said in a small voice.

"No, the children will be along soon."

Jeanne turned and stared. "The children?"

"Yes," Robert said, his eye trained upon her closely. "I was not sure they would be here with him tonight, so I did not tell you. The lady I spilled the drink upon and the rather flamboyantly-dressed man with her are my children."

Jeanne flushed. "You could have told me. You only said we were to make positive the man I saw with Paul was The Hawk."

"I did not wish to increase your stage fright."

"Mon Dieu," Jeanne said, a comical look of dismay crossing her face. "What will they think of me? They will think me a tart!"

"They will think you splendid. It is not as if their guises are any more flattering—a moment." Landreth raised his hand for silence. "Someone comes."

"Voyens, what do we do?" She whispered.

"Play our parts, of course." Landreth swept Jeanne quickly into his arms and before she could inquire further, he bent and kissed her. Her fingers balled into a fist, ready to cuff, when suddenly she remembered her role. She allowed herself to relax into his embrace. All thoughts of her role melted away, however, in the heat of the passion he ignited within her. Her fingers unfurled and entwined themselves in Landreth's hair as she stood upon tiptoe to kiss him more deeply. He responded by lifting her off the ground as he melded her shorter frame to the long length of his.

"Aha, here is the buffoon who spoilt your dress, Miranda," a foppish voice observed in amusement. "He evidently seeks to disarrange yet another's clothing."

Landreth tensed and lifted his head, loosening his grip on Jeanne. She, stunned and unable to speak, slid down slowly until her feet touched the ground. Blushing, she stared foolishly at Landreth. He returned her gaze with an odd, unsettled expression of his own. Then he deliberately set her free and turned to the man and woman observing them with keen interest. "Hello, my dears. It is good to see you two."

"Even if we interrupt?" Armand asked dryly.

Jeanne flushed and Landreth smiled. "We were expecting you. Children, this is Jeanne—she is here possibly to help us."

"Yes, yes," Jeanne said swiftly, embarrassed at what the two must think. "I am not what I seem. I am perfectly respectable, not a—a trollop. I only play the role, non?"

"Yes, we see," Armand said gravely, approaching and lifting her hand for a graceful kiss. "And if you can help us, we will be ever grateful."

Jeanne flushed and then laughed. "The son, he is very much like his father, non?"

"True," Landreth said, casting Armand a frown. "Now enough of all this, I will explain about Jeanne later. What news have you to tell me? When I asked for you at Lady Daniella's, Hinton merely said that you would advise me. What have you two done? It must have been something, to make old Hinton so nervous."

Julia and Armand cast each other a glance, and Armand coughed. "Nothing much. But—but we are engaged."

"Tiens!" Jeanne breathed. "Is that not—what you call—eh, incest? You do much for your country—very much indeed."

"We do not intend to go through with it," Armand said quickly, observing his father's darkening brow.

"I certainly hope not. I do not care to give my only daughter away to my only son; I would certainly have idiots for grandchildren. How did this happen?"

"How else?" Armand snapped. "We were caught in the same situation as you were a few minutes ago. Only we were not kissing, I assure you, Madame," Armand said swiftly to Jeanne. "Merely appearing to do so. It is a common ploy of ours in such cases."

"So I see," Jeanne said, a lilt of laughter escaping. "You also learned it from your father." Then she frowned and cast Landreth an accusing look. "You did not tell me only to make it appear so instead of—you did not tell me."

Landreth looked disconcerted a moment, then said, "There was no time. And you, Madame, are not my sister." He turned his gaze back to Armand. "Anything else?"

"Not much," Julia said quietly. "We have befriended Chlorinda and I feel she is not party to Rendon's plans. I—I do not think she helped in Lord John's death. Armand thinks differently."

Landreth studied his silent and tense son. "What do you believe?"

"I think she was involved," Armand said, "but I do not believe she did it knowingly. I cannot fit the pieces together yet."

"Try," Landreth said. "It would ease my heart to know that she was not involved."

"I shall endeavor. I also have heard . . ."

Landreth raised his hand quickly. "Hush, someone is coming."

Jeanne, who had been listening wide-eyed, turned to him. "Bien, we all 'pretend' to kiss each other again, non?"

Landreth grinned and whispered, "No, it would be a positive orgy—too French, my dear. No, start a fight with Armand—he's called you a trollop!"

"Aha, we do it the English way! Make war, not love!" Jeanne spun on Armand, raised her voice in indignation, and shook a finger at him. "How dare you call me a whore? I am no such thing, you fancy little man!" She delivered a barrage of light slaps at Armand's chest.

Landreth, with a slight, approving chuckle, turned to

Julia and, leaning into her threateningly, bellowed, "I ain't paying fer no damn dress and that's that! Ye nobs are all the same!" Julia, in Miranda-like obtuseness, said she had not asked it but her fiancé had. Landreth bellowed all the more.

Alas, those who approached were not strangers who would have discovered an argument in progress and quickly left the scene. They were Jason and Chlorinda. The couple paused a moment and Chlorinda exclaimed, but then they both reacted in a very interesting manner.

Jason, seeing Landreth towering over Julia and threatening violence, strode up to him and spun him around. Landreth, not expecting this, was unprepared for the iron fist he received in his face. He went flying backward, dusting the ground with his inexpressibles. Julia exclaimed and threw herself in front of Jason to restrain him, for her enraged defender appeared to harbor every intention of continuing the attack.

Chlorinda, alas, had not observed her fiancé's efforts, for as Jason had instantly stepped toward Julia and Landreth, she had immediately sped toward Jeanne and Armand. Jeanne had achieved full Gallic steam by then, delivering a series of dramatic blows to the retreating Armand. Chlorinda, with unaccustomed grimness upon her fair face, maneuvered around Jeanne and grabbed at her shoulders in an attempt to tear her away from Armand, who was "Gadzooking" and "Gadshounding" in foppish defense. She secured only a handful of Jeanne's dress, however, and while she tugged in one direction, Jeanne surged forward in the other. Jeanne's cherry-striped dress might have been strong in color, but it was not so in construction. It ripped loudly, sending buttons to flight.

Jeanne gasped as she suddenly felt the night air upon her back and spun in outrage to discover an astonished and guilty Chlorinda, who still clutched a piece of cherry-striped material. "You tore my dress!" Jeanne accused, approaching her with unfeigned ire.

Armand, realizing the scene was out of control,

quickly encircled Jeanne's waist before she could reach Chlorinda.

"Let me go! She ripped the dress monsieur gave to me!" Jeanne fumed, an armful of struggling fury.

"You were attacking Sir Horace," Chlorinda returned tartly, her chin rising pugnaciously.

"Faith, ladies," Armand breathed in amused exasperation. "Let us not have a fight."

Chlorinda flushed at that and dropped the incriminating cloth. "I'm sorry—but I knew you would not strike a woman and—"

"—And came to my defense. Zounds," Armand said, "I am unmanned."

"Let me go, you pig," Jeanne exclaimed, though she had stopped struggling, for her attentions were now directed elsewhere. "That large man, he has hurt him!"

"Hurt who?" Armand asked, startled. He let loose of Jeanne, and all three turned to discover Landreth sprawled upon the ground, a rather curious expression upon his face, while Julia stood with her hands upon Jason's chest, speaking in low, desperate tones.

Jeanne ran to Robert and sank to the ground, wrapping her arms about him. "Are you all right? The rock—he did not hurt you?"

"Certainly not, ma chérie," Robert said softly, his eyes alight as he watched Julia haranguing Jason, both oblivious to the others. "The mountain merely grazed me. He appears a man of passion after all."

"Beast!" Jeanne called accusingly, finally gaining Jason's attention.

"I quite agree," Julia said angrily.

"Forgive me," Jason said, his features once again settling into an attitude of calm attentiveness. "It merely appeared that this man was accosting Miss Miranda and you, Sir Horace seemed—er preoccupied."

Armand turned a slight laugh into a cough and trotted up to them. "Indeed! Faith, to be attacked by a woman—egads, the unnatural thought of it. But your fiancée, bless her tender heart, came to my aid." He turned to Chlorinda with a quizzical look.

Feeling all eyes upon her, Chlorinda blushed red. "It was nothing."

"Nothing!" Jeanne said, hugging Robert closer. "She tore my dress."

"I fear we should be retreating—er, leaving." Armand said with amusement, looking to Jason. "Do not you agree, my dear man?"

"Most definitely, Sir Horace," Jason said. He looked at Julia with an impenetrable gaze and then turned to Chlorinda. "Shall we go, Miss Everleigh?"

"Certainly," Chlorinda agreed swiftly, refusing to meet anyone's eye. She quickly moved to take the arm Jason offered.

"Come, my love," Armand said haughtily. "let us leave this place—and these people!"

"Yes, begone with you," Robert said, blustering as Freddee once more. "Else I'll take the large toff on again, and this time he won't level me so fast."

"I would find that a pleasure," Jason said, a gleam of amusement in his eyes, "but I fear Miss Miranda would level us both for it, and she is not a lady to cross. Now we must leave—my fiancée's chaperone is sure to be looking for us."

"Tipped her the double, did you?" Robert asked appreciatively.

"Yes," Armand said, taking Julia's arm while nonchalantly leading the other couple away from the two upon the ground. "I did wonder where that good lady was."

"We lost her somewhere in the crowds at the fireworks," Jason said. "And is this where you hoped to find vinegar, Sir Horace?"

"Faith, man." Armand's voice could be heard as they disappeared down the dark path. "That churlish sailor may have been impossible, but I rather liked his one idea. My love and I are affianced, after all."

"And so are we," Chlorinda could be heard to respond

defensively.

Landreth chuckled, shaking his head. "That man Jason is interesting, and far too bright, I fear."

"He is a brute." Jeanne turned Landreth's face to hers to study it. "This bruise does not look good." She directed his head down, gently. "We must attend to it soon."

Landreth's gaze, with his head obediently bent, could only fall on Jeanne's shoulders, from which her ripped dress had slipped. His gaze travelled further down and he sighed. "Ah, I do believe we must attend to something much sooner—your neckline, ma belle. It is delectable but rather low-cut, even for Sheree."

Jeanne gasped and disentangled herself from Landreth in order to straighten her neckline. Landreth, sighing again, rose and extended his hand to Jeanne. "Come, my dear."

"But how," Jeanne said, rising and clutching her torn dress, "how am I to go anywhere like this?"

Landreth shrugged out of his jacket and placed it over her shoulders. "It clashes with your dress, but it will suffice. Come, before someone else appears."

"Yes, let us leave," Jeanne said apprehensively. "Me, I do not believe I can fight again."

"And with your dress the way it is, we dare not kiss again," Landreth said softly and took her arm to lead her down the path.

Chapter Fifteen
The Hawk Circles

Chlorinda frowned pettishly at her sewing. She had closeted herself within the parlor, spending the whole of the morning upon it. She had not, however, advanced much upon the piece, taking out a stitch for every two she put into the material. The dreadful scene the night before played itself over and over in her mind. She had actually engaged in a lowbrow fight and had even ripped another woman's dress. What had possessed her?

She sighed again. She did not know whether she was on her head or her heels. Things were happening too fast — an abduction, the stranger in the garden, her betrothal, and now a fight at Vauxhill. It was all so confusing, and so were her emotions, which seemed to sway in every direction like branches in the wind.

Distracted, she once again jabbed the needle through the cloth, stabbing her thumb in the process. She cried out in pain and pulled her thumb to her mouth.

"Are you all right?" a concerned voice asked huskily.

Chlorinda started in shock and looked up. She nearly fainted. She must be hallucinating, she told herself, for one of the men just then in her thoughts stood before her — her stranger. He sat as calmly as you could please upon the opposite settee. "You," she breathed. A joy shot through her, until reality asserted itself. "How did you get here?"

"Your butler let me in?" her stranger asked with a smile.

"No, he did not," Chlorinda accused. "He would have announced you otherwise. Filton always announces everyone."

"Very well. So Filton does not know of my presence. Why disturb him? I'm sure he's a very busy man."

"I didn't even hear the door."

"Nor did you hear me sit down." Her stranger grinned, his sparkling brown eyes encouraging her to smile. "You were very intent upon your sewing. Does it deserve the wrath you bent upon it?"

Chlorinda flushed. "You, sir, should have made me aware of your presence."

"What, and miss that remarkable little face that you were making? No, it was far too charming to do that."

"You still should have warned me, sir." Chlorinda's voice rose.

"Quietly, fair one. Since no one knows I am here, why inform them? I—er, also took the precaution of securing the door, if you don't mind."

"You locked the door?" Chlorinda asked in alarm and confusion.

"Please, do not be upset," her stranger said sincerely. " 'Tis only I wished to hold private conversation with you, and you must own that in the normal course of things, that would not be allowed. I promise, I will not importune you. I won't touch you. I merely desired to see you one more time."

"You did?" Chlorinda asked coolly, attempting not to be swayed by his flattery. "And why must it be in this clandestine manner? Why have I not seen you anywhere else? I've looked for you, but didn't see you." She turned away from the fire flooding her stranger's eyes.

"You did look?"

"Yes, I—I feared I had dreamed you that night."

"Then you did not consider it a nightmare?" he asked

in a self-deprecating tone. "I do not forgive myself being so ungentlemanly that night. I am not always so rude and rough."

"I see." Chlorinda swallowed, afraid to say any more, lest she betray her feelings. "Why—why then have you come?"

He shrugged, rising to study a painting upon the wall. "I merely came to inquire upon your welfare. I have heard that Edward Carstairs has quit town. Does that relieve you?"

"Yes, indeed it does," Chlorinda said softly, then bit her lip. "He engaged in a duel with—with a man, and left town directly."

"Ah, yes." The stranger's voice was muffled. "Sir Horace Farouche. I have seen the man about town, a fop of the first water."

"Do not say that," Chlorinda said angrily.

He turned from the painting, stunned. "You defend the poppinjay?"

"No—yes, in this case I do. I cannot fault his actions— why, how could I when he has been of service to me? I own he cares for naught but the cut of his jacket—which caused him to fight Edward—but nevertheless, he has been of service to me. And he—he can be kind, on occasion."

"It sounds as if you have a tender for him," the man said accusingly.

"Do not be ridiculous," Chlorinda said quickly, flushing. " 'Tis only that . . . I've come to respect the man."

Her stranger strode swiftly to her side. "I would have fought Carstairs myself if I could have, but—but Farouche beat me to the match."

"I understand," Chlorinda said, refusing to look at him.

"No, you don't," he said urgently. "Chlorinda, you must listen to me. You cannot, must not, fall in love with Sir Horace!"

Chlorinda's eyes flew to his indignantly. "I beg your pardon?"

"Damn," Her stranger said, running an agitated hand through his hair. "What a coil, that I would be jealous of Sir Horace." He took a quick turn about the room and returned to her, his eyes stern. "You must not fall in love with Sir Horace, you simply must not."

"Why not?" Chlorinda asked. "Is there something you know about him that I do not? Is he evil? Is he dangerous?"

"Evil?" He looked taken aback. "No, no. He does not mean to be. And dangerous? No, never to you. Only — only he is not exactly what he seems, and that's all I can tell you. Please only say that you are not in love with Sir Horace."

"I told you once that I was not in love with him," Chlorinda said very stiffly. "He is my best friend's fiancé, after all."

Her stranger forced a smile. "Of course. Forgive me." He returned softly to her side and sat. "Now that Edward Carstairs is gone, do you still have fears?"

Chlorinda, her eyes darkening, nodded her head slightly. "I still have the nightmares."

He lifted her hand in a gentle clasp and held it there when she would have pulled it back. "Tell me, fair fatality, what was it that your father and uncle fought over? How came you to be under your uncle's care rather than your father's?"

"I — I cannot tell you that," Chlorinda whispered, though her hand clasped his convulsively. "I — I am ashamed."

"Ashamed? Ashamed of what?"

"You may not know, but my father worked for the state department as my uncle does now. My father — was good friends with the traitor Landreth."

"And you were ashamed he knew him and thus left your father's house?" The stranger's voice was rigid.

276

"No, of course not, but my uncle had come to me with the—the news that my father had not only known Landreth but was in league with him—had aided him in treason."

"My God! You believed this of your own father?"

"The evidence was—was conclusive. The letters and papers were in my father's handwriting."

"Do you still have them? the stranger asked tensely.

"No, no, my uncle burned them for me."

"I see. You burned this so-called evidence and then deserted your father without even confronting him."

"I had to," Chlorinda said desperately. "Uncle promised me he would do anything he could to save my father, but it was important I go with him. He told me I—I could only be in the way of the escape plans he made for Father, that I could hinder it if I did not come with him."

"I see." The stranger's tone was grim. "Very clever. You were your father's pride, and your uncle took you with your permission."

"What do you mean?"

The stranger, his eyes cold granite, released her hand, stood, and walked away. Fear grew within her. "What do you mean?"

He turned to her, his gaze piercing. "Tell me this. The letter you sent your father asking him to come to you—did you write that with your uncle?"

Chlorinda's eyes fell. "No, that was of my own doing. My uncle did not wish me to write it."

"What?"

"After I had more time to think, I realized that—that I could not believe Father was a traitor, no matter the evidence. I went and told my uncle that my place was with my father, and I wished to return home. He told me he would not allow it—that my father was a traitor and that my returning home would interrupt a very delicate operation."

"I have no doubt."

277

"I—I felt so terrible. I wanted to talk to my father and couldn't wait as Uncle told me to do. I wrote my father to meet me at the back entrance."

"And how did you send it? Did you have your uncle frank it?"

"No. I told you Uncle did not approve. I sent it through my maid. If only I had not written that letter, my father would be alive today."

The stranger was suddenly there beside her, his firm hands upon her shoulders. "No," he said firmly, forcing her to look at him. "I am sure you eased your father's pain in letting him know you still believed in him and loved him. Never regret that. The rest—the accident—it was not your fault."

"I—I try and tell myself that. But always, I have this feeling that I could have prevented it. Something I failed to do. But I can't remember."

Strong, comforting arms enfolded her. "Hush. It was not your fault. Thank God it was not your fault."

Chlorinda pulled slightly away from him, searching his eyes desperately for reassurance. She found what she was looking for. A hesitant, grateful smile touched her lips and she leaned further into his comforting embrace. She felt so safe with him. She could not determine when, but slowly her need for comfort and safety streamed into a different yearning, one she could not totally define. Her stranger must have felt it, for he suddenly pulled back from her, a rueful smile on his lips.

"Forgive me, you must think me a cad. I promised you would be safe from me."

Chlorinda's lashes covered her eyes and she flushed. "But I do feel safe with you. It is not at all like the last time."

He laughed shakily. "I told you I am not always such an ill-mannered lout."

"I think," Chlorinda said shyly, "that it would be best if—if I were to see you in this vein a little more—so as

278

not to remember when you were—were rude."

She could hear her stranger catch his breath as he stared at her. Her own breath lodged within her throat at her temerity. "Indeed," the stranger said, a golden timbre to his voice. "I would that your remembrances of me would be kind." Slowly his lips touched hers. They were gentle and warm as they brushed over hers once and once again. His hand rose to trace the graceful line of her neck tenderly. It was the softest of touches and Chlorinda shivered. A deeper shiver coursed through her as his lips followed in the path of his hand, lighting gently at the hollow of her neck. She gasped slightly and his lips, as if in response, returned to hers. As in a memory, she opened her mouth to his. His lips were soft, his tongue but a feather-touch to hers. A warmth was tickling its way down her spine, and it was she who drew him nearer, searching for more closeness.

Finally, he pulled back. Both were shaking. "Forgive me, fair one. I have once again taken advantage."

"No. For you were not rude, or . . ."

"No." He rose abruptly. "I take advantage in a manner you could not fathom. I must leave. Could you please go and see if anyone is in the hall?"

Chlorinda only stared at him, bemused at the lightning change in him. Choking, she rose and went to the door. Unlocking it, she went into the hall to ensure no one was present. "There is no one about . . ." she reported as she returned, then stopped in confusion. The room was empty—her stranger had vanished. "Stranger?" she called softly, closing the door. She called again and garnered no reply.

He must have slid by her when she was in the hall, she realized. But why would he leave her without even a goodbye? What had she done? She flushed; would she ever see him again?

She sighed and sat down upon the settee again, absently picking up her sewing. Questions buzzed within her mind. Who was he? Why did he disappear like that? She stared at her sewing a moment, then Chlorinda Everleigh — quiet, biddable Chlorinda — lifted her sewing and threw it across the room with an astounding force.

Jeanne hummed softly as she pulled the last piece of clothing from the line and folded it into her basket. She picked up the basket and walked toward the house. She intended to bake a batch of biscuits next — her son's favorites. She wondered if Robert Landreth would like them as well. Then she smiled. Not in her wildest dreams would she have imagined that one day she would be planning to bake biscuits for the dangerous and daring Fox and debating if he would like them.

Then she frowned. What was she thinking? Robert Landreth was still a dangerous man, and she would do well to remember it — even if he did have a sweet tooth. It was her patriotic duty not to become attached to the man; he was merely a means of protection to her and her son. She had given her love to a spy once before, and now he was dead. She'd not do it again.

She shifted the wash basket to her other hip. No, she decided, she would not make any biscuits. Her eyes roamed the yard of the small farm where they presently resided. Not far from London, it was well off the main road, quiet and charming. Michael thrived on the country air, while John was a patient wonder with the boy. Jeanne opened the door to the cottage and exclaimed as Sophocles bounded up, rocking her on her feet. In one split second, Sophocles had snapped at the corner of a towel that hung over the basket's edge and jerked it away. He tore off with the towel, and it flapped beneath his teeth like a proud banner. Verbally maligning Sophocles, Jeanne dropped the basket and gave chase. "Sophocles, you wicked monster, give that towel back!"

She pursued him into the living room, attempting to

catch his waving tail. Sophocles, mischief shining in his mismatched orbs, tucked his tail in swiftly and she failed at every try. He then dove under the dining table and bolted out the other side. Jeanne circled after him and they went round and round as if the table were a maypole. Sophocles taunted Jeanne with a few good tosses of the towel, and Jeanne maligned not only Sophocles' heritage but that of his mother as well.

Either her insults must have reached him or Sophocles was growing dizzy, for he finally broke the cycle and bounded for the open living room. Jeanne, muttering dire threats, stalked him until she cornered him between the sofa and a chair. "Aha, you thief, you lowly towel-snatcher, I have you now. Give it over!"

Sophocles hesitated a moment, his eyes searching nervously, and then he leaped the chair, sending it crashing. "Sophocles!" Jeanne sputtered. "What is the matter with you! Look what you have done—*cochon!*"

She dashed after him, all the more determined to win back the towel. Sophocles, his nails scrabbling on the floors, swerved into the master chamber. Jeanne was in hot pursuit behind him. "Monster! I want that towel upon the instant!" Her words suddenly caught in her throat, and she skidded to a halt in dismay.

Robert Landreth stood before her, wet and naked except for the towel she had demanded be returned to her. He was just then securing it about his lean hips. Sophocles hunkered down quietly beside his master with what could only have been considered a canine smirk. "Mon Dieu!" Jeanne breathed.

Landreth looked up and cocked his brow. "Er, you wish this towel—and upon the instant?"

"Non, non," Jeanne stammered, flushing. "Please, keep the towel."

"Are you positive?" Landreth asked, his hands moving to the towel's knot.

Jeanne's eyes followed, mesmerized. "No, I do not

need it — I mean, I do not desire it — " She stammered and then blushed fiery red at what she had just said.

Landreth's chuckle drew her eyes back to his face and his features came into focus. She stared all the more. His face was, for once, clean-shaven, devoid of moustache or beard. It revealed the strength of his features as well as the set of his firm jaw. His hair, which she had seen in varying shades of brown and black, was silver — not white, not blond, but silver. "Your hair — " she whispered. "Is it real?"

"Yes, my own color. Do you not like it?"

Not like it? Jeanne could not draw her eyes away from it — or from him. Her husband Paul had been the true dark Frenchman, slender and much shorter. Landreth was tall and fair. Yes, his skin was fair, fairer than hers, but there was no impression of softness; the muscles rippling beneath belied it. Rather he reminded her of a Greek statue carved in white marble. Jean bit her lip, for she realized she was gaping at him the way a school girl would react to her first sight of a Greek art exhibit. She sternly collected her wits and performed a creditable shrug. "It is very English."

The blue in Landreth's eyes deepened, and he stepped toward her. "That is because I *am* English. Do you still detest the English so much?"

Jeanne looked down and shrugged again. "I did not say that."

"I would understand. Nanette could never like England. The only thing English she made an exception for was me."

Jeanne's eyes rose to his despite herself. "And so you lived your life in France and still worked for your own country?"

Landreth smiled gently. " 'Twas not difficult. I cared for France, also — just not its politics. Or Napoleon."

"Yes, Napoleon," Jeanne said sadly. "First, he led our men for France. Now, he leads them only for himself. So

282

many fine men dying just for him."

Landreth stepped even closer. "You do understand."

Jeanne's hand flew up to ward him off as her heart pounded. "B-but that does not mean I will help you, monsieur. Now—I—I think it best to go."

Landreth smiled. "Yes, one should never discuss politics in the bedroom. I am remiss."

Jeanne's eyes began to sparkle. "It shows your English nature, Fox. You English will talk politics anywhere."

Landreth chuckled and his hand rose to cup her chin. "Would you care to change the subject—to one more French, perhaps? Maybe we could lay our differences to rest, so to speak."

Jeanne trembled, and she quickly pulled his comforting hand from her face. "You truly are a Fox. I am going now—and we will never lay anything to rest, monsieur, so do not even think it." She backed away, and then her eyes fell to Sophocles, who had padded up to join them. "And you!" She shook a finger at the dog. "You are just as bad as your master. Next time ask for a towel, do not just grab it."

Sophocles tipped his large shaggy head to one side and barked. Jeanne shook her head sternly at him. Sophocles, tail thumping, cracked open his canines and with another joyful bark grabbed hold of the bottom of Landreth's towel. Before either Jeanne or Landreth could protest, he had snagged the covering away.

Jeanne had always thought Michelangelo's statue of David was beautiful. Now she knew that in her estimation, Robert Landreth surpassed that beauty. She breathed one more "Mon Dieu," dragged her gaze away, and sped from the bedroom. She reached the safety of the small parlor and collapsed upon the sofa, closing her eyes and gasping for breath. The heat of a blush ran through her. She had never been so embarrassed. She had never been so enthralled.

She felt a movement at her skirts, and her eyes snapped

283

open in wariness. It was but Sophocles—with the towel still dangling from between his teeth. He gazed at her in deep apology. He raised a large paw to rest on her and placed the towel in her lap as an offering. "What do I want with this towel now, imbecile?" Jeanne said in aggrieved tones. Sophocles whined. She sighed and picked up the damp towel. Suddenly, a smile transfigured her face, and she chuckled, holding the towel close. *"Bien, bien.* The Fox says you must learn everything you can about your enemy. Me, I think I know more about The Fox now than I did this morning." Her blush returned. "Much, much more."

A sharp rapping at the door drew her from her reverie. She arose from the sofa and cautiously walked to the door. What should she do? Surely if it was an enemy they would not be considerate enough to knock? "Who is it?" she demanded, twisting the towel in anticipation of an answer.

" 'Tis I, Sir Horace, with Miss Miranda and the Lady Daniella."

"Ah, the children," Jeanne breathed. She happily swung open the door. "Hello, hello." She waved the towel in excitement. "Do come in. Monsieur Landreth will be glad to see you, yes?"

"That remains to be seen, I am sure—Sheree." Armand smiled. "I mean Jeanne, is that correct?"

Jeanne flushed, ringing the towel in her hands. Soon Landreth would tell these charming children her last name, and who she really was. How would they react? "Yes, yes, that is correct." She coughed. "Monsieur will be here soon, I am sure. He is done with his bath now and—" She gasped, suddenly embarrassed to be holding the towel. She attempted to hide it unobtrusively behind her back. "I mean, I'm sure he's dressed by now . . ." She gasped again. "Peste', I mean—"

"She means I am here." Landreth strolled into the tiny parlor, impeccably dressed and obviously at his ease.

"Hello, my children. I am glad you could make it. I fear we have much to discuss, do we not?"

"Don't we though?" Armand cast an amused glance at the embarrassed Jeanne.

"Yes." Landreth chuckled, walking over to Jeanne, placing a supporting hand on her shoulder. "First, may I reintroduce this lady. She is Jeanne—Jeanne Lecroix, wife to Paul Lecroix."

All three visitors stared at her. It was Julia who spoke first, her eyes filling with warmth. "I am pleased to make your acquaintance, Mrs. Lecroix. I was sorry to hear of your husband's death; though we fought on separate sides, he was a fine agent."

"Thank you." Jeanne swallowed hard.

"Then there was something havey-cavey about Paul's involvement after all?" Armand asked intently.

"Yes," Landreth said. "And Jeanne here has had the rare but unenviable distinction of seeing Rendon as The Hawk, as well as hearing him plot with Paul to frame us."

"Huzza!" Armand said. "Here is the link! The link we have been looking for!"

"Faith," Julia said, looking at Jeanne with respect and concern. "And you are still alive."

"Your father, he outran The Hawk to me first and—ah, spirited me away."

Julia laughed knowingly. "Whether you wished it or not?"

"I find all this fascinating," Armand said. "You have been very busy, Sir."

"And so have you. Marrying each other is a notion I would never have thought of," Landreth said dryly. "I had always hoped you both would marry—but certainly not to each other."

It was Lady Daniella who answered, both brother and sister looking chagrined. "Never fear, Robert, the rig is moving along swimmingly. Why don't you three go and brew up your plots while Mrs. Lecroix and I have a coze? Or do you need her as well?"

"I certainly need her." Landreth's eyes were intent upon Jeanne. "But the lady is unwilling to become involved."

"And could you blame her?" Lady Daniella replied. "Now go — I'm sure your plotting will only cause her and me to shake like blancmanges."

"I very much doubt it," Landreth said good-naturedly. "You have far too much love for intrigue and Jeanne is simply bloodthirsty. Come children, let us discuss your wedding. Is the date set as yet? I do hope we clear up this matter before I am forced to walk you down the aisle."

The family left laughing and Lady Daniella merely shook her head in mild reproof. "Come, let us go sit." Both ladies entered the parlor and seated themselves comfortably. Lady Daniella gave Jeanne an appraising look and chuckled. "They are too much sometimes, are they not?"

Jeanne laughed. "But you enjoy it, non?"

"Ah, you have found me out," Lady Daniella said with a charming smile. "Indeed, I haven't had as much fun since my husband and Robert worked together."

"Your husband? He was also a —"

"A spy." Lady Daniella nodded pleasantly. "As was yours. I sympathize with you on his passing. Although you live with the expectation of their death, when you truly lose them, it is not the same, is it?"

"No, no, it isn't." Jeanne bit her lip and looked away; the other woman's understanding had brought tears very close to the surface. She shrugged then, to cover her emotions. "But he died doing his work — he would not have had it any other way."

"So did my Quentin," Lady Daniella said. "We women who are foolish enough to love a spy must face the fact that we will probably be left to survive the best we can. Only Robert has outlived his Nanette."

"How did she die?"

"She died of a fever—very unexpected. Robert always said it was wrong that she went before him. But I am not sure. He was everything to Nanette; at least Robert still has his work, and his children, of course."

"You—you do not think he will remarry?" Jeanne asked as nonchalantly as she could.

"No, I highly doubt it." Lady Daniella laughed, still caught up in memories. "Though many women would like to have him. He does attract them so effortlessly. The man is blessed with a dangerous amount of charm, don't you think?" She turned her eyes towards Jeanne and caught a glimpse of Jeanne's emotions; her smile faded. "Oh my dear, how careless of me. I have upset you."

"Non, non," Jeanne said quickly. "If I am upset, it is only because it is so sad, non?"

Lady Daniella studied her closely, but Jeanne had herself well in hand, smothering her betraying emotions. Jeanne smiled at Lady Daniella and evidently succeeded in fooling her, for the lady sighed in relief. "Thank heavens. I feared you had formed an attachment for Robert, and I could not truthfully say that he will ever fall in love again."

"You do not need to explain, for I—I loved my Paul the same way as he did his Nanette," Jeanne said, even as she realized she lied. "But still, it is sad to think of these things, non?"

"Then let us not think of them," Lady Daniella said quickly. "Instead, tell me how Robert found you."

"He found me at the bakery. I thought him a ghost at first."

"It must have been a shock."

"Yes. I threw bread at him."

Lady Daniella's eyes widened. "You threw bread at Robert?"

"And the bread knife, of course."

"But of course." Both women started laughing. They were still having a fine time discussing how Landreth had

287

spirited Jeanne away when he and his children returned.

"I see you two are enjoying each other," Landreth said with a smile.

"Yes, indeed," Lady Daniella said, rising. "Jeanne has been regaling me with the story of her life since you entered it. You are fortunate she is a woman of such courage and strength. Many other women would have broken under the strain, or shot you dead for your bullying."

"As I told my children, Jeanne is a jewel of great price," Landreth said. He looked toward Armand. "We shall be in contact again. I do not care for the sound of this clerk. It could be a trap."

Armand shrugged. "Do we have anything else to go upon?"

Landreth gazed at Jeanne and then looked back. "No, I guess not. I still say it is best to leave the matter alone. I do not like the feel of it."

"Yes, Sir," Armand nodded after a moment. "We will not rendezvous with him."

"Excellent," Landreth answered as they walked toward the door. They said their goodbyes and Landreth closed the door, deep in meditation.

Jeanne studied him and then asked, in slight embarrassment and pleasure, "You told your children I am a jewel?"

Landreth's blue eyes grew intense as he looked at her. "I did, and you are." Jeanne's eyes lit up, and she blushed. Then he continued, "I still believe you are the only answer to bringing Rendon down. You are the witness we need."

The light disappeared from Jeanne's eyes, and her fists clenched. The man enraged her. "Ah, is that why I am your jewel? Because I may become an informer? Well, I told you before and I will tell you again, I will not aid you in this."

He stepped toward her in confusion. "You are angry. I'm sorry if I made you so."

288

Jeanne turned her back on him quickly, hiding her face. "I have no doubt, for you do not want this jewel of yours to refuse to help in your plotting, non?"

He placed his hand upon her shoulder. "We cannot play this game much longer, Jeanne, not without Rendon discovering us."

"Game? That is all I am, is it not? A pawn in this game you are forever playing. No, monsieur, I am more than a pawn, I am a woman who must think of herself and her child."

"Jeanne, please. Armand has told me of a clerk who may have evidence against Rendon, but I feel it is a trap. I've dissuaded him from meeting with this clerk, but he grows restless. I cannot be assured he will listen to me."

"He is like his father then, non?"

"Perhaps, but if you could be persuaded to come forward with your story, we could end all this."

"No." Jeanne turned around, refusing to allow his closeness to affect her. "I cannot do that. You are so charming and clever Fox; you will discover a way without my help. This I believe—you can do without me."

His hand tightened on her shoulder. "I cannot do it without you." He shook her ever so lightly. "I need you, don't you understand?"

Jeanne's breath caught at his vehemence. "You need me for what?"

His fingers dug into her shoulder convulsively. "I need you because—because—dammit!" He pulled in his breath, his face suddenly devoid of emotion. "I have no other way to bring Rendon down! I can't find another way!"

Voyens, you English, you are so very obtuse. And yet you think you know everything. You have only to ask politely, is that not so?" Jeanne was seething. "Well, I will not help you. Go find yourself another jewel." She jerked from his grasp and crossed her arms defiantly.

"What is it you want, Jeanne?" Landreth's voice rang

out passionately. "How can I persuade you to help? Could I pay you? I could ensure your security and Michael's for years to come."

Jeanne stared at him, then jeered. "The mighty Fox stoops to bribery! Is that the best you can do, Reynard?"

He stepped closer, his eyes darkening. "Think on it, Jeanne. The quicker you help me, the safer you will be, and the quicker you will be able to go back to your precious France. You will never have to deal with us dreaded English again. Is that what you would like? I promise you, I will take you there immediately after you help us."

Jeanne suddenly laughed. She stepped closer until they were eye to eye. "I do not intend to tell you what it would take for me to help you. You are the almighty spy, the one who always knows his enemy. You find out what my price is, monsieur, for you are not anywhere near it."

Landreth stiffened and his jaw tightened. "Then there is a price?"

"I am a jewel of great price, am I not?" Jeanne mocked. "Well, monsieur, you must pay more for that jewel than you expect." She tapped him on the chest once and turned, humming as she left. She cast a laughing glance over her shoulder. Landreth was still frozen in place, a look of sheer consternation upon his face. "Ha!" she laughed, and resumed her humming.

Jason was admitted into the Duke of Rendon's spacious study. It was a graciously appointed room with a gleam of polished wood and the smell of books. A large Adams fireplace ranged the opposite wall. A magnificent picture of a very distinguished gentleman hung above it. The man in the painting was indeed handsome, but the most startling aspect of the portrait was the blue of his eyes. Jason halted a moment to study the features.

"That was my late brother, Lord John," Rendon's voice said from behind him. Jason turned to discover the duke rising from his desk. "This was his favorite room."

"I can see why," Jason smiled, walking over and taking the seat before the desk. "It's clear Chlorinda inherited his eyes."

"Yes, indeed." Rendon sighed. "I see her eyes and think of my brother; I miss him very much."

"I can understand," Jason said, surprised to hear such a sentiment from the normally contained Rendon.

"Here are the settlement papers to my niece's marriage if you would care to study them," Rendon went on smoothly, handing the papers across the desk.

Jason reached for them. As he took them, they upset a small miniature on the side of the desk. Jason, murmuring an apology, moved to right the oval, but froze on the spot. The miniature was of a beautiful young girl with white skin, laughing brown eyes under dark, flared brows, and a coil of silver hair at the nape of her slender neck. The dress was demure white and blue lace, obviously of French design. Without thinking, Jason picked up the picture and leaned back, mesmerized. "Who is she?" he asked quietly.

"The traitor Julia Landreth." Jason's hand clutched the miniature and he looked at Rendon. The duke's eyes were piercing. "Why, have you seen her, perhaps?"

Jason hesitated a moment. "Only in my dreams." With an effort of will he returned the miniature to Rendon's desk. "She's very beautiful."

"Her beauty has caused many men to betray their country. Even nobles and princes have vied for her easy favors. Yet they say she has caused the deaths of as many men as she's taken to her bed."

"Indeed . . . with those stunning looks, one would think she would be easy to locate."

"No, for she is the mistress of disguise," Rendon returned quickly, "just as her sire was before her. She can create any character, any of which a man cannot resist."

Jason thought of Granny and choked back a laugh—

though, in truth, in his heart he did not feel like laughing. "She looks young in the picture. How old is she now?"

"Twenty-five, and steeped in depravity already," Rendon said. "Raised in espionage from the age of three."

I have been blessed to do and see things other women would never dream of doing, his sprite had said once. No, other women were not trained in espionage, Jason thought—nor were they traitors. Jason's eyes rose to meet Rendon's, which were studying him closely. He forced a lazy smile. "Then let us hope you capture her soon, my lord. That such a she-devil lives is beyond belief."

"Yes, we believed we'd killed her and her brother, but alas, they escaped," Rendon said, shaking his head.

"What do you mean, 'we'?" Jason asked, eyes sharpening.

Rendon paused, then smiled. "Why, we of the department. We knew they were traitors just like their father, long before the public knew. Now, if you would care to look over these contract papers?"

Jason nodded quickly, and for the next half-hour they dealt only with the settlement terms. Once the papers were signed, Jason took his leave of Rendon and returned to his house. Two hours later, he began making his routine social calls. One call, however, was to the Lady Daniella Manchester and her charge, Melinda Waverly.

Julia started up from the letter she was writing as the parlor door flew open. Jason Stanton, Earl of Wynhaven, stood upon the threshold, filling the doorway with his large frame. Hinton could barely be seen behind him. Julia looked into the iced hazel of Jason's eyes and knew. Her stomach turned over, and she said, as calmly as she could, "It is perfectly all right, Hinton. I will see the earl."

"Are you positive, Miss Miranda?" Coming from behind Jason, Hinton's voice was slightly muffled.

"Yes," she said numbly. "Please leave us."

She heard Hinton's consent, then Jason entered the room fully, closing the door behind him. Julia felt as if she had been shut in with a Bengal tiger. She breathed in deeply and said, "And how are you today, my lord?"

He trod silently up to her, and Julia had to force herself not to back away. "I would ask the same of you, Miss Landreth." Julia twitched and turned pale; even though she'd known, it still hurt to hear him speak her real name with such contempt.

"I—I believe I do not feel quite the thing," Julia choked out, and went to sit in a chair away from the towering Jason.

"I wouldn't imagine you would. Now that I know the full truth about you."

"Do you, my lord?" Julia's hand tightened into a claw on the chair's arm. "Or do you just think you know the truth?"

"You deny that you are Julia Landreth."

Her chin lifted. "No, no, I do not."

"Ah, then you deny being a traitor to England?"

"Yes, I do."

"Clever to the last. Rendon said you were wily."

"Rendon?" Julia gasped. "You—you heard this from Rendon?"

"Yes. I would say he is a reliable source, would you not?"

"No, I would not," Julia said, shaking her head softly. "How—how long has he known that I am here?"

Julia rose, crossing to him with despair in her eyes. "Please, at least let me know the time I have left."

It was Jason who backed away now. "My God, so beautiful and so deceptive. Rendon said you've caused the deaths of as many men as you've taken to your bed."

Julia gasped, a fire finally entering her eyes. "And do you believe that? Did I kill you? Did I not save you

293

rather than leave you to die out in the wilderness?"

"Yes, but I wish to God you had left me to take my chances. I do not care to be beholden to a traitoress," Jason said, his words cutting like knives. "But I am, and therefore I did not tell Rendon I knew you. I had seen a miniature upon his desk and asked who you were. He told me."

"A miniature? It must be the one I sent Lord John," she said quietly. She looked into Jason's angry eyes and, unable to face his contempt, she crossed to the fireplace to grip the mantel for support. She forced herself to think. "So you haven't told Rendon who I am? What are you going to do?"

"So cool, aren't you? Still trying to protect your traitorous hide."

"A traitor's death is not a pretty one. And it is particularly galling when you are not a traitor."

Jason's laugh cracked through the room. "Ha! So you are not a spy, then. Just a sweet innocent, running away from her evil uncle."

"No, I am a spy." Julia tried to hide her trembling. "But only for England. I'm no traitor—Rendon is the traitor."

"Damn you, woman!" Jason growled. In two steps he was upon her, grasping her shoulders and pinning her to the mantel. "Do not lie any more!"

"I do not! Rendon is the traitor, and he's framed us for his crimes!"

"Stop it!" Jason shook her harshly. "I will not believe any more of your stories! Do you know how it feels," He said, drawing her close to him, forcing her to look into his scalding eyes, "to have fought for one's country, to bear the scars for one's country, and then to discover one has protected its enemy? Do you know how it feels?"

Julia's hands unwittingly rose to his shoulders. "I am not England's enemy, Jason. You have done no wrong."

Jason held her close, and he looked as if he wanted to

believe her. Then his eyes hardened, and he dropped his hands from her shoulders as if he touched a brand, and spun away. "Damn you, woman," he said over his shoulders. "Damn you to hell . . . I will give you an hour. An hour to escape and then I will tell Rendon everything. I will put him on your trail as sure as the sun sets, so do not waste the time you have, vixen. Find yourself a hole."

Julia straightened. An hour would be nothing. It would not be enough time to warn her father and Armand. It would destroy everything they had done. "No. I will not be hunted down again. I cannot do it again."

He turned. "Then face your traitor's death, Miss Landreth."

"No." She said it softly, her eyes direct and determined. "You once made an oath to me. You promised you were mine, body and soul. Word of a Stanton." Jason stiffened and the cords on his neck tightened. "I call upon that oath now."

"I should kill you."

"Then do it now, for I will not relieve you from your oath."

He was silent. The room was charged with electricity, and Julia bit her lip so hard it bled. "What do you want from me?" he finally asked.

"You will tell no one who I am," Julia said, tears coming to her eyes. "You will allow this game to be played out to the end. That is all I ask."

"All you ask? It is too much."

"I ask it anyway. I want your word upon it."

"Very well. You have my word I will tell no one. But my debt is paid to you then."

"Yes—yes, it is. You will owe me nothing more. You will be freed from your debt." Jason nodded abruptly and turned to leave. Julia wanted to call out to him, wanted to plead with him to believe she was not a traitor, that he did not betray his country, but she could not. She let him walk away, closing the door upon her without another look. She went and sat upon the chair, pain frozen within her heart. The man she knew she loved thought her a traitor, and if Rendon won and she died, he would always think her so. She did not think she could bear it, and she prayed to God, prayed as she never had before.

Later that evening, Armand stopped before Julia's bedroom door and rapped lightly. "Julia, it is I."

"One moment," Julia's voice came from behind the door. She opened it slightly and Armand stepped in.

"I received your note. What is so important that—" Armand stopped in mid-sentence as he gained a clear view of Julia. She was rigged out in her Granny outfit with only the wig left to don. "Why are you dressed like that? We are to attend the Grearson ball this evening."

"I am not going to the ball," Julia said, adjusting her wig at the dresser.

"You're not?" Armand said courteously. He knew Julia's tone and didn't like it. "Where are you going?"

"I intend to meet our courier at the Shield and Arms to see if he has learned anything from that clerk about Rendon."

Armand sucked in his breath. "I thought we all decided that it was not wise and that we would let that lead die."

"I have decided otherwise. We cannot wait any longer, and any possible lead is important."

"Sir expressly told us not to. We should trust his instincts."

"I know, but—but I must try." Her voice shook.

"Why, my dear?" Armand walked up to her and studied her face in the mirror.

Julia's eyes met his in the glass; hers were painted. "I must. But I am the only one going. It should mitigate the danger."

Armand placed firm hands upon Julia's shoulders. "What is the matter? You know it's crazy. You yourself

296

said you did not like the feel of the whole thing."

"We must end this masquerade soon," Julia said tightly. "I am not sure how much time we have left."

"What do you mean?" Armand's voice was sharp.

Julia couldn't meet his eye. "Jason—Lord Stanton knows who I am."

"My God. How?"

"He—he saw a miniature on Rendon's desk. The one Lord John had. Rendon told him who I was." She hesitated. "And he had already seen through Miranda . . ."

"Then we have no time. We must decamp as soon as possible."

"No. I have his oath he will tell no one."

Armand's hands fell from her shoulders in surprise. "You have his oath?"

"Yes. I held him to the fact that I saved his life."

Armand whistled. "My God, Ju', you play with fire."

"I know. I believe he wanted to kill me before giving me the oath not to betray me."

Armand stared and laughed. "And he'll probably kill you for certain once he finds out you are not the traitor he thought you were."

Julia's smile was fragile. "I'd far rather have it that way. He—he thinks some dreadful things about me."

Armand's face turned sympathetic, and he came to kneel before her, his hand turning her chin so he could look at her. "And does it matter so much?" Julia could only nod mutely. "I see . . . sits the wind in that quarter. Well, then, we must be about exonerating ourselves. How—how long do you think Jason's honor will hold out?"

"I am not sure. That is why, if Jacob has any information tonight against Rendon, we need it."

"Very well. We may be setting our heads in the noose, but we'll go to the rendezvous."

"No, Armand. If it is a trap, it's better only one of us is caught."

"If it is a trap, it's better we are both there to help each other. You go with me, or not at all."

Julia studied Armand's face and sighed. "Very well. But you must hurry if we intend to catch Jacob."

The Shield and Arms was crowded, and amongst the roistering bodies, the silent old lady and seedy dockhand at the corner table could easily have been missed. The old lady, taking a sip from her tankard, leaned over to the man and said quietly, "Jacob's late."

"Yes. We give him a few more minutes, and then we leave, agreed?" The dockhand's eye roved the room nonchalantly, particularly the door. He stiffened then, and muttered an oath under his breath.

"What is it?" Julia asked. "Is it Jacob?"

"No, but if I am not mistaken it is our clerk."

"What? Impossible. Why do you think that?"

"How many clerks do you know that patronize this place? He's even carrying a damn satchel."

"My God." Julia turned her head slightly. She saw a small man, baldheaded with glasses, picking his finicky way through the crowd. She might as well have stared openly, for the rest of the rough clientele was doing so. "Yes, it's got to be him. What is going on?"

They saw the little man stop at a table and could hear him ask in a high, nervous voice for a man named Jacob. "Get him," Julia hissed quickly, "before he asks any more."

Armand was out of his chair even before she finished. He approached the little man and soon both were returning to the table.

"Who is this?" the little clerk asked suspiciously as he sat down and glared at Julia.

"Another friend of Jacob's," Armand said curtly. "Now order a drink, for God's sake."

"No. I don't intend to stay long."

298

"Why did you even come?"

The little man looked about nervously and leaned over to them. "Tell Jacob everything is off! I want the copies of the papers I wrote him back. Now. And if he tries to use the papers, I'll deny everything."

"Jacob is not here, as you can see," Armand said coolly, "but he'll be along shortly. You have the original papers, though?"

"Not any more. I burned them."

"You burned them? Why?" Julia asked sharply.

"Because I've decided against it, that's why." The little clerk twitched. "I know Rendon—"

"Shut up." Armand ordered. "Don't mention names."

The clerk drew back, offended. "Well, he's bad. And helping my country is a fine thing to do, but getting killed for it isn't worth it. Even the money Jacob offered isn't enough."

"Why? Do you think they are onto you?" Armand asked tensely.

The man shook his head. "No, and that's the way I want to keep it. I'm leaving London tonight. Disappearing. I'm not taking any chances."

"But don't you realize running will draw them to you?" Julia asked urgently.

"No, it won't. I told them I must visit my sick sister. I've got official leave."

"Let us help you," Armand said softly. "We can hide and protect you."

"Not on your life! I don't trust you either."

"You're in danger," Armand said. "We know how to protect you better than you do. You're an amateur against these men."

"I'll take my chances." The clerk stood quickly. "I'm not waiting for Jacob any more—you tell him what I told you! The deal is off." He clutched his satchel closer to his chest and left them quickly.

"What do you think?" Armand asked as he watched

the little clerk bob his way through the crowd. "The man is a fool."

"Yes, but we must leave. I don't like the fact that Jacob hasn't appeared."

"I know. Things are getting too warm. I do believe Sir Horace and Miranda should make their farewells to society. This could be potentially dangerous and I would not trust your mountain's patience any further either."

"Yes," Julia nodded, a pain shooting through her. "I don't think Sir will be happy with us when we tell him about this wild goose chase."

"Let us pray that's all it is. Now, we've allowed enough time to elapse. You go first."

Within a course of twenty minutes, two customers of the Shield and Arms departed its doors. The old lady turned to the left and toddled down the narrow street. The dockhand, when he followed later, turned to swagger to the right towards the wharves. Upon each departure, a shadow slipped from a single alleyway to trail far behind. Left behind in the alley was a sprawled body, still clutching a mangled passport and ripped satchel.

"You say she went into the back entrance to Lady Daniella Manchester's and did not return?" Rendon asked over his shoulder as he looked up at the large portrait of Lord John in his office.

"That's it." The shadow stood respectfully at attention behind him. "I figured the old woman most likely worked there, so I waited around until a maid came out from the house, and I asked her about the old woman. She said she couldn't be sure but she thought the old woman sometimes helped the Waverly girl—but not regularly. She's only seen the old woman once in a while.

"What'd she have to do with Landreth, I wonder?"

"Lady Daniella was a good friend of Landreth's, and no doubt would help his children as well. Though she denied it before, I have no doubt she could be aiding them."

A knock at the door disturbed the two men and another man entered at Rendon's command. "What do you have to report?" Rendon asked as the man took up a stance next to the other.

"I followed the man who met the clerk when Tom here followed the old lady."

"Yes? And?" Rendon asked with slight impatience.

"It stumps me, but the man there switched streets a couple o' times and then went inter this room at a tavern. I waited for him to come out, but the only bloke who came was this flash cull. So's I asked the landlord whose room it was, and he said it was a John Smith's room. So's after a while I still don't see the man come out of the room, so's I rather jimmied the lock and went in. Nobody was there. Room was clean as a whistle. No window, either, so's I don't know how the man got away. 'Twas queer."

Rendon stared at the man and then sighed. "Not really. The man that went into the room evidently exchanged clothes and dressed as the flash cull you saw. How did this man look? The flash cull?"

"A real Nancy, if you know what I mean. He wore paint, for God's sake. Had on pink and carried a hankie."

"Sir Horace," Rendon murmured. "No other man of the *ton* dresses like that." He stared off into space a moment, then tensed. "Yes, of course. Sir Horace is the man who met our clerk. And if that is so, considering what information our little clerk was trying to sell . . ." His eyes narrowed and a smile snaked across his lips. "Then, gentlemen, we have just uncovered the whereabouts of one Armand Landreth."

"What?" one of them asked, confusion upon his face. "How do you figure?"

Rendon's eyes turned cold. "Do not take your impertinence too far. Suffice to say I have had my eye upon Sir Horace for some time now. His skill with the foils is rare. This last piece of information solidifies my suspicions."

"Who's the old hag, then?" the other man asked. "What's he doing with an old woman? She can't be much use, after all."

Rendon smiled. "You cannot guess? Where Armand Landreth is, so will Julia Landreth be. They are a team. That old hag, as you call her, must be Julia Landreth." Rendon frowned. "She helps Miranda Waverly—no, bedamn, I would wager she *is* Miranda Waverly! That is why Daniella would sponsor such a fright. Why didn't I think of it before?

"Finally we have them, gentlemen. You have done excellent work and shall be rewarded. I shall take control from here."

Neither man chose to remain longer; the duke's ice-blue eyes seemed to glow with a cold malice.

Rendon, smiling, turned to the large portrait of his deceased brother. "Well, John, I do hope you can see this. As I hope Landreth can. His children will soon be joining you both in death. I'll own they were exceptionally cunning, just like their father—and so unlike you, who were such easy prey." He laughed, quietly exultant, and strode from the room.

Chapter Sixteen
Fox-Cubs At Bay

Lady Daniella's butler had been a faithful retainer to that good woman for years. He had been her husband's butler before that. When he heard a sharp rap upon the door in the late hours of the night, he went to peer out a small, unobtrusive window by the side of the door. It had been a few years since he had resorted to scanning the streets before admitting entrance, but since the arrival of Miranda Waverly, he had once again returned to his old routine—a routine he relished, for it reminded him of the good old days of adventure and spice.

His eyes widened and he whistled softly, however, when he discovered who his impatient guests were. He turned, only to gasp, for Tobias, the youngest and newest footman, had his hand upon the door, ready to open it to the awaiting entourage.

"Tobias, stop," Hinton hissed, speeding to the footman's side with more energy than dignity and jerking his hand from the doorknob. "What do you think you are doing?"

The young footman, startled and blushing, stammered, "I'm sorry, sir. I—I didn't know you was—were—here and the guests, they seemed real impatient like."

"But of course," Hinton sighed in exasperation as the rapping turned to steady pounding. "But the bloke—er, gentleman, can bloody well wait this time. Now please remove yourself from this hall, and never forget it is my duty to open the door and nobody else's. Is that clear?"

"Yes, sir." Tobias scurried from the hall, only too glad to escape Hinton's censure, and whoever pounded so imperatively outside.

Hinton had not turned from his place when lady Daniella entered the hall from the drawing room. "Hinton, pray tell, who is pounding so upon the door at this hour?"

Hinton cleared his throat. "It is the Duke of Rendon, ma'am, with a minor contingent of soldiers."

Lady Daniella looked startled at first, but then a slow smile crossed her lips. "Indeed? So Converse brings soldiers. Hold a minute, Hinton. Miranda is upstairs. I shall be down within the nonce."

"Certainly, my lady." Hinton bowed, but it was to thin air. Lady Daniella was already taking the stairs with such a sprightly air Hinton could not help but smile. She appeared as she had some thirty years before, when she had arrived as a bride in the house. Hinton shook himself from his reminiscing, however, and donned his most imposing and dignified butler's mien. Slowly, and with great ceremony, he unbolted the door and opened it. "Yes?" He looked down his nose at the covey of soldiers upon the door stoop.

The Duke of Rendon, who held center position, pushed Hinton aside rudely and strode into the hall, his eyes surveying the room coldly. "I wish to speak with Miss Miranda Waverly. You were quite a time answering the door—why?"

"I am sorry, sir. I was under instruction the ladies intended to retire early. I wasn't informed that they were expecting guests at this hour."

"They weren't." Everleigh smiled icily. "But we are here, and we will have words with them. It is upon official business."

"Hinton, who are you talking to?" Lady Daniella's voice could be heard before she appeared upon the stairs. "Converse," she said in surprise, drifting down the stairs with regal composure. "What brings you here at this hour—and with soldiers, as well?"

"We have come, my lady," Everleigh purred, "for Julia Landreth."

"Julia Landreth?" Her brows raised in query. "But isn't she the traitoress? Why would you come here?"

"The game is finished, Daniella. You know full well that Miranda Waverly is Julia Landreth."

Her ladyship stared at him as if he had just made a successful escape from Bedlam. "Miranda is—the Landreth woman?" She burst into laughter. "Converse, don't be ridiculous. Tottyheaded Miranda is Julia Landreth? You are roasting me. I love Miranda dearly, but not by any stretch of the imagination could one believe such a tarradiddle."

"I am not playing games, Daniella, so do not attempt to lie."

"My God." She widened her eyes in shock. "You are serious." She raised herself to her full height. "What gammon. I told you once before, Converse, that I didn't know anything about the Landreth chit, and for you to persist in this fashion, and bring soldiers, yet, into my home, is the outside of enough! I have been through with such cloak and dagger activities ever since Quentin passed away, and I will gladly prove it to you. I will bring Miranda down to you so you may speak to her yourself, and see what an impossibility your idea is." She lifted her skirts in majestic anger and stalked back up the stairs.

The soldiers watched the irate lady steam away and cast each other furtive, questioning glances. Everleigh, however, only curled his lip and turned to the silent Hinton. "Tell me, Hinton, were you aware your mistress was aiding and abetting a traitoress?"

"Sir, we harbor no traitoress. You know the mistress and master were ever loyal to the crown in their work—though there hasn't been any of that since the master passed on, God rest his soul."

"No?" Everleigh's lip curled.

"Converse!" Lady Daniella's voice expressed great agitation as she reappeared, rapidly treading the stairs. "I cannot find Miranda. She isn't in her room, she isn't anywhere—where could she be?"

The duke's face clouded. "Sergeant Halley, search the house immediately!"

"Yes, your grace." The sergeant nodded curtly and gestured to his men. They veered in various directions like so many ants from a hill.

"Converse, don't be so ridiculous," Lady Daniella said. "You surely don't believe Miranda's disappearance means she's the Landreth woman." At his steady stare, she moaned and swayed slightly. "No, oh dear God, no, she can't be!"

"Madame," Hinton cried, running to catch her as she swooned gracefully. He waved impatiently to one stray soldier and between them, they placed the slowly reviving woman in a chair.

"I'm all right," she said weakly after a moment. "I—I only felt faint . . . Miranda . . . Miranda could not be that awful woman . . . she simply couldn't be . . . But wherever is the dear child? It's not like her to—"

Her flutterings were interrupted by a shout and heavy feet pounding on the stairs. An excited sergeant and another soldier puffed into view. "Your grace, we've found this wig, and this paint box! There is every kind of masquerade paint in here!"

"What?" Lady Daniella sat up in shock, then leaned back with a cry. "Hinton, my smelling salts! It can't be! My sweet Miranda is the Landreth jade. But she couldn't be . . ." she repeated in such a pitiful voice that the sergeant flushed and cleared his throat in embarrassment. The other soldiers displayed equally sheepish sympathy for the grieving, distressed woman.

"I—I am sorry, Madame," the sergeant said, "but I fear 'tis so."

"Oh, no," she moaned. Actual tears welled from large, pained eyes, streaming down her face. "I cannot believe it. I have been betrayed—used—I presented her to the *ton*, guided her . . . oh, God," she wailed suddenly. "They'll think I meant to aid her—a traitoress!" She burst into great sobs then, bringing her hands up swiftly to hide her face.

"Now, now, Madame," Sergeant Halley said uncomfortably, "don't carry on so. The Landreth woman's known to be a great conniver. She's fooled more and better ones—beg your pardon, more knowledgeable ones, I meant to say—than you. We understand how she could have deceived you."

"You do?" Lady Daniella said pleadingly. "Oh, thank you—but how, how can I forgive myself? I introduced a traitoress to society—I helped her! My husband—he was such a loyal patriot, you know. He worked for the government—he must be turning in his grave." She burst forth in fresh sobs.

The sergeant reddened to beet hue. "Yes, my lady, I know. He was a great gent. We know that and I'm sure no one would ever think you would knowingly help a traitor. Would they, your grace?"

"I would believe she could," Everleigh said coldly.

Lady Daniella looked at him with brimming eyes. "Oh, Converse, how could you say such a dreadful thing? I know you disliked Quentin—and I know I turned down your proposal of marriage—" All the soldiers looked elsewhere about the room at this. "—But surely you could not accuse me of such a crime. Why, it was Lady Heartly herself who recommended Miranda—Julia Landreth—to me, and asked me to sponsor her." She looked woefully towards Sergeant Halley. "Sir, I promise you, I did not know. Lady Heartly could testify, too. I can—"

"Er, that won't be necessary, my lady," the sergeant said gruffly. "We understand how a lone widow like yourself could have been hoodwinked by such a hussy."

"My God," Rendon muttered in exasperation.

"It took us, who have experienced like, to even find this here evidence. It was tucked far away in a bottom compartment. I wouldn't expect an unsuspecting lady like yourself to catch on to that sort of stuff. And the traitoress is already gone—she's nowhere in the house, your grace," he added, turning to the duke.

Everleigh studied the rather determined sergeant's face. His gaze flicked to the embarrassed soldiers, then to Lady Daniella, who presented the perfect picture of weak, distressed womanhood. "Very well, let us waste no more time here. She has evidently escaped. Sergeant, take your men and join them with the others. I wish a moment with her ladyship to — comfort her."

The sergeant looked as if he wished to object, then nodded. "Yes, your grace. Madame," he said, nodding to Lady Daniella, "do not worry. We will find the traitoress who betrayed you, never fear."

"Oh, thank you!" She thanked every soldier before they left.

Everleigh waited until the door was shut, then crossed to Lady Daniella and handed her a handkerchief from his vest pocket. "That was a superb performance."

"Thank you, Converse." She took the handkerchief calmly. "I'm pleased you enjoyed it."

"How could I not? It was masterful. I assume Julia is still hidden somewhere in this house, since I have had it watched since she returned to it this evening."

"Have you? Every moment? Well, assume what you like, Converse." She wiped her eyes daintily and returned the handkerchief. "Thank you."

"You're welcome. You know I will find her, do you not? It makes no difference if she is here or elsewhere."

"Oh, I don't know." She smiled brightly. "I think you underestimate your lady, Converse. But then again, that has often been a failing of yours with women."

His jaw tensed. "I see I underestimated you, Daniella — but I did love you, you know?"

"Love me?" she said sharply, rising. "Was it love when you attempted to kill the man you knew my heart was given to? No, Converse, you have never loved anyone but yourself — and gold, perhaps. Now, would you please leave my house? I do not care to harbor a traitor, after all."

His hands clenched at his side. "I will capture the Landreth children. And you will see them die. Don't think you won't see it, Daniella."

"Will I? You are so very confident, aren't you, Converse—as you say, we shall see . . . Now, if you will please leave? I am exhausted from the shock of this evening."

"Very well. I believe it will quite amuse me to see you try and spirit Julia past me. I know she is here, and my men will be watching."

"Will they? I fear they will be quite bored, the poor dears." Lady Daniella waved him to the door and Everleigh merely laughed as he left.

"Shut the door, Hinton," Lady Daniella said promptly. "Let us hope we need not entertain any more sludge this evening." Turning, she picked up her skirts, and this time took the stairs slowly, in deep meditation.

She proceeded to her bedroom, and after closing and securing the door, went straight to the bed. It was a large fourposter, and not until she crawled down on all fours and pulled at the side did she discover it contained a hidden, wooden platform. The side swung down and Julia rolled out.

"This is magnificent," Julia breathed, rising to her feet. "Though highly unoriginal—hiding under the bed."

"Indeed," Lady Daniella laughed. "But Quentin always said there was no place he would liefer hide than in my bed." Then she blushed.

Julia chuckled and sat down upon the bed. "Now tell me, what happened?"

Lady Daniella's humor faded, and she sat down besides Julia with a serious face. She covered Julia's hand. "He knew everything, my dear. He knew you and Miranda were one and the same."

Julia sat quietly a moment, then said in a soft, lost voice, "It must have been Lord Stanton. He informed on us."

"I fear so. How else could the duke have been so very positive—and he was, condescendingly so. I had no need to feign shock when he asked for you by name."

Julia, her face pale, nodded and rose, pacing across the room with her back to her ladyship. "I should have known Jason would break his vow to me. His compliance was too much to ask."

"Perhaps it was not he. Converse could have discovered it some other way."

"No. You did not see Jason's face when I demanded he hold to his vow. I thought he'd kill me then." She sighed. "Evidently, he wished to wait until now."

"The game still isn't over—" Lady Daniella hesitated. "What will you do?"

"I must go and warn Armand."

"But you can't! I forgot to tell you—Converse is having the house watched. He knows you must be here."

"Damn him! But I must warn Armand—he is in danger!"

"Yes, but he can take care of himself. We must decide how to make your escape—but it cannot be upon this instant."

"But—"

"No, Julia, there is nothing else we can do—and you know that is true. We must pray to God that Armand is safe, and that we figure a way to help you escape."

Armand, travel bag in hand, opened the door from his room at the Putney. There, before him, his hand raised to knock, was an officer of the law, with two stalwart underlings behind him.

The officer, after a surprised moment, cleared his throat and asked gruffly, "Are you the man they call Sir Horace Farouche?"

The phrasing was not lost on Armand. "Yes," he replied with a sniff, "I am he—and who might you be? And who might these fine, gorgeous gentlemen behind you be?" He gave an effeminate wink that set the men squirming.

"I am Captain Thomas and I—"

"Heavens silly me, a man of rank and here I leave you standing in the hall. Come in, Captain, and your men also."

Before the captain could frame an answer, Armand turned and traipsed back to his room, setting his bag down and leaning nonchalantly upon his cane. "Do, do come into the room, gentlemen. The hall is so drafty, and there is always someone interrupting."

Captain Thomas, after a moment's cogitation, realized the truth of Armand's words—the Putney was a discreet hotel. His two beefy minions were much slower than he to enter, for Armand watched them both with an appreciative eye. They closed the door diffidently at their leader's signal; after a quick glance around the neat room, he straightened and said, "I am here to arrest you on charges of high treason, Armand Landreth." He watched Armand's reaction cautiously, and his face fell when Armand but smiled benevolently upon him.

"You called me Armand Landreth? Why would you think I am he? I am Farouche."

The captain stiffened. "We have knowledge you are one and the same; I am ordered to bring you in."

"Yet perhaps I am not he."

"It makes no difference to me. My orders are to bring you in, and that is what I will do."

"Very well," Armand sighed. "I only wished to determine the strength of your dedication to such a foolish cause." He twirled his cane and in a flash, it became a small sword. "Shall we discuss this further, Captain?"

Any passerby to Sir Horace's room would have likely stopped to listen as curses, thumps, and ominous bumps sounded from within, along with howls of pain and the crack of splintering wood. Fortunately, no one was passing at that late hour, and the sound soon halted.

The door opened and Sir Horace stepped forth. A dark cape swung from his shoulders and he employed his walking stick with one hand, shielding his other arm within his cloak. His wig, alas, was slightly disheveled, but nonetheless, he minced along in his usual strutting manner.

The door two rooms down opened and a sleepy, grizzled

311

head, topped by a wrinkled nightcap, popped out. "Eh, that you, Farouche? What's going on in your room down there?"

"Oh dear me, dear me, a thousand apologies, Sir Jasper. I fear I invited some chance acquaintances over, and they turned out not to be quite the thing—in their altitudes, and refusing to be quieted. I do beg your forgiveness."

"Hurmph, very well—just see it don't happen again. The missus and I don't rack up here to be awakened in the dead of the night by your wild parties."

"I assure you," Armand said fervently, "I cherish no desire to repeat the experience if I can possibly avoid it. I found the fellows rude and boorish."

Sir Jasper, after another gerumph and a stern gaze, nodded and closed the door.

Armand's shoulders slumped for a second, and he leaned heavily upon his cane. The hand beneath his cloak slipped out, blood-covered. Breathing deeply, Armand stiffened his spine, grasped his cane more tightly, and proceeded down the hall to the grand staircase. He paused at the head of the stairs, looking down. Two officers paused at the foot, looking up.

"S'death, but I am a popular fellow tonight," he muttered.

His unadoring fans, after a brief hesitation, charged up the stairs. Armand remained poised until the first of them came level with him. His cane snaked out to rap the approaching man smack in his teeth. The man's head snapped back, and he lost his balance. He fell backward into his crony, and soon both men were a rolling mass of arms and legs, bumping their way back down the stairs.

"Tsk, such clutter," Armand sighed in disapproval. Throwing back his cape, he smoothly mounted the gleaming side banister and slid down. As he glided past the entangled men, descending in a much slower and more painful manner, he called out cheerfully, "Toodles, old chaps!" He reached the bottom of the stairs in record time and dismounted with an ease that would have engendered deep envy in any schoolboy's heart. He wasted no time in observing if anyone in the lobby applauded his feat, but barrelled towards the front door, and freedom.

He skidded to a halt in the middle of the lobby's large, marble floor as two officers entered by that door. "Persistent devils," he murmured, falling into a defensive stance, quickly unsheathing his sword-cane. "Very well, have at it gentlemen — faith!" Suddenly more men appeared, coming from every direction.

A saner man might have laid down his sword at this out-numbered juncture, but Armand merely shrugged and, with an unholy howl and his sword flashing, charged the men. Surrounded by so much flesh, Armand slashed his mark across his foes. Indeed, the hotel clerk later said the gentle-man's sword was an awesome sight, and the avenging angel Gabriel couldn't have done no better.

But alas, numbers are numbers; soon, Armand was but one fallen, huddled shape amongst a group of wounded, hostile men. One man with a gash across his forehead was giving Armand a heavy kick when a quiet, authoritative voice sounded from the door. "Stop. I want him alive, not dead."

The Duke of Rendon slowly approached, flanked by his own men. The others fell back from his cold, aristocratic presence. Everleigh halted before the fallen man, studying him. "Turn him over."

One man reached down and rolled the still body onto its back. Armand groaned, then opened his eyes. "Ah, Ever-leigh — so nice of you to join us. No party would be complete without your charming presence."

"Quiet, Landreth. You are under arrest for high treason."

"My crimes — of which you know well. In truth, even bet-ter than I."

Everleigh paused a moment, then he surveyed the men around him. "An excellent job. My men will take him from here."

"Tut, tut." Armand sat up with a grunt. "Don't be so shabby to these gentlemen — after all, they are the ones who bagged me. It's only right they receive the glory of bringing me in, don't you agree?" He looked at the battered group, many of whom were holding their hands to bloodied limbs and sides. Rather than agree, they seemed to step backward as one. "Come on, chaps, don't give up on me now. I promise to be as docile as a lamb if you will take me in."

"Enough," Everleigh said. "My men will take you."

"I thought you might say that." He gritted his teeth as two of the duke's men hoisted him to his feet. "You really are too kind."

"Tie him up." Everleigh turned on his heel, leaving the lobby to Armand's weak laughter.

The laughter died as the men roughly bound Armand and pushed him out of the hotel and into a covered carriage, the Rendon crest clearly emblazoned upon it.

"I ride in style to gaol," Armand observed, leaning against the plush cushions. "Though I doubt that is where I am destined to go, am I, boys?"

The darker of the two men laughed and jabbed him curtly in the ribs. "You're too bright fer your own good, ain't ye, Landreth?"

"A failing of mine," Armand muttered. "Since you dare not take me in for questioning, I presume I am slated to have made a desperate attempt for freedom, only to be shot down by you two heroes of England, no?"

"No." The man's grin was feral. "You're going to live, though you'll wish you hadn't."

"My, my, for what reason this honor?"

"We've missed your darling sister—seems she's even smarter than you. The duke's thinkin' it will be easier if he just holds you until your sister comes ter us fer ye." He laughed. "He rather likes the notion."

Armand tensed. "I fear I will be your guest for an extended stay, then. She's already on her way out of the country."

"We've got time. The duke plans to make good use of it, too—he's got some questions for you, as well."

"Questions for me?" Armand feigned surprise. "How so? Everleigh always knows everything, doesn't he?"

"That he does—but what he doesn't know, he'll take out of your hide. Strip by strip."

Noises filled her fitful sleep—men's voices, cruel laughter, a man's groan. Chlorinda tossed her head, willing the voices to go away. They persisted, commanding her emergence into consciousness.

She finally lay fully awake, eyes open, staring into the dark and waiting. Was it all a fragment of her dreams? She had unobtrusively avoided taking the draught of laudanum her uncle and Mrs. Bendley had been requiring she take the past few nights. Since her uncle's return, he had ordered the sleeping draughts out of concern for her health. She couldn't explain that she would rather have her nightmares than the deep and formless sleep the laudanum caused.

She closed her eyes after a moment, only to snap them open. The noises were there again. Chlorinda arose silently. Trembling, she tiptoed to the door and flitted out into the darkened hall. Further down she could see a shard of light seeping from under a door.

Drawing in a deep breath, for the voices were clearer now—and one was her uncle's—she padded, barefooted, to the door, and found it slightly ajar.

She bit her lip in an attempt to steady it and, placing her hand upon the door, she softly opened it wider. A cry rasped through her chest and throat.

Two soldiers stood over a man bound to a hardbacked chair. Her eyes focused on one of the soldiers; his hard, brutish face seemed familiar, yet she could not remember where she had seen it. His visage, nonetheless, filled her with a haunting dread.

She tore her gaze from his unsettling face and focused upon the man in the chair. "My God!" Despite the masses of bruises and the smeared paint obscuring his face, it was un-

315

deniably Sir Horace. His jacket, always perfection, was tattered; his torn shirt exposed a chest covered with welts.

"Chlorinda." Her uncle spoke and she tore her horrified gaze from the battered Sir Horace. "What are you doing here?"

"I—I—" She swallowed hard, forcing herself to meet his penetrating stare. "I heard noises." Her eyes unwillingly strayed back to Sir Horace.

He raised pain-glazed eyes to her. "Dammit, Everleigh, she doesn't need to be here. Get her out!"

The soldier who had drawn her attention before backhanded him. "Shut up! Who are you to give the orders?"

"Slowly, Marcus." The duke raised his hand. "You'll have my Chlorinda confused about what is happening here." His smile sent a chill through her. "I'm sorry, my dear, but you see, we have discovered Sir Horace is not who he pretends to be."

"He is—" Everleigh strolled over to Sir Horace and tore the wig from his head. "—the veriest fraud!"

Chlorinda choked, her hand flying to her mouth. It was her stranger. "No. You can't be both."

"You have what you wished, Madame," he whispered. "You have seen Sir Horace stripped of his finery."

"Who—who are you, really?"

"Still your fool." Pain—and something else—filled his eyes.

"He's nobody's fool, Chlorinda," Everleigh purred. "He is Armand Landreth."

"Landreth?" Chlorinda murmured it as if she had never heard the name before. "Landreth . . . oh, my God!"

"That's correct, my dear," her uncle said. "He's the son of the man who caused your father's downfall. He is a spy, masquerader—and murderer."

"You betrayed me!" Her eyes filled with sudden tears. "I was the fool, was I not? All the time taunting me as Sir Horace, and—" she faltered. She couldn't speak of how he'd betrayed her before these men. "I hate you."

"Forgive me."

"Forgive you?" The words exploded from her. "Forgive you—that's why you were always asking me that! You knew the day would come when I would know who you were and despise your dark soul. You cur!"

Marcus barked out a laugh. Angrily, Chlorinda gazed at him, then started. For a moment, she seemed to fall into a trance, then she shook herself slightly and dragged her eyes away. She deliberately turned and walked up to her uncle, her visage grim. "You will have him killed?"

"He will." Armand answered. "Never doubt that, my lady."

Her eyes remained locked on Everleigh, who laughed fondly. "So you are my niece, indeed. Do not concern yourself, my dear. He will receive proper punishment."

"You will not let him escape, will you? Promise me that."

"I won't—that's why we hold him here and nowhere else."

"Will you kill him tonight?" Her eyes were tearing. "I would like that."

"No—we must keep him for a short time, I fear."

"How long will that be?"

"Only as long as it takes to draw his sister to us. Perhaps a day or two, no more."

"That long?" She shook.

"Yes, my dear, only that long. Now, I fear you are becoming overwrought; you must go back to bed. I will send Mrs. Bendley in with a sleeping potion."

"Yes," Chlorinda nodded through her tears. She turned from Everleigh and moved slowly over to Armand. He met her gaze stoically. "I will never forgive you. You will die for this!" She raised her hand and slapped him resoundingly.

Armand's head snapped back; when he looked at her, there was agony in the depths of his eyes. "I see she is more of you, Everleigh, than of her father."

"Yes," Everleigh said approvingly. "I begin to believe so as well."

Chlorinda stiffened, eyes ablaze. She gave Armand another ringing slap, spun, and walked from the room without glancing back.

Within two minutes of her return to her room, Mrs. Bendley arrived, carrying a glass and vial. "My poor lamb," she clucked. "His grace told me you have had an upset. This draught will help you, however. Don't you worry."

"I don't want it," Chlorinda said dully.

Mrs. Bendley's face grew severe. "Your uncle said for you to take it, and so you shall, else I will go and tell him. He is very concerned for you."

"Very well," Chlorinda sighed wearily.

"Now there's a good girl." Mrs. Bendley poured a generous dollop from the vial into the glass and stood over Chlorinda, waiting, like a stern schoolmistress.

"Th—thank you." Chlorinda started to weep. "Could—could you please open the window a crack, I feel so flushed and faint."

"Of course, my dear. Poor chick." She hastened to the window and drew it open.

Turning back, she saw Chlorinda downing the last of the glass and smiling weakly. "Thank you. I'm finished. Perhaps—perhaps I can sleep now."

"Of course," Mrs. Bendley said kindly. "That is just what you need."

Chlorinda lay back upon her pillow and after one pitiful little sob, drifted off. Mrs. Bendley stood and watched her for a while to ensure she slept, then she left.

Chapter Seventeen
Dawns The Morning

Lady Daniella trod softly down the stairs the following morning, a frown marring her brow. Julia was just then upstairs, donning the clothes of her hostess's personal maid, intent upon leaving the house in such a disguise. Would it do, her ladyship fretted. She prayed it would, for Julia was determined to escape as quickly as possible, her fears for her family distorting what might have been her better judgment.

Lady Daniella shook her head as if to clear her doubts. It could work, she thought, for Hinton had reported the posted soldiers had left sometime in the early hours. She could not fathom Converse's plans—perhaps he'd been forced to employ his guards to chase Armand.

The door knocker thumped and Lady Daniella halted, shaken by a sudden presentiment. She waited silently on the stairs as Hinton entered the hall. He crossed and viewed the street from the window.

"It is the duke again, my lady," Hinton said softly.

She tensed. "Open it, Hinton."

Hinton nodded and unbolted the door, opening it on the smiling Duke of Rendon. "Ah, Converse," Daniella said, forcing a smile to her lips as she walked down the stairs. "What brings you here so bright and early this morning? I was just now going to break my fast."

"I will not keep you. I stop to ask you to deliver a message to Julia Landreth."

"Tsk, I have told you that she was not here last night, nor is she here this morning."

"A pity," Everleigh murmured. "For I am sure she would care to receive this message. You have, no doubt, discovered the soldiers posted here last evening are gone?"

"Are they?" She feigned boredom, cursing the man to his very soul. "I had not noticed."

"And would you like to know why?"

"I find it of no interest."

"But you should, my dear. They are reportedly out scouring the neighborhood for Armand Landreth, who escaped after only one hour of captivity."

"Did he? My, how nice." Amusement entered Lady Daniella's eyes.

'Please warn Julia not to fall prey to them."

Lady Daniella stilled warily. "My, such a display of concern. Why would you warn her of that, since they are your hounds, after all?"

"Quite. And they must have something to do, after all. Only warn her to steer clear, for I far prefer she comes directly to me to be captured."

"Lud, that I can well believe," her ladyship laughed. "But surely a rather impossible desire, Converse."

"Not when she knows I, personally, have Armand Landreth—at my townhouse, no less. Very much bound and chained, lest she think he might remove himself from there."

"What?" She couldn't keep herself from paling.

"Yes, well-guarded—and well-beaten." Everleigh reached into his pocket and withdrew a golden ring with a square-cut emerald. "Give this to Julia Landreth with my compliments."

"Why are you doing this?" She accepted the ring with a slightly trembling hand.

"I have grown weary of this chase. It ends now. Tell

Julia where her brother is, and that I am impatient. Every day that passes, I will come to you, my dear Daniella, with another—token—of her brother's. Today, it is his ring; perhaps tomorrow, the finger upon which he wore it. Armand Landreth will surely die, that she cannot stop—but if she wishes him to die mercifully, why, then she will come to me. Do you understand?"

"Indeed I do."

"I thought you would." He bowed and turned to leave, then stopped, his smile sure. "You see, I do not underestimate you women after all, do I?"

Lady Daniella closed the door upon him, clutching the ring in her hand. She turned, and her eyes rose to the top of the stairs. Julia stood in her maid's clothes, a blond wig covering her hair. Her face was frozen and pale as an alabaster statue. "You heard?" Lady Daniella said weakly.

Julia nodded. Without a word she walked down the stairs, reaching out her hand when she stood before Lady Daniella. Daniella mutely placed the ring in her trembling palm. "I should kill him," Julia said softly.

"Rendon?"

"No, Jason," Julia said, shaking her head. "It's all my fault! Armand may die because I—I—"

"No. Don't think it. Go to your father. Tell him." Her voice was low and urgent. "It's not over yet. You can save him."

Julia looked up, her eyes stark. "Yes, perhaps." She leaned over and hugged Lady Daniella. "Yes, but first I shall—" She stopped.

Fear entered Daniella's heart. "You will what, Julia?"

Julia shook her head. "Never mind."

Lady Daniella drew back, studying Julia's suddenly enigmatic face. "Julia, are you all right?"

Julia hugged her close; Daniella couldn't see her face. "Of course. Now I must be going, I really must. Pray for us, dear—pray for me."

Jason had just finished his breakfast, though much remained upon his plate. He had drunk too much yesterday . . . and last night. The hangover gave him a slight headache, but the knowledge that Granny Merton, Miranda Waverly, and his sprite were all one and the same as Julia Landreth, traitoress, twisted and knotted at his stomach. He would not accept the fact that his heart fared as poorly as his stomach.

Pushing his plate away, he reached for his newspaper. "No need to open it, my lord," a woman's voice said. "I can tell you what it says—and what it does not."

"I beg your pardon?" He looked up, and discovered a blond maid eyeing him with disdain. Astounding; rarely did maids address him in such a manner. She was most definitely not one of his regular staff.

He peered closer—and his jaw clenched. "What are you doing here?"

"Surprised to see me, my lord?" Julia taunted, approaching him ever so softly. "I am sorry to disappoint you, but Rendon did not catch me last night."

"What do you mean?" Jason asked sharply.

"What else could I mean?" Julia's eyes were slits of anger. "You set Rendon onto me, but I outsmarted him and escaped." Her body all but shook.

"How—unfortunate," Jason said, as calmly as he could. His emotions were in a riot, but his concern was for Julia. She seemed close to crazy. "However, you are in the wrong of it—I did not tell Rendon. If he came for you last night, he discovered you by himself."

"Liar!" She spat the word. "Liar! The great honorable Lord Stanton, who cannot bear the presence of a—a lowly, common deceiver like myself, breaks his oath, destroys his trust—"

"Stop it!" He didn't want to hear the pain and disillusionment in her voice. "I do not know what happened

322

but I did not break my oath to you."

"Yes, you did!" she rasped. He'd never seen her like this. Indeed, he had never seen any woman like this; her body was as tense as that of a lioness about to spring. "You could not even give me a day. I was not even worth a day to you, was I, my lord? I trusted you, and because of my stupidity, my—my trust, my brother will die. I should kill you!"

She reached out to slap him, but he grabbed her wrist quickly and gripped it hard.

"No!" His rage rose to meet hers—how dare she call him the betrayer? How dare she accuse him of dishonor! He jerked her to him, toppling her into his lap. It seemed he held a volcano, but he only held her the tighter, cruelly pinning her to him. "I didn't do anything—I don't even know your damn brother."

"You didn't have to. Once Rendon knew me, it was easy to know Armand—and now he holds him hostage! He will torture him, damn you!" Her voice hoarse, she pulled and struggled against him, demanding all his considerable strength to hold her.

"Stop it, sprite," Jason said, his voice as rough as hers. "Stop it!"

"My name is Julia!" Suddenly she became still, her white, ravaged face a stone mask. "Call me Julia." He looked into her demanding brown eyes; the name of the traitoress stuck in his throat. "Say it. Call me Julia this one last time."

"What do you mean, last time?" An unreasonable, numbing fear crept over him.

"Do you think I will leave Armand to Rendon? I will go to him. At least Armand and I can die together." She wasn't weeping. There was only a deep, deep sadness in her, one that seemed to seep into him, invading his very soul.

He fought it with anger. "What game are you playing now? Rendon will not kill you! That is up to the crown—

you must go on trial."

Julia snorted. "That's it, my lord, salve your conscience. Say it over and over. You did not betray me." Her hands moved slowly, until one arm broke free and slid around his neck.

"I did not, damn it! Enough of the Cheltenham tragedy—!" He broke off, stunned to feel the cold blade of a knife at the side of his neck. She must have had it hidden in the cuff of her dress—but how had he not noticed it?"

"I should kill you," she said hollowly. "Kill you before you can help Rendon again."

"Kill me then," he said slowly, his eyes locked with her ravaged ones. "Finish what you started—Julia."

Her face twisted. He knew he couldn't have hurt her more if he had hit her.

The knife slid away from his neck; she brought it out and around, until it rested between their two chests. Her hand relaxed. "Take it—Jason. *You* finish it."

Rage welled within him as he looked at her, knowing she played with her life and his. "Damn you . . ." he let his arms fall away from her. "Leave now. I never want to see you again. Ever."

A racking sob came from her as she shoved away from him and ran to the door. "Sprite," he called as he saw the last of her skirts disappear. "Julia," he said more softly. "Julia . . ."

"Armand," Chlorinda said softly to herself. "His name is Armand . . . Armand Landreth."

She shook her head. It hurt, but for once it seemed clear. A small, retching sob escaped her throat. Indeed, it was clear. She had remembered.

The scene she had witnessed in that terrible room had brought back a sliver of memory. Then she had returned to her own room to face Mrs. Bendley. She had waited for Mrs. Bendley to turn her back and open the window, so she might pour the laudanum into the nearest place she could find—her slipper, lying on the floor by her bed. She'd sipped just a taste of the liquid when Mrs. Bendley turned around.

When the chaperone finally left the room, Chlorinda opened her eyes. A scene was playing itself out on the stage of her memory, the scene she had been trying to remember, the scene that had haunted her.

Rushing down the stairs to escape the house early and meet her father at the bridge, she had slowed as she came to her uncle's library. Though the door was closed, she could make out voices, and she was afraid to make a noise lest her uncle hear it and appear.

"Soon it will be over," she heard him say. The tone arrested her, for it was said with a malicious joy she had never heard him employ. Curious, hoping that the conversation dealt with the escape plan for her father, she crept to the panelled door and peered through the keyhole. She could not see her uncle, but she could see a man, sitting in a chair—the man, Marcus, whom she had just seen standing over Armand Landreth.

Her uncle's words were clearer now. "Tom will be cutting the bridge now. It should not be too difficult. My dear brother won't be prepared for an ambush, since the letter came from his own darling daughter. You, needless to say, will go and insure the business is finished, if my brother is tiring enough to survive the accident."

"What about the girl?"

"I will work to detain her from her meeting."

"What if you don't—should I kill her?"

"Never fear, I shall detain her. And if you kill her, your life will be forfeit—is that understood? She has a fortune in her own right from her mother's side, and it will not come to me if she dies. Her mother always was a strange one . . . But as her loving, trusting guardian, I will gain her fortune, never fear. She's such a naive, stupid chit, but she is quite pretty and will also sell very well on the mart. *N'est-ce pas?* That's your problem, Marcus—you never look ahead."

Chlorinda didn't wait to hear Marcus's answer; she picked up her skirts and ran. She thought of fleeing to the stables for her horse, but she checked herself; if her uncle had control over the stable boys, they would hold her. She took off running, praying she could make the bridge in time by foot.

She could remember the terror and her constant prayer that she would not be too late. She remembered her horror as she reached the bridge, winded and near faint. And then she saw her father's carriage approaching. She had tried to scream to him through her dry and winded vocal cords, but he had not heard. She had been forced to stand, helpless, and witness the rest.

Now, with ugly memories flowing back, she realized she had not fainted. She could remember the blinding, painful blow from behind before blacking out.

Chlorinda opened her eyes. They were dry. Through her stupidity, she'd killed her father—and how could she not have remembered this? Fear chilled her; if she had remembered, what would have become of her?

Cold determination grew within her. She'd been a pawn of her uncle's, used to kill his brother. She would never allow him to kill another man she loved, never! Armand Landreth might be a traitor, but she no longer cared. She loved him, and Uncle Converse would pay for what he had done.

She lay there then, waiting. The room had turned gold with the morning's early rays when she finally heard the voices of the guards passing her door. She waited a minute more, then slipped from her room to flit stealthily down to the last door of the hall.

The door was closed and her heart beat wildly—what if it was locked? She tried it softly, and it clicked open. The fools!

She slowly cracked it open, not knowing what she'd do

326

f there were another guard in the room.

"Dear God . . ." No guard, just a solitary figure, slumped over in his bonds. "Dear God!" There were no guards because they'd already killed him!

She ran to kneel beside the silent man. "Sir Horace, please, please be alive . . ." She patted hesitantly at his face, attempting to avoid the largest bruises, but that proved impossible. Then he stirred. Breath entered her body again.

He opened one eye slightly. "Come to finish me off, English rose? Just can't wait, can you?"

"Hush," Chlorinda admonished. "Help me, what shall I do?"

Incredibly, a grin touched his lips. "You ask me to advise you on my own death. Make it short, sweetings, make it short."

"No, no, the guards will return soon—"

"Not them, they have to go break fast. Cruelty can make one so hungry."

"Thank God! Here, should I untie you? She went behind him and with shaking fingers tugged at the bonds. The knots were tight, buried in his skin. "My God, I can't undo them."

"Yes, you can—you must. Take a deep breath and try again. Look closely at the knots; concentrate only on them. Tell me how they look. I'll help you."

Chlorinda nodded. Sucking in her breath, she attacked the knots again, determinedly ignoring Armand's gasp of pain. Once the fear was out of her eyes, she could see how the knots could be loosened, and after a struggle, they fell.

"Wonderful girl." Armand pulled his hands free and gingerly rubbed them. "Now my feet, if you could? My hands—too numb."

"Of course." Chlorinda hastened to do his bidding. "Now what should we do?" she asked nervously. Armand looked as if he'd fall from his chair any second.

"Help me up."

"Can you make it?" she asked. He flinched as she helped him rise and she loosened her grip contritely.

He leaned on her, heavily. "Take me to the green bedroom."

"The green bedroom? But that's my room."

He definitely grinned. "Is it now? How nice. Let's go."

Blushing slightly, Chlorinda helped him toward the door. They weaved and staggered until she shakily brought him to her bedroom. She gratefully deposited him in a chair and swiftly crossed and locked the door. "How will this help? They'll search in here as well."

"Go to Matilda over there." He raised his hand weakly and waved at a painting of a stern dame, hanging on the bedroom wall.

Chlorinda stared. The austere lady on the wall was a long-ago ancestor of hers, whose name, indeed, had been Matilda. "But how—how did you know?"

Armand merely smiled, much as a tired drunkard would have. "Never mind. Just move the old tartar aside."

"I beg your pardon?"

"Move the painting."

Chlorinda, certain now that he suffered from delirium, nonetheless trod to the painting and tipped Matilda's sour features akilter.

"Do you see it?" he asked.

"See what—oh!" She saw it—a small crack in the plaster, and the tip of a small lever visible within it.

"Pull it down."

Chlorinda obeyed. A small click sounded and a portion of the wall moved and jolted open. She ran her hand along the edge of the crack and opened the wall as she would a door. A small room lay behind, with a stairwell in the corner. "Help me?" Armand said weakly.

Chlorinda didn't respond for a moment, so dumbfounded was she. Finally she turned, eyes alight. "How

328

did it get there?"

"This is your father's house, remember? He was a man of invention. Now help me, please." Chlorinda flew to his side and helped him into the sequestered little chamber. "I—I must sit."

Chlorinda, feeling the weight of his weakening body dragging her down, nodded gratefully, and together, they slowly slid to the floor. There they sat, entwined, trying to catch their breath.

Armand broke the silence. "Why are you aiding me? I've treated you foully."

Chlorinda flushed, though she smiled. "I fear it is I who am your fool."

"No, never that," Armand said softly. His eyes were oddly humble. "Thank you."

Chlorinda, unable to meet his look, asked, "What are we to do now?"

"You must leave me here."

"No, I cannot. You must be tended to, or have a doctor—"

"I will be fine: do not think on it."

"I don't want you to die here." Panic filtered into her voice.

"I shan't. I find I have much I wish to live for. But you mustn't tarry. When you can, you must go to my father."

"What?" Her eyes showed her fear. "Please, sir—Armand, let me tend to you, you are not well."

"No, I am not crazy. My father is still alive."

"Alive?"

"Yes. You must tell him I am here. I—I can't make it out of here without his help. I won't endanger you."

"Very well," she said soothingly, for his voice was fading. "Only give me the directions."

She had to lean closer as Armand whispered the instructions. She listened intently, as a priest to a dying man's confession. The thought made her shiver, and she held him all the closer. "I understand. I'll go to him

329

directly."

"Thank you. Be careful. I—I couldn't bear it if anything happened to you, English rose."

"Hush," she said, blinking back tears and standing resolutely. "Nothing will happen. Uncle Converse has used me for the last time." With one last look at the silent Armand, she closed the secret door and meticulously arranged the picture over it. She stared at the haughty face of her ancestor; it seemed to return her stare in full measure. "Take care of him for me, Matilda, take care of him." She stiffened her back and flew to her wardrobe.

It was a cozy group that sat down to breakfast at the small farm just outside of London. Robert, Jeanne, John, and Michael were enjoying a large repast.

Jeanne watched in amusement as Robert laughed at a precocious antic of her son's. He had been somewhat sober this morning, saying he intended to meet with his son and daughter today. He couldn't wait for the appointed rendezvous time. Something bothered him, yet he could not say what.

Now he was laughing at Michael's childish attempts to capture his attention. She marvelled at the nature of the man; Robert Landreth was evidently not one to hold a grudge. She'd held fast in her refusal to aid him, yet he had not allowed it to deter his friendly behavior toward her or her son. A slight feminine smile curved her lips. That was not to say that he was not covertly wary when alone with her, but that had nothing to do with the war between England and France.

The small group stilled as a knock sounded at the curtained door, but relaxed as they recognized the pattern in the rapping.

"Julia," Robert murmured, frowning. He arose and went swiftly to the door, opening it. At first, Jeanne thought a simple housemaid stood before them. In another moment, she recognized Landreth's only daughter beneath the mobcap. Mon Dieu, but she would never accustom herself to this family's chameleon-like propensities.

"What has happened?" Robert inquired sternly, pulling a silent, pale Julia into the kitchen and rebolting the door after her. Julia's gaze encircled the group and fell pointedly on Michael.

Jeanne easily read her thoughts. "Michael, you may go play now."

"But Maman," he objected, his eyes wide upon Julia. "I have not washed the dishes yet."

"No matter, go and play." Michael's face was that of a martyr as he reluctantly left the adults.

John rose, worry in his eyes. "I shall watch the boy." He left the room quietly.

"Now sit and tell me," Robert said tersely.

Julia sat and expelled a wavering breath. "Everleigh has captured Armand."

"Mon Dieu," Jeanne breathed as she saw the blue in Robert's eyes deepen to black and his jaw stiffen.

"How?" he asked quietly.

"It was all my fault, sir," Julia said. "All my fault. The Earl of Wynhaven discovered my secret and he must have told Everleigh."

"What!"

"But how can that be your fault?" Jeanne asked.

"He discovered my real identity yesterday. He told me I had an hour to leave town before he told the duke."

"And you didn't go?" Robert asked. "The man was doing more than you could have expected."

"No, I—I swore him to secrecy upon his oath—that he was mine for saving his life."

"He swore that?"

"Yes. I thought he would honor it." She said wretchedly. "He did not."

"Something is awry." Robert's eyes narrowed. "You say

you wrangled his vow of secrecy—though I don't know how you did it—and then he broke it?" He sat a moment, then shook his head. "No. He is a man of honor."

"Man of honor or not," she said tightly, "he betrayed us. Though he swears he did not."

"He swears . . . ? How could he swear that?" Robert's eyes were stern.

Julia's eyes went down in embarrassment. "I—I just came from him.

"You what?" He exclaimed.

"I—I just came from there."

"Why?" Robert looked at her as if she were two-headed.

"I wanted to kill him," Julia said softly.

"Ah, yes. That makes much sense," Jeanne nodded wisely. "Did he bleed greatly?" she asked, rather eagerly.

Julia's eyes flew to Jeanne's in shock. Then a small smile touched her lips, and the first sign of life entered her eyes. "No. For I did not kill him."

"*Voyons,* but he betrayed you," Jeanne exclaimed, confused. "Why did you not kill him then?"

"Because she is not as bloodthirsty as you are, my little madwoman," Robert said, though a smile played upon his lips as well. He looked oddly at Julia, who was now biting her lip. "Indeed, it is my Julia I can depend upon to be cool in a situation, unswayed by such emotions—usually, that is. Please, dear, start from the beginning and leave nothing out." He cast a stern eye to Jeanne. "And you, not another word. I do not wish my daughter to be killing everyone she dislikes. That is, if she does dislike him," he mused, his eyes turning back to her. "Julia?"

"Of course I do," Julia said stiffly, pain filtering into her eyes again. Drawing in her breath, she told the story in a clipped, concise manner, only her eyes betraying her agony. Robert's brow darkened alarmingly when she told him she and Armand had met at the Shield and Arms against his express wishes. He nodded shortly when he heard the story about the clerk. "There lies the problem."

"What do you mean?" Julia asked.

"Something happened there. It was a trap—The Hawk's decoy, most likely."

"You don't think Jason betrayed us?" Julia said. It appeared to Jeanne to be a flare of excitement, perhaps of hope, flashing through Julia at this. Ah me, Jeanne thought, she has a care for the man.

"Exactly," Robert said. "The Shield and Arms was the trap."

"And now Everleigh has Armand," Julia said, the hope of the moment before extinguished. "He has sent a message that he will torture Armand until I come to him and surrender myself."

"Non," Jeanne breathed, aghast. Robert's only son was in the hands of a monster. Robert had saved her son, but she'd denied him her aid in saving his own.

"Does he indeed?" Robert said softly, smoothly. "He was ever an insolent man . . ." He stopped speaking as yet another knock sounded upon the kitchen door, hesitant, with no recognizable pattern.

Julia rose swiftly. "I'll answer it." She peeked through the curtains. "My God, it's Chlorinda."

A strained moment passed as another furtive tap sounded. "How did she know we were here, sir?"

"She must have come from Everleigh," Robert said. "Strange . . . see what she has to say."

Julia unbolted and opened the door slightly. "Here now, wot do yer wont?" she asked in a low voice.

"Please, is—is Mr. R. Smith here?" Chlorinda asked in a quivering voice.

"He ain't at home."

"Not at home?" Chlorinda stammered. "Oh no, he must be here, he simply must be. It is of dire importance."

"Ye want ta tell me wot it is?"

"No, no, I must tell him myself."

"Ye want ter wait fer him?"

"No, I cannot stay long, my uncle will discover I'm gone soon."

Robert stood up. "Let her in, Julia."

She nodded and opened the door. "Come in, Chlorinda. It Is I, Miranda."

"Miranda?" Chlorinda repeated stupidly, bewildered. "What are you doing here—and dressed like that?"

"Never mind," Julia said quickly. "I thought you knew. Come in."

"Thought I knew what?" Chlorinda asked. She studied Julia a second, then her eyes widened. "You—you aren't Julia, are you? You can't be—Armand's sister?"

Julia's eyes deepened in compassion at Chlorinda's stunned expression. "Yes, dear, I am."

Chlorinda shook her head to clear it and then tears welled up in her eyes. "Oh, Miranda—Julia—Uncle has Armand!"

"I know," Julia said softly, enveloping the smaller woman in a hug. They clung to each other. "Your uncle sent a message to me this morning . . . how did you know of Armand? Do you know if he's—still alive?"

"Yes." Chlorinda stepped back. "For the moment. But you and your faster must rescue him soon."

"How may we do that?" Robert stepped toward her and she drew back. It seemed as if she shrank within herself as she focused upon Robert Landreth.

"You—you are Armand's father?"

"Yes, I am." His voice was suddenly devoid of emotion.

"I could not believe you still lived."

"I do. Does that displease you?"

"No, oh, no." She shook her head slowly. Her eyes shimmered with tears. "I am glad of it—at least my foolishness did not destroy you as it did my fa—I only came to tell you about Armand, and then I will leave."

"If that is your wish," Robert said coldly.

334

"No." The tears slid slowly, silently down Chlorinda's face. "I know you cannot forgive me, but I do not want you to hate me. I loved my father and I did not mean to kill him."

The eyes of Robert Landreth, The Fox, appeared slightly moist. He said gently, "I loved your father, child. He was my dearest friend. I never meant his death either; forgive me for being unable to stop it."

"Forgive you? No, no, forgive me!"

Robert shook his head. "I never wanted to blame you. I always believed deep down that you were innocent." He opened his arms wide. "After all, you are my best friend's child."

Chlorinda flew to his arms, crying. "Ah, child, do not carry on so," he said. "You must be strong. Julia will take you to compose yourself, and when you come back, you will tell us all. Then you must be on your way."

Chlorinda sniffed and nodded. As Julia led her out of the kitchen, Robert stood looking after them, deep in concentration.

"Monsieur," Jeanne said quietly, rising, "I am sorry, too."

Robert turned to her and suddenly, unbelievably, his eyes brightened with amusement. "You also?"

"You know it is my fault," Jeanne said in a small voice. "I would not help you when you asked it of me, and now your son is in danger."

His eyebrows rose. "But you heard Julia say it was all her fault, and Chlorinda claims the same."

"Bah! It is mine! You must permit me to help rescue your son now."

Robert's amusement dissipated, and his face became sober. "No, I will not permit you."

"Yes, yes, you must. If I had helped you before this, your son would not be captured, non? I must be allowed to help—I will do anything."

"Then you will remain here tonight."

"Non! I wish to make the amends. I will help tonight; you cannot stop me."

Robert's face became pensive as he advanced towards her. "You do not understand. I must know that you are safe tonight."

"Safe? You know there is no safety for me. Let me help!"

"I will let you aid me another time — tonight I want you here, safe and sound." He observed her stubborn expression and a certain look entered his eyes. Jeanne recognized it.

"Do not look so. I know already that look — you think to cozen me out of this!" She backed away from him, shaking her finger. "It will not work, non!"

"Yes," Robert said, softly stepping toward her. "I do mean to 'cozen you' out of it."

Jeanne trembled, for suddenly he stood very close. She felt drawn to him by an inexplicable force. She cast a quick, nervous look at him, then anger filled her; he felt the physical power between them, too, and he was using it. "Ah, you Fox. Do not come closer, stay away."

"But I only wish to comfort you." He stepped closer, despite her orders.

"Comfort me? Bah! You do not seek to comfort me."

The smile left Robert's face, and he stopped. "No, perhaps not. Perhaps it is I who seek comfort. He has my son, Jeanne. I cannot let him have you, too."

Jeanne's eyes widened, then it was she who advanced. She put her arms about the silent man and felt a tremor run through him. She held him closer. "He will not have me, monsieur. I will stay here, safe and sound. And you will have your son safe and sound, too, very soon. You are the great Fox, non?" She pulled away, that she might run a soothing hand down his cheek.

His eyes darkened. "I am but a man."

Jeanne's hand froze, and she swallowed hard. "I know this, too."

"An English man."

"Yes. And for all three, I will do whatever you ask of me."

His hand rose to smooth Jeanne's brow. "Do not fear, ma belle, I will never ask too much of you."

Jeanne sighed and quickly hid her face against Robert's shoulder. She held him tightly and blinked away a quick tear—if only he *would* ask more of her! "No, monsieur, I know that. I know that all too well."

Julia's heart beat in rhythm to the desperate pounding of her horse's hooves. She glanced back and spurred her mount faster. They were close behind, so very close.

No matter, Armand and Father are safe away, her exhausted thoughts chanted. All had gone so well; Armand and her father had already been horsed and on their way, she remaining behind to close the secret passage. Then the footman discovered her, and the alarm had been sounded.

She had made sure they had followed her. They were bloodhounds, slavering on her scent, too intent on tracking her to think of Armand or her father. Oh, but they were persistent dogs, easily relaying with new men as their horses grew weary. She had only herself and her mount.

She could not continue, she knew that. Where could she go? Exhaustion from the past days dragged at her, engulfing her. Her horse was frothing at the mouth, heaving. Sanctuary. There was none for such as she.

One weak desire rose in her heart and threaded through her weary, benumbed soul. He never wanted to see her again, he had said. But if she must die, she wanted to see him. Only one more time, no matter the cost.

Jason laid the book down upon the side table, rubbing

his eyes. He could not read tonight. He laid his head back against the chair and his eyes roamed the shadows of his bedroom. He looked at his bed, already turned down for him, and he knew he would not sleep.

Still he thought of her. His sprite. His traitoress. The raw pain on her face as she had left him haunted his memory. Gossip that day had spread of where she and her brother were, what they had done, and what they had not done. He had said nothing as they had all talked around him at the club. Some of the stories were so fantastic as to be unbelievable—yet the woman herself was unbelievable. So beautiful, but so cunning.

His fist clenched and he pounded the chair's arm. Even as he prepared to marry Chlorinda Everleigh, he realized his heart belonged to the traitoress, Julia Landreth. Damn her!

His eyes widened slowly. A shadow had crossed his balcony doors. He sat silent as the doors softly creaked open, and the shadow slipped softly into his bedroom. The shadow took form and shape into the woman who haunted him. Julia stood before him, a torn gray cloak enshrouding her, her silver curls matted and unruly.

She stood mute, staring at him, her body swaying slightly, her ragged breathing the only sound in the room. "I'm sorry," she said hoarsely, her eyes agonized, "You don't want to see me. But they're after me."

Jason remained frozen. He truly had not expected ever to see her again. "So you came here? To kill me?"

"No," she said, her voice but a whisper.

"Am I to hide you then?"

"No," she said more strongly. She stepped forward. "Only allow me to hide myself." He didn't say a word as she walked past him, toward his bedroom door. "If I am caught, you must deny knowing I was here." She reached for the door handle.

"No," Jason said sharply, rising. "They will find you if they search the house."

338

A pounding sounded from the depths of the house, the sound reverberating even to where they stood. They stared at each other.

"Get undressed," Jason said softly. "Get into my bed, and I will do the rest."

"No, stay out of this—it would never work! They will uncover me and hold you responsible for harboring me."

"Do as I say!" he said sharply. He could not let her be taken. Ever. He knew that now. The banging at the door increased, and they could hear voices from downstairs. "Hurry!" He grabbed her by the shoulders and spun her towards the bed.

"No, I won't, I won't endanger you!"

His fingers tightened upon her. "Either you do what I say, or I will take you down to them immediately. You came to me for help . . ."

"I did not," Julia whispered.

Jason gazed at her and almost asked her what she could mean by that. The pounding at the door brought him back to the moment at hand. "You will take what I offer or nothing at all."

Julia stared at him, eyes wide. "Very well."

"Now hurry. I will stall them. Blow out the candle—and for God's sake, do something to cover that hair!"

Jason did not waste a minute more to see if Julia obeyed, but walked out the door. As he descended the stairs, he unbuttoned his shirt and pulled it from his pantaloons, undoing the cuffs. He ran his hand through his hair, rumpling it. As he approached the lower level of the townhouse, he called in an imperious voice, "Canton, what in blazes is going on down there?"

"Soldiers, sir—looking for a traitor."

"What? A traitor?" Jason descended the last steps and found his butler in the midst of a squad of soldiers. He looked to a small, gruff man who seemed to be in charge. "Hallo, I'm Stanton. Now what is this about a traitor?"

339

The little man straightened, almost coming to attention. "Sergeant Clover, at yer service, my lord. You might not remember me, but I was of the 5th Foot."

Jason relaxed into a smile. "Were you? Then you certainly saw some action, didn't you?"

The sergeant's eyes strayed to Jason's open shirt and scarred chest. "So did you, sir." He coughed. "I'm glad you made it through."

"So am I, Sergeant, so am I. Now, what is this about a traitor?"

"Julia Landreth, my lord. We've chased her here to this street. We have reason to believe she might be hiding in one of these houses—particularly yours. May we search it, my lord?"

"Most certainly." Jason looked grave. "The sooner she and her brother are apprehended, the better for England." Then he frowned, looking hesitantly over his shoulder. "Only there is a slight difficulty."

"What is it, my lord?"

Jason coughed and lowered his voice, knowing the men would listen all the more closely. "Could you, perhaps, not search my chambers? I will most certainly vouch that no one—that is, no outsider—has entered them."

The little sergeant looked nervous. "My lord, we have orders—and she might have slipped in, unbeknownst to you while you were sleeping. She might be hiding there now."

"Sergeant Clover, I have not been—sleeping. Far from it. And I am not alone."

"Oh . . ." The sergeant nodded with dawning comprehension, then frowned. "But, my lord, oughtn't we to search? The Landreth woman might have slipped in when you were—er, otherwise occupied, as it were. They say she's very wily, and most likely a thing like that wouldn't deter her like it would a decent woman."

Jason, controlling a sudden anger, looked at the flushing, but determined sergeant. He sighed. "Very well, sergeant, let us—you and I—search my chambers while the other men search the rest of the house. My 'companion' is a high-born lady and I'd not care to cause her any embarrassment with a large contingent searching the room. Also, it would be better if her presence here were not common knowledge—understand?"

The sergeant coughed. "Yes, I fully understand. Let us do that then." He turned to the men, who were all attempting to look in other directions. "Gerald, Hearst, you take the kitchens and basements. Kirkland, Davies, take the rest of the downstairs. Bradshaw, Clements, the upstairs—except for the master's chamber. My lord and I will search those rooms."

Jason smiled and escorted the little sergeant up the stairs. They approached the bedroom door and Jason tapped lightly upon it. "My love? My Love? Are you awake?" They received no reply. "She must have fallen asleep—we had a very, ah, strenuous evening. Come along, then—if we do it quietly, she might never know we've been here. And that, I assure you, would be far preferable. Her temperament is not the mildest."

"Yes, my lord." Sergeant Clover nodded fervently. "When are they ever?"

Jason chuckled and opened the door gently. They entered the room and he crossed and lit the taper. Holding it high to illuminate the room, he smiled grimly as the little sergeant breathed a barely audible "Cor."

Julia had done her part well. A petticoat lay on the floor in front of his poster bed. Stockings dangled from the bedboard. The blankets were rumpled and tossed as if, indeed, it had been a passionate night.

Yet it was the figure in the bed itself that drew the eye most. Wrapped only in a sheet, alluring feminine curves met the candle's light—one smooth, creamy leg, a rounded shoulder, and an arm bared for scrutiny. Under her arm she held two pillows so as to completely mask her face.

341

"My God," the sergeant whispered. Jason realized the man was just as transfixed as he.

"Sergeant, let us get to it," Jason said, attempting to hide the sternness he felt.

"Yes, my lord." The sergeant jumped as if he'd been pinched.

They proceeded to search the armoire and the corners of the room. The slumbrous figure in the bed did not stir.

"The door to the balcony is open, my lord," the sergeant whispered urgently.

Jason grinned. "Never mind that, my man. I did that. It was getting much too hot in here."

Sergeant Clover's eyes strayed again to the bed. "I can believe that, my lord."

"Should we, perhaps, check under the bed, Sergeant — though if the Landreth woman's hid there, she must have had one bumpy time of it."

The little man chuckled. "I wouldn't dare look, my lord."

"Wait." Jason raised his fingers to his lips. He crossed noiselessly over with the candle and went down upon the floor, looking under the bed. The sleeping lady only stirred slightly. Jason could tell the sergeant was holding his breath — so did he, for the expanse of smooth white shoulder had increased with the motion.

They heard a slight, feminine mutter, then the very lightest of snores. Jason picked himself off the floor and moved hastily to join the sergeant, attempting to control his urge to laugh. "Are you satisfied that we are traitoress-free, sergeant? I hope so, for the lady will have both our heads if she awakens and discovers us here — especially since we now know she snores."

The sergeant chuckled despite himself. "They never will admit to that, will they? It looks like you've worn her plumb out, at that."

"Her? Only think of me, man!"

The sergeant shook his head. "I'll certainly not take

pity upon you—but I will leave now, in case you do need your rest."

"Thank you, sergeant. I still have the morning to go, you know." Jason ushered the sergeant from the room and down the stairs. They were met by the rest of the men, who reported having found nothing.

"Well, my lord," Sergeant Clover said as they exited, "I'm sorry to have bothered you. We will be on our way."

"It was no problem. I respect your diligence and I hope you catch the woman," Jason said, waving them good-bye.

He closed the door and went swiftly up the stairs into his room. He set the candle down quietly upon the bed-side table, reached over, and jerked the pillows from Julia's head. She gasped and grabbed at the sheets to keep them from sliding away under his sudden motion.

"They're gone," Jason said as coldly as he could. Julia stared up at him, her brown eyes large and shadowed. He stared back at her—the woman he knew he loved, naked in his bed. Yet she was a traitor, both to him and to his country. He had kept her safe, but that was all he would permit himself to do. "You may get dressed now and leave."

He walked swiftly away and sat down in his chair, refusing even to glance in her direction. He could tell there was movement, and his eyes strayed once in her direction, just in time to glimpse a sheet-clad Julia disappear behind the dressing screen. He looked away again, a pulse starting in his jaw.

She came from behind the screen and stood before him. "Thank you."

"Don't thank me. I don't know why I did it. I've aided and abetted a traitor—a woman who's betrayed my country and me."

Her eyes teared. "Don't think it, Jason. I've never betrayed you—I have lied to you, but I've never betrayed you. And you have not hurt your country, I swear that to

343

you." Of a sudden, she was kneeling before him—not as if in supplication, but as a liege woman before her lord. "I thank you, Jason, and the Landreth family thanks you. And though it may be short-lived, I owe you my life." She smiled wryly as Jason studied her features. "It is now I who owe you my body and soul, no matter how dark you think that soul is. Perhaps someday I can repay my debt to you." She leaned over and quickly kissed his hand, then rose swiftly and walked toward the balcony.

Jason stared at his hand, where the warmth of her kiss still lingered. He had told her to leave, but she was exhausted and hurt. Men searched the street for her. "No, stay—" She did not stop. "Julia, stop." She hesitated. Looking straight ahead, he said, "They will not search this house again tonight—it's safe here. Go get your sleep—I will stand guard for this evening." She remained frozen, and he turned to look at her. Her head was bowed though her shoulders remained stiff. "It will be safe here—do not be foolish." Finally, she nodded her head slightly. "Take my bed." Then he smiled. "You are safe there, as well." Her eyes lifted to his on this, and something twisted inside him, for tears stained her face. He wanted to rise, to take her into his arms and comfort her, but he merely clenched his fist all the harder and said, tightly, "Go." Julia said not a word, but walked to the bed and lay down, fully dressed.

Jason sat there until he could hear her even breathing—she slept. He sighed and rose to lock the door, then went softly over to the sleeping woman and gently pulled the covers up around her. He returned to his chair, adjusting his large frame in it, and closed his eyes for sleep, though he knew he would not.

Chapter Eighteen
To Dine With Foxes

Jason awoke to a soft but persistent rapping at his door. "My lord," Canton whispered, "there is a noble here to see you."

"Send him away." Jason sat up, groaning as his cramped muscles protested their nocturnal stay in the chair.

"But my lord, he says it is very important, and that he will refuse to leave until he has met with you."

"Does he?" Jason said, becoming more alert. "What is his name?"

"He would not say. He only says that he wishes to discuss the events of last night."

Wide awake now, Jason cast a hasty glance towards Julia. She still slept, unmoving. "Tell the gentleman—at least, I hope it is a gentleman—that I will be down directly."

Jason dressed stealthily and left the room, turning the lock in the door to ward against curious servants. He descended the stairs and was greeted at their foot by a very distinguished, handsome gentleman. A shock ran through Jason, not because of the man's distinctive bearing, but because of his dark, flaring brows and eyes of blue, which gave him a rather saturnine face—and because of the fact that his hair was the silver of old coins.

Jason nodded politely as he reached the last step. "Hello, sir. Canton said you wished to speak with me, Mr.—?"

"You may call me, Mr. Smith." The gentleman's eyes appraised Jason, slowly and meticulously. Jason towered over him, but he showed no signs of being intimidated—indeed, his manner seemed rather stern. "I wish to discuss a subject that is close, very close to my heart."

Jason smiled slightly. "In that case, let us go into the study. It is much more private."

"That would be wise, son," the older man said, following calmly.

"Would you care for a drink perhaps?" Jason asked, as the man settled himself easily into a chair.

"A brandy will do."

Jason poured a glass for both his quiet visitor and himself. He handed it to the gentleman, then sat down across from him. It was Jason's turn to study the man, who appeared to be savoring his brandy quite happily. Jason smiled and took a sip. "I did not know that dead men could drink brandy."

Mr. Smith glanced at him, then smiled approvingly. "Julia said you were uncommon intelligent."

Jason laughed. "I should be honored, but it was no great feat. There are very few who possess the features you and your daughter share—Mr. Smith."

"Call me Robert," Landreth said with a wave of his hand. "I'm really quite pleased with your astuteness; I didn't intend to go through much roundaboutation."

"Of course not, else you would not have appeared here as yourself."

"Exactly. I am Julia's father, after all, and I am here as her father. Do you know where she is, perchance?"

"She is safe upstairs in my bedroom, sir."

His brows rose high on his forehead. *"Safe,* did you say?"

"Merely exhausted," Jason said blandly.

"Indeed . . ." Setting his glass down firmly upon the table, Robert rose and stood before the fireplace, his back to the mantel and his hands before him. "And as a father, may I ask what exactly ensued last night?"

"Which details are you lacking?" An amused smile

346

touched Jason's lips as Landreth's face darkened dangerously. "It appears you already know quite a lot, since you came directly to me."

"I know," Landreth said with an edge to his voice, "that Julia was chased to this area of town; since she knows you and your house, I assumed she might have come here for aid. But that would only be so if she were pressed to the utmost." Jason nodded coolly at this, his smile leaving his lips. "And then, John happened to overhear certain — tales — at the Shield and Arms last night. It seems the soldiers searched your house.

"The occasion apparently ranked very high in their memory. You impressed them no end with your 'prowess' with a certain 'lady' in your bedroom . . . was that lady perchance Julia?"

"Yes."

Landreth's shoulders stiffened and his eyes narrowed. "And Julia did not leave your bedroom after that?"

"No, she stayed."

"Did she? Of her own free will?"

"Yes." Jason's eyes sharpened.

Landreth's jaw clenched. "I refuse to believe that, sir."

"Believe what? That she was utterly exhausted and too weak to leave, so she accepted my offer of sanctuary while the soldiers searched the other houses? She needed the sleep, which she got; I didn't, because I slept in the chair."

Landreth stared at Jason very hard, then he sighed. "Forgive me. My only excuse is that I didn't get any sleep myself. And a father has to watch out for these things, especially with a woman like Julia. Many mistakenly believe that because of her line of work, she would be more relaxed about certain issues."

"Indeed?"

"And I'm not saying there aren't women who use that method in spying, but the truly expert ones don't need to resort to such — and my Julia is very good."

"She is a master at it, in fact."

Landreth grinned. "I may be biased, but yes, I consider

her so." Then he sighed. "Yet, expert as she is, you can't expect a father not to be protective. I must tell you, if you'd played with her affections, I would have had to call you out and kill you."

"Are you then as proficient with the foils as your son?"

"My son will be just as proficient as I am in a few more years."

Jason laughed. "Then I'm glad I have no need to cross swords with you."

"So am I." He smiled. "I believe I was fond of you from the moment I heard about you."

"And you like me far better now, I have no doubt."

"Yes," Landreth said, laughing. Then he looked at Jason, considering for a moment. "Since you have already been so kind to Julia, would you care to carry it one step further?"

Jason's eyes became hooded. "How?"

"Help us."

"Why should I help you?"

"Because you will finally discover the truth about Julia one way or the other. You will either uncover her as a traitor or uncover the real traitor."

"But if you are the real traitors, then I will be your dupe—and I already have first-hand knowledge that your daughter is superb at playing me for a fool."

Landreth laughed heartily. "You must know you taxed her ingenuity to no small degree. Come now, do help us. I may be wrong, but I have a feeling you've already made your decision upon our innocence, else you would not have sheltered Julia last night."

"I helped Julia last night despite believing she was guilty."

Landreth's brows rose, then he looked away, saying, quite casually, "Your fiancée is already aiding us. Perhaps, if you were to speak to her, she could enlighten you on the matter."

A deep silence fell for a few moments.

"How interesting," Jason finally said. "My fiancée is already involved in this?"

"She was from the start, though she didn't know it."

Suddenly, Jason smiled. "Then by all means, if she is already helping, I see no reason why I should abstain."

"I was hoping you would see it that way," his companion said with a smug smile. "And indeed, it is but a small favor I ask of you . . ."

Julia emerged from a deep, haunting sleep to feel a persistent shaking upon her shoulder. She opened her eyes and looked up at Jason, whose large hand was upon her shoulder. For a few moments, she merely stared into his smiling hazel eyes. "Hello," she finally said, her voice husky with sleep.

"Hello. You have a visitor."

Fear rocked her; she'd slept so heavily she couldn't remember what had happened. Jason might have turned her in to the authorities after all. She pulled herself up to a seated position and searched the room fearfully. She quickly discovered her father sitting on the other side of the bed. "Father, what are you doing here?"

"Merely coming to retrieve you from Jason's good care."

Her eyes narrowed; both men appeared to be in fine spirits. "Jason, is it? How did you know I was here? Is Armand safe?"

"Yes, Armand is safe," Landreth responded. Then he looked uncomfortable. "And we, ah, traced you here—through deductive reasoning, as it were."

"Oh." Julia frowned. "But if you knew I was here, why did you endanger yourself by coming?"

"My dear, I wished to ascertain not only that you were here, but that the earl had not taken advantage of the situation."

Julia flushed, refusing to look at either man. "Your worry was quite unnecessary. Jason—the earl—would never have considered such a thing."

With her downcast eyes, Julia failed to catch the look

that passed between the two men: Jason's look was wry and Landreth merely raised his eyes toward heaven. "You see why I said I must protect her?"

"What?" Julia asked suspiciously, raising her eyes.

"Nothing, my dear," Landreth said quickly. "I'm pleased to tell you the earl has decided to aid us."

"What?" Suspicion flared in Julia's eyes as she looked to Jason. "Why would you do that?"

"I have decided I wish to know the truth. And Landreth tells me Chlorinda is involved and aiding you as well."

"Oh, I see — that would explain it. You certainly must aid your fiancée. But it could be dangerous, very dangerous."

"No more than my life has already been since I met you."

"Indeed." Julia's chin lifted, and her eyes turned to her father's in haughty anger. "Are you sure you wish this, sir?"

"We need their help, my dear," he replied.

"Very well," Julia said with ill grace, "but I do not like it."

Her father's lips quivered, but he kept a straight face. "Yes, well, it cannot be helped. Jason, let us leave Julia, that she may refresh herself and join us later."

Jason's face was just as controlled, only a glint of amusement showing — for Julia's was a display of sourness and pique. "Yes, I believe that would be well."

"Excellent," Julia said tightly. "Now that I would like — I will join you later."

Both men left quietly, and Julia fell back against her pillow. She still ached and her head felt dizzy. Jason was going to help them, for Chlorinda's sake; life was getting more complicated, more fey. It was madness, all of it, and if she managed to survive, what then? There would always be Jason and Chlorinda together and she, with an empty heart.

"Please have a seat, Chlorinda — Lord Stanton." Castlereigh studied the couple before him, particularly Chlorinda Everleigh. "I'm glad to see you again, my dear. Permit me to congratulate you on your upcoming nuptials."

350

"Thank you, my lord." Chlorinda smiled. "I appreciate you allowing us a moment of your time so I could introduce my fiancé."

Lord Castlereigh smiled and nodded to Jason. "Your name has certainly come across my desk before. I am pleased finally to meet a man who has served his country so well."

"I have done very little, my lord, but I thank you all the same," Jason said. "Chlorinda respects you very highly, and I know your opinion is of great moment to her. That is why I would like to invite you to dine with me tonight at my personal residence."

Lord Castlereigh was taken aback, though he attempted to hide his surprise. He was quite accustomed to men using any connection possible to bring them into his political sphere, but his initial impression had been that Stanton was not such a man. Such an instant and immediate invitation seemed quite out of the ordinary.

"I am sorry, my lord," he said politely, "but Lady Castlereigh and I are promised to another function this evening."

"Please, my lord," Chlorinda spoke quickly, with an unusual urgency, her blue eyes pleading. "I would dearly love it if you could—could find your way to dine with Jason tonight. I—I know my father would wish for it, too, if he were still alive."

"My dear—" Castlereigh felt quite confused. "I will be only too glad to accept your fiancé's kind offer at another time."

She shook her head firmly. "No. It needs must be tonight."

"What my fiancée means," Jason said, putting a calming hand on her arm, "is that tonight is rather special. I quite understand that yours is a very busy schedule, and it would be difficult for you to rearrange it, but I promise you, my lord, if you choose to dine with me alone tonight, it will prove very—intriguing."

"Intriguing? How so?"

"I can guarantee the finest dinner conversation—not

only entertaining, but enlightening."

Castlereigh glanced at Chlorinda, who was nearly on the edge of her chair with nervousness; then he looked back to Jason, who was sitting in the semblance of a relaxed man, but with eyes frighteningly intent. "You hold yourself to be that fine a conversationalist?"

"Tonight, I promise to be. I am quite shy of crowds, and I know if you will but dine alone with me, we can be — more open with each other."

"Alone? Mrs. Castlereigh will be quite disappointed to be excluded."

"Then you will come?" Chlorinda said hopefully.

"Yes, I do believe I shall." Castlereigh's senses were alert. The couple before him had a purpose and his curiosity, his instincts, would not allow him to deny them. "But tell me, what am I to tell Mrs. Castlereigh?"

"That you wish to meet me and insure I am a proper husband for Chlorinda," Jason said. "I believe you should tell anyone else who might be interested the same."

"I see . . ." He frowned. "So it is now to be my idea to dine with you, is that it?"

"Indeed, my lord, and such an excellent notion it is, too."

"Very well." Castlereigh's eyes narrowed at the challenge. "But I do expect to be 'enlightened' tonight. I will not take it kindly if I am disappointed."

Jason's eyes glinted back. "I assure you, my lord, whatever tonight may bring, it will not be disappointment."

That night, Castlereigh sat in Jason's elegant salon, sipping an excellent brandy and feeling quite confused. Confusion, moreover, was bringing on irritation. He had expected Jason to impart something of magnitude from the way he had spoken earlier. Yet here they sat, urbanely discussing politics and military strategy over a drink; though he was pleased to discover the earl was not only well-versed in such things, but brilliant in his ideas, he was not pleased to be passing his time in such a fashion, not when he'd left a very wroth Mrs. Castlereigh at home.

At that juncture, the earl's butler entered to announce that dinner would be served.

Jason smiled and rose. "Lord Castlereigh, let us go in. I do hope you will enjoy what I've had prepared for you. My chef is superb, and his efforts with sauces are outstanding."

Castlereigh rose, a polite smile pinned on his face, and followed his host into the dining room. His eyes scanned the table, and his irritation changed to suspicion. Two extra place settings gleamed upon the table. "I thought you said you and I were to dine here tonight."

"I said I wished for you to come alone and dine with me. I also promised you rare entertainment. Please be seated."

Castlereigh sat, his irritation burgeoning. Servants entered and he watched as they served him turtle soup, ladling some into the two bowls across from him. "Well, Stanton, your 'entertainment' is late."

"Indeed." Jason smiled. He rang a bell, and the side door opened for a couple, man and woman, to enter. The man was tall and silver-haired, the woman petite and pretty. Though she appeared haughty, he could feel she was nervous, looking at Castlereigh as though he might eat her. The man beside her struck Castlereigh as familiar, though he did not know why. "My lord, permit me to introduce Madame Jeanne Lecroix and Robert Landreth."

Castlereigh froze. "I beg your pardon?"

The silver-haired man approached, his hand stretched out in welcome. "My lord Castlereigh, I have been desiring to meet you for over a year now. I am sure you have heard the ill-natured rumor I was dead, but I certainly would not have wanted to die without meeting you first."

"Is this a hoax?" Castlereigh said, outraged. "Stanton, what is the meaning of this?"

"It's no hoax sir, only the truth," Jason said.

"My God, you've truly invited me to dine with a traitor? A dead one, at that?"

"No, sir, I've invited you to dine with a very live and loyal

353

Englishman who wishes a conference with you."

"Shall we sit down, my lord?" Landreth said kindly. "Our soup will grow cold."

Castlereigh, his anger high, spun to leave. Two stalwart footmen mysteriously appeared before each exit. "Do I have a choice?"

"Certainly," Landreth chuckled. "However, since you are here, and I have taken great pains — extremely great — to meet you, I think it would only be proper for you to listen to me. Besides, the earl does not boast when he says his chef is excellent. It would be a pity to waste such a fine meal."

Castlereigh, after considering a moment, sat down with ill grace. He feared he was in Bedlam. The others also took their seats.

"Now, my lord," Landreth said as he picked up his soup spoon, "I am sure you have many questions you would care to ask. Which do you wish to ask first?"

Castlereigh, seeing everyone else had begun to eat, picked up his spoon and sampled the soup. It was superb. "How is it you are still alive, when all reports have it to be otherwise?"

"Well, you see, my lord," Landreth said, "I have an enemy. He had taken such great measures to ensure my demise that, though I escaped the fire he had set, I decided to allow him to believe me dead. Being alive was becoming extremely exhausting."

"Was it?" Castlereigh's voice was hard, but he couldn't help feeling slightly amused. "Gracious, John always told me you had an extreme sense of humor."

Sadness entered Landreth's eyes. "Yes, John was a fine man. That is another reason I determined to remain dead: I was not about to allow his murderer to kill me before I met you, or before I personally mete out punishment for his crime."

"His murderer!" Castlereigh's spoon splashed into his soup. "John was not murdered — he died in a carriage accident!"

"Just as I was to have died in a convenient, but accidental, fire."

Castlereigh silently returned Landreth's steady gaze. "If—if this is so, who might the murderer be?"

"Converse Everleigh, the new Duke of Rendon."

"Preposterous! Absolutely preposterous!"

"Non, non," the little brunette woman said. "It is he. He is a ver' bad man, The Hawk; he killed my husband, too."

"Your husband?" Castlereigh turned his eyes toward her. "Madame—?"

"I am Jeanne Lecroix. Paul Lecroix's wife."

"Paul Lecroix . . . you're the wife of a French spy?" Castlereigh turned to Jason for confirmation; Jason nodded. "You have asked me to dine with a French spy's wife!"

"See?" Jeanne exploded, hands flying up, angry eyes turning on Landreth. "I told you he would not listen to me! The English never listen. Now he will take me to the, the— ah, bah, what do you call it? The gaol, and my son, he shall be an orphan. Oh!" Her eyes widened in terror; she turned back to Castlereigh, unaware she'd quenched his rage with her own. "Monsieur, I—I lied! I do not 'ave a son, I do not!"

He studied the woman, whose eyes were dark with consternation. "Madame, calm yourself. I do not care if you have a son. And please explain yourself—although I am English, I will strive to listen."

Jeanne hesitated, but then she began to talk. "You see, m'sieur, The Hawk, he killed my husband too."

"The Hawk?"

"Yes, yes, The Hawk—Everleigh. That is what we call him in France. Certainly he would not have used his own name, non? Just as we—"

"We?"

"My husband and the others that work for our cause. Just as we call Everleigh The Hawk, we call M'sieur Landreth The Fox. We have always known of his work, but never exactly who he was. He was so clever; we could never really determine this, so we called him The Fox."

355

"She presents a charming picture of me, does she not?" Landreth said dryly.

"But that is the truth, yes. That is why you are such a great spy," Jeanne said. She turned accusing eyes to Castlereigh. "He says you did not know he was The Fox. This, I do not comprehend. He worked for you, non?"

"I did not know he worked for us," Castlereigh said. He felt decidedly on the defensive, which seemed ridiculous.

"I would say I worked for John, my lord," Landreth said apologetically. "It seemed best, considering how secrets can be stolen. I was usually the unknown but reliable source he would mention."

"You were?" Castlereigh said, amazed. "I see."

"That is why," Jeanne said sternly, looking at both men with displeasure, "the pig man decided—"

"The pig man?"

"She means Everleigh," Landreth said.

"I said that," Jeanne said, irritably. "That is why The Hawk had to slay M'sieur Fox. So he falsely accused him, non? He wished you to kill The Fox for him."

Her tone condemned Castlereigh; he sighed. "Madame, all the evidence was against Landreth. We didn't know he was working for us, and he did not come forward to defend himself."

"But of course not!" Jeanne huffed. "You mad English would have chopped off his head—he is The Fox, not an imbecile!"

Castlereigh turned beseechingly toward Landreth. "Kindly explain this to me. And you had best be convincing."

"But of course." Landreth smiled.

"I have not finished my story," Jeanne said, offended. "That is what you brought me here to do. Why does he not listen to me?"

"He is, my dear." Landreth chuckled. "But I believe I must tell him mine first, after all."

Landreth's story was far clearer and more distinct. Though Castlereigh found it hard to credit, the strength of his testimony was confounding. Landreth had access to knowledge only Castlereigh and Lord John had shared. At the end of the explanation and examination—in which, try as he could, he could not catch Landreth out or sway Jeanne's vehemence—he sighed. "If what you say is true, Landreth, how do you propose to uncover Everleigh? How do you intend to prove to me that it is he, not you, who is the traitor?"

"Oui." Jeanne nodded in agreement. "How do you plan it? I told you. Monsieur Castlereigh, even though he seems reasonable for an Englishman, would not just take our word for it."

"I intend," Landreth said quietly, "to prove it to you—and only you, sir."

"That is a start," Castlereigh said slowly. "But if you prove it only to me, how do you expect me to bring him to public trial?"

"I do not wish him to be brought to public trial."

"What? What do you mean?"

"If you bring him to trial, you will defame the Everleigh name. Chlorinda Everleigh will be stripped of all the lands and live in infamy, even if she has been loyal. John was my dearest friend; I will not see his family ruined because of Converse's treachery. His death would not be avenged in such a case—indeed, Converse once again would have won if he destroyed John's loved one."

"But—"

"I would also not care for Whitehall to appear the fool in this matter—nor the Regent who has bestowed his favor upon Converse."

Castlereigh's mouth closed. "Indeed, you have me there. What do you propose?"

"I will prove to you beyond doubt that Converse Everleigh is both traitor and murderer, if, in return, you grant me one boon."

"And what is that?"

"I will be his judge, his jury—and his executioner."

"You will be his executioner?"

357

"Yes. He killed my dearest friend. He has tried to destroy my family and tarnish my name. He dared to think he would be master of Landreth lands. I have the right. I and I alone shall execute him." The man's voice was calm, implacable.

Castlereigh controlled the chill that passed through him. Generations of family pride and honor seemed to look out at him through the demanding eyes of Robert Landreth. Eyes that called for personal justice, the eyes of a man who would clearly settle for nothing else. He was beginning to believe this man's story. He was also beginning to pity Rendon if it were true. He cleared his throat. "And for you to do this, I presume I am to permit you to go free? How do I know I am not letting the true traitor free to falsely implicate, then kill, the Duke of Rendon?"

"Impossible!" Jeanne stood up angrily. "This man is impossible! He does not believe us!"

Landreth's hand clasped Jeanne's. "No, chérie, he is merely cautious. Very reasonable – I expected no less. Now, sit." Eyes shooting sparks, Jeanne stared at him. "Please, my dear." She sat down with a small nod.

Landreth turned to Castlereigh. "I understand your dilemma perfectly, my lord; that is why I offer into your care my most cherished possessions. Possessions that guarantee I will come back to you. As for killing Everleigh, I could have done that many times since reaching England. I wish for justice to be done and my family honor restored. He is the only man who can do that, and I will not kill him until it is done."

"I understand you offer me a security," Castlereigh said with interest.

"Yes, I do, but you must guard it with your life. I must have your word of honor upon that."

Castlereigh paused, turning to study Jeanne, who gazed now at Landreth in bafflement. He glanced next at Jason, who also appeared tense and suspicious – obviously, both were as confused as he. Landreth played a deep game.

He considered cautiously another moment, then nodded. "Very well, I give you my word of honor—if the security is great enough to satisfy me."

"The security is great enough," Landreth said. His face was solemn, no longer nonchalant, and he clapped his hands loudly. "You may come out now . . ."

Another couple appeared from the same door Landreth and Jeanne had entered by—a woman with Landreth's silver hair, and a man with his nonchalant style.

"No!" Jason rose from his chair with a start. "You didn't tell me of this, Robert. I will not allow it!"

Landreth rose more slowly. "It must be done, Jason." He turned from the volcanically imposing earl back to Castlereigh. "My lord, may I present my children, Julia and Armand Landreth."

"My lord." Julia curtsied.

"Pleased to meet you," Armand said, executing a graceful leg.

Castlereigh drew in his breath, completely stunned. "I see. Yes, I see. Er—how do you do? Yes, they are certainly sufficient security."

"No, they are not!" Jason bit out. "For I will not permit this!"

"Jason, you must." Julia came to him, hands reaching out. Castlereigh felt amazed at her temerity, for Jason exuded a dangerous energy. "Please, this is the only way."

"The only way?" He clasped her hands. Castlereigh could see the grip was hard enough to be painful, but the lady did not flinch. "You have some scheme cooked up, I have no doubt, but what if it goes awry? What then?"

"It won't! We must prove our innocence; was it not you who said you wanted the truth?"

"Not at the cost of your life."

"I thought you wanted to kill me yourself," she said with a wry twist of her lips. It was a pitiful attempt at a smile.

"I didn't mean it."

"Don't you see, Jason, there is no life for me this way. I cannot live forever running, forever masquerading. I cannot live without honor."

"You tricked me again, Madame." His voice was gentle. "I would not have aided you in this."

"She didn't trick you, son." Landreth stepped toward them. "I did. I knew you would not allow it if you knew, but she is my daughter—I would not play with her life needlessly."

The two men gazed at each other, deadlocked. Finally, Jason nodded curtly, and his eyes turned to pierce Castlereigh. "Landreth chooses to offer up his children to your care. I will let you take them for now, but if they become endangered in any way, I will come, too. Unlike Landreth, it will not be to turn myself in. I will take them back, is that understood?"

"Jason, no!" Julia exclaimed. "You don't know what you're saying."

"Yes, I do, and I say it."

She trembled a moment, then turned to Castlereigh. "We are ready to go with you, sir."

"Very well." Castlereigh felt he'd just made an agreement with the devil—or a host of devils. He chanced one more glance at Jason, who was now tautly under control. Unable to meet his stare, he turned to the father of his 'security'. Landreth stood tall and dignified—and his intent gaze seemed deadly serious.

If ever Castlereigh prayed for everything to go perfectly, he prayed now. He knew that if he took the Landreth children into custody, there would be two men to reckon with if any harm came to them. One would face death if need be; the other would tear down the prison walls. Not a pleasant prospect, not a pleasant prospect at all.

"At least they're being treated well," Jason said bleakly. His eyes scanned the streets from his townhouse window. He wasn't looking at anything in particular—in fact, he wasn't seeing the view at all. Slowly, he turned towards the forlorn woman sitting on his sofa.

"Treated well," Chlorinda repeated. "In a cell, fed bread

360

and water?"

"Castlereigh cannot offer them any other treatment without arousing suspicion—especially your uncle's."

A ghost of a smile touched Chlorinda's pale face. "He does not seem too wary—just wroth he is unable to reach them now."

"Indeed, he attempted to send an assassin in last evening, in the guise of a warder with food," Jason said. "Armand—" He checked in midsentence as Chlorinda swayed. He was beside her at once, a comforting arm around her shoulder.

She swallowed. "Yes—what of Armand? He—he wasn't hurt, was he?"

"Of course not—the assassin, however, was a bit worse for wear."

Chlorinda laughed lightly. "Indeed, I should have known."

"I am sorry I alarmed you like that," Jason said gently. "You're shaking."

She hid her eyes from him. "Thank you—I'm fine. You—you're very kind, my lord."

"Kind, yes." He pulled her chin up in order that she might look at him. "But not the man you love, I believe."

Agony filled her eyes. "I—I am sorry, Jason."

"Do not be," he said with a wry smile. "There was a time when we would have made a good marriage, safe and conventional. But now . . ."

"Now it is different, is it not?" Chlorinda asked, almost in bewilderment. "Things have changed so much."

"Yes, ever since we became embroiled with the Landreth family. *Safety* is not a word that comes to mind in their case."

"Neither is *conventional*." The blue of Chlorinda's eyes softened as she smiled. "You love Julia, don't you?"

"Yes. I fear I do."

The two clasped hands then and sat together in silence. "I pray they may come out of this safely." Chlorinda finally said. "The trial is tomorrow."

"I know," Jason sighed. "Landreth says he will satisfy Castlereigh tonight, before the trial, that all will work out—but I do not see how. If anything should happen—"

"Don't think about that," Chlorinda said quickly. "It will work out. My father always said Robert Landreth was the coolest man he knew, and that was what made him so successful. We must believe he will satisfy Castlereigh before tomorrow morning. We simply must."

It was late, and the Duke of Rendon still sat at his office desk, working on papers. A slight frown marred his brow, and his cold eyes scanned and rescanned the pages. Other than that, he appeared calm and composed.

The gold-leaf clock upon the shelf chimed the hour of midnight, and the shadow of a man quietly slipped in from the window. He stood a moment, his gaze resting upon the large portrait of Lord John. Then, softly, he walked up to the desk.

Everleigh's eyes rose from the document. He froze. Disbelief filled his gaze, chased by a flicker of fear.

"Hello, Everleigh," Landreth said, his voice softly chilling. "I've come to haunt you."

"Landreth! How . . . ?"

"You tried to burn me in my own house. Not only did that show bad manners, but folly as well. A fox's den always has a foxhole—an escape neither above ground nor obvious to the eye." The glint in his eyes deepened. He withdrew a pistol from his pocket, training it upon the seated duke.

Everleigh leaned back, his hands slowly sliding into a drawer. "It's not there, Everleigh. I removed it. I came merely to talk with you, but seeing you now, after a year of your hounding, I fear I cannot abide your presence on this planet another minute."

"You take justice into your own hands?" Rendon said, a tic starting in his jaw. "Not very honorable."

"Justice—or revenge." His voice was hoarse. "Have it

362

what you will. My children are incarcerated, to be tried as traitors on the morrow. I cannot aid them—I thought I could, but I cannot. I have failed at that—but I will not fail in killing you."

Sudden hope flared in Everleigh's eyes, and he leaned back, laughing softly. "Kill me, Landreth, and you will indeed be unable to save your children. I am the only one who can do that, for only I know of their innocence."

"And you intend to testify against them tomorrow." Landreth's hand shook with the strength of his emotion. "I won't allow that." Walking around the desk, he placed the barrel of the pistol deliberately at Rendon's temple and cocked the hammer slowly. "Are you ready to go to hell, Converse?"

"Wait!" Sweat beaded on Everleigh's forehead as a tremor ran through him. "I can save your children—I can, I swear it!"

"How? How can you do that, bastard?"

"I—I can confess. I can tell everything. Th-that it was I who committed the treason. That I made them seem the traitors. I will, I swear it." His breath came in gasps, his voice breaking. "Don't kill me, for God's sake, don't kill me!"

Landreth slowly uncocked the gun. He withdrew it from the duke's temple. "You will admit you are The Hawk?"

"Yes, of course."

"And that you gained the aid of spy Paul Lecroix to ensnare us in your lies, only to kill him later?"

Everleigh visibly relaxed. "Of course, but that was a mere detail. He was of no account, easily handled."

"Careful, Converse, your conceit is showing."

"And should it not? I am a mastermind. I even outwitted you, the great Fox, so secret no one knew your name. But I unmasked you—I, The Hawk!"

"Only because your brother came to you with the knowledge."

"Oh yes, dear John. Respected by all, responsible, reliable, powerful. His power proved futile against me."

"You boast of killing your brother?"

Everleigh smiled, coolly amused. "You made it so easy for me, Robert, I could not resist. Admittedly, until you gave him the evidence against me—and he, honorable dullard that he was, confronted me with it—I would never have thought to kill him. I always despised him, but never saw the way to kill him, to gain what he had, until you forced me to see it clearly."

"For that you will die, Converse."

Everleigh laughed. "No, I will not! I can save your children; I created the evidence against them, I can uncreate it. But you're a fool if you think I will ever confess to anyone what I have told you. Once again, The Hawk will triumph over The Fox. I will set your children free—when you swear to allow *me* to go free. That is my offer."

Landreth smiled grimly. "You seek to bargain. But you're wrong, Converse. I will not let you go free. Your time is at an end. I know your treachery and I will be your executioner."

"You would shoot me in cold blood?"

"No—I am going to grant you a chance to prove once and for all which of us is the master. We will fence one final time."

Everleigh's grin became feral. "Excellent. I will cut you down."

Landreth bowed. He walked slowly back to the window, his eye never leaving his adversary. He reached outside and drew in two rapiers.

"You've planned this." Everleigh rose slowly and drew off his coat.

Landreth barely contained his anger as he threw the duke one of the rapiers. "I may not be able to save my children, but this I know I can do. You will die."

"I doubt that." Everleigh tested the foil, smiling. "You consider yourself the master in fencing, but you will see I am your master here—as in everything else."

"Begin."

The men slipped into an en garde crouch. Their blades

met, clashing with sure skill, high, low, lunge, disengage, riposte. Everleigh feinted high, then dropped his blade for a low thrust, only to have Landreth parry and deliver a lightning riposte. The duke barely parried the stroke.

"You lose ground," Robert murmured. The tip of his sword almost slid under Everleigh's guard.

"Unlikely." Sweat trickled down the duke's jaw. "I still control the game!" He knocked the blow aside, then thrust.

"Conceit." Landreth parried coolly. "You're a puppet master who has lost control of the strings—and I shall use them to strangle you."

"You lie." Beat, parry, lunge, parry, riposte—Everleigh hissed as Landreth danced back out of range. "I have left no clue, no trace—"

"The widow, Converse." Landreth closed again, not attacking, only parrying Everleigh's ever-more-frantic thrusts. "You shouldn't have let her slip away. I have her."

Everleigh hesitated a second. Landreth thrust, darting around the duke's blade, scoring the man's arm lightly. The duke retaliated, desperately trying to break Landreth's defenses. "There—is—no—widow!"

"There is. She witnessed your meeting with her husband. She knows you and can testify against you."

"So?" Both their shirts were damp with sweat, and Everleigh's sleeve glinted crimson in the lamplight. "Who will believe a French slut?—"

Landreth batted the duke's sword out of line and slashed a long, deep cut across Everleigh's chest. "Do not say that again."

The duke gritted his teeth. His parries had slowed; yet Landreth took no advantage, slowing his own attacks to match.

"And then there is Chlorinda." Another cut, as Landreth spoke, down the duke's thigh.

"Chlorinda? Chlorinda is nothing!"

"She remembers everything. She remembers hearing you give the orders to kill John—and she will testify."

"Lies! She lies!"

"It was your greed, Converse—you really should have killed her, too. She helped Armand escape; John's child foiled you."

"No! Damn you, Landreth, damn you to hell!" Skill and training forgotten, he swung his sword like a berserker.

"No." Landreth parried every blow. "No, Converse, damn *you* to hell." He drew back, then lunged again, slipping past Everleigh's rapier as if it didn't exist.

His sword-point slid smoothly between the duke's ribs. Everleigh's fevered, angry face glazed over with surprise, and he fell, looking astonished that fate had finally called him to account.

Landreth dropped his rapier and bowed his head. "It's all right now, John." His head rose and his pain-filled eyes found the eyes in the painting. "Has justice been done? Has justice been done?"

After a second of silence, there came a gentle click and the panel beside the fireplace swung open. Castlereigh, pale and solemn, entered the room. He went over to Everleigh's body and stared down into the death mask. A shudder ran through him. "Yes, Landreth, yes. Justice has been done."

Chapter Nineteen
Treason's Aftermath

The rays of the morning sun were both cool and warm as they filtered into the dim courtroom. It didn't matter that it was early—people crowded into the room. Many waited outside, impatient for news of the traitors' fate, just as their countrymen did within.

The crowd was an entity in its own right, strong with anger and bloodlust. It murmured, it rustled, it growled as the two prisoners were shoved, manacled and chained, into its seething presence. Neither the barristers nor the judge noted the battered, disgraceful condition of the prisoners. The crowd openly approved of the torn, dirty clothes, the haggard features, and the bruised faces of Julia and Armand Landreth.

"Oh, my God," Chlorinda moaned. Her hand convulsively clenched Jason's arm. "Look at them! Oh, my God!"

"Damn Landreth," Jason hissed. His eyes flared with impotent rage and pain. "Why did he permit such mistreatment? Where the hell is he?"

"He will come," Jeanne whispered tightly, though her eyes shimmered with tears. "Mon Dieu, those poor children. These English beasts, bah!"

The two prisoners stood as straight as their chains would permit. As if divining the sole island of kindness within the mob, Julia raised her eyes to her friends. Her gaze met and melded with Jason's. He appeared to start and almost rose. She shook her head slightly, but a new strength seemed to fill her eyes. She straightened her shoulders completely and turned a dignified, determined gaze upon the rest of the room.

The watchers noticed and a low rumble began. Armand raised his head at the sound and his lips slowly curved into a smile. He bowed sardonically to the angry crowd, his manacles clanking with the motion. His guard cuffed him roughly.

The crowd exploded with howls; the judge frowned and called for order.

As the room fell silent, he barked for the prosecution to get on with it. A slight confusion and hesitation occurred amongst the barristers. Finally, an uncomfortable, red-faced spokesman rose. He coughed. "I—I'm sorry, your honor, but his grace, the Duke of Rendon, has not yet arrived."

The judge frowned forbiddingly. He opened his mouth, obviously to deliver a stinging reprimand, when the back doors suddenly flew open, drowning him out. Lord Castlereigh entered, stalking down the center aisle, looking very official and very serious.

The onlookers watched, slightly subdued by his presence, as Lord Castlereigh approached the barristers. Whispers hissed as he flashed a legal-looking document to the men, who reacted with stunned amazement.

The barristers immediately requested a council with the magistrate; eyeing the tense, maddened crowd, the judge quickly agreed. Someone handed him Lord Castlereigh's document and barely a second after scanning it, he called for a recess. The crowd broke into excited yaps and mutters as judge and lawyers disappeared together.

"What does this mean?" Chlorinda's blue eyes were large in her pale face.

"It's Monsieur, of course," Jeanne said, nodding her head in a positive manner. "The Fox, he has caused this.

Enfin, I cannot wait to see what he has done."

Jason's grim face had brightened. "I believe, Madame, you may be correct."

The magistrate re-emerged from his chambers. He did not take his seat, but stood, looking sternly out across the crowd. "The crown has withdrawn its accusations against the Landreth family." The room reverberated with the crowd's uproar and he raised his hand. "The Prince Regent himself has ordered it done and set his seal upon it. New information has proven the Landreth family to be not only completely innocent of treason, but loyal English patriots ensnared by a nefarious French plot. Therefore, the Prince offers the Landreths clemency, and lauds and honors them for their steady faithfulness to their country."

The judge hesitated; the room was still, clinging to each word. "This heinous plot against loyal subjects was uncovered through the efforts of Converse Everleigh, Duke of Rendon. His Majesty grieves that in his efforts to bare the French intrigue, he was slain. We mourn him."

"He is dead!" Jeanne squealed, clapping her hands in delight. She lowered her voice immediately. "The Hawk is dead!" Suddenly, a look of sheer consternation crossed her face, and she turned to Chlorinda repentantly. "Ah me, my wicked tongue. Forgive me."

"No." A gentle peace had settled on Chlorinda's fair features. "I, too, am happy — save that he went unpunished."

Jason clasped her hand and squeezed it. "It is Landreth's memorial to your father — and his gift to you."

She blinked and nodded mistily. They turned their attention back to the magistrate as he spoke again. "And though we mourn the duke's passing, we can rejoice that another patriot, thought slain, survives. Despite the vile French scheme, Robert Landreth still lives!"

Jason chuckled, then broke out laughing as the room roared in a frenzy. Ladies fainted, and men who would earlier have spit at the news now applauded. He shook his head, hazel eyes glimmering. "Faith, they've done it! Against all odds, the family has done it!"

Landreth Court shone with the brilliance of glowing chandeliers and glittering aristocrats. Since the Regent's announcement, the upper ten had become charmed and smitten with the Landreths. Not one would have missed this, the Landreths' debut ball.

Talk, inevitably, centered on the family, now totally unmasked and far more amazing than they had ever been before. Men and women alike shook their heads in wonder at Armand Landreth, not only tastefully dressed but virile as well. That he could have been the effeminate Sir Horace still confounded them.

The men shook their heads even more, eyes aglow, when they looked at Julia. With her tall, willowy figure and gleaming silver-blond hair, she resembled a moon goddess. She was such a far cry from drab, skitterwitted Miranda Waverly no one quite believed it, in spite of the facts.

Indeed, the Landreth offspring were in high demand for the evening. Jason stood beside Chlorinda as they watched Armand dancing with a vivacious brunette.

"You have not told him our engagement is at an end?" he asked softly.

"No," Chlorinda said in a sad voice, her eyes never leaving Armand. "I—I have not seen him much since the trial, and when I do . . . it never seems to be the time to tell him."

"Yes," Jason said wryly. "England has been so busy feting them, it is difficult to talk to them alone."

"Then you have not told Julia?"

"You must tell Armand, first. I wouldn't feel it right or honorable to tell Julia until then."

They were both silent a moment. Jason looked at Chlorinda with gentle understanding. "They really have had much to do. What with opening up the Court again, and making their entry into society as themselves, that is."

"I know," Chlorinda sighed, "but I feel as if Armand is intentionally avoiding me."

"I believe it is important for you to tell him," Jason said—and he left her.

Chlorinda frowned. Tell him, Jason said. Did he not understand how difficult it would be? Would it not be obvious to Armand that it was because she loved him that she was not marrying Jason? What if he did not love her as she thought he did? He had just returned to his rightful place in society. He could choose any woman he wished—some beautiful, fascinating woman who had never failed her father or had an Uncle Converse.

She tensed; the dance had ended, and Armand was looking toward her. Worse, he was approaching. "Good evening, Chlorinda."

"Good evening."

"Would you care to dance? It's a waltz."

"Yes, thank you."

The couple moved silently to the floor. The music began, but conversation between the two did not. Chlorinda peered up at Armand and saw him watching her with an unreadable expression.

"Your home is very lovely, sir," she said weakly.

"Sir? Can you not call me by name?"

"Armand." She blushed. "Your home is beautiful."

"And so are y—" He broke off.

Her heart fell. "Yes?" she prompted.

"Nothing . . . it's a beautiful evening."

She couldn't bear it any longer! "Jason and I broke our engagement."

"What?" Armand stiffened and their waltzing came to a grinding halt.

"I said—" Other couples careened into them but he stared only at her; she wished she could fall through the floor. "—I said Jason and I broke our betrothal."

A light flared in Armand's eyes that Chlorinda didn't know whether to fear or welcome. He grabbed her by the wrist and pulled her from the dance floor toward the bal-

371

cony doors.

"What are you doing?" she protested as he dragged her down the steps and out onto the lawn. He did not reply, but kept leading her on until they finally came to a small, private garden.

"Here." He turned abruptly to face her, and his look took away what little breath remained in her. "Here's where I have wanted to bring you for so very long. It reminds me of the night in your garden. The first night we met."

"You mean the first night I met you as my masked stranger?"

"No." He drew her gently into his arms. "Not as your masked stranger, but as your fool. Marry me, Chlorinda."

"Wh-what?" Chlorinda gasped, her heart hammering.

"I've waited so long to be able to ask you. If you're free of Wynhaven, I will wait no longer."

"Oh—is that why you've been avoiding me?"

"Yes, of course; what else did you think it could be?"

"I thought it was because you might have decided you didn't care for me after all. I thought you'd gone back to—to how Sir Horace felt."

"I forced Sir Horace to hate you," Armand said. "You see, I wanted to love you, even when I didn't know if you were my enemy or not. Even when you were pledged to another."

"And I—was rather envious of Miranda," Chlorinda confessed, shamefaced. "And how you—I mean Sir Horace—made love to her."

Armand chuckled. "Sir Horace could never make love to you as I intend to do."

Chlorinda shivered as his gentle, demanding lips found hers. She floated in a mist of sweet passion that was slowly turning into a fire from her toes on upward. She sighed as he finally drew away.

"Do you forgive me for deceiving you?" Armand asked, his voice slightly rough.

"Oh, yes. If you had not, I would never have been free

372

of Uncle Converse, or my guilt."

"And you do not love Jason?"

"You know I never did. Although I own he has never kissed me as you have — nor have I ever desired him to do so as I do with you."

"Then say it, English rose. Say you will marry me!"

"Yes, Armand, yes! I love you so very much." Smiling, he bent to kiss her.

"Armand," a stern voice commanded from behind them. The two lovers turned to see Robert Landreth watching. "What do you think you are doing?"

Armand sighed. "Attempting to kiss my fiancée." Then he smiled. "Chlorinda and Jason finally broke their engagement."

"I certainly hope so," Landreth said sardonically. "It was high time." He smiled warmly at an apprehensive Chlorinda. "I had expected the two of you to sever that bond far sooner. You've caused my children considerable grief."

"I am sorry, sir," she said, smiling, "but I intend to make it up to your son."

Landreth laughed. "Excellent!" Then his voice lost its bantering tone. "I am proud to have you in the family, my dear. Your father and I always intended it to be this way."

"What?" Armand said in surprise.

Landreth smiled complacently. "We knew you two were made for each other — now don't poker up, Armand; you've already asked her, so you certainly cannot renege now. After Jason, that would be far too much."

"You know I never would," Armand said. "Besides, who am I to disagree with fate?"

"I'm glad we didn't upset your plans, sir," Chlorinda said, laughing, but a warm glow suffused her heart. Her father would have approved her choice of a husband, had even wanted it.

Landreth nodded, then his look became distracted. "Has either of you two seen Jeanne?"

"No," Armand said slowly. "She said she would join us,

but I have not seen her."

"Well, I'm sure I will find her," his father said. "Congratulations, children." He turned and left, a frown hovering upon his brow.

Armand stared after him with an arrested expression and then laughed. "I believe Jeanne may be the one person who does intend to upset Sir's plans."

Chlorinda giggled. "I fear so. Now, sir, you may kiss me again—after all, it is merely what your father intended . . ."

Landreth threaded his way through the crowds, his blue eyes intently searching the room for the petite Frenchwoman. He was unrewarded, but he discovered Julia coming from the retiring room. "Do you know where Jeanne is, my dear?"

Julia frowned. "No, sir, I have not seen her yet. I had imagined she had already come down; perhaps she did not feel well. She did seem to be acting rather strangely this afternoon."

"Perhaps," Landreth said. "But then she would have sent word—never worry, I shall find her, no doubt." He swung away, distracted, but then turned back, his eyes glinting with mischief. "By the by, dear, Jason and Chlorinda are no longer engaged. Armand and Chlorinda are, though. He just proposed and she accepted—but I see them approaching. I will allow them to tell you the tidings."

"But father—" He smiled at her stunned expression and departed.

After circling the room again, he went and found his new butler, Jennings, and asked if he'd seen Mrs. Lecroix.

"No, sir—I presume she is still packing."

"Packing?"

"Yes, she said she still had much to do before your journey."

"Journey?"

"Yes, when you take the madame back to France. She

374

said she might pack tonight rather than attend the ball since she only had a few more days—sir?" Jennings asked as his employer cursed and spun away. Shaking his head, he went back to his duties.

Jeanne sighed as she closed the lid of another trunk. Downstairs, the cream of English society was dancing and chatting, and here she was packing with a sadness in her heart she could not chase away. Robert probably wouldn't even notice she was missing, although he had sent her a green satin ball gown that shimmered and tempted her each time she looked at it lying on a chair.

No, do not be foolish, she scolded herself. She didn't need to go down amongst all those snobbish, cold Englishmen. She did not need to see Robert Landreth mix with his own, nor to taste his champagne, when she had only a lonely France to go back to. A lonely France with no silver-haired man waiting there.

The door to the salon opened and she turned. Landreth stood upon the threshold, every inch the fine aristocrat, in black satin with silver lace at the cuffs. Her heart twisted within her at the look of anger and hurt upon his face.

"What are you doing?" he asked quietly as he entered and closed the door.

"I am packing," she said with a feigned nonchalance. "You promised I could go back to France if I helped you."

"But why tonight?" His voice was sharp. "There's a ball in progress downstairs. You never said you would not come to it."

"I decided to pack instead. Why should I meet these English pi—people, when I will be back in my France soon?"

"Why? Because I bought you a dress for it. Because we all thought you would join us tonight—we all *wished* you would join us tonight." His eyes roved to the green dress upon the chair. "Was the dress not to your liking?"

"Non." Her eyes looked longingly at the dress. "Non, it

is most beautiful. I—I just do not wish to go to the ball."

Landreth's blue eyes flared. He walked stiffly over to the dress, picked it up, and brought it to her, holding it out. "You gave everyone the impression you would come to the ball. Many wish to meet you. You will disappoint the children if you do not come. Now, put on this dress and come downstairs."

"Non." Her small body stiffened and sparks flashed from her eyes. "Who are you to order me about? The great aristocrat you may be, with all your silly English falling all over you, but not me! I am not your—your lackey! I do what I will."

His free hand shot out and grasped her, dragging her close. "You will put the dress on, or I will do it for you."

"Mon Dieu!" She had never seen him like this, but she still shook her head. "I do not believe you—I will not!"

The ball gown slid down between them, and Landreth clasped her shoulders with both hands. "Do not try me."

"You—you are mad! *Enfin,* I do not wait, I will leave tonight! Let me go, you brute!"

Robert's right hand slipped to the back of her neck and efficiently undid the top button. "Don't!" Her second button snapped open. "Stop! I—I will go to the ball!" The third button joined the others. "I said I will, I will go to the ball."

"I want you to stay, chérie," Landreth said softly, almost in surprise.

"I said I will—non, do not touch another!"

"I want you to stay, and not just for the ball." He caressed the nape of her neck, entangling his fingers in her hair. "Stay with me here in England. I cannot go back to France now."

Jeanne's mouth fell open. The insidious man took the opportunity to cover her mouth with his, kissing her warmly, fully. She felt no shock, just a sense of rightness she had never felt before, even with Paul. She melted into him, feeling her softness flowing to his hardness. Passion ran between them, scalding and chilling her to the marrow.

"Non," she whispered as her body thrilled to his touch. "Non, monsieur, I cannot stay, I—I cannot be your mistress." The words were torn out of her.

He stiffened, and his arms tightened around her like bands of steel. "I want you as wife, Jeanne. Understand me, I want you as wife or as nothing."

She felt as if she would faint; the strength of his hold had already stopped her breathing, without his stunning words. "Let me go!" His arms dropped as he stepped away; she nearly fell, so swiftly did he withdraw. She closed her eyes, breathing in deeply, trying to settle her swirling world. Then she opened them again. He stood before her, concern, fear, and even hesitation in his eyes. "You—you want to marry me?" she stammered; almost afraid she hadn't heard him correctly.

"Yes. I know it's terribly English, but I could not tolerate being your lover, then having you leave me for France."

But—Lady Daniella said you would never marry again."

"I thought I never would. I never imagined I'd find love again. But I love you, Jeanne. If I could go back to France with you, I would, I truly would. But you know I can't."

Jeanne smiled, mischievous, purely feminine. She stepped towards him, her arms sliding around his shoulders. "I find I like England very much. It is not so cold, you see. And some English, why I love them very much— but will your English lords and ladies ever accept me?"

Landreth laughed, lifting her off the ground with his hug. "Just leave that to me, *mon cher*. With the story I will tell, they will accept you with open arms."

Jeanne's giggle was muffled against his chest. "Yes, M'sieur Reynard, I believe you will manage it." She pushed him away as he bent to kiss her, her eyes sparkling with love and laughter. "Non, no more of that. I have a ball to dress for. You have been of much service but I think, if I am ever to go, I must have my maid instead."

"Very well, he sighed. "But you will marry me soon."

Jeanne flushed. "Yes, as soon as you wish. We are in England, non? We will behave as the English do. We will be respectable, non?"

Julia had frozen when her father so carelessly dropped those yearned-for words—*Jason and Chlorinda were no longer engaged.*

She shook herself back to reality and smiled with true warmth when Armand and Chlorinda came to her, to share their news, love and excitement filling their eyes.

"Where is Jason?" Chlorinda then asked happily and totally without embarrassment.

It was the very question Julia had been asking herself. "I don't know. I saw him earlier."

"Oh, there he is," Chlorinda said, pointing across the large and crowded room. "Come, Armand, we must go to him." Armand rolled his eyes at Julia, shrugged fatalistically, and allowed Chlorinda to lead him away.

Julia watched, amazed. Chlorinda evidently still considered Jason a friend, implying they'd broken off the engagement without rancor. Or was that only on Chlorinda's side?

How did Jason feel? He had danced with her earlier and never mentioned it. Was it too painful for him to talk about?

She quickly turned her head away from the group, lest she be caught studying them. When she glanced back in their direction, they had disappeared.

Julia forced her social smile to her lips and circulated amongst the guests. She talked and danced her way through her daze until her father and Jeanne finally appeared, Jeanne resplendent in green satin, her father with a look on his face she had never seen before. As they approached her, she knew beforehand what they were going to say. It was obvious in their eyes and faces, and when they finally told her, she congratulated them

378

warmly.

"Are you not surprised?" Jeanne asked.

"No, not at all. I wondered when you two would realize you were in love."

"Ha," Jeanne said. "Me, I was totally surprised."

"So was I," Landreth said. "It appears my daughter was before us on this."

Jeanne smiled warmly at Julia. "Now we must tell Armand and Chlorinda. Will we surprise them, Julia?"

"I don't think so."

"Eh, bien," she said happily. "I am pleased. Is this not a great night?"

"Yes, it is," Julia said, though her smile waned.

"Where is Jason?" her father asked.

"I don't know—he disappeared." Julia attempted a shrug.

"I see." Landreth said nothing more and for the second time that evening, a happily engaged couple left Julia's side. It was harder and harder to keep smiling.

The night seemed endless. She laughed, she ate, she danced, she did everything a woman enjoying herself should do. Jason never appeared.

She was beyond grateful when the last goodbyes were said, and she could drag herself up the stairs and head toward the haven of her room. She opened the door, sighing—and the sigh turned into a gasp of surprise.

The room was aglow with myriad candles. Her maid was nowhere to be seen. When her eyes found the bed, she blinked and blinked again. It was strewn with soft rose petals, so heavily carpeted with them she could not even see the coverlet. Two glasses and a bottle of chilled champagne rested upon the bedside table.

Her heart lurched as Jason stepped quietly out from behind the dressing screen.

"Hello, sprite." There was a soft smile on his lips. "Do you think this is decadent and romantic enough to suit Granny's tastes?"

Julia could only nod, dazed. "Yes. Yes, I do believe so."

"Excellent," he murmured, treading softly toward her. "I would not wish her to think me lacking in romantic fervor."

He drew Julia's unresisting hand into his warm grasp and pulled her to the bed. He sat her gently down upon it while she gazed at him in a trance. It dissipated when he knelt down and lifted the hem of her skirts. "Jason, what are you doing?"

"Merely kissing the hem of your dress." He grinned and lifted the silk to his lips.

Julia broke into laughter and her hands went to his shoulders. "You're being ridiculous!"

"Am I?" He rose swiftly and kissed her with a fervor that sent Julia reeling. They fell back upon the bed.

The scent of roses only slightly invaded Julia's awareness, for the feel of Jason's hands, lips, and body commanded all her attention. She shivered as his mouth found and nuzzled the sensitive spot behind her ear. "I am no longer engaged to Chlorinda," he whispered.

"I—I know—" She seemed to be having trouble breathing.

His lips blazed a tender, warm path back to her mouth, then hovered there. "Will you marry me, Madame?"

"Yes . . ." She pulled his head down, bringing the warmth of him back to her. She kissed him with all the depth of her emotions, nothing held back, no masquerading.

"Lord, Julia," Jason said, pulling back and laughing softly, "I loved you the best."

"What?"

"Since meeting you, I've been falling in love with all kinds of women. A sprite at a pond, whom I thought an illusory dream. A crotchety old woman. Faith, that was when I really feared I was going mad—to fall in love with a woman old enough to be my grandmother!"

"And the traitoress? What of her?"

"Though I could not admit it, I loved her, too."

"But—can you trust her?" Julia asked fearfully.

380

"I loved them all, but you are the one I can trust," he said softly. "You were the woman I've been chasing through them all, the one I've always wanted."

"I love you, Jason." Her voice was husky. He kissed her in reply, and any worries she had melted away.

"Ah, excellent." They both froze and looked up to see her father watching them from the foot of the bed, Armand and Jeanne behind him.

Jason sighed. "At least I'm not being shot at for kissing you this time." He sat up and pulled her up beside him.

"I believe this means you are suitably engaged, Jason?" Landreth asked appreciatively.

Jason grinned. "Yes, my lord, it does."

"Gads." Armand looked wonderingly about the room. "I must hand it to you, Jason—I didn't think you had it in you."

"Oui," Jeanne nodded, "the mountain, he is not so dull an Englishman, is he?"

Julia's eyes glowed as she looked to Jason. "No. No, he isn't. Not at all."

"Champagne, too." Armand walked over and looked down at the tray. "But only two glasses, tsk."

"Eh, bien," Jeanne said laughing, "that is no problem." She pulled out a glass from behind her. Robert and Armand followed suit.

"Now that is better," Landreth said.

"Is it?" Jason asked under his breath.

"Come now, old man." Taking the bottle, Armand poured champagne into his glass. "We've been waiting all night for you to get on with it."

"Besides, my friend," Landreth said, handing over his glass, "I knew you would need a chaperone about this time."

"Did you?" Julia's eyes narrowed.

"But of course." Jeanne accepted a glassful. "The gentleman, he has French flare, no?"

Julia laughed and took a glass herself. "In that you are correct, Step-mama."

"And we are now in England and must be respectable, no?" Jeanne went on.

Landreth sighed sadly. "She has suddenly decided that is the proper thing for us all."

"Gad's," Armand yelped. "I hope not. I didn't fight for my life only to settle down to that."

"And I didn't learn everything from Julia, Madame, for me to fall back to that," Jason said. "Respectability is highly over-rated."

Jeanne grinned complacently. "I told you, Monsieur, I like your family."

Landreth grinned back and raised his glass. "A toast. To the regaining of the family honor."

Jeanne raised hers. "To England."

Julia raised her glass. "Yes—to love."

Jason raised his and all held, awaiting his toast. He smiled. "To the most loyal of traitors, the best of spies . . . and the not-too-respectable future!"

SUSPENSE IS A HEARTBEAT AWAY —
Curl up with these Gothic gems.

THE PRECIOUS PEARLS OF CABOT HALL (3754, $3.99/$4.99)
by Peggy Darty

Recently orphaned Kathleen O'Malley is overjoyed to discover her long-lost relatives. Uncertain of their reception, she poses as a writer's assistant and returns to her ancestral home. Her harmless masquerade hurls Kathleen into a web of danger and intrigue. Something sinister is invading Cabot Hall, and even her handsome cousin Luke can't protect her from its deadly pull. Kathleen must discover its source, even if it means losing her love . . . and her life.

BLACKMADDIE (3805, $3.99/$4.99)
by Jean Innes

Summoned to Scotland by her ailing grandfather, Charlotte Brodie is surprised to find a family filled with resentment and spite. Dismissing her drugged drink and shredded dresses as petty pranks, she soon discovers that these malicious acts are just the first links in a chain of evil. Midnight chanting echoes through the halls of her family estate, and a curse cast centuries ago threatens to rob Charlotte of her sanity and her birth right.

DARK CRIES OF GRAY OAKS (3759, $3.99/$4.99)
by Lee Karr

Brianna Anderson was grateful for her position as companion to Cassie Danzel, a mentally ill seventeen year old. Cassie seemed to be the model patient: quiet, passive, obedient. But Dr. Gavin Rodene knew that Cassie's tormented mind held a shocking secret — one that her family would silence at any cost. As Brianna tries to unlock the terrors that have gripped Cassie's soul, will she fall victim to its spell?

**THE HAUNTED HEIRESS OF WYNDCLIFFE
MANOR** (3911, $3.99/$4.99)
by Beverly C. Warren

Orphaned in a train wreck, "Jane" is raised by a family of poor coal miners. She is haunted, however, by fleeting memories and shadowy images. After escaping the mines and traveling across England with a band of gypsies, she meets the man who reveals her true identity. She is Jennifer Hardwicke, heiress of Wyndcliffe Manor, but danger and doom await before she can reclaim her inheritance.

WHITE ROSES OF BRAMBLEDENE (3700, $3.99/$4.99)
by Joyce C. Ware

Delicate Violet Grayson is hesitant about the weekend house party. Two years earlier, her dearest friend mysteriously died during a similar gathering. Despite the high spirits of old companions and the flattering attention of charismatic Rafael Taliaferro, her apprehension grows. Tension throbs in the air, and the housekeeper's whispered warnings fuel Violet's mounting terror. Violet is not imagining things . . . she is in deadly peril.

Available wherever paperbacks are sold, or order direct from the Publisher. Send cover price plus 50¢ per copy for mailing and handling to Zebra Books, Dept. 4231, 475 Park Avenue South, New York, N.Y. 10016. Residents of New York and Tennessee must include sales tax. DO NOT SEND CASH. For a free Zebra/Pinnacle catalog please write to the above address.